FOREST OF DREAMS AND WHISPERS

KATHERINE MACDONALD

Forest of Dreams and Whispers

The Fae of the Forest Book One

Katherine Macdonald

Copyright © July 2022 by Katherine Macdonald

All rights reserved.

No portion of this book may be reproduced in any form without written permission from the publisher or author, except as permitted by U.S. copyright law. Small quotes may be used for the purpose of review.

This is a work of fiction. Any similarity to actual persons, living or dead, or actual events, is purely coincidental.

Cover Design by: Rebecca F Kenney (RFK designs)

Chapter headings/front page: Elisha Bugg (Inkwolf Designs)

ISBN: 9798831387155

Follow author at:

Twitter: @KateMacAuthor

Instagram: Katemacdonald89

Tiktok: @Katemacauthor

Website: Katherinemacdonaldauthor.com

FOREST OF DREAMS AND WHISPERS

Contents

Prologue		3
1.	Prince of Thorns	9
2.	Return from Autumn	18
3.	The Witch of the Wilds	26
4.	The Tournament	40
5.	Dreamless Nights	49
6.	The Boon	56
7.	Daggers in the Dawn	65
8.	Briarsong	68
9.	The Dreams Returned	73
10.	The Road to Autumn	81
11.	Lady of Autumn	95
12.	The Road to Acanthia	105
13.	Daggers and Disguises	115
14.	Paper Grief	126
15.	A Call in the Dark	131
16.	A Dance and a Debut	138
17.	The Agony of Want	145
18.	The Road to Summer	151
19.	The Night Before	160
20.	The First Drop of Blood	174
21.	At The Summer Court	190
22.	Upon a Dream	197

23.	Into the Woods	203
24.	The Sickness and the Cure	216
25.	The Lament	226
26.	The Girl by the Sea	238
27.	Rivers and Grindylows	245
28.	The Way to Winter	254
29.	A Fighting Dance	259
30.	The Winter Quarry	269
31.	Hollow	281
32.	Shadows and Ember	285
33.	Beneath the Sea	290
34.	The Witch Returns	299
35.	The Valley of Memories	313
36.	The Sacrifice	325
37.	The Last Words	330
38.	The Road Home	341
39.	The Autumn Gate	349
40.	City of Thorns	358
41.	The Tower of Thorns	371
42.	The Sentence of the Unseelie King	376
43.	A Heart Shared, A Heart Bared	383
	Excerpt from the Royal Records	395
44.	Epilogue	398
	Acknowledgments	400
	Afterword	401
	About the Author	403
	Also by Katherine Macdonald	404

For those who dream of finding faerie,
Of being both the prince and the princess—

The savior and the saved.

KATHERINE MACDONALD

PROLOGUE

Juliana did not remember the curse being cast. She was there, of course, a small child of only one. Too young to have any memory of it. But the story had been told to her so many times by so many people, she felt as if she had been there. She'd gathered together all of the details over the years, stitched them together like a tapestry, a constellation of memories.

Alia, the court bard, told her the sounds the guests had made, the quiet mutterings, the screams of terror, the clang of steel.

Eoghan, the jester, told her the words that were spoken, each line of the curse, committing the horror on the Queen's face to poetry.

Cedany, the court painter, told her every shade of the room, each shadow and shape, her tongue describing what her paint could not.

Her father told her the most, how her mother had bravely defended the Queen and had cut down a dozen Unseelie creatures whilst holding Juliana in her arms.

Juliana often wondered what tale her mother would have told, if she had ever had the opportunity to ask her.

From her patchwork story, Juliana knew this:

It was the day of Prince Hawthorn's naming. He was a much longed-for prince, born a century after his mother's reign began. Faeries were infertile by nature, but a century was a long time to wait for an heir, especially when the parents were 'trying so hard.'

But finally, *finally*, the child had come. All Faerie births are celebrated with aplomb, but none more so than a royal one. A ball was hosted in his honour, and although Juliana knew it was statistically impossible to fit *everyone* in the kingdom inside the grand hall, it apparently seemed like everyone was there.

Well, all of the Seelie court, anyway.

The Unseelie were not invited. They never were. Only a few lived within the capital—the occasional tame werewolf, a nixie who'd deserted her sisters, a minotaur guard admired for his strength—none were invited in numbers, as if their presence would sour the crowds.

The great hall was strung with banners of white and gold. Blossoms bloomed in the enchanted vines that inhabited most of the Acanthian palace, weaving through walls, over stones and ceilings. Musicians fluted and piped, the music sweet and harmonious, the great feast much the same: mountains of honey cakes, thick, creamy cheeses, dense breads, custard apples, dragon fruit tarts, pastries in the shapes of flowers and crowns.

It was, according to Alia, a scene as soft as rosebuds and the feathers of a day-old duckling.

"Not a smile was painted on that day," Eoghan reported. "People wore joy like medals. It was as bright as pure summer sun."

At least, Cedany added, to begin with.

Midway through the celebrations, before anything had gotten too chaotic, and while Juliana was hiding under one of the tables eating honey cakes, the main doors to the palace had burst open in a cloud of black, shimmering smoke. It drowned the lights, shrouded the windows, expunged the music and plunged the room into a grey-black sea.

At the centre of the room stood Ladrien, King of the Unseelie, proud and tall as a griffin, with skin like shimmering moonlight and long black hair darker than night. Two long, towering horns grew from his temple, and two dark leathery wings sprouted from his back. He wore a crown of thorns and robes woven with raven's feathers, and carried nothing else but a gnarled staff cut from the core of an elder tree.

According to all onlookers, his eyes were pale, like sunlight sheathed in mist, and he was all at once elegant and terrifying.

So terrifying, so regal in his wildness, that even Juliana's own father, one of the bravest knights in the kingdom, didn't dare pull his sword.

"It would not have been wise," he would tell Juliana, years after the event.

A few of the palace guards raised their weapons. The Unseelie King laughed, and held up his hands. "Come, come, now," he said. "There is no need for that. I only come to offer a gift to the young prince, on this most auspicious day."

In Faerie, refusing a gift could bring on all kinds of trouble.

"Of course, King Ladrien," said Queen Maytree, rising from her throne. "If you come in peace, you are always welcome here."

To mark the occasion, the Queen wore a gown of white lace and rose petals. It drifted down the stone steps like a cape. Juliana could remember nothing of the day, but that picture formed clearly in her mind's eye, the steely gaze of the blue-eyed queen facing down the Unseelie King, her chestnut curls woven through her golden crown.

King Ladrien just smiled. "Year by year, the mortals in their kingdoms swell," he said. "Within a few decades, they will expand enough to press into our borders."

"Our realm is all but hidden from mortal eyes," Lord Aspen, the queen's consort, retorted.

"All *but*," Ladrien sneered, and his eyes settled on the mortal servants, on Juliana's own parents. "Too many invade your lands as it is."

"The mortals here are our trusted servants," Queen Maytree retorted. "We have no reason to fear—"

"We have every reason to fear a creature that can lie, that cannot be held to the promises it makes," Ladrien insisted. "And they outnumber us. They always have."

A dark murmur whispered through the crowd. The Queen pursed her lips. "What of your gift, King Ladrien? I do remember you mentioning one."

"Ah, yes. A gift." He smiled, dark and sinister. "I offer you an army of Unseelie, the likes of which the world has never seen before. Take it, and purge the mortal lands. Expand our territory. Let the mortals know who was born to live in shadow, and who was born to rule."

The room went silent. No one had dared suggest such a thing before. Faeries needed mortals; needed them to fill their ranks, to wet nurse their children, to create the kind of art that only mortality could inspire. Their mages liked them, too. Mortal's dreams and wishes and tears could be used in all kinds of spells... even their hearts, Juliana would learn later, although such practises were usually outlawed.

Faeries bargained with mortals for their skills and services, offering them magic, riches, extended lifespans.

No one had ever suggested just *taking* these things before. Or if they had... they had been cast out of history.

"We will not invade the mortal lands," the Queen said stonily, as the silence gave way to whispers. "We have peace here in Faerie. We have no need of a war."

"You have the peace of a graveyard," Ladrien warned. "The mortals will turn on you. They will outnumber you. And they will destroy you."

More terrified murmurs echoed throughout the room.

"Have you some gift of foresight, King Ladrien? My soothsayers have foreseen no such thing."

King Ladrien growled. "Not yet," he said darkly. "But they will."

"Be that as it may, I will not risk the safety of my people on a gamble."

"Then you refuse my gift?"

"Regretfully, King Ladrien, we must."

"Very well." Ladrien turned instead to the child in its cradle, a tiny, shrivelled thing, pointy-eared with tufts of dark hair. Innocent for the first and only time in his life. "Then I offer this instead: a gift to all Faerie. When the prince comes of age, at the first drop of blood he spills from his body, I will bring my army to this kingdom. Not a faerie shall be harmed, for all shall fall into a deep, dark sleep. For one hundred years will you rest, and after, awaken to a new world, a paradise for all faerie kind. There, I shall rule as king, with both Seelie and Unseelie as my subjects, and mortals shall be slaves to us all."

At the utterance of his words, wind tore through the hall, the vines themselves shirking against the walls. Dark whispers whistled beneath.

"Your counter-curse," the Queen declared, face still white with shock. "No curse is complete without one."

"Ah, quite right. Young prince, I offer you this escape: if your chosen fae bride offers a kiss to your sleeping form, you shall awaken immediately, and I shall withdraw my armies and surrender myself to your judgement."

"Well, that's easy—" cried a courtier, somewhat foolishly, "We'll just—"

"All fae will fall victim to my sleeping curse," Ladrien interrupted. "None shall be free from it. And who in all of Faerie would ever agree to marry this cursed prince?"

"No!" said the Queen, rising from her seat. "You shall not take my child, or my kingdom. Guards—seize him!"

Ladrien smiled. "The curse is already cast."

That didn't seem to matter. Immediately, the guards sprang into action, a cacophony of steel. But when their blades rose to meet the monster, he vanished into smoke.

Shadows sprung from where he stood, demonic creatures that scuttled like spiders.

They went straight for baby Hawthorn's crib.

The Queen screamed, racing towards him, dragging roots from the floor to bar their passage.

Juliana's mother, Cerridwen, got there first, her own child in one arm, a sword in the other. She cut the first creature in two, giving the Queen time to pick up the wailing infant.

"Come, Your Majesty!"

And yet the Queen did not move. She stood in the centre of the room, vines limp around her, holding the screaming child.

"Your Majesty!"

Finally, the Queen moved. Cerridwen cleared a passage to the back of the room, where Queen Maytree opened a vine-covered door and rushed inside, together with a few of her handmaids. While Cerridwen fought monsters, Juliana was thrust into the Queen's arms.

"Guard her, Your Majesty, so that I may guard you!" Cerridwen begged, shutting the door tightly behind her.

The Queen, who was, like most faeries, unused to children, suddenly found herself in charge of two. One howled in her arms, the other went stiff with terror.

So did the Queen.

No one knew what was going on in her mind at the time. Juliana had never asked. But the handmaids later reported that the Queen held on tightly to them both, and that after the fighting was done, nothing short of her own parents could pry Juliana from the Queen's arms. She had found some safety in whatever comfort she had offered.

The reports on what happened next differed. Some said the fighting was over in a matter of minutes and the party resumed within the hour. Others said it took weeks to weed out the creatures that had spread to the corners of the castle, that no one smiled or danced for weeks, that the days after were filled with meeting after meeting, all debating how best to avoid the curse, to delay it, to punish Ladrien.

Naturally, the entire of Faerie was scoured. "Not a leaf left unturned" reported the mortal storytellers, whose tongues were crafted for metaphor. No sign of the Unseelie King was ever found.

Every mage and sorcerer was consulted: the curse could not be broken. On the Prince's 18th birthday, Ladrien would return, and the kingdom would plunge into slumber. Unless, somehow, a bride could be arranged, made immune to the curse, and delivered to his sleeping form after the event.

Juliana liked to imagine creeping up to Hawthorn's crib at the end of the day after all the chaos had ended, and staring at his little scrunched face. She liked to imagine, that if she could talk properly, if she'd known then what would happen next, she would have looked at the faerie boy and said,

"Little prince, you may have doomed us all."

1. PRINCE OF THORNS

THREE MONTHS UNTIL THE CURSE AWAKENS

It was Juliana Ardencourt's day off, and she was trying to make the most of it. The thing was, she was never sure what to do with time off, and it almost felt lazy to be sitting beneath one of the trees in the castle's orchard, polishing her sword.

You've earned this, she reminded herself.

But had she?

She looked down her palms, scarred and calloused from years of handling the blade, yet they'd grown softer since she became the personal guard of Crown Prince Hawthorn. Aside from the occasional training mission or sparring in the knights' ring, she rarely got the chance to practise any more.

Well, aside from the occasional failed assassination attempt, which did happen with surprising frequency.

More so, of late, with his eighteenth birthday only three months away. People were keen to spill his blood *before* he came of age, to avert the curse from happening at all.

There were days when Juliana was sorely tempted to let them have him. The prince had been a definite *thorn* in her side growing up. Despite Queen Maytree's insistence that mortals were treated with respect in her kingdom, the reality was that spoiled faerie children were the same as spoiled human children, and that growing up beneath the thumbs of folk who could literally summon sparks from their fingers was far from easy.

One day in high summer, Hawthorn and his friends had manipulated the roots of the apple trees and tied up the mortal children as a game. Of course, Juliana had cut her way out with one of the knives she hid about her person, and rigged a bucket of cold water over Hawthorn's fancy bed in retaliation.

"The thing about fae is they always expect everything to be magic," Juliana's father had told her. "They're never prepared for mortal tricks."

So Juliana became the master of them. Every time Hawthorn and his group frightened a friend of hers with fire, every time they glamoured spiders to scuttle out of books, every time they pulled at braids, or tied them up, or locked them away, she returned it back ten-fold.

One time she even tied his hair to his bedpost as he slept. He hadn't worn his hair long since.

Not once had she ever been caught.

The pranks had come to an abrupt end, when, just after her thirteenth birthday, her father had packed up their bags and moved the two of them to a hut in the middle of the Autumn Forest.

For three years.

Juliana had hated it at first. As much as she loathed Hawthorn, she'd missed the palace. She missed her friends and the fellow servants, like Iona, the cook that had half-raised her. She missed the palace gardens where all seasons reigned, the enchanted library where books flew, and the vines that hummed and murmured against the walls. She missed the feasts and the gowns and the revelry.

Her father never fully explained why they had to go, only that it would be 'character building'. He barely explained when they returned, either, three years later on Hawthorn's fifteenth birthday, or why Juliana had to suddenly serve as Hawthorn's guard. He insisted it was all for her, and as Hawthorn had promised her knighthood and riches after his eighteenth birthday, she hadn't complained.

Much.

Often. *Lately.*

Hawthorn hadn't pulled a prank on her since they were children. That did not mean he was easy to work with.

For, she reminded herself. *You work* for *him. Not with. You are not one of them. You will never be one of them.*

She sighed, sheathing the sword she was polishing, and packed up the rest of her equipment. Really, it was foolish to be spending any of her day off thinking of *Hawthorn* of all people.

She swung her bag onto her back, and continued through the gardens.

Faerie was made up of four regions: Spring, Summer, Autumn and Winter. The capital of Acanthia stood at the centre, and was blessed with the climate of all four seasons. This was never more apparent than in the palace gardens, where a fountain marked the centre of all Faerie. The grass around it shimmered with frost and bronze, gold and green, showing the exact point where the seasons shifted.

None of Acanthia resided in Winter. That court had fallen long ago to ruin. It was a snowy wasteland, reserved only for those banished from the other courts, a punishment so severe it had not been done for centuries.

Juliana still liked to walk the frost-covered gardens, to watch the snowflakes glitter on the trees, although she rarely went deeper, to where the trees grew dark and the snow deep and endless.

You could not stray into Winter accidentally. A sheer mountain stood between the gardens and the rest of the region, and the narrow passage between the two could only be opened by the immediate royal family.

It was safe. Everyone assured her.

But darkness lingered there, and for all that she was brave, there was something in the air beside those mountains she could not name, a chill that slithered along her spine, and Juliana feared anything she could not strike down with a blade.

She walked to summer instead, down to the lake, and upstream a bit to a more secluded spot. She ate the food she'd packed with her that morning, and stretched out along the bank, unbraiding her tawny-coloured hair to bask in the sun's glow.

Although she had never lived in the mortal realm, she had heard the tales, how the world shifted round the sun, experiencing only one season at a time. How dull a place to live. She was glad she would never see it, even if—

No. She shook her head. *No dark thoughts today.*

She soon grew too hot, but it hardly mattered. It was a bright and glorious day, and no one was around. She stripped off her brown tunic, trousers, boots and shirt, left them behind a bush (once Hawthorn and his friends had stolen her clothes) and dived into the lake. The cool waters shimmered over her skin like a sheet of blue satin.

Perfect. Heavenly.

Who would ever want to live anywhere else?

For an hour or two, she swam and floated, occasionally leaping out to bask on a rock. The need to *do* something quickly abated (and anyway, swimming was training). She could have stayed there forever.

Footsteps sounded along the bank. Juliana looked up, judging the distance between the intruder, herself, and where she'd left her sword.

Silly, really. She ought to be safe here, especially with no Hawthorn to guard. No one was going to try and assassinate *her*.

"Are you sure, Jules?" Hawthorn had said to her once, when she'd voiced a similar opinion. "You have a lot of highly undesirable traits."

"I do, Prince Prickle, to be sure," had been her retort. "Yet only one of us is wearing a sword."

Juliana groaned again as she swam closer to her weapon.

Stop. Thinking. About. That. Prince.

As she drew closer to the bank, the features of the intruder became clearer. Dillon, a squire, friend from childhood, and one-time paramour.

And Hawthorn's relief guard.

"Dillon?" she questioned.

Dillon bristled, turning swiftly on spot. "Ah, Juliana."

"What are you doing here?"

"I, um, well…"

"Spit it out!"

"I'm sorry!" Dillon cried, practically weeping. "He gave me the slip!"

Juliana sighed. Poor, sweet, useless Dillon.

"It's fine," she said. "I'll deal with it."

Almost three years ago, when she'd first come into Hawthorn's service, the two of them had struck a deal; he would never go anywhere without telling her.

This bargain, alas, didn't extend to telling *others* where he was going if she wasn't around.

He could also be a bit vague with the details. "I shall be going outside the palace" was not exactly as specific as she needed it to be.

She clambered out of the water, naked and dripping, making Dillon blush. It wasn't anything he hadn't seen before—and honestly, given the faerie tendency to dance naked under the moonlight or wear nothing but leaves to a party, he really ought to have been used to it. But for all Juliana was fairly unabashed by nudity, most mortals were not so free with their bodies.

She patted herself down, pulled her clothes back on, and belted herself up.

"You better come with me," she said, stepping out from behind the bush. "If the Queen discovers you've mislaid her son, she'll mislay your *head*."

Dillon gulped, massaging his neck. "But I really like my head..."

Juliana laughed, slapping his back. "I'm fond of it too. Come on, Prince Haw can't have gone far."

"You know he hates it when you call him that."

"He hates it when I call him anything."

"You would think that," Dillon remarked under his breath, "but you would be wrong."

Juliana split from Dillon as soon as they reached Down-Water, a part of the capital that stood downriver, in a part of Autumn so cold that it fringed the mountains of Winter. It was a place of ill-repute, known for seedy taverns, black markets, dens of extreme highs and bitter lows.

While the Summer and Spring sections of the city were known for their upmarket saloons, it was this thin sliver of town that Hawthorn chose to frequent whenever Juliana's back was turned.

He was most likely to be in one of the district's three taverns. He never visited the seedier dens, the places filled with magical highs, and although she'd *once* discovered him in the local whorehouse, she found him there fully clothed and covered in glitter, being spoon fed honey by the madam herself. She wasn't entirely sure what he'd gone for, but she was fairly sure it wasn't the sex, and he'd never been back.

No, the taverns were the most likely.

"You head to *The Hideous Swan*," Jules instructed. "I'll check *The Why Knot*. Meet at *Owen's* if we don't find him?"

Dillon nodded. "Aye-aye!"

He shuffled off without another word.

Juliana sighed, glancing at the sky. It was getting dark. That was no problem for a faerie, whose eyes were made for night, but as a result, they kept their light to a minimum, and as a mortal, it would be harder to find her way.

She hurried along to the first tavern, seizing the remains of daylight. She ducked as she entered, a tankard flying over her head. Two burly fauns charged into the street, their antlers locked together. A half-dressed nymph with bright pink skin and flowers for hair hurried out after them, alternating between screaming at them to stop and goading them onwards.

Juliana slipped inside. Only three of the six tables were upright, half of the patrons seemed to be on their backs, and a pixie was flying overhead dousing everyone with cheap ale.

This was chaotic, even for Hawthorn. He'd never risk spoiling his fancy clothes.

She gave the tavern a quick once-over, surveying the horizontal customers, and quickly slipped away.

Owen's was just around the corner. It was owned by a burly mortal man named Owen who had fallen into Faerie two decades ago, fell for a werewolf, and opened a seedy tavern close to the outskirts so she could go hunt freely in the forest once a month or stay locked in the cellar if she preferred. Not that Owen's clientele would be particularly perturbed by a rampant wolf launching itself across the bar; half of the chairs already had bite marks in.

Juliana ducked into the tavern, the floor sticky with ale. A bard was on a table strumming his lute, singing about some silver-haired demon hunter who had left him for a witch, and a bunch of drunk patrons were hurling coins at his feet. Three nymphs were performing a semi-naked dance in the corner, for entertainment or their own amusement, Juliana wasn't sure.

She spotted Owen behind the bar, cleaning tankards with a calm serenity that did not belong amidst the noise. He looked up as she approached, nodding his head at the back door.

Although plenty of Hawthorn's would-be assassins over the years had been faeries, mortals tended to dislike him more. After all, they were the ones that Ladrien had promised to enslave, who had more to lose if the curse came to pass. Even those who had no intention of harming him seemed to despise him for existing.

Owen, thankfully, didn't seem to mind, although the ridiculous sums of money Hawthorn lost at his tavern might have had something to do with that.

Not that Juliana could talk, she tolerated Hawthorn for the money, too.

She headed into the back room. Half a dozen fae were seated around a table, playing a game of exploding cards—thankfully the less violent kind that involved theatrics rather than actual murder. The main rule of the game was to get rid of the exploding card before it, well, exploded. The rest of the rules were lost on her.

"Juliana!" Hawthorn crowed from the table, his black waves tousled, silver circlet askew. "My sweet, despicable villain! You're looking just as hideous as I remember."

Juliana narrowed her eyes. "You left your guard."

"But you found me!"

"Sadly, I did."

Hawthorn laughed. He climbed shakily to his feet, kicked back his chair, and gave a bow so low that he hit his head on the table. This was, apparently, hilarious. "Alas ladies, gentlemen, I must do as my mistress bids."

"I am *not* his mistress," Juliana hissed, although no one seemed to be listening.

"If you are not my mistress, then why do I come whenever you bid me?" Hawthorn cackled, staggering towards her. "I am quite at your mercy."

"You're at the mercy of liquor, that's what you're at the mercy of."

Hawthorn pitched forward, stumbling, catching himself on Juliana's shoulders. He laughed maniacally, squeezing her. "You're always there for me to lean on."

He could be worse, she told herself. *He could be so much worse. He* was *so much worse.*

She seized his arm, the rest of him still slumped against her shoulders, and dragged him from the tavern.

They met Dillon at the door.

"Ah, Dillon, there you are!" Hawthorn laughed. "I suppose I should apologise for giving you the slip."

"That's all right, Your Highness."

"Ah, mortals. Such sweethearts, such liars. Well, apart from Jules, of course. Tell me, Dillon, would you call Juliana a sweetheart? She's about as sweet as a bee's arse."

"Um..." Dillon started uncomfortably.

"Don't answer him!" Juliana hissed, and flicked the back of Hawthorn's head.

"Ow!" he winced, "Careful, you may bruise me!"

"You're a bloody faerie prince, you barely bruise at all."

"My feelings, alas, are far more delicate."

I could drown him, Juliana told herself. *I could just drop him in that fountain over there. Alcohol would do the rest for me. It's my day off. I was never here.*

Sometimes Juliana worried about her propensity towards murder to solve even the slightest of inconveniences, but it was not when she was dragging a very inebriated prince across town on her day off.

"Have you got everything you need, Your Highness?" Dillon asked, trying to be helpful.

"Kind, thoughtful Dillon! You could learn a thing or two from him, my sour-faced viper."

"The only thing I'm interested in learning from him is how to lose you."

"Ouch," said Dillon and Hawthorn at the same time.

Juliana muttered an apology to Dillon.

"Why does he get an apology and not me?" Hawthorn slurred.

"I mean it when I insult you."

"That is... fair, I suppose," he said, a little sadly. He tapped his midsection. "I appear to have mislaid my coin. Oh well, no matter."

"I can fetch it for you—" Dillon offered.

"Leave it," Juliana warned. "Maybe he'll learn something. Make some poor sap's day."

Getting the drunk prince back to his chambers without anyone noticing was no easy feat, but Juliana had perfected the art over the years. She knew every passageway, every guard rota, every entrance and exit. Before too long, the prince was flung back into his room and collapsed on the thornwood bed. The vines groaned in welcome, crawling around the bedposts. Hawthorn raised a hand to touch one, a bud blooming as he made contact.

"At least someone is pleased to see me..." he sighed.

Dillon set to work removing his boots.

"Oh, leave it," said Juliana, waving a hand. "My day's already over. I'll deal with it."

"If you're—"

"It's fine."

"I'm sorry—"

"Not your fault."

Dillon left without another word, slinking into the dimly-lit corridor.

Juliana turned back to Hawthorn, who'd successfully managed to remove his boots and was now tugging off his wine-stained shirt. He flung it to the floor and stared at her as her eyes moved over the flawless panes of his chest.

He smirked. "Well?"

"What?"

"Does it meet with your approval?"

Juliana's cheeks heated. "Nothing about your appearance makes up for how absolutely loathsome I find you."

"Ah, so you *do* find me attractive!"

"Did you hurt yourself, making that stretch?"

"You sound angry, Jules dear."

Juliana rolled her eyes. She almost missed the days when he called her *filthy mortal* and put worms in her food. "You ruined my day off."

"Did it ever occur to you that I might miss you?"

That was typical fae speech: phrasing something as a question because you couldn't state it as a fact. Juliana wasn't fooled. She'd grown up around the fae—how could she be?

"No," she said sharply. "Does it ever occur to you that I really, really hate this job?"

"Ah, Jules, it does, but yet you stay with me anyway."

"I don't have a choice."

"You do," he said. "You could leave any time you wanted. Mortal vows are made to be broken, after all. I guess I just enjoy testing you. My dearest Jules, my most loyal companion, it is nice to know that someone will always stay with me."

It was only after she rolled him into bed and he'd fallen asleep that she thought about his words. He couldn't say anything he didn't mean. Was she honestly his most loyal companion?

When she'd returned from her three years in Autumn, the majority of his friends had returned to their own courts. The new ones he made never seemed to last long. She'd always assumed he tired of them... but what if it was the other way around?

And why did this prince who had everything he wanted have no one in the world?

2. RETURN FROM AUTUMN

THREE YEARS UNTIL THE CURSE AWAKENS

A crisp breeze blew through the woods on the edge of the Autumn Court, brushing the branches aside and turning the leaves as gold as flecks of paint in the still evening light.

It was fifteen years, almost since the day, that Prince Hawthorn was turned into a living bomb. To mark his fifteenth birthday, a grand tournament was being held, and every knight in Faerie was journeying to the capital for the event.

Markham, Juliana's father, was no exception, although it had been three years now since he'd quit his position, gathered his daughter and a handful of possessions, and fled to the forests of Autumn like a criminal committing a crime.

Not that, as far as Juliana could work out, he'd done anything wrong. "I just fancied the change of scene," he'd tell her. Or, worse, "It'll do you good, daughter. You'll see," with no elaboration whatsoever.

That was the best and worst thing about being mortal, Juliana had decided. The fact that you could lie and be lied to.

Although Juliana initially hated living in the woods, she soon came to find enjoyment in it. Life there was definitely more difficult, but Juliana found it easier in so many other ways. Yes, you were at the mercy of the elements, and you could go hungry if there was no food to be found. Some days you couldn't get warm or clean or dry, no matter what you did. There was no magic to fix you if you got hurt.

But there were also no fae with their tricks and glamours, no lies that weren't lies, no bargains and markets where you could haggle with flesh and bone and memories.

And no spoilt princes, barking orders, pulling your hair, putting frogspawn in your morning tea or moving your chair away as you tried to sit.

She missed the food, though. And the magic.

"Are you going to tell me why we're returning, yet?" Juliana asked, staring at her father.

Markham smiled. He was a handsome man, with brownish hair, warm, sun-speckled skin, and green eyes like the forests that he shared with Juliana. He appeared somewhere in his mid-thirties, although she knew his actual age to be twice that. His ageing had slowed when he entered faerie as a young man. If he stayed, he'd live to be a hundred, maybe more. If he left...

You could only enter Faerie once. The way closed for mortals if they left. No one was sure what rule applied to mortals born in Faerie, and Juliana wasn't about to find out first hand. Why would she even want to leave? She'd heard the mortal world was dull and ordinary, that people died young, that women were denied the sword, that water came from wells, and everything was cold and drafty.

That world has nothing for me, she told herself. *Nothing at all.*

"I already told you," Markham explained. "We're attending the tournament."

"You told me what," she said, "not why."

"The winner is granted a boon."

"You want to win it?"

"I'm fairly sure I will," he said.

"We packed a lot."

"Your point, daughter?"

Juliana sighed. She half-wished he'd give her an outright lie if he wouldn't speak the truth. "Are we staying, Father? Are we moving back to Acanthia?"

"That depends on the outcome of the tournament."

Juliana shook her head, not bothering to chastise him for not telling her earlier. There was no arguing with her father, no dragging information he didn't wish to divulge.

I miss Iona, she thought wistfully. She missed Iona and Cedany and Aoife and Alia and Eoghan and Albert and Dillon and—

Her father told her the ache would grow less, in time, like they were a scab that would heal over. But instead they were a scar, one that would rise up unbidden, out of nowhere, impossible to heal.

Soon, she told herself, *you'll see them soon.*

Shortly before dark, the trees grew sparse, and they hit the main road. There were three entrances to the capital, three gates in its great thorn walls—Autumn, Spring, Summer—each entrance as grand as the last. The Autumn Gate was wreathed in red-gold leaves, like the plumage of a fat bird, trembling in the quiet breeze. Beyond it, the cobbles trailed up the hill towards a silvery palace tumbling with vines, giant blooming flowers spilling out of the turrets on the sides of Spring and Summer, mushrooms and lichen clinging to the part shrouded in Autumn.

Home, whispered Juliana's thoughts, although she tried to squash them.

It didn't matter. The word curled around her heart like the vines at the palace gate, blooming with wistful sentimentality.

"Happy to be back?" Markham asked.

"I bet the food is nicer here."

Markham barked a laugh. For all that she could lie better than most mortals, Juliana was used to faerie speech, dodging the truth but speaking no falsehoods.

She had grown to love the woods and the freedom they offered. She was still happy to be back.

She didn't want her father to know that, though.

They made their way towards the palace, passing by the marketplace brimming with food: fat suckling pigs glazed with cider, pheasants soaking in red wine or smothered with blackberry sauce, thick, dense breads packed with dates and raisins.

Her belly grumbled.

"There'll be food at the palace," her father told her. "Competitors eat free."

Juliana quickened her gait, moving through fire-breathers and jugglers, self-flying kites in the shape of dragons and butterflies. Magic twitched on the fingers of acrobats twirling on golden ropes, spitting out illusions as they turned and tumbled.

A dozen sights utterly unchanged.

Nothing in Faerie changed. Juliana could never be sure if she liked that or not.

People were trickling in at the palace gates for the welcoming feast, open to all partaking in the tournament tomorrow. Faces she knew rose to greet her, although none she knew well enough to run to. There were a few smiles and nods of heads thrown in her direction, a few more that passed over her. She'd grown some in three years. She couldn't blame them.

"Well, well, if it isn't Ser Markham," boomed a voice overhead.

Juliana glanced up. At the guards' post above the gates stood Miriam of Bath, a fellow mortal knight and old friend of her parents, although the smile she gave wasn't as warm as Juliana remembered. Miriam was as strong as an ox, muscles bulging beneath her golden armour, engraved with the thorned crest of the royal family. Her muddy brown hair was cut close to her head, her skin freckled and bronzed by the sun. Though she looked ordinary and mortal, a wisdom of ages shone in her steely eyes. She was as immortal as the faeries she served.

Markham bowed, arms open. "Ser Miriam. You look well."

"As do you," she replied. "Although... Vines, Juliana, is that you?"

Juliana smiled, glad to be recognised by someone. "Good to see you, Miriam."

"You look well, child." The knight smiled. "Like your mother."

Markham put his arm around Juliana's shoulders and pushed her under the gate, jaw tense. "We shall speak later, Miriam," he said tersely.

"Perhaps during the tournament."

"Will you be competing?" His jaw looked stiffer than before; Miriam was the only knight that stood a chance of beating him, although there was no telling who might have risen up the ranks in their absence.

"I have not yet made up my mind," Miriam declared. "We shall see."

Markham nodded, and followed the road up the barracks. The smell of the stables raced up to greet her like an old friend, all damp hay, mud, horse. Not waiting for her father's approval, she rushed off to inspect the mounts. Several were unfamiliar to her, brought by contenders from other parts of Faerie, but there, in their old stalls...

Applejack, Bobtail, Fairweather, Merfoot, Raven—all her old friends.

She rushed to greet each one, to stroke their velvety muzzles, to play with their manes. Some steeds were traditional horses like the ones from the mortal realm, but others were sea-green with manes of seaweed, or dazzling white with golden hooves, or not horses at all but giant stags or enormous toads.

All beautiful. All missed.

"Juliana?"

Juliana turned and found herself face to face with Albert Woodfern, the stable master. He was a shire horse in human form; broad, tough, proud. The greys in brown hair were more pronounced than they once were, his face a little more beaten than she remembered, but he wore the same kind smile as always.

"It *is* you!" he cried. "My, look at you, child. You've grown."

"In height and wit," she responded. "Although I only have my father's word for the latter, so others might not agree."

He patted her shoulder, still grinning, and gestured to a large hulk of a lad sweeping in the corner.

"You remember my son, Dillon?"

Juliana blinked. She remembered Dillon being a scrawny, sparrow of a boy, capable of flitting from the rafters like a bird. This boy—man, really—looked like he could break floorboards if he breathed on them.

"Juliana," he said bashfully. "Good to see you. Staying long?"

"As long as my father bids me."

"You must be hungry," he said. "Shall I escort you to the kitchens?"

Juliana couldn't understand why he needed to escort her when she was perfectly capable of finding her own way there, but it was good to be seen by someone, so she took him up on his offer. The kitchen was a bustling hive of activity, clanging bowls and steaming cauldrons, but the sight was as welcoming to her as an old blanket.

"Julie!" screamed a voice, and Juliana found herself swept up into the ample arms of Iona, the head chef, and the woman who'd half-raised her. *Everyone* in the castle had had some hand in that, with her father away half the time and the general belief in Faerie that childhood was a short, fleeting and slightly inconvenient period of existence that no one dedicated much time to. Juliana had spent hers being watched by everyone and no one and frankly wouldn't have had it any other way.

Iona steered her away to an alcove, pressed a bowl of stew into her hands, and gave her a careful appraisal. Before long, Juliana's ears fit to burst with all the tales of the past three years. As the evening wore on, more and more people drifted in to see her.

So, she thought, *this is what it's like to come home.*

Her father found her shortly before the feast was set to begin, and she was sent to the barracks to change into a clean tunic. She felt a bit ridiculous in the plain woollen garment, next to the splendour of the night and the swirling gossamer of the guests. She almost wished she could wear her travelling clothes; those were allowed to be plain and messy.

A few months after they'd left for the woods, desperate for something pretty in her rugged life, she'd tried to embroider flowers onto the hems. She'd done an appalling job, and it was only made worse by the finery flocking towards the great hall.

She tugged on her cuffs.

"No one will care what you are wearing if you don't," her father whispered as they walked towards the hall.

"I'm not sure that's true."

He shook his head. "When I first met your mother, she was scrubbing bloodstains out of a tunic. She saw me gaping and snapped that if I had time to stare, I had time to help her. She was the most ravishing thing I ever saw."

Juliana almost stumbled, relishing this new little story. Tales about her mother were rare, treasured, Markham so seldom spoke of her. Whenever he did, though, the world seemed to narrow. He spoke of her like the great storytellers spoke of the stars.

"Come," said Markham, annoyed at her dallying. "The feast is beginning."

They passed under the boughs of the great hall, an enormous domed chamber composed almost entirely of branches, vines and blooms. Currently, white flowers carpeted every surface, humming with fireflies, a swirling mix of spring days and heady summer nights.

Queen Maytree sat on her throne of thorns wearing a midnight gown stitched with constellations and fringed with raven's feathers. Her chestnut locks were scraped back from her face, pinned behind a star-like crown, and ran in curled rivulets down her back. Although all accounts of the Cursed Day mentioned something about the queen freezing, Juliana couldn't imagine it. Queen Maytree didn't freeze, she *froze*. The fiercest warriors cowered before her shadow, and the most powerful of creatures trembled like a leaf in frost.

Juliana bowed.

"Ser Markham," said the Queen. "Welcome back to our halls. Your daughter, too. It is good to see you both."

No further words were spoken at this time, for a line had formed behind them. Juliana's focus fell from the Queen to a smaller throne of similar style where her consort, Aspen, sat.

And next to him...

Hawthorn.

He'd grown some since she'd last seen him, tall and lean rather than small and skinny. His spider-silk shirt was open at the neck, revealing chiselled marble skin. The smile he wore suggested he knew it. His face had lost the boyish roundness, sharpening at the nose and cheeks, his black waves cut just above his shoulders. He grinned at Juliana over the rim of his goblet, as if they were old friends... or Juliana was a delectable piece of meat he was trying to work out how to cut.

She wasn't sure.

Nothing in Faerie changes, Juliana reminded herself. *Don't let a pretty face fool you. There's a spider at the centre of that frosted web.*

A dozen people came to speak to her, servants, knights, entertainers and old school friends. She was filled with food, drinks pressed into her hands, plied with questions till her ears felt fit to bleed.

She was quite sure she spoke more that night than in a full year in Autumn.

Her goblet dry, she dismissed herself from her present company and headed towards one of the fountains for a refill, before noticing the glazed expressions of some of the mortals dancing around it. She frowned; they were still wearing their wards of rowan berries. They couldn't be glamoured. Had someone spiked the wine?

Deciding it would be better to open a new bottle, she moved towards the tables instead, picking up one that a card assured her was suitable for mortal consumption.

"I wouldn't try that wine," said a voice behind her. "Someone has switched the labels."

A long, elegant hand reached out to swap around the cards. Juliana stilled, following the black feathery cuff up the slender arm to an unsettlingly familiar face.

The face smiled. "Juliana."

Juliana unclenched her jaw, just enough to speak. "Prince Prickle."

The smile twisted further. "Not completely forgotten me, I see."

"Believe me, I gave it my best shot."

Hawthorn barked a laugh. "You haven't changed at all."

"I'd say the same for you, but it wouldn't be a compliment."

Only, he had. He was finally taller than she was, almost by a head. Everything about him was smoother and sharper. He moved like water, and his smile was liquid sin.

As was the look in those ridiculous aegean-blue eyes of his. Juliana had stared at those eyes for years, hating how she had no name for them and how they plagued her late at night. Not dark as the lake. Not bright as the sky. Not blue as cornflowers. Some ancient, ageless blue, stony and smooth, softer and more beautiful than they had any right to be.

One day, she came across Cedany painting a seascape in a corner of the gardens. Juliana had never visited the sea before, but she longed to, especially when she saw images like this. One of the colours Cedany was mixing was the exact shade of Hawthorn's eyes.

"What's that?" she'd said, pointing.

Cedany, far from being annoyed at the interruption, had smiled. "Be more specific."

"That colour. What's it called?"

"Aegean blue, child. Like the seas of the summer court."

Juliana pursed her lips. She ought to have been happy she finally had a name for the beautiful, accursed colour, but somehow she was not appeased.

"Do you like it?"

Juliana's face twisted further, and then, with a kind of painful honesty like the ones exhibited by faeries when the truth was wrenched from them, she said, "I wish I didn't."

Those same eyes—both hated and admired—were riveted on her now, even as he poured out a measure and handed her a goblet. "A drink?" he offered.

"No."

"You don't trust me?"

She ought to, as he couldn't lie. He would not be able to say the labels had been switched if they weren't. But perhaps they'd been switched multiple times at his behest. Perhaps he'd swapped them round twice himself. There were plenty of ways to deceive even when your tongue could only speak the truth.

"I trust you as well as I can throw you," she snapped. "Which, given your recent growth spurt, is not as far as I once could."

Hawthorn smirked, harder. His lips felt like daggers to her, groaning against her insides. "Ah, so you have noticed. Makes me look more dashing, don't you think?"

"Better target practice," she admitted, stepping closer. "Easier to aim for."

Something flickered in Hawthorn's eyes at that, something dark, almost fearful. "Enjoy the rest of the night," he said tartly, and strode back to the rest of the dancers.

3. THE WITCH OF THE WILDS

THREE MONTHS UNTIL THE CURSE AWAKENS

Juliana could not remember meeting Hawthorn. He'd always been there in the background, a shadow over her life in the kitchens, a glaring presence at feasts and festivals and tournaments.

She remembered meeting Princess Lucinda of the Autumn Court, daughter to the noble High Lady and Lord. She breezed into their lives the summer before Juliana turned thirteen.

Most high ladies sent their children to the capital to be educated with the other noble children at the age of seven, but Lucinda's parents had declared she was "not yet ready." It did not take Juliana long to realise what that truly meant.

Lucinda was fourteen when she swept into the castle, two years older than Hawthorn and beautiful beyond measure. She had skin like milk and hair like fire, eyes of brilliant gold, and a voice like honey.

In that honeyed voice, she poured poison into Juliana's ears, reminding her she was worthless, weak, pathetic, a worm in a house of peacocks. She made Hawthorn twice as bad as he had ever been.

Hawthorn was a stone in her boot—she could remove it at any time and hurl it away from her. Lucinda was an infection she could not expunge.

And Hawthorn adored her.

Although he was only twelve, he found himself ensnared by her flattery, devoted to her whims. Before long, there were talks of a betrothal. Lucinda could be escorted out of Faerie prior to his eighteenth birthday and escorted back again under every protection to break the curse not long after it came to pass.

"They already seem to adore one another," Lucinda's mother would croon whenever she came to visit. "They make such a beautiful couple. How lucky to have found each other so young!"

Lucky for you, thought Juliana.

One day, she caught Lucinda talking to her mother. Juliana was hidden in the vines, playing her own private game with them. The minute the two entered the room, the vines cocooned around her, shielding her further from view.

Lucinda's mother's eyes darted around the room, checking for eavesdroppers, but she did not see Juliana, suspended in the space above them.

"Have you secured his word yet?" the mother asked.

Lucinda shook her head. "He is mindful of giving it to me."

Even a foolish, lovestruck boy was more careful than that when he was fae, when a vow could not be broken.

"You need to act quickly," Lucinda's mother urged her. "I've heard there are other houses vying for his favour. It's a shame he's not a little older. Perhaps too young for you to seduce him—"

"He won't be too young for much longer."

Juliana's insides twisted uncomfortably at the horrid smile on Lucinda's face, at the thought of seducing someone so young. The was no exact law in Faerie regarding the age someone was allowed to bed—only very strict laws regarding consent, including manipulation. And this—this was that. She had noted how the Lucinda's flattery tended to fall on Hawthorn's features and skills, never praising who he was or what she liked about him. Not that Juliana thought there was much to like, but she never for one moment suspected the girl was quite *this* unfeeling towards him.

For days after, Juliana wondered what to do with the information. She didn't like Hawthorn, after all. What was it to her if he married someone who hated him?

But it didn't sit right in her gut, like she'd swallowed a needle.

She'll be queen one day, if she marries him, Juliana realised. *Do you really want her as your queen?*

She told herself that was all that she was protecting when she went to speak to Queen Maytree. It was for the good of Faerie, nothing more.

Plus she really, really hated Lucinda.

Juliana trembled as she stood before the Queen, her courage already failing her. Maytree had always been kind to her—at least in the way that faeries could be—but that didn't make what she was about to do any less terrifying.

Especially as Lucinda's mother was standing right beside her.

"Well?" Maytree prompted. "Go on, child."

So Juliana told. She said that Lucinda only wanted Hawthorn's crown, that she didn't care for him at all, that her mother had put her up to it and she was planning to seduce him.

"How dare you!" screamed the Lady of Autumn. "Mortals are liars! Filthy, disgusting worm. How dare you spread such vile accusations in front of your betters!"

There was no way to prove she was telling the truth, of course, and no one dared question such a noble lady, even when the Queen's eyes shone darkly.

The next day, Hawthorn and his friends attacked Juliana for her lies, pushing her to the ground and driving her face into the mud. Hawthorn's eyes were far darker than his mother's, his face twisted.

"Filthy mortal," he hissed. "Never speak of my lady that way again."

"What reason have I to lie?" she hissed back. "I *despise* you. I don't care if you marry someone who hates you. I told the truth because..."

Hawthorn's eyes flickered. "Because *what?*"

"Who cares," she said, "since I can lie? But why don't you ask her? Ask her if I am lying. Ask her if she cares for you."

Hawthorn turned to face Lucinda, who was standing far away from all this. Her smile immediately dropped.

"Well?" he said. "Tell her, Lucy. Tell her what a liar she is."

"All mortals are liars," she said swiftly, with only the slightest of tremors. "That worm more than most."

Juliana spat out mud, ready to speak, but it was Hawthorn that did so next. "But is she lying about *this?*"

"I don't know what she thought she heard—"

"What do you want more," he asked, "me... or my crown?"

At this, she could not speak.

And Hawthorn had his answer.

The morning after Hawthorn snuck away to *Owen's* after giving Dillon the slip, Juliana woke bright and early, combed her locks into a braid, and forewent her uniform (a black tabard adorned with green thorns) for plain clothes; a soft pair of brown trousers, a loose lilac shirt, and a long waistcoat that gave some semblance of respectability.

She pounced into the next room, ignoring the fact that Hawthorn was spread out naked on the bed, and flung open the curtains.

He winced at the sudden intrusion of the light, hissing as he grabbed a blanket to cover himself.

"Juliana," he groaned, "I wish I could say you're a sight to wake up to."

"Even my mortal tongue could not find the words to utter the lie, 'it's good to see you, too'."

"So cruel, Jules." He ran a hand down his face. "My head hurts."

"As long as I live, I will never get over your incredible ability to get drunk quite so easily."

"I require water."

"Say 'please'."

"*Please.*"

Juliana took the jug of water from the nightstand and threw it over his face. Hawthorn screamed.

"You—*what was that for?*"

"For running away from Dillon!"

"I said I was sorry!"

"You could have cost him his job! 'Sorry' doesn't cut it!"

Hawthorn shifted up in bed, removing his sopping sheet and flinging it to the floor. His scowl twisted into something else. "You're being very protective of him—"

"*That's* what you're concerned about?"

"I wouldn't want you to be distracted on the job."

"Have you ever known me to be distracted?"

"I don't know," said Hawthorn, stretching out his long, cat-like body on the bed. "Maybe occasionally."

"Stop that."

"What?"

"You know what."

Hawthorn picked up the wet sheet and lay back against the damp pillows with the damp part draped over his eyes. "So, you're not secretly pining after Dillon."

"I am not," she assured him. "I like him, I don't want him to lose his position, and that is all."

"You were close in the past."

Juliana's cheeks heated, remembering a particularly charged moment involving all three of them they'd all silently agreed never to mention ever again. "That's in the past," she said swiftly, hoping he'd drop it.

He did. "Fetch me my robe, will you? I have no intention of getting properly dressed today."

"Good," said Juliana, throwing a robe in his direction. "For I am taking today off. There're guards outside. Promise you'll stay here?"

"I promise," he sighed, as if it was some great sacrifice he was making. "But only if you take dinner with me."

Juliana scowled. "*Why* do you want me to take dinner with you?"

"Because I take much delight in torturing you, at least in this way."

She rolled her eyes, returning to her adjacent room to finish buckling on her sword. "I'd be insulted, but honestly, I understand that."

"You did just throw a jug of water at my head."

"I did. And I thoroughly enjoyed it."

"There are other ways to hear me scream."

"I've slept next door to you for almost three years. I'm well aware of the different ways to make you scream. Not interested in anything that doesn't involve actual torture, thank you very much."

"I might be all right with that."

"Come again?"

"I thought you said you were going out?"

Juliana pursed her lips, wondering if she'd truly heard what she thought she'd heard. He was being evasive. "Fine," she said. "I'll see you later."

"Enjoy your day."

"Without you in it? Hard not to."

Hawthorn muttered something under his breath that she didn't hear, already halfway out of the door and off on her mission. Hawthorn's word to her was no longer good enough to keep him out of trouble, and as the assassination attempts were likely to increase the closer to his birthday they got—

It was time for a different tactic.

Her first port of call was the great library.

It was a collection of enormous vaulted rooms in a myriad of dark, muted colours: rich earth reds, forest greens, deep-sea blues. Windows of crystal adorned the ancient walls, but nearly every scrap of stone and glass and bookcase was hidden beneath the twisted vines of the castle, parting only around the books and entrances. Impish librarians patrolled the shelves, guarding everything from venerable lore, forgotten magic, and a rather fine collection of mortal novels that she had found some solace in in her youth.

As she stood in the enormous foyer, she felt a soft nudge at her back, like a cat on a shelf demanding to be fed. She turned to find the vines behind her, lifting volumes up to the highest of shelves.

"Morning," she said, reaching out a hand to stroke them.

The vines dropped a thick tome in front of her. Juliana picked it up. It was some sordid romance called "*The Wicked Prince.*"

"Not really my genre," she replied, holding it back up. The vines rustled, their leaves shaking like the feathers of a perturbed bird. The next volume hit her squarely on the head.

"*The Reluctant Bodyguard*," Juliana read. She rolled her eyes. "Very funny."

Vines couldn't snicker, but the shaking mimicked the action so well she could easily be convinced otherwise.

A tiny, barefoot girl appeared from behind the dusty bookcases. She had the appearance of a startled duckling, wide-eyed, streaked with dirt, with feathers in her tangled hair. Aoife.

Abandoned as a small child on the borders of Faerie, Aoife had a wild, impish look. Her parents had mistaken her for a changeling child and left her for the faeries to claim, although she was as mortal as Juliana was. They'd grown up together in the castle, although Aoife had never cared for bloodshed or knighthood, preferring books and quiet. It was her lifelong goal to read every book in the library's vast collection, and whatever she read, she remembered.

"Morning," said Aoife cheerily, picking up a loose feather and slotting it carefully back into place. "How's His Royal Pain in the Arse?"

"I think you answered your own question there."

"I'm good at that. Here for a book?"

"Maybe. Got anything on, 'how to keep tabs on a wayward prince?'"

"Oddly specific," said Aoife. "Maybe in the romance section."

Juliana groaned. "I need something. A spell. A way to keep track of him."

"Spellbooks, I have," Aoife said, "the means to cast them, though…" She leant against one of the shelves, eyes flickering, as if skim reading some great invisible tome. "Market day today."

"Come again?"

"You need a witch."

"A witch?" Juliana grumbled. "Must I?"

"Best option."

Witches were mortals learned in magic. Although they could not do what faeries could—casting glamours and manipulating elements—they could spin potions and enchantments with the right equipment and ingredients. Although some witches were benign, most dealt in stolen years and bottled dreams, and the general view was that they were not to be trusted.

"Second weekend of the month," Aoife continued. "Mabel will be there. She's… knowledgeable. Fair."

"If you say so." Juliana kept her dealings with witches to a minimum, and kept her sword with her just in case. "Thanks for the advice."

"Any time. Pick up a book next time you're here. Best way to have a very safe adventure."

"Safe isn't exactly my style."

Aoife sighed. "Of that, we are all aware."

Juliana turned to go.

"Juliana?"

"Yes?"

"Is he worth it?"

Juliana frowned. "I'm not doing this for him."

"What are you doing it for, then?"

"I don't know. Honour, glory, riches?"

"You sound unsure."

Juliana tensed. "I have no other reasons," she declared. "I'll see you later."

Faerie markets, like the markets Juliana had heard existed in the mortal realm, sometimes dealt in coins. Some stalls were full of mundane wares; slabs of meat, wheels of cheeses, baskets and ribbons and trinkets. Other stalls held fabrics cut from night, glass slippers forged from mortal tears, vials of luck, charms to bring about love, pockets of rain, cloaks of fire, chickens that belched bubbles every full moon, small flying reptiles like miniature dragons, unicorn hairs, bottled dreams and just about everything else under the sun.

For many items, money was never enough. Merchants wanted blood or tears, dreams or years of your life. Mortal years were worth a lot to them, but Juliana had never bargained hers away.

"How does it work?" she'd asked her father once. "What if, say, I'm destined to get knocked down by a carriage tomorrow?"

Markham shook his head. "It doesn't work that way. As long as you are healthy and hale, there's an energy attached to you... they take a sliver of that. It doesn't hurt. You likely won't miss it."

Juliana paused. "Have *you* ever bought something with your years?"

Markham hesitated. Although her father lied, she knew he never did so without thought. "Once or twice," he said eventually.

"Father!"

"I did not bargain much away, and I have years to spend, a knight of faerie."

"What did you spend it on?"

"I cannot say," he said. "But it was worth it."

Juliana couldn't imagine wanting anything that much. Her lifespan was minute enough by Faerie standards as it was. She didn't want to part with any more of it.

Hawthorn had asked her once, over a year ago, what she'd do if she had forever. She hadn't wanted to answer, but somehow he'd tugged it out of her.

"Travel," she said. "See *everything*. Mortal and Faerie and all that lies between."

There were other things, of course, but nothing she wanted to share. Even that felt too much, because she couldn't leave Faerie. It didn't matter how long she had.

But if she had forever, she could become the best knight in the kingdom. She could master every weapon, conquer fear itself.

If I had forever, I wouldn't be afraid.

Locating Mabel the Witch wasn't too tricky. There were only two witches at the market that day, two ancient old crones, pruned and wrinkled. Their magic tended to keep them alive beyond their mortal lifespans, but it did little to lift the effects of ageing.

"*Beware the young witch,*" she had been warned as a child, "*and what she has done to appear that way.*"

The ancient ones were more likely to be benign, but Mabel's appearance was unsettling in a land of youth. Her snow-white hair looked brittle as straw, woven in a loose braid and threaded with feathers. Her skin was colourless, her once-rich robes threadbare. Everything about her was worn and shrivelled—except for her eyes, sharp and orange as an eagle's. An unusual feature for a mortal.

Juliana wondered if they were hers at all, if she had traded a faerie for them, or cut them from a bird to bestow her with enhanced sight.

She cleared her throat. "Are you Mabel?"

"Aye," the witch rasped. She coughed loudly. "Sorry. Sore throat."

"I'm surprised you don't have a potion for that."

"I use my ingredients in other things," she said, with a soft cackle. "See Drusila if you want a herbal remedy. I suspect you're after something more, prince guard."

Juliana stiffened. She wasn't wearing her uniform. There was no reason for Mabel to—

"Calm yourself," said Mabel, which annoyed Juliana more. Did she honestly look so startled? She needed to keep her wits about her, steel herself—

"Oberon's arse, you're a jittery one, aren't you?" Mabel continued. "Rest assured, girl, your face betrays nothing."

"How—how are you doing that?"

"Well, when you get to my age, you gain a few powers of observation..."

Juliana stared at her, not entirely convinced.

Mabel tutted, rolling her eyes. She pulled back the feathered collar of her cloak and revealed a dozen talismans underneath. She held one up for inspection. "Helps me read emotions," she declared.

"You've quite the collection," Juliana remarked.

"Well, I'm quite old." She seemed to find this amusing. "What can I help you with, dearie?"

"I need a way to keep track of someone."

"Long term or one off?"

"Long term, regrettably. At least the next three months."

"A pendant or charm then, no straightforward spell. Is the person willing to be tracked?"

"They could be made willing."

"Makes things easier..." The witch turned back to her stock, examining jars and vials, twisted bones, pieces of metal. "Can be done. Not cheap, though."

"How much?"

"Six months of your life."

Juliana grimaced. It wasn't much, she supposed, especially if she lived to be old. Maybe it would be like her father suggested, not a thing she would miss.

"What else would I need?" she asked, unwilling to commit to a cost just yet.

"A droplet of blood from you both," the witch replied. "To ensure the connection."

Juliana tensed. Witches were capable of lies. There were any number of things they could do with blood, and handing over Hawthorn's... what if someone paid her for it? A skilled mage could kill someone from afar with a droplet of blood, or devise a poison to only kill their mark—

"A droplet only, and you can watch me do it," the witch assured her. "Not a sliver shall be kept."

"How does it work?"

"You both carry a trinket of some sort. Should the person move some distance away, you'll feel a pull towards them. It's hard to explain, easy to feel."

"All the time?"

Mabel shook her head. "Only when you wish it."

Juliana paused. Six months of her life for three months more of keeping him safe. Was it worth it?

You won't get your knighthood without it, rate he's going, said a voice inside her.

And then another, louder than it had any right to be, *Do you really want him to die?*

No, she realised. Much as she detested how reckless he was being, she didn't want him dead. And not just because of her knighthood, either.

"Fine," she said. "I'll be back with the blood."

Convincing Hawthorn to donate a droplet of blood in the name of self-preservation was not a particularly arduous task. Walking back to the market with him was.

"Your dedication to my safety is unparalleled," he said, smirking. "Really. It's quite touching. I do hope my mother is paying you enough."

"Not enough," she said through gritted teeth. "Don't sound so happy. I'm only doing this because you seem quite determined to put yourself in harm's way."

"Sounds like you care."

"It's my *job*."

Finally, mercifully, they reached the stall in question. Mabel had gathered all her ingredients around a few wooden pendants. "Pick whichever of them you like," she said.

Hawthorn tried on every one, lamenting the crude workmanship before finally picking a black thorn. He pushed a carved flower onto Juliana.

"There needs to be something sweet about your appearance," he told her.

Juliana scowled.

"And you keep giving me yet more proof. These two, please, good woman." He laid the pendants down on the surface.

Mabel took out a ring with a sharp claw on the end, and stabbed the inside of Hawthorn's wrist, letting a single droplet of blood splash onto the thorn.

"Oww," Hawthorn gasped, clutching his arm.

"Really?" Juliana hissed. "'Twas a pinprick, Prince Prickle."

"Not all of us are tough and calloused, all right?"

Juliana watched Mabel clean the claw, throwing the rag into the fire beneath her cauldron, all while under her steady gaze. The witch came back for her blood. Juliana was half-tempted to cut herself with her own dagger, just to prove how tough she was, even though she knew that was wildly impractical.

And why should she have to prove herself to *Hawthorn* of all people?

The witch took the second sample and threw both pendants in the cauldron. Hawthorn took Juliana's hand, inspecting the prick. "Need me to kiss it better?"

"I will chuck you in that cauldron."

"Wouldn't do much harm," the witch muttered, stirring the pot. "Not nearly hot enough. No lethal ingredients."

Hawthorn blinked. "Are all women obsessed with murder, or is it just you two?"

"The common denominator in this equation is you," Juliana said pointedly. "A lot of people want to murder you."

"That is harsh and also fair," Hawthorn admitted. "Witch, when shall our trinkets be ready?"

"Give it another minute or two. Can't rush magic."

"Depends on the magic," Hawthorn responded, summoning flames and making them flick through his fingers like coins. He glanced sideways at Juliana, as if expecting her to be impressed by this trick she'd seen him do a hundred times. Sensing her displeasure, he cupped the fire together, opening his palms to reveal he'd fashioned it into a tiny dragon which he let scurry over the tabletop before vanishing into smoke.

"You think there would be more practical applications for fire magic," Juliana said coolly.

"I could burn the market down, but that seems a little extreme."

Juliana groaned. "Why are you *never* serious? You're supposed to be king one day!"

"Am I?" he said. "News to me. I'm the Cursed Prince, remember? No one expects me be anything but a bomb."

Juliana stilled. *But I do*, she realised, glad he couldn't read her thoughts. Because for whatever ridiculous reason, she believed he could be better, do more.

Adjust your expectations, warned a voice. *He will only disappoint you.*

There had been a few times over the years—well, more than a few—where she'd seen him be different, *more*. He'd offer kind words to a troubled citizen, get caught speaking plainly and softly to a wounded animal or worried servant... even, once or twice, to her. But then a wall would go up, and he'd be back to barking orders and complaining about spots on his shirts, and all traces of a benevolent ruler would vanish.

Hawthorn was used to disappointing people. Juliana wondered if he'd be different if someone believed in him.

He hates you, she reminded herself. *Or barely tolerates you. He is not interested in what you think.*

"Done!" Mabel declared, hoicking out the pendants with her ladle. She placed them on the side to cool. "All yours, once we've extracted payment."

Juliana cringed as the witch pulled out a long glass object.

"Extracted...?" Hawthorn's eyes widened, latching onto the instrument. He turned back to Juliana, face pale. "What did you promise her?"

"Six months," Juliana returned. "No big deal."

"Of your *life?*"

"I've got plenty to bargain with, I assure you."

"You literally don't," Hawthorn snapped. "Forget it. We don't need them. Juliana, I promise I shall stay beside you every day for the next three months, if that is what you wish—"

"Are you trying to terrify me? No. We're taking them."

"I won't step foot in a single tavern—"

"I don't trust you," she said, and a stoniness dropped over him. For a moment, something like guilt prickled over her, like the kind she felt whenever she accidentally trod on a cat's tail. "Besides," she added, "what if someone sneaks in and carries you away? Or you're seduced by some beautiful mermaid who leads you off to water to drown you? This could be the difference between life and death."

Hawthorn gritted his teeth. "Fine," he said, and turned back to Mabel. "Witch, you will take the payment from me instead."

Mabel shook her head. "Six months of Fae life is nothing to anyone."

"Then take six years. I don't care."

"Immortal lives are worth far less than mortal ones."

"She can take the six months," Juliana insisted. "I don't mind."

"Well, perhaps I do," he said, eyes narrowing.

Perhaps is an excellent word for liars to use, she'd been told as a child. And it was. There was no way he really minded. Why was he doing this?

"I will have some mortal energy," Mabel insisted. "It was promised. That charm was not cheap."

"Two months of hers, then," Hawthorn bartered. "Five years of mine."

The witch narrowed her eyes. "Two months' of her life, five years of yours, and a month's worth of dreams... hers, of course. I don't much care for yours."

Hawthorn did not look pleased, but he deferred to Juliana.

She did not want to be in his debt, but neither did she want to bargain more of her life away. And the charm was for him, after all. Why shouldn't he pay?

She'd never be around to miss him for those five years, anyway.

"Fine," she said, holding out her hand. "Do it."

Mabel pressed the extractor into her palm. There was no wound this time, just a bright, hot pain, the sensation of something being pulled from her. A gold mist appeared inside the glass container.

Hawthorn was next. He winced, but said nothing, his whole body tight.

"Done," the witch declared, taking the extractor away. She passed them the pendants.

Juliana took hers and looped it around her head. It rested against her chest, like a small, hot lump of iron, buzzing faintly.

"Watch out for side effects," said the witch.

"Side effects?" Hawthorn screeched. "Like what?"

"Mild headaches whilst you get used to them, mostly."

Juliana raised an eyebrow. "*Mostly?*"

The witch shrugged. "There may be other side effects. Other ways you find yourself bound."

"And what does *that* mean?"

"I've no idea, dearie. I don't control the magic, after all." She gave them a cheery wink, and turned towards another waiting customer.

Juliana muttered something cross under her breath, sensing she'd get no more out of her. What did it matter, anyway, as long as she could track him?

She tugged on Hawthorn's arm and pushed him out of the marketplace, now heaving with life and sound, highlighting the silence growing between the two of them.

"Why did you do that?" Juliana asked as they walked home.

"You are going to have to be more specific."

"Why give her some of your lifeforce?"

"Six months of your life is a good chunk of it," he replied, not meeting her gaze. "I have almost forever to play with. And the charm was for me, not you. It made sense."

He didn't want to be in her debt, either. It made sense. There was no need to thank him.

There would never be a need to thank him.

4. THE TOURNAMENT

THREE YEARS UNTIL THE CURSE AWAKENS

The rest of the night before the tournament passed in a beautiful, hazy blur. She danced and chatted with Dillon and Aoife and a dozen other old friends, about old times and adventures in Autumn. She gorged herself on honey cakes and sweet wine and blue-veined cheeses, slivers of red meat she hadn't butchered herself, thick, warm, crusty bread, sugar apples and dates. She danced and laughed and talked till her feet ached, her sides hurt and her mouth went dry, until colours smudged together in a dark rainbow and music swam in her veins.

If it was magic, it was of a different kind.

Finally, blissfully, she crawled back to her cot, and sank into a dark, delicious slumber.

She woke late morning to her father standing over. He did not look best pleased.

"Make rather merry last night did we, daughter?"

Juliana chanced a grin. "I did, rather." She climbed out of bed, forcing a spring in her step. "Didn't drink too much though. Honest. Just enough to make it *look* like I did."

He patted her head. "Good girl. Others were not so smart." He picked a leaf out of her hair. "You should have gone to bed sooner, though."

Juliana ran her fingers through her tangles, picking out other leaves and bits of twigs. She'd strolled into the gardens at one point and lain down in the downy grass with her friends, like moonlight was a thing they could absorb. "I was enjoying myself."

"Clearly." Markham placed both hands on her shoulders. "No distractions."

"No distractions."

"Good. Inspect your kit. Training starts in an hour."

The tournament set to begin after midday, most of the competitors would spend the morning in the training ring. Most kept to simple warm-ups, others used the chance to show off their prowess to intimidate their competitors. Juliana's tactic was to appear mediocre, to show off nothing but minimal skills, and to learn as much as possible about every other participant.

Her father joined her after an hour. "What have you learned?"

Taking care that no one was watching, Juliana rattled off a list. There were a lot of young would-be knights, eager to test their metal, but only a few of any note. A merrow from the Summer Court, built like Neptune himself; a fox-faced rogue from Autumn, quick as a sharp breeze; Ser Miriam, if she decided to participate; and a hardy knight from Spring, rumoured to be part ogre.

Markham did not seem daunted by any of them, even though at least three were older and more experienced.

Juliana knew she was a fine warrior, but she had nowhere near his level of confidence.

I will destroy half the competition here, she thought. *But the other half may well destroy me.*

Before long, the trumpets were blazing, the drums beckoning all to the fayre. Ignoring the fire-tamers and the jugglers and the mermaids dancing with water, Juliana made her way to the competitor's tent.

There was no fighting fair in Faerie. The smallest squire could find themselves facing an ogre in round one where the only rule was that magic not be employed... at least not in the first few rounds. Everything else was fair game, even if it was like fighting a claymore with a twig.

Once they were registered, the competitors drew lots from enchanted marbles at the next station and queued up to take their places.

A ring in the garden outside had been set up with hay bales and barrels, a few stone shelters. Not that it did the gangly-squire any good in the first round against a werewolf. Although they typically only shifted during the night of the full moon, most could tap into their strength any day of the month.

And this one did. He almost took his arm off.

Juliana winced.

"He'll be fine," said Dillon, heading out the tent for his first round, whilst the werewolf took a break. "Bit of faerie magic will fix him right up."

Juliana knew this was true, but the boy's mangled shoulder and muffled cries were still hard to stomach.

That won't be you, she reminded herself. *You can do better. You'd never face a werewolf head on. You'd use the levels, gain the higher ground. And he'd never get past your sword.*

The next few rounds were similarly short-lived—all over in seconds and celebrated with little aplomb. Dillon won his first round, and winked at her as he left the ring. "Nervous?" he asked her.

"Rarely."

Which was true, although glancing around at the half-ogre and Miriam of Bath, Juliana knew her courage might falter later in the day.

Finally, her turn came. The ring was reset, and Juliana stepped forward to take her place.

An unknown squire from Spring, who must have been from one of the other courts, was Juliana's first opponent. She was small and slight, a little shorter than Juliana, but quick on her feet and not entirely incompetent with a blade. After a minute of sizing her up, Juliana knew she could beat her in seconds.

She didn't.

Don't give away your advantages, her father had taught her. *Hold back for the first few rounds. Don't give anyone the chance to evaluate you.*

So she played poorly, deliberately misstepping, using her left hand, letting the squire get in a few half-decent jabs. She let her opponent hit one of the hay bales, and made disarming her look almost like a fortuitous accident.

A lacklustre applause ended the match, and they shook hands.

Juliana took her seat for the rest of the first rounds, trying to focus on each fight, analysing who was holding back, each skill, each weakness. The second round saw the fox-faced rogue lose to the merrow, but the ogre, the werewolf, Dillon, Miriam, Markham and several other impressive characters all persevered.

Juliana's next round saw her paired with another squire, almost twice her size but clumsy with his blade. A short laugh whispered through the crowd as they approached each other, clearly thinking this would be an easy match for the lumbering oaf.

I can bring down a bear, Juliana hissed. *You're the one that's no match for me.*

She'd calculated the easiest way to topple him from the moment she saw him swing, but she played the mouse a little while longer, scurrying away from his crude swipes even though he'd left himself wide open. A few jabs at any point could have sent him toppling.

She made her eyes wide, let out a few little gasps, betrayed little more about her true skill other than the fact she was nimble.

She ended it by leaping up a hay bale, pushing one of them into his face, and disarming him whilst his mouth was filled with straw.

That earnt her a laugh from the crowd.

Hawthorn didn't laugh. His face was rigidly fixed in place, the same as hers, betraying nothing. The only movement he made was to twist his blackthorn ring.

Juliana moved swiftly up the ranks. Miriam took out the merrow. The werewolf fell to Markham. The number of competitors started to thin.

Soon, Juliana found herself pitted against Dillon. "I won't go easy," he warned her.

"You won't need to," she told him.

Dillon was the first to present any kind of challenge, and it was impossible not to reveal she'd been holding back a little when their blades clashed and she didn't buckle.

The crowd 'ooed'.

Dillon frowned, his eyes drifting to the sword in her hand. "You're right-handed?"

"And stronger than I look, right?" She kicked him in the stomach, sending him reeling. She shot him a smile. "I won't go easy on you."

They traded swipes, darting around the ring, sliding in and out of range. It was like a dance. It was the first fun she'd really had.

Focus, she said. *This isn't a game.*

It occurred to her that Dillon could actually win. He was stronger than her even if he lacked her speed, and resourceful, too—she'd seen him flick dirt into an opponent's eye earlier. He had good stamina.

Flirting her way into a position of power actually didn't seem like a bad idea.

She flitted behind one of the shelters. "You're stronger than I remember," she whispered coyly.

A blade swung over her head.

"You're faster," he said, as she rolled out of the way.

"Am I prettier than you remember, too?"

A brief pause before another swipe, a pinkness in his cheeks, not from the exercise. "Definitely," he said.

She rolled under his arm, jabbed him in the side, and leapt onto his back. She let her breath tickle his cheek as he tried to shuck her off.

"Feel like yielding?" she asked.

"No," he said, groaning as she gripped his neck. He moved towards the edge of the ring, attempting to fling her out of it. She held on, tighter.

"I don't *particularly* want to hurt you," she said. "Would put quite the dampener on our relationship."

"Relationship?" he croaked.

She waited until his attempts to remove her got weaker. If he fell, but she landed outside the circle, he'd still win if she hit the ground first. She detached her legs from around his middle, found her footing on his back, and vaulted over his shoulders. Whilst he was struggling to stay upright, she rolled over the ring, snatched up her blade, and placed it to his throat.

"Sorry," she said, "no hard feelings?"

He smiled at her, massaging his neck. "None whatsoever."

"Drink later? On me?"

"I look forward to it."

Juliana glanced up to the stands, and found Hawthorn smiling even less.

The number of remaining contestants was dwindling. As the tournament progressed into the final few rounds, new rules came into effect. The barrels and hay bales were replaced with powerful glamours. Some fulfilled the same function as before, other obstacles would turn to sludge at the slightest touch, or dissolve into bubbles. Some containers would spill open butterflies, others bees, and contestants would have to risk the potency of the glamour or charge through them regardless.

At the beginning of each round, competitors would be offered three vials, each offering a different skill or handicap. Some housed potions for extreme strength, speed, flight... others made an arm go numb, covered a person with boils, made their fingers turn to leaves, slowed them down to a snail-like pace, rendered them half blind, doubled everything in weight or turned their blade to rubber.

Once, in the past, Juliana had watched a body-swap mid match. It started an hour-long argument about who had won; the soul inside the victorious body, or the victorious body itself.

They hadn't used that one since.

"Never take the vials," her father had warned her. "You have no need of a boon. The risk is not worth it."

Juliana always found herself agreeing when she witnessed a fight where a seasoned warrior found themselves stumbling around the ring, eyes streaming with uncontrollable tears while their opponent shook the ground with quakes, but her mind quickly changed whenever she witnessed someone with super-strength split apart the obstacles, searching for their opponent imbued with super-speed.

And, when she found herself facing Miriam in the semi-finals, she knew exactly what she needed to do.

The vials were presented to both of them. Miriam watched carefully, waiting for Juliana to decide first.

I can't win without a gift, Juliana knew. At best, she could hope not to be defeated straight away, to put up a good fight. Maybe Miriam would allow her that. Juliana could not achieve a victory, not against a woman of her skill and prowess. She'd be a pebble against a wave. But with a gift, maybe... just maybe...

She glanced up at her father, saw him shaking his head.

She seized one of the vials.

The crowd 'ooed' again, but their clamouring increased when Miriam reached out a steel-gloved hand and took one as well.

Miriam never used them. In sixteen years of watching the tournaments, Juliana had never, ever seen Miriam take a vial. She had triumphed over ogres imbued with flight, pixies gifted super-strength, and werewolves with enhanced speed.

Juliana didn't know if she ought to be flattered or very, very scared.

Miriam's steely eyes met hers, and she offered her a curt smile. They nodded their heads and necked back the vials.

The liquid crawled down Juliana's throat like ice, sharp and tingling, spreading to every corner of her body. After the immediate effect, she found herself feeling no different as she took her place in the ring. She was no stronger, no lighter. She hadn't sprouted wings. She wasn't deaf, she wasn't blind—

Although, there was *something* different about her vision. Colours seemed enhanced, everything clearer, sharper. She could see beads of sweat on Miriam's face, detect the slow blinking of her eyes. Details she couldn't have picked out before.

Fae sight. She'd been gifted with fae sight.

And Miriam...

Well, that was for her to figure out.

The trumpet sounded.

Miriam and Juliana circled each other, touching nothing, making no move. Of course they did. Juliana had learned that from her, to let the enemy expose themselves first. Which one of them would move first?

The crowd held their breath.

Juliana watched Miriam's footsteps, trying to work out if she had received strength, if she trod faster or slower than before. Everything was impossible to discern; Miriam gave nothing away.

So Juliana would have to make her.

She charged towards her, changing her course at the final moment before they collided, swooping under her arm and slicing through one of the nearby barrels.

Her father always taught her to avoid them in the final rounds, but he also likely hadn't expected her to be up against *Miriam.*

Butterflies splurted from the barrel as Juliana skittered out of reach. They were harmless, by the looks of things, and Miriam seemed to know it too. She walked out of the cloud calmly, betraying nothing still.

There's something, Juliana knew. The vials were never empty. But whatever Miriam had drunk, was it aiding her or hindering her?

Juliana's mind whirled as she tried to make sense of it. If she had a gift, why wasn't she using it? Was she trying to be kind to her, to give Juliana a chance of a show?

Finally, Juliana swung. Miriam's blade met hers with force and precision, making her heels creep backwards in the dirt. The ground cheered.

Juliana withdrew, darting for an opening, Miriam's blade colliding with hers again. She was slick and fast and showed no mercy. Juliana was sweating in seconds.

Still no signs of boons or weaknesses, and Miriam wasn't letting her out of her sight.

She wasn't letting her out of her sight.

Even when the butterflies were swirling around her, Miriam had kept her eyes on Juliana, as if determined to keep track of her.

Why? What happened if she went out of sight?

She had to test it.

Dropping to the floor, she let Miriam's blade slice overhead, and kicked up a cloud of dust in her face, scurrying behind one of the shelters. She kept her ears open, waiting for Miriam's approach, certain it wouldn't be long. A little dust wouldn't stall her, and Juliana was breathing too hard to disguise her location.

But Miriam didn't come.

She had no visible boon. She hadn't received extra strength or speed. She could see—

But could she hear?

"Over here!" Juliana called.

Nothing.

Still not daring to trust it, Juliana carefully peered around the corner. Miriam's back was to her, examining another shelter. She wouldn't be the first to fake a handicap, but it didn't seem like Miriam's style.

Juliana picked up a loose stone and threw it at a bucket not far from Miriam.

She did not move when it clanged.

The crowd let out a low gasp, realising what Juliana had suspected; Miriam was deaf.

One-on-one, that hardly dented her capability as a fighter. Miriam was just as strong, just as formidable. She would doubtless register Juliana's presence if she rushed at her now, and she'd never knock her out of the ring with strength alone.

Juliana needed to be smart. She had enhanced sight. How could she use that to help her?

She sighed. If only it were dark already, and she could use her fae sight to see in the dark. With *two* of Miriam's senses lost, maybe, *just* maybe, Juliana stood a chance of beating her.

Her heart stopped for a moment. She couldn't make it night time, but maybe one of the barrels could. There were three left. One earlier had swamped the ring with blackness. If it had been reset...

It was her best chance.

She glanced at all three of them, planning her moves, trying to anticipate how quickly Miriam would turn, where she would go, if she'd have time to stop her before she could strike—

She seized her moment, Miriam's back still turned, racing into the open and smashing through one of the barrels.

Water. Just water, nothing more.

The contents raced across the ground, splashing against Miriam's calves and alerting her to Juliana's location. Juliana didn't care. It wouldn't stop her. Already she was racing across the ring, second barrel in sight. It exploded upon contact, filling the entire ring with—

Bees.

Fat, huge, blood-red bees, the buzzing thick and wretched, chomping through the air, searching for her skin—

Juliana pushed through. Let them sting her if they could. She'd been through worse. She only had to—

She charged into the final barrel and knocked it to the floor. Blackness erupted over the ring like a flood, expunging everything. The bees disappeared. The surfaces vanished. Even the crowd faded from view, their noises muffled and far away.

Juliana turned. She could hear Miriam close by, breathing hard. She forced herself to steady her own breath as her eyes adjusted to the sudden change. Crates slid back into focus. The ring burned, silvery and bright. Miriam's broad form grew wide and obvious.

Carefully, Juliana crept towards her, aware that Miriam was doubtless still using her sense of touch. Too close, she'd start to fight back. Too far away, she'd never gain the winning hand when the blackness cleared.

She took her space, and waited.

When the conjured dark finally peeled away, the crowd found Juliana's sword pressed to Miriam's neck.

And Miriam, far from looking annoyed, smiled.

5. DREAMLESS NiGHTS

LESS THAN THREE MONTHS UNTIL THE CURSE AWAKENS

Juliana had bargained away dreams before, but never so many for such a length of time. It was an odd sensation, made the nights feel short and empty, the mornings heavy and drugged. It felt unnatural to have nothing between sleeping and waking, no mushy thoughts as consciousness slipped away. It made her more irritable and clumsy.

They'll come back, she reminded herself. *Only another couple of weeks...*

One day, as she took lunch with Hawthorn in solid silence, Juliana found herself cutting into the table with her knife. She hadn't even realised she was doing it.

Hawthorn sighed. "I'm happy to find you something to butcher, but could you refrain from attacking my table?"

Juliana dropped the knife with a clatter. "I didn't realise."

"Evidently." He folded away the book he was reading. "I've gambled away dreams before, you know, when I've been out of coin. It never feels like a sacrifice until you're paying it." He paused. "Why did you do it?"

"Do what?"

"Pay with your life."

"It was the price she demanded."

"You could have gone elsewhere."

"Wasn't sure of the trouble you'd get into in the time it took me to find someone else."

"Is knighthood really so important to you?"

What else would I be trading for? "Must be."

"You don't sound so sure anymore."

"The older I get, the less sure I am of anything." She sighed. "Strange, that, don't you find?"

Hawthorn fixed her with a long, curious look. "No."

Juliana wasn't sure what he meant, and wasn't sure she wanted to ask. "There's a revel tonight," she said instead. "What are your plans between now and then?"

"I'm saving myself for debauchery and will be remaining safely within the confines of the castle, you'll be pleased to hear."

"Excellent."

"Do you wish to go anywhere?"

Juliana stilled. Hawthorn never asked her what *she* wanted to do. She had no idea how to answer. Why even ask?

"Not that I can think of."

Hawthorn tilted his head. "What do you do on your days off?"

When she was younger, she and her friends would go to the markets or run through the gardens or bathe in the summer lake, time an irrelevant thing that mattered to no one. But by the time she'd returned from Autumn, most of her friends had sought positions outside of the palace, new lives, new loves—new families, even. She had seen so little of them since her return, her circle shrinking to merely Aoife and Dillon, and even them she barely saw with her time monopolised by Hawthorn. If she had a day off, it was rare they did too.

"Train," she admitted, still unsure about where these questions were going. "Visit the gardens. Go to the lake. Take a ride in the woods."

"Hmm, a ride," said Hawthorn wistfully, staring out of the window, "it's been a long time since I went for a ride. In fact, that sounds like a delightful way to spend the rest of the day. Saddle my horse, my significant bother!"

Juliana glared at him.

"What? You said you liked riding."

"Say please."

Hawthorn sighed. "Please, my darling Jules, sweetest of my guards, song of my soul, won't you prepare our horses so that we may go for a ride?"

She got up from her seat, sweeping into a false bow. "As His Highness desires."

Hawthorn grinned as she swept towards the door. "I quite enjoy you bowing towards me. You should do it more often."

"In your dreams."

"Only once or twice."

"What was that?"

"The horses, woman!"

She rolled her eyes, asked one of the guards stationed outside to watch him, and headed off to the stables.

Juliana ought to have enjoyed the ride, and perhaps she would have, if it had been another day, different company, a different circumstance.

Because even though it was a fine day and Hawthorn was in high spirits and he didn't, thankfully, demand they go outside the palace gardens, it was still hard to keep track of him. Every time he raced on ahead she pictured disaster unfolding—some unseen assassin leaping out of the bushes, trolls scurrying up from the earth, perhaps a merrow appearing from the lake.

None of those things had happened, but it didn't stop Juliana imagining them.

Being on high alert all the time was exhausting.

It was one of the reasons she both longed for and hated her days off. She liked handing over that mantle to someone else, but at the same time, she could never quite shake it. It wasn't that simple. She still imagined disaster befalling him in her absence and after all these years, the weight was almost like a crutch—she didn't know how to stand without it.

What would it be like when the curse was finally over?

What would her life be like without him?

Hawthorn paused at the summer lake, the shadow of his great black mount spreading out across the still waters. He waited for Juliana to reach him, and they stood beside each other for some time as the sun began its descent, turning the lake to liquid fire.

Their horses nuzzled each other.

"If only we could get on as well as they do," Hawthorn sighed.

Juliana did not remove her gaze from the sunset. "You want to nuzzle my neck?"

Hawthorn went quiet for a moment. "It seems as friendly a thing to do as any."

"We are not friends."

Hawthorn scoffed. "Liar. Race you that tree over there."

"You aren't going to demand a neck nuzzle, are you?"

Hawthorn grinned. "Only if you lose," he said, and raced off.

A short time later, a sopping wet Hawthorn and a decidedly dry Juliana made their way back to the castle.

"You didn't have to do that, you know," Hawthorn said, handing the reins of his horse to Albert and sliding in through the back door, boots squelching.

"You didn't have to try to nuzzle me, and yet you did."

"I won."

"I made no agreement. Even by faerie word, I'm off the hook."

Hawthorn grumbled, pulling off his shirt as he ascended the stairs, and handing it to a passing maid who received a wink for her troubles and went away giggling. Juliana supposed she ought to have been happy he didn't just leave it in a pile for someone to trip over, as he'd done frequently when she first took the job.

"The joke is entirely on you," Hawthorn insisted as they climbed, "for I shall now be taking a very long bath with the door open."

"I don't think that's the punishment you're implying it is."

Hawthorn's grin turned wicked. "Why, Juliana, you *do* think I'm a delight to behold!" He walked into his bedroom and dropped his trousers.

Juliana walked away from him, back to her own room. "I think there is such a thing as doors."

By the time Hawthorn had finished with his bath, climbed into a velvet suit, curled his hair to perfection and painted his face with silver, the revel was already in full swing.

Once more, Juliana was on high alert, watching as countless fae flocked to Hawthorn's side. All had been checked for weapons before they entered, but that didn't mean they couldn't find some other way to hurt him. Once a spritely-looking nymph had seduced him into an alcove and tried to strangle him with her hair. It took way too long for Hawthorn to realise he was in danger, almost too long for Juliana to get to him, and not nearly enough time before he returned to flirting with everything that moved.

So Juliana watched. She took note of everyone who spoke to him, where they went afterwards, who they spoke to, how much they drank. Most people attempting an assassination would be trying to keep their wits about them, although that didn't rule out opportunists. Juliana had once stopped a very drunk faun who was trying to murder him (unsuccessfully) with their minute horns. "It seemed like a good idea at the time," had been his only defence.

Maytree had cut off his horns in retaliation, and several other parts of him before she got to his head. It decorated the Spring Gate for a full month.

No one tried again for the better part of that year.

Hawthorn appeared beside her, clearly drunk and lolling against her shoulder. "You don't seem to be enjoying yourself tonight, my queen of grumps."

"Doesn't it bother you that people here may want to kill you?"

"You apparently want to kill me all the time and yet I keep you around."

Juliana scowled.

"*Fine.* If you must know, I'm not scared because I have you here. Threats of violence aside, I trust you to keep me safe."

He placed a very loud, very long kiss on her cheek, and returned to the throngs of dancers, hooting with laughter.

Juliana raised a hand to her cheek, wondering if she wanted to wipe it away or hold it there.

Not long after, Hawthorn selected three guests to bring up to his rooms, and Juliana sat next door in her own, in case any trouble should arise. Hawthorn had been very insistent from day one that no one was allowed in his chambers when he was 'entertaining'—no matter the risk to his person.

"People don't just want to kill me," he'd insisted. "They want to kill me *and get away with it.* They'll have a hard time doing that with you posted outside."

Juliana, who did not particularly relish the thought of watching whatever he was doing, agreed.

Listening was almost worse, and she *had* to listen, just in case moans of pleasure turned into screams for help.

She really wished he'd stop inviting people up.

She'd suggested it, once.

"You can join us, if you wish," had been his only retort. "I don't think I'd mind you watching if you were *participating*."

She put an end to that idea pretty sharply.

Finally, the sounds of enjoyment slid into silence. Giggles turned to murmurs. Someone started to snore—probably the minotaur.

Sensing that her attention was likely no longer required for the night, Juliana checked the other guards were stationed outside his room, and started to undress, folding her uniform onto her chair, ready for the next day. She slipped silently between her sheets, the vines curling around the bed posts.

A short while later, halfway between sleep and the soundless dark of her not-dreams, she heard the adjoining door click open. A shadow hovered over her bed—

Juliana was yanked from sleep in an instant. She seized the knife from beneath her pillow and reached out to grab the assailant, flipping him over her shoulder onto her mattress and pressing the dagger against their throat.

"Jules, it's me!" Hawthorn clicked his fingers, and the candles blazed back to life. "Still keeping knives under your pillow, I see."

Juliana did not lower her blade. "What are you doing here?"

"Ah, so, the downside of inviting three people into my bed—especially when one is so, so large"—he stared wistfully into the distance for a moment—"is that there is shockingly little space left for you."

"So you've come to *mine*?"

"Yours was closest! And already warm. You can sleep somewhere else, if you prefer. Don't worry, I'll keep my hands to myself if you decide to stay, if you promise the same. I know I'm ravishing—"

"You mispronounced 'irritating'. You're irritating. The most irritating person I know, in fact."

"*Please*, Juliana. What if this is secretly some long-winded ploy by a very dedicated assassin to kill me in my sleep and then slip out before anyone notices?"

"You could wake them up and kick them out."

"It's rude to wake people who are sleeping."

"You woke *me*."

Hawthorn paused. "I'm sorry," he said, with a devilish grin, moving forward to take her fingers. He brought them to his mouth and kissed them. "Forgive me?"

"Ugh!" Juliana wrenched her hand away, stuffed the knife back under the pillow, and rolled over in the bed.

"Is that a 'yes'?"

"I'm too tired to argue," she said. "Just go to sleep. And don't touch me in the night."

Hawthorn chuckled. "I'd say 'I wouldn't dream of it', but..."

"No filthy thoughts in my room, thank you."

"Not even yours?"

"I don't have any filthy thoughts around you!" she hissed.

It wasn't entirely true, and she thanked the stars for her mortal tongue in that moment.

Hawthorn sighed, wriggling under the covers and scooting over to the other side of the bed. "*No* filthy thoughts at all?"

Juliana pursed her lips. "None whatsoever."

"Are you lying?"

"No."

Hawthorn elbowed her in the back. In retaliation, Juliana placed her freezing cold feet against his warm sides.

"Witch!" he hissed.

"You deserved that."

"I could learn to dislike you."

"Don't you dislike me already?"

"Not as much as I used to... although the bar was extremely low."

"Go to sleep, Prince."

"As my lady bids. Goodnight, Jules. I shall dream a dream for both of us and give you all the sordid details in the morning."

"If you do that, I'm leaving."

Hawthorn fell silent. "Jules—" he began at last.

"Oh, what is it now?"

His silence stiffened again. "Never mind," he said. "Sleep well."

6. THE BOON

THREE YEARS UNTIL THE CURSE AWAKENS

Miriam was taken away to the healer's tent and her hearing swiftly returned to her. Juliana followed, partly to follow protocol and ensure her boon was removed in time for the next round—the final round—and partly to ensure her former instructor wasn't angry with her.

"You did well," Miriam said, tapping her ears to ensure their functionality. "I am rarely bested in battle. You have grown much in three years."

"You took a vial."

Miriam swallowed a smile. "I thought I might need it."

Juliana could not imagine higher praise than that. She submitted herself to the routine tests, took a vial to wipe the boon from her, and allowed herself some refreshment. It wouldn't be long now until the remaining matches were done.

"What did you get?" Miriam asked. "Your ability? You had something. What was it?"

"Fae sight," Juliana admitted, blinking. Her eyesight felt blurry, even though she knew it to be keen for a human's.

Miriam sighed. "I've experienced it a few times in my life. Beautiful, isn't it?"

"Almost too much," she admitted. "Imagine seeing the world like that all the time."

"I don't think they appreciate it," Miriam continued. "Or use it to their best advantage. Would you, if you had it all the time?"

"Probably not. At least, not after a while." She stuffed a small bread roll in her mouth, moaning as the fruit erupted on her tongue. "I am going to miss this food..."

Miriam raised an eyebrow. "You're not staying?"

"I don't know. Father wasn't exactly clear."

"You know, he never quite told me why he left in the first place."

"He never told me, either."

Miriam opened her mouth, but before she could speak, the trumpet sounded.

"Is that the end?" one of the attendants asked. "That was quick."

A servant bustled into the tent, breathless and wide-eyed. "That half-ogre chap has finally fallen," he rushed. "Which means..."

Juliana did a quick elimination in her mind, and found her stomach dropping.

"Well, well," said Miriam, rising to her feet to clap Juliana on the back, "father against daughter. This really should be interesting."

Juliana had fought against her father a hundred, a thousand times before. But never like this. And never in all her imaginings since her father announced their participation in the tournament, had she imagined this. She never dreamt she'd make it so far.

"Scared, daughter?" Markham said as they approached the silver tray of vials.

"You taught me better than that."

The truth was, she *was* a little nervous. She could be fairly sure of surviving this—Markham's lessons sometimes hurt, but he would never publicly shame her, and he took no joy in causing her pain—but that didn't mean she didn't have other fears. She didn't want to let him down. She didn't want to let the *crowd* down, either.

But Markham knew her every weakness, and she wasn't sure she knew all of his. He was so much better than she was. How could he not be?

She tried to recall if he had an injury she could exploit, but he would doubtless have had everything seen to by the healers before now. He was stronger, fitter, larger than she was. She had the barest of advantages of speed.

He knew her every move, her every pattern, like the stitching on a cloth he'd sewn over years. She was carved in his image.

She couldn't beat him.

She wanted to. She *really* wanted to.

She waved away the offer of a vial. Somehow, this victory would mean nothing if she couldn't do it as herself—and she certainly couldn't risk a handicap instead.

Markham didn't look at her when he reached out and took a vial of his own.

Juliana's eyes widened, certain she must be seeing things. He *never* took the vials, and to take one against her, when he knew she wouldn't present him with a challenge, when she hadn't taken one of her own—

She spared no thought for the idea that he'd taken it *hoping* to be weakened, that he might provide her with an advantage; Markham wasn't like that. He fought to win.

She kept her eyes on him as they moved into the starting position, waiting for signs of the potion's effects. Markham held her gaze now, smiling quietly.

He was still smiling when the trumpet sounded and he launched forward with such speed that Juliana barely had time to draw her sword.

The impact with which his sword met hers was so strong it sent her reeling, a shock she felt down to her shoulder blades. She spun out of position, rolling out of his way just quick enough to miss the point of his blade.

It cleaved the ground in two.

The crowd gasped.

This was more than Markham's usual skill. He'd received strength from the vial.

The spectators were stirred into a frenzy. What they must think of this man, charging after his own daughter. They'd think he wanted to hurt her.

He certainly wasn't holding back. But although there was probably a lesson here, Juliana knew her father better than they did. He knew how fast she was. He knew when to pull back. His reflexes were finer than any fae's—finer because of the hard, constant work he put into his training. Finer because he never took anything for granted.

The swing of his blade inches from her face still made her stomach turn, and she fought back as if there was nothing between them at all, as if he were a monster who would cut her down without mercy. She zoned out the crowd, zoned out everything—concentrated on the space around his sword and nothing else as she dipped and stumbled and twirled to avoid it.

It took her a long time to acknowledge that she couldn't win this match, that all she was doing was delaying the inevitable.

And still she couldn't stop. Still, she found herself knocking over barrels, scrambling in the dust and the dark and the glitter, searching for an escape, a way out—

Until Markham had destroyed the ring, until all shelter, all surprises were gone. Until there was nothing left but the two of them and their swords.

She raised hers to meet his final swing, and the blade snapped like a toothpick.

Markham held his against her chin. "Good match, daughter," he said, "do you yield?"

Juliana unclenched her jaw. "I yield."

The crowd erupted into cheers of applause as Markham lay down his sword and helped her to her feet, holding up their hands in a sign of victory. Juliana tried to smile, but the action was forced.

"Why did you take the vial?" she asked him, as the clapping continued.

"Why did *you* take the vial, despite my teachings?"

"I wasn't going to beat Miriam without it. I would never have beaten you. Was this another lesson?"

"That depends on what you learned."

I learned that the rules don't apply to you.

Queen Maytree rose to her feet, and the applause quickly died down. "A splendid end to the tournament, Ser Markham, Juliana."

The two of them bowed.

"It was an honour," Markham insisted. "And a fine welcome back to court."

More cheers went up.

"You have won yourself a boon," the Queen continued. "Please, ask it of us. You already have knighthood for yourself, but perhaps for your daughter..."

Juliana's heart leapt. She'd never allowed herself to believe she could win, so she hadn't even dreamt of what she'd ask her. Knighthood? At her age? She'd be the youngest mortal knight to ever—

"Your Majesty is very gracious, and we are humbled by your generosity," said Markham. "But I have another request in mind."

Juliana's heart sank.

"Name it," said the Queen.

"I hear your son is in need of a personal guard," Markham began.

"That seems a little beneath your talents, honoured as we would be."

"Beneath mine," Markham continued, "but a fine use of my daughter's."

Juliana blinked, certain she'd misheard. "I'm sorry, what?" she said, at the same time as Hawthorn. He'd finally detached himself from his seat.

The Queen surveyed them both carefully, as if searching for a trick. "Your daughter is a fine warrior, as we have all seen. But His Highness' safety is our top priority—"

"Your Majesty, may I approach?" asked Markham.

The Queen scoured the crowd, all peering in. "You may," she said.

Markham came forward, guiding Juliana with him. Certain he was out of earshot of any but the royal family and their advisors, he asked, "How many assassination attempts have there been?"

The Queen's eyes flared. She chanced a look at her consort and her handful of advisors, as if searching for an explanation.

"Worry not, My Queen, I have heard no such rumours. I merely understand how people work. There will be more, you know, the closer he gets to eighteen. More people eager to avert the prophecy the only way they know how... by ensuring his eighteenth birthday never comes."

Juliana chanced a look at Hawthorn. His eyes were screwed to the floor, looking like he was trying to twist his face into a mask of indifference. It didn't quite work, especially as his skin turned pale and there were marks in his armrests where his fingers had been.

There *had* been attempts. Some recent, some close.

No wonder he'd baulked at her target-practise joke last night.

She wished she didn't feel guilty about that.

The Queen glanced at her advisors—sparing no look at her son—before turning back to Markham. "And you think that this... that Juliana can offer him more protection than we have currently?"

"She has already demonstrated her skill with the sword and her resourcefulness in a fight," Markham went on. "But consider that she is also mortal. How many guards do you have of her calibre? How many capable of *lying*? Of hiding the Prince and being able to say, 'he went that way!' to any errant assassins? She's pretty enough to pass for fae at a glance. People do not question lies in this kingdom. She can protect him in a way no others can. Besides," he added, shifting a look to the rest of the guards, "I hear none of the other guards appointed to the prince have lasted long."

A stillness passed over the party. The Queen's steely eyes flickered, unsure of what to say.

"Well," said Hawthorn, rising from his seat, "I think it's a fine idea. But mother, perhaps I could have a word with Juliana in private?"

The Queen's shock furthered. "Of course," she said. "We shall begin the revelries whilst you converse."

She clicked her fingers. Immediately, a band started up, and pixies arrived seconds later carrying goblets of wine and silver trays of rich delicacies to disperse amongst the crowd. Two guards leapt forward to escort Hawthorn and Juliana away from the inevitable chaos.

"To my room," Hawthorn instructed, "dally not."

He swept into one of the side entrances of the castle, up a winding staircase, and emerged into a short corridor. One of the guards entered his chambers first to give it a swift check.

"Wait outside," Hawthorn instructed.

"But, Your Highness—"

"I dislike repeating myself," he said in reply, and clicked at Juliana to follow.

She did so, her eyes narrowing. Hawthorn's bedchamber had changed little since she used to sneak into it to place frogs in his bed or fill his shoes up with mud. It was dark, all black velvet and green satin, with gold embellishments everywhere from the mahogany furniture to the giant bed of thorns.

Hawthorn sat by the window, poured himself a measure of wine from the silver jug on the table, and drank slowly. "Would you like a glass this time?" he asked. "Or would you still think I was trying to poison you?"

"This is a terrible idea," Juliana said, finally finding her voice.

"Agreed," Hawthorn admitted. "I completely forgot to check this wine for poison first, but after today, I almost think it's worth it." He necked back the drink. "This isn't some trick, is it?"

"Trick?"

"You haven't been sent by my enemies to spy on me?"

"Believe me, I'm as surprised by my father's request as you are. If *he's* been sent to spy, he didn't inform me." She paused, trying to think what his real motives were, and if he'd ever bother explaining them to her. "Not, of course, that my word means much."

"Yes, I've missed your delicious mortal lies, but generally speaking, you don't lie about the big things."

Juliana stilled, a little taken aback that he remembered that about her... that he remembered her much at all, really. She'd been expecting cruelty at worst, thorny indifference at best. Not this kind of strange familiarity. "If you're talking about the girl from Autumn, I only spoke up because I hated her a *little* more than I hated you. Nothing more."

"Indeed," said Hawthorn, although he did not sound convinced.

"This is ridiculous," Juliana rushed. "I'll go back to my father and speak to him. Or you can tell your mother this isn't going to work. I suppose I could utterly fail in my duties and have them dismiss me—"

Hawthorn paused, surveying her over the rim of his goblet. "Let me get this straight... your plan is to behave as badly as possible in the hopes you'll be dismissed?"

"That is correct, yes."

"But, my dear Jules, what about your knighthood?"

"To get away from you, I would give it all up in a heartbeat."

Hawthorn gasped, clutching his chest. "Words can hurt, you know."

"I doubt you have a heart to break."

There was a knock at the door. "Not now—" Hawthorn started.

"Have you discussed it?" came the Queen's voice. "Does she please you? We ought to issue the proclamation before the guests get too... wild."

Hawthorn stiffened, as if he were quite unused to his mother's presence in his chambers. He looked at Juliana, and then a slow smile slid across his face.

"Indeed, my dear mother, I have yet to see a knight that quite matches Juliana's level. We would be fools indeed to consider another candidate. Tell Markham we accept."

"Oh," said the Queen, sounding as surprised as Juliana felt. "Well, if you're sure—"

"I've rarely been surer," he insisted. "Give me a moment, Mother. I shall be down again presently."

There was the sound of skirts swishing along the cobbles, then silence once more.

"I hate you," Juliana hissed, the minute they were alone. "Why did you do that?"

"For many reasons, the most pressing being that I really enjoy teasing you, and, if I'm honest, though I find your presence loathsome, you are the most tolerable of all my prior guards."

"Tolerable? You hate me."

Hawthorn frowned. "Whatever gave you that impression?"

"You used to tie my school bag to the trees."

"You put frogs in my bed."

"Because you pushed me in the mud!"

"Only because—actually, I don't remember why I did that."

"Because you *hate me*," she reminded him.

"You vexed me," he said simply, as if this explained everything.

"Well, that's an entirely mutual feeling, I assure you," she declared. "So what's changed?"

"I have a vested interest in staying alive," Hawthorn said, still smirking. "And you seem awfully good with that sword."

"A lot of people are good with swords."

"A lot of people have already left my service, as your father so kindly pointed out. Running short of decent guards willing to put up with me."

"And what makes you think that *I'll* put up with you?"

"Because I intend to make you an excellent offer," he said, with the same serpentine smile. Juliana wanted to rip it off his face and shove it somewhere unpleasant. Did he *ever* stop smiling?

"I'm listening," she said through gritted teeth.

"Be my personal guard until my eighteenth birthday. If the curse is broken, I'll secure your knighthood. If the curse comes to pass, I'll devise some way of securing you vast riches so that you may live exceedingly comfortably in some land free of the curse."

"There are other paths to knighthood. Less... distasteful ones."

"It'll be an easy job and you know it. You'll still be the youngest mortal knight in the kingdom. And in the meantime, you get a life of relative ease. Finest food in the kingdom. Excellent cakes. Far better than anything you could get in that hovel of yours, I'm sure."

Juliana paused.

"You're actually tempted by the cakes, aren't you?"

"I... I like food, all right?" She pursed her lips. "*Fine.* I'll be your guard until your eighteenth birthday. Under a few provisos."

"Name them."

"You tell me where you're going to run off to. Your mother will have my head if I lose you, and it'll be hard to secure my knighthood without it."

Hawthorn rolled his eyes. "You exaggerate. My mother has always liked you. For some strange, unfathomable reason. But all right. I shall tell you when and where I'm running off."

"Good. Secondly, I want a sword."

"Don't you already have several swords?"

"A *fancy* one."

He sighed, half chuckling. "One fancy sword."

"Thirdly, you were right, I *am* tempted by the cakes. I want to eat anything I want for the next three years."

Hawthorn grimaced. "Even from my plate?"

"I'll keep my hands off your precious plate, Prince."

"Then agreed. Anything else?"

"No calling me filthy mortal or words to that effect."

"Fine. Are you quite finished?"

"I think so," she said. "Yes."

Hawthorn smiled, as though he had just won some great victory. "Juliana Ardencourt," he said, like he was issuing some great proclamation, "be my guard until my eighteenth birthday. Keep me safe from harm, and upon the day, I shall award you with a knighthood. Should I be unable to complete my vow, riches shall be awarded instead. Accept my offer, and I shall ensure that you are informed of my whereabouts whilst I am in your care, that you receive a fancy sword, that the kitchens will offer you anything they hold, and I shall refrain from calling you a filthy mortal. Do you accept our terms?"

Grudgingly, Juliana held out her hand. "I accept."

Hawthorn took her fingers and kissed them. "This is going to be a very interesting three years."

Looking at that beautiful, sinister smile of his, Juliana couldn't help but wonder if she hadn't just made a terrible mistake.

7. DAGGERS IN THE DAWN

LESS THAN THREE MONTHS UNTIL THE CURSE AWAKENS

"Where is the Prince?" shrieked Dillon's voice in the next room, yanking Juliana from sleep. She groaned, tumbling out of bed and shrugging off the arm that had somehow found its way around her in the night.

Odd. She ought to have woken up the minute he touched her. She was usually a light sleeper, prone to waking at the slightest noise, the slightest indication that something wasn't right. And yet somehow she'd managed to end up somehow... *entwined* with him?

She shook the thought away, pulling a robe over her nightgown and walking into Hawthorn's chamber. His menagerie from the night before were cowering on the bed, trembling under Dillon's hovering blade.

"Stand down," she told him. "He's right here."

"Morning," said Hawthorn, appearing behind her, shirtless and dishevelled. "How are we all?"

"You... you're... Your Highness." Dillon hastily dipped into a bow. "Forgive me, I was concerned—"

"I am unharmed, as you see. Jules was kind enough to let me bunk with her last night when these three took over my bed."

"Your..." Dillon's eyes caught Juliana's. "Your bed?"

"It's not what it looks like," she said quickly.

"It really wasn't," Hawthorn sighed, crossing the room to help himself to a glass of water. He inspected the goblet carefully before drinking.

"We... we should probably go," said the minotaur, shucking off the bed and reaching for his discarded clothing, taking care not to tangle his horns in the vines.

The other two bedfellows slid out of the sheets to dress. Juliana's gaze turned to the room. It was littered with short blades, none of which could have come in with the party. "Why are there knives all over the floor?" she asked, pursing her lips.

Hawthorn kicked one under the bed. "Ah, yes, those, um, you see—"

"How come they're allowed knives in the bed and I'm not?"

"These are on the floor," said Hawthorn swiftly, as if he'd just said something really clever.

"They weren't last night," the pink-skinned nymph whispered, deftly picking up one of the blades with her foot and running it underneath his chin.

Hawthorn's cheeks twitched.

"That was fun, Your Highness," she breathed in his ear. "Please call on me again... any time you're feeling *adventurous.*"

Juliana stared at him as the rest of his 'guests' slunk from the chamber, Dillon closing the door behind them and resuming his post outside. Juliana sighed. "I'm not even going to ask."

"Thank the stars." He sat down on the bed, smirking like he'd just discovered gold. "Last night was fun."

She looked up at the ceiling where a piece of stray clothing dangled from the chandelier. "Looks it."

"I wasn't talking about that. I was talking about you and me."

"What? *We* didn't do anything."

"You're a cuddler."

"I am *not* a 'cuddler'—"

"And yet I cannot lie."

Juliana's cheeks turned scarlet. "If you ever come to my bed again—"

"Without your permission?"

"Without—*I will never give you permission!*"

"If it's all the same to you, I'll make no vow to that end. I want to keep my options open."

"I will keep your *guts* open if you try anything—"

Hawthorn winced. "I'm so, so glad you can lie. That would be a really horrible end to a potentially lovely evening if you had to be held to that."

"Ugh!" Juliana held up her hands. "I'm going to get dressed."

"For the record, I have no problems with you guarding me dressed in your current attire. Bed hair really suits you. Also, you have lovely ankles."

"I hate you."

"Semi-naked really suits you too."

Juliana slammed the door between their two rooms. *Nine weeks,* she told herself. *Just nine more weeks of this.*

And then what?

All being well, she'd have her knighthood. She'd be able to go anywhere—anywhere in Faerie, at least. She'd have freedom and respect and purpose.

Why did she suddenly feel like she'd be losing something?

A vine dropped from the ceiling and curled around her cheek. She reached out to touch it. The vines never bloomed at her touch like they did for Hawthorn's, but they seemed to hum against her skin.

She would be sorry to leave here, to leave them, to leave her room.

Was that all she feared losing?

She sat down on her bed, not even straightening out the sheets. They were still warm.

And last night, although she had not dreamed, she woken restful, that feeling of emptiness abated.

"I hate you," she whispered to the shape in the sheets.

It was easier than admitting anything else.

8.
BRIARSONG

THREE YEARS UNTIL THE CURSE AWAKENS

After accepting Hawthorn's offer, Juliana was escorted to a small door at the side of his room she'd always assumed to be some kind of closet.

"Your room," Hawthorn explained. "I do hope you like it. Might not be homely enough for you, though. No mud."

Juliana scowled, but moved forward to wrench open the door.

She had to stifle her gasp.

She had expected it to be a provincial, rudimentary thing, little bigger than a closet with nothing more than a cot to sleep in and a trunk for her clothes. If she was lucky, she thought, she might get something a little cosier, like the room she occupied as a girl in the servants' quarters. This... this was something else. Although smaller and less grand than Hawthorn's, and devoid of gold embellishments, it nevertheless seemed fit for a royal. A substantial bed made of black, blooming thorns stood at the centre, hung with curtains that shimmered like dragonfly's wings. The bed and all the furnishings were piled high with deep blue-green velvets, rich purple satins. Everything was dark and sleek and soft.

I belong here, she reminded herself, wishing she could burn the clothes on her back. *I belong here. This is mine.*

"Is it to your liking?" Hawthorn asked.

"It'll do."

A smile flickered in his face, different from the others he'd worn in the past two days. Almost... almost warm.

"Perhaps you'd like a little while to settle in, maybe clean up? The party has barely begun."

"Right," she said, realising for the first time how much of a mess she was. "Of course."

He turned to leave.

"Hawthorn—" she started, and then stopped herself. What an informality. "I mean, Your Highness—"

"We successfully managed almost our entire schooling together without you being so civil, let's not ruin that now."

"Well, Prince, then."

"What is it?"

"Happy birthday."

Hawthorn paused, as if the words were alien to him. Had anyone spoken them at all to him today? There had been no proclamation, no toasts in his honour—

But of course they hadn't. The point of the tournament was to cover it up, pretend it wasn't happening. No birthday. No time passing.

But plugging up your ears doesn't stop the clock from ticking.

Three years until he turned eighteen.

Three years until the curse was unleashed.

And now Juliana was right there at the centre of it.

Going straight from a hut in the woods to the plush royal quarters of the Acathian Palace was quite the change, but Juliana was nothing if not adaptable. By the end of the first week in Hawthorn's service, she had memorised every guard change, every shift, and knew the faces of every servant in the palace. Most, of course, had not changed since she was a child, and it helped that she already knew every alcove, nook and cranny of the sprawling palace of silver and vines.

The newest member of staff was a food tester by the name of Mithel, a thin, spindly chap with a permanently sour expression. He only seemed to exist at mealtimes and vanished into the shadows between them. There were a few others new to her, but no one of note.

The main problem with her new position—other than it was exceedingly dull—was Hawthorn.

She had not quite considered when she accepted the job how much time she would actually be required to spend with him. Or, if she had considered it, she assumed that she'd be just watching him, standing outside his room, lurking in the shadows.

But no. Far, far too often the job involved actually *talking* to him.

In fact, Hawthorn rarely seemed to stop talking. He'd bark at the servants one minute and treat them like old friends the next. He took forever to dress in the mornings because he'd stop to rattle off an anecdote about gambling or the best way to make wine or some old folk story he couldn't quite remember the name of. He'd ask Juliana's opinion on just about every frivolous thing, from the colour of his tunic to which ridiculous ruffled shirt he ought to wear.

She never gave her honest opinion.

And he never listened.

He was also exceedingly free with his body. Juliana was no means embarrassed about her own, but Hawthorn had a way of... flaunting it. She was aghast the first time he'd summoned her into the adjacent washroom and found him soaking in the bath with nothing but a creamy film of bubbles hiding what was beneath.

"Wine, Jules, if you don't mind," he declared, stirring the water with a long, pointed finger.

Juliana's cheeks went bright red.

"You look flushed," he remarked. "Are you too hot? Mayhap you should have a cold soak when I am done."

It was impossible to tell if he was doing it on purpose.

She half missed the days he used to torment her.

Markham had vanished not long after the tournament had ended, giving no time to explain himself. He re-appeared before the end of the week, bringing with him a sleek horse the colour of waxy honey or fields of wheat, and a grin that Juliana hated almost as much as Hawthorn's.

"Are you giving me a horse as an apology?"

FOREST OF DREAMS AND WHISPERS

Markham handed her the reins. They were embroidered with green thorns that matched her palace uniform. "Only if it works."

The horse nudged her cheek, velvet-soft. Juliana felt her anger ebbing away. "Do I get an explanation as well as an apology?"

"I have my reasons," Markham returned. "But I think this is where we should be for now, with the curse approaching..."

Juliana stroked the horse, her fingers playing with her mane. "Do you think it can be broken?"

"All things have a way of being broken," he said sagely.

Juliana sighed. "You should have been a faerie, the way you play with words."

"It never hurts to speak like one of them," Markham continued. "Just remember—we *aren't* them. And they aren't us. Do not forget you're mortal, Julie, no matter how he comes to treat you."

Juliana wasn't paying attention. She was too busy plaiting the horse's mane and deciding what to call her, planning on where to ride her first. *Cercis*, she thought. A tree that grew in Autumn she was rather fond of. Yes, that would do nicely.

Markham patted her on the shoulder and headed off towards the barracks. "I'll see you on your next day off."

Juliana's promised sword arrived by the end of her second week, wrapped in velvet and ribbons. She lay it on her bed after her shift was over, carefully peeling it from its trappings.

She inhaled sharply, half grasping at her chest.

She had asked for 'fancy', but had never expected Hawthorn to follow through, not to this degree. She assumed he'd find something practical with a little embellishment and declare it was fancy enough for a mortal guard. This... this was something else. The grip was braided leather, the pommel set with a large green stone, and the guard was fashioned in the shape of thorns, the pattern of which descended down the silver-black blade. When she dared to clasp it, she found it light yet strong, and sharp enough to slice through air.

Beautiful. Impossible.

Hers.

She didn't mention it for days, half afraid it was a mistake, that it would be snatched from her the moment she let herself announce it. She didn't even take it out to practise, instead admiring it from the safety of her room.

It was almost another week before she buckled it on and dared to stroll around the castle with it, and even longer before Hawthorn said one evening when they were alone in his chambers, "You've not yet mentioned the sword. Is it not to your liking?"

"No!" said Juliana quickly. "That's not it, I just..." *I'm trying to work out why you gave it to me. I'm trying to see the trick in it.*

Because it had to be a trick, right?

But she didn't voice this. Letting him know she was confused was giving him power. "I just need to find a name for it, first," she lied. "A mortal superstition. Bad luck to thank someone for a nameless blade."

"Is that so?" Hawthorn twirled a curl with a long finger. "And have you thought of a name for it yet?"

Juliana paused, biting her lip. "Briarsong," she admitted. It was the first time she'd said it out loud.

"Pretty," he agreed.

"It's because it'll make a lovely sound when I cut people down with it." She unsheathed the blade and slashed it through the air. "Listen to it sing, isn't it beautiful?"

Hawthorn blinked at her. "It's terrifying, that's what it is."

"Do not fear the blade, Prince Prickle. Fear the one who holds it."

"I assure you, I am mighty cautious of that too." He stared at the pointed tip. "I'm half surprised you didn't name it Princeslayer."

"I'd have to kill a prince with it first."

"Ha!" he barked. "Wait, why are you looking at me that way?"

It was the first time she'd made him look uncomfortable since she assumed her new position. She decided she rather liked it.

"Rest assured, I'll never spoil this weapon with your blood, Dear Prince."

"That is not particularly comforting, I must say."

"I won't hurt you," she told him, "doesn't mean I won't threaten to."

Hawthorn flashed her one of his rare soft smiles, devoid of any sharpness, any teasing. She wasn't entirely sure what it was supposed to mean, and she was afraid to ask.

9. THE DREAMS RETURNED

LESS THAN THREE MONTHS UNTIL THE CURSE AWAKENS

Finally, Juliana's dreams returned to her. She'd almost gotten used to the nothingness of sleep when she woke one morning with the memory of dancing in her head.

The dancing part had been fun. The weird, fuzzy image of her taking off her clothes in front of Hawthorn? Less so.

Disturbed, and more than a little confused, she tip-toed into Hawthorn's room and into the adjoining bathing chamber. Technically, she was supposed to use the servants' one next to the kitchens, but Hawthorn had swiftly declared this ridiculous and they'd been sharing ever since.

It was one of the only good things about him.

Well, not quite the *only* good thing, she thought as she turned on the taps full-blast and added a generous helping of apple-spice soap to the foaming waters. Aside from his moments of generosity and no-nonsense behaviour, he could be kind when he wanted to be. Why, just the other day, when they were sent up a tray of over-cooked meat, he'd not complained—instead asking after

Iona. When he heard she was unwell and that one of the lesser-experienced cooks was substituting for her, he'd had flowers sent to her room.

"I hear it is a mortal tradition," he told her, "I rather like it. Feel free to send me flowers should I ever be bedridden again, sweet Juliana. Flowers, confectionaries, notes of your undying affection—"

It was at that point she threatened to send him a series of threats on fancy paper instead, and he quickly shut up.

It was one moment, she reminded herself, seeping into the waters and scrubbing at her skin. *One moment doesn't erase a lifetime of cruelties and poor, poor choices.*

Although it had been a very long time since he'd done anything cruel to anyone.

His poor choices, however, remained.

The bathing-room door clicked open. "Juliana—don't scream, it's only me—have you seen my finest silk shirt?"

"I'm not screaming!" said Juliana, sinking further beneath the bubbles. She hoped their presence didn't alleviate the impact of her scowl. "I never scream!"

Hawthorn's eyes brightened, flame-blue. "I could make you scream."

"Doubt it," she hissed. "And your shirt is on top of the chandelier. One of your 'guests' must have thrown it up there last night."

Hawthorn stepped out of the room again. "Ah! So it is. My thanks, cruel mistress. Also, it's nice you knew which one was my finest silk shirt. Really. I'm touched."

"You'll be dead in a minute, if you don't leave me to my bath!"

"Hmm. Not your finest insult, I have to admit. You need to try harder."

Juliana picked up a brush from the side of the bath and hurled it at the still-open door. There came a *thunk* as it collided with the floor.

"Missed!" said Hawthorn, and then poked his head around the door frame again, brush in hand. "Do you need this?"

"Out!"

Hawthorn dropped the brush, held up his hands, and retreated behind the closed door. She sighed, wishing they could install a lock. Unfortunately, Maytree had had it removed some year ago after Hawthorn had climbed into the bathtub drunk and almost drowned. "People are trying to *kill you!*" she'd raged. "Why do you insist on giving them a helping hand?"

Juliana had since realised that Hawthorn rather suspected someone *was* going to kill him at some point, and rather preferred death at his own, decidedly drunk hands.

She tried not to think too much about that.

Finally clean, she dressed and marched back into Hawthorn's room. He sat beside the window, writing in a notebook he'd had for years. He folded it away the minute she emerged. "You look vexed."

"This is my natural expression."

"Regrettable. Anything I can do to turn that frown upside down?"

"Accompany me on my errands this morning."

Hawthorn shrugged, rising to his feet in a languid, elegant fashion. He moved like a cat and she hated it. "As you wish."

She buckled on her sword, grabbed her basket, and headed for the door, Hawthorn keeping close beside her. He nodded to the guards as they passed, exchanging pleasantries with the servants and occasionally flirting with them. He stopped as soon as they were outside the palace grounds. He was always a little more wary with the locals, although she supposed he had reason to be—he could never be sure who was wishing him dead.

"Don't worry, I'll protect you," she'd told him once, half-jokingly.

"Ah, but can you protect me from their barbs, their stares, their dark thoughts?" he'd responded.

"Come again?"

"Do not think on it," he'd said, avoiding her gaze.

But he could not tell her it was nothing.

She'd asked Iona about it later. For all that the woman rarely gossiped, never giving away information unless asked, she seemed to know everyone's secrets, like she inhabited every hearth.

"Someone spat on him once," Iona had told her, making sure no one else was listening. "He's had stones thrown at him too."

Juliana paled, because even though she wasn't his biggest fan back then, the thought of doing that to anyone—least of all a prince—was unthinkable. "Maytree would have had them whipped."

"Aye, she would have," Iona confirmed, nodding her head sagely, "which is why he never mentioned it, and why I found him trying to apply sage to a scrape he'd sustained during an incident."

"Sage?"

"He knew herbs could take away the sting but didn't know which ones, and didn't want to go to the healer in case she told his mother. I sorted him out."

Juliana hadn't known what to make of that. She still didn't.

"You look pensive this morning," Hawthorn remarked, strolling beside her. "Care to share your glorious thoughts? Am I in them? Am I dashing?"

"I have not the imagination to create that image," she said, jaw tight.

Hawthorn sighed, clutching his heart. "The lady wounds me so! May I hold your basket?"

"What—why would you want to hold my basket?"

"I am hoping that it might make me look less conspicuous."

"You—you are wearing finest spider-silk!"

"Well, I couldn't exactly bring myself to dress in those rags the peasantry call garments...."

Juliana sighed so deeply she felt her breath cut against her ribcage. *I can't believe I ever felt sorry for him,* she thought, and thrust her basket at his face. "Here, hold this. Nice and high, so I don't have to look at you."

Hawthorn made no complaints, and diligently accompanied her as she swept through the market, purchasing more oil for her sword, a buckle to replace one that had broken, and a small pot of ink.

Purchases complete, she turned to head back towards the castle, almost bumping into a young mortal woman carrying a small baby strapped to her front and a large basket.

"Bree?" Juliana said, recognising her warm brown face and dark eyes immediately. She was the widow of a young knight they'd lost on an expedition into Winter a few months ago. Juliana hadn't seen her since just after the baby had been born. She'd been meaning to check in on her. "How have you been?"

A terrible question to ask a faerie, bound to honesty. How would most be having lost a husband and gained a child?

But Bree was mortal, and answered as a mortal would. "Oh, fine, or as well as can be expected! This one keeps me busy, of course. She's starting to sleep better now, which helps."

Juliana nodded, trying not to notice the dark circles under Bree's eyes or how frayed and patched her dress was. She'd been compensated when Jack died, of course, but that was a while ago, and rumour had it he'd never been that great with money.

She bit the inside of her cheek. "Can *I* help at all?" she asked, hoping she wasn't being rude.

Bree smiled, more warmly than before. "Honestly, if you asked me a few weeks ago, I'd have jumped at the offer, but then my brother came into a bit of money. Shouldn't be glad of it—gambling, you know—but this time he actually gave some of it to me and bought his way into an apprenticeship. Said he's going straight and going to help us. Wish he was a faerie and I could hold him to it, but even our words are worth something."

It was at this point, the baby squirmed, hitting out with her fist and accidentally catching it on a spiky, low-hanging plant, making her wail. Bree made her goodbyes quickly, kissing the fat little hand as she bimbled away.

Hawthorn, who'd remained examining a stall by the side while the two conversed, now appeared at Juliana's shoulder. "If I was hurt, would you kiss me better?"

Juliana glared. "Oh, shut up."

"That wasn't a no..."

She flicked his chest, and the two of them walked back to the castle in silence.

Something niggled at the back of Juliana's mind. Something about Bree's brother's turn of good fortune, his sudden coming into gold—his desire to do better.

I seem to have misplaced my coin.

"Did you know Jack?" she asked.

For a moment, Hawthorn was quiet. "I did."

"What about Bree's brother?"

"We've met."

"Lucky he came into that money when he did."

"Indeed."

Hawthorn was rarely so elusive. It irked her more than it should. "Be quite the coincidence if he was the one that came into your misplaced coin."

"Quite the coincidence indeed. But a fortunate one which works out best for all involved, wouldn't you agree?"

"Oh, certainly." She stopped for a moment, pursing her lips. "Prince?"

"Yes?"

"Have you ever glamoured someone for their own good?"

Hawthorn smiled, but he did not meet her gaze. "Maybe once or twice."

Juliana bit the inside of her cheek, resting her hand against Briarsong's hilt. "You're infuriating."

"Perhaps," he said, "but sometimes I think you rather like me that way."

At the inner gate, Juliana and Hawthorn were met by Kieran, Maytree's personal guard. He was reed-slim and silver haired, a creature of lakes and moonlight.

He'd been in Maytree's service for close to a century, and was as solemn and serious as stone. Juliana quite liked this about him, and respected his prowess as a warrior.

"Her Majesty requests your presence in the council room, Your Highness," Kieran said.

Hawthorn groaned, but Juliana elbowed him and he diligently marched ahead. She moved to follow him, but Kieran cut across her.

"I can escort him," he told her.

Juliana frowned. There'd been precious few times she wasn't allowed to follow him into the council chambers. "Why can't I—"

"Your father has returned," Kieran said, with a merest hint of a smile.

Juliana's heart jumped. He'd been gone for over a month. Rarely did missions take him so long. She knew better than to worry—or perhaps had grown used to it—but still...

"Where is he?"

"Down by the training ring. Arrived maybe an hour ago."

Nodding in thanks, she tore away from the gate and headed down to the training ring. Trust her father to go straight there rather than to his lodgings in the barracks.

She spotted him immediately, sparring in the ring with a young squire—a small, spritely boy not yet fourteen by the name of Ian. Despite his size, Ian's swings were decent, but his footwork was clumsy at best.

Markham hit the side of Ian's left calf with the flat of his blade. "Turn, boy. Tighten your stance. Be less of a target."

Someone in the stands jeered he was hardly a target at all at his current size, which made his cheeks redden, and his swings worse. He missed his next attack, tumbling past Markham and landing poorly. He let out a sharp cry.

"On your feet, boy, walk it off."

Ian climbed unsteadily to his feet, wincing on his wounded ankle. Not broken, but maybe sprained or twisted, an injury easily fixed with faerie magic. Juliana had pushed through dozens of injuries when she'd had no other option, and not thought much of it, but this was only training, and the boy was only young.

Markham's swings grew wilder. "Come on, lad. Defend yourself."

To his credit, Ian was really trying, but it was hard to fight back whilst shouldering the pain. Markham's attacks pushed him further and further back, losing footing. Sweat beaded his brow.

If the lesson was about footwork, the objective had been lost. It was now about pain.

She was just about to intervene when Miriam's blade cut across them. "That's enough," she said. "Get yourself to the healer's, Ian. She'll sort you out."

The boy hobbled away, head bowed gratefully or in embarrassment, it was hard to tell.

Miriam turned to Markham. "That was unnecessary. The boy was injured."

"He needs to learn to fight through pain."

"He will," Miriam said, "if he needs to. But not today. That wasn't the lesson."

"War won't wait for him," Markham said darkly. "You know what might be coming."

Miriam's eyes narrowed. "I know having his ankle seen to today won't make tomorrow any harder."

"You're too soft."

"And you're too hard!" Miriam spat back, harder than Juliana had ever heard her. She shook her head, sighing. "What happened to you? You're not the knight you once were. Not the *man.*"

Markham shrugged, turning away. He did not yet seem to have noticed Juliana. "Everything good about me went with her."

Juliana's stomach churned uncomfortably. Miriam, too, seemed to tighten her face, the awkwardness palpable. "You've had a long journey," she said quietly. "Take some time to rest."

Markham said nothing, and Miriam turned away. Pretending she'd only just arrived, Juliana slid into the ring and bounded towards his side.

"Father!" she said, half leaping into his arms.

Markham clung to her, and for just a moment, she felt like the child he'd left behind all those years ago, when nothing else in the world was better than his return.

"How was the mission?"

"Oh, you know, wiped out some ogres, took down a giant—the usual."

"No trace of Ladrien's supposed army?"

Her father shook his head. "They must be somewhere, but that land is almost impossible. Besides, we won't find Ladrien there."

"No?" Juliana frowned. "Where else could he be so well concealed, for so long?"

"He never liked the cold," Markham responded. "Or so the old faeries say. Avoided it wherever he could." He waved a hand. "I digress. How are you, daughter?"

Juliana shrugged. "Nothing to report. It's been painfully dull around here."

"And the Prince? Still pulling at your braids?"

"If he tried it now, he'd lose a finger."

Markham smiled, and patted her head. "That's my girl."

He put his arm around her, and they walked back to the barracks together. For a moment, Juliana let herself believe that all was fine.

But only for a moment.

10. THE ROAD TO AUTUMN

LESS THAN THREE YEARS UNTIL THE CURSE AWAKENS

A few months after Hawthorn had asked Juliana to become his guard, his mother decided to take the entire royal procession to visit the Autumn Court, a visit declared 'long overdue' somewhat awkwardly, seeing as the family had had little communication with Autumn since the incident with Lucinda almost four years ago.

Hawthorn would have liked to have declared he'd not thought of Lucinda since the day she left court, but he'd be lying. He'd thought a lot about how she'd made him feel, and why he hadn't found that with someone else.

And he thought a lot about why Juliana had reported her, knowing the trouble it would get her in, knowing she wouldn't be believed.

He wasn't quite sure he believed her declaration that she simply hated Lucinda more. He liked thinking there was something else to it.

He didn't like liking it, though.

For safety reasons, several carriages were taken on the journey, some completely empty to confuse any lurking assassins. As a further act of diversion, Queen Maytree and Aspen were in a separate carriage entirely, leaving Hawthorn and Juliana by themselves.

It was a three-day trip.

For the first day, Hawthorn talked nearly the entire time. He challenged Jules to countless card games, recited poetry, educated her on several historical facts and at one point tried to serenade her.

It didn't end well for him, and he had no idea why he'd even attempted it.

Juliana didn't seem amused. She was tightly wound the entire time, barely muttering a word. Come to think of it, when was the last time he'd seen her smile?

He kept his eyes on her all evening when they rested at an inn. It was like she was standing on a bee's nest. She never relaxed, her brow rarely anything but furrowed.

"You don't smile much," he remarked that night, as he changed for bed.

Juliana stepped out from behind the screen. "I have nothing to smile at."

Hawthorn didn't quite understand that. He had people wanting to kill him all the time, and he still got smiled at. *Most* people smiled when he was around, come to think of it. And why shouldn't they? He was hilarious.

He tried not to think about Juliana's lack of smiles, but it provided a better distraction than thinking about what might await him at the Autumn Court.

The next day, he couldn't *stop* thinking. And he couldn't summon his usual smiles, either.

"Are you nervous about seeing Lucinda again?" Juliana asked mid-afternoon as they trundled through the Autumn forests.

Hawthorn glared. The truth was, he *was* nervous. Or at least awkward. He was almost certain now that he was older, she was definitely going to try seducing him again. He was very worried he wouldn't be able to resist.

"I was twelve years old when I last saw her, a foolish boy," he said swiftly. "I've grown a great deal since then." *Outwardly. Outwardly, I've grown. Inside I am afraid I am just the same.*

"Doesn't answer my question."

"Are *you* nervous? You and Lucinda never precisely got on."

Juliana half-smiled, but it was devoid of warmth. "I'm armed," she said, patting her sword.

"You aren't allowed to cut down nobles."

"Correction," she said, as he sipped from his flask, "you're not allowed to get *caught* cutting down nobles. No body, no crime."

Hawthorn snorted wine up his nose. "You aren't nervous, then?" he asked, whipping out a silk handkerchief to mop up the damage. He ought to be annoyed if his shirt was spoiled, but he found he didn't care. The laugh was worth it.

"I am never nervous."

She certainly never *looked* nervous, but that wasn't exactly the same thing.

The carriage jolted to a sudden stop. Juliana's arm flew out, pinning him to the seat. "Don't—" she started.

A cry sounded at the head of the procession. A horse brayed. A crash splintered through the air, like the ground was being ripped apart. The carriage rocked, once, twice—

Juliana's sword was out in an instant. She kicked open the door. Hawthorn kept close behind her, peering out at the rest of the procession.

A massive club came swinging towards them. Juliana grabbed his arm and flung him out of the way, her sword slicing upwards at the fist of an enormous ogre.

Hawthorn had never seen a full ogre before. They tended to live in the mountains around Winter. He'd seen them in illustrations, met the occasional half-ogre at court. They tended to be broad characters with heads a little smaller than most, but otherwise appeared to be much like other fae citizens.

But this creature was far from fae, far from human. It was almost twice his height, broader than a bear, a huge, grey, lumpy creature, like stone rendered flesh.

Juliana's blade barely scratched it.

And it wasn't alone.

Black shadowy creatures had descended upon the party—long, ragged limbs, wings like torn capes with shapeless faces and white, empty eyes.

Sluaghs.

Twisted unseelie creatures composed of the souls of the dead.

And there were dozens of them.

Miriam of Barth ran forward, swinging her claymore, decapitating one and streaming towards the ogre. She slashed its hamstrings, bringing it crashing down, driving her sword through the base of its neck.

"Protect the prince!" she cried.

Hawthorn stood screwed to the spot, aware of sound, of noise, of a sickening, debilitating thumping in his chest, but his muscles wouldn't move. He *couldn't* move, not even when he heard his mother screaming, saw her running towards him and throwing up a wall of vines, covering him from the sluaghs.

Queen no longer, but a warrior.

And he was a statue.

Juliana dragged him round the corner of the smashed carriage, pressing him into a crevice as a sluagh flew over his mother's barrier. Her blade glistened with black blood as it twisted through the air, slicing through shadow.

And Hawthorn stood there once more.

"Juliana!"

Markham's voice now, shouting at his daughter as he fought his way towards her.

Something sharp and cold fastened around Hawthorn's shoulder. A sluagh was perched above him. He let out a cry. Juliana twisted round, cutting off the hand at the wrist, dissolving the limb into flesh and shadow until the remains fell with a wet, shuddering thud. Another pounced behind her, slicing across her arm.

Unthinking, Hawthorn bolted forward, summoning fire in his fist and hurling it clumsily in the rough direction. It seared against its wing.

Juliana spared a second to blink at him before running it through.

"Juliana!" her father called again. "Run! Protect the prince!"

Juliana nodded, grabbing Hawthorn's arm, and shoved him forward into the forest. He wasted only a second to look back, seeing his mother perched on an overturned carriage, bending the roots to her whims as the onslaught continued.

She was no longer a queen, regal and refined. She was power and chaos, nature in the shape of a woman. He didn't think he'd ever seen her look quite so terrifying.

And yet he didn't want to run. He knew he couldn't fight, but he didn't want to leave.

But he knew better than to try and stay to help. His fire had barely grazed the sluagh. Swallowing his resolve or summoning his courage, he shoved aside all feeling, and bolted with Juliana away from it all, heart pounding, lungs burning, the ripping and screaming still clawing at his ears.

The forest dissolved into shapeless colour, dark and disordered, a frenzied mess of leaves and brambles. He was conscious of nothing, the sounds of battle sliding away, replaced by the demented thud of his own heartbeat pumping through his ears. Everything and nothing hurt.

They might have run for hours, slipping down banks, sliding in the mud, spoiling his silken clothes. He had no notion of time.

Finally, Juliana stilled, slowing to a stop in a ditch and resting against a fallen log. She took a few moments to steady her breathing. "Are you hurt?" she asked.

He shook his head, quite forgetting to ask about her. His words had turned to slush.

He could still hear the battle raging behind them. Was that good? It meant that everyone was still alive.

Hopefully.

Juliana surveyed their surroundings, glancing at the sky. "We need to keep moving."

"Where to?"

"Back towards Acanthia."

Hawthorn buckled. It was over a day away by carriage. On foot he didn't want to think. So much lay between them and their destination, a myriad of disasters— "It's too far—"

"I spent years in these woods," she reminded him. "Our old cottage isn't too far away. We should reach it before nightfall."

Hawthorn nodded, not sure what else he could do. Uselessness gnawed at him like a rodent. He followed Juliana further down the twisted path, pulling on the frayed cuffs of his shirt, trying not to look at his scuffed, mud-soaked boots or the flecks of blood and flesh splashed across his garments. He'd never been so filthy in his life.

He hoped the others were all right.

Not long before nightfall, they reached a tiny cottage beside a stream, swallowed up by the trees and half made of earth. It was a shallow slip of a building, the sort that looked like a strong breeze might blow it away.

Inside was barely any better. It had one main room, no proper space for bathing, and a tiny bedroom in the attic. A rudimentary kitchen was set around a fireplace. Most of the furniture was rough and crude, all sharp edges, no softness.

Easy as it was to imagine Juliana here, he felt she was better suited for palace life.

"Don't," Juliana growled.

"What?"

"I know how provincial it is."

"I didn't say anything."

She shifted into the kitchen of sorts and started digging through cupboards. The place didn't look picked clean, exactly. It was more like it had never had much in the way of belongings to begin with.

Juliana emerged from the cupboards with a small wooden box. She put it on the table, taking out dried herbs so old they'd practically disintegrated, needles, thread, and a small clear vial of something Hawthorn assumed was alcohol.

Wincing, she at last unbuckled her sword, hauling off her tunic and rolling up what remained of her shredded shirt.

Her upper arm was slashed. Why hadn't he noticed?

"Not too bad," she declared, dousing it with the alcohol. "Doesn't need stitches."

"Stitches?" Hawthorn recalled. "As in... sewing? Mortals *sew their flesh?*"

"We don't have other options, not..." *Not out here.*

Because whenever she'd been injured as a child, she'd been treated by the same faerie healers he had access to. Mortals were more breakable, but fae magic healed them just as well.

But there were no healers out here.

"Here," said Hawthorn, moving forward and grabbing her wrist, "let me."

Juliana hesitated, but soon relented. His hand moved towards her wound, noticing other tiny silvery scars as he went. His palm hovered over her cut, and he tugged on the energy he'd always had, as a faerie, as a prince. The ability to change and manipulate matter in the way others could clench their fists.

Light poured from his fingertips, knitting her flesh back together. It wasn't flawless, wasn't perfect, but it now looked like it had happened days ago rather than hours.

"I've never been particularly adept at healing magic," he said.

Juliana glanced down at her arm. "I still need to bind it."

He shuffled off his own muddied doublet and found a patch of his silken shirt that remained unspoiled. It hardly seemed worth keeping at this point, and he didn't much care for how filthy the rags in Juliana's box looked.

He tore off a strip and wrapped it round her arm, binding it as tightly as he dared. "Decent?"

"It'll do." She waited for a moment. "Thank you."

"You're hardly indebted to me. Reckon you've saved my life at least once today."

"Right."

She started clearing up, inspecting the entrances and exits, the condition of the beds. In the months the hut had lain dormant, a thick sheet of dust had settled over every surface, and something had made a nest in the corner, destroying her father's bed. The mattress upstairs apparently remained 'serviceable.'

The sun set. Hawthorn stared at the dusty hearth, wondering when Juliana would be starting a fire or be barking at him to do so instead. She seemed busy enough checking everything was safe. She probably *expected* him to start the fire. It was getting cold and dark, after all.

He pulled out a few logs and shoved them into the space, clicking his fingers for flames.

The moment the flames hit the cold hearth, Juliana bolted from her spot, knocking him to the ground as she stamped out the embers. She whipped out her dagger, as if expecting the sluaghs to materialise in the room. "Are you trying to kill us?"

"Um... no? You're the one with a knife out. Are you trying to kill me?"

Juliana's eyes narrowed. "It's tempting, sometimes, Prince Prickle. It really is."

"So... why can't we have fire?"

"It brings attention to us. We don't know how many of those things are still out there. It's best to be safe."

"How will we cook dinner?"

"We aren't having dinner."

"No *dinner?*"

"There isn't anything to eat and we can't risk hunting right now. It's not ideal, but we'll live. It's just a couple of meals."

Hawthorn was aghast. "I've never not had dinner before."

"Clearly."

"Have you?"

"Yes," she said through gritted teeth. "It's not pleasant, but survivable."

"But I'm *hungry.*"

"It's survivable as long as you don't complain to the girl with the dagger that you're hungry."

He sighed, shoving her off him, and went to inspect the few things she'd dragged from the cupboards. The only consumable was a pot of ancient tea.

There was water, at least. She'd drawn some up from the stream. It was easy enough for him to heat that with magic, and mix it with the leaves. It helped a little with the hunger.

"We'll need to share a bed," said Juliana, finishing her cup. "Not much space. Slightly safer up there. We can always escape using the window."

"Great," he said, surprised he could say that truthfully.

There was nothing else to do with the evening, and the cold soon started to stiffen around them. They made their way upstairs, removing what little of their clothes they dared and bits of jewellery certain to cause discomfort. Hawthorn's blackthorn ring rolled against Juliana's necklace of berries.

He doubted she was removing it because she trusted him not to glamour her—she definitely had another piece on her somewhere. When they were children, Hawthorn and his friends had devised a bet over who could glamour the most of their mortal classmates. Several of the children were not easily tricked, but after a while, pretty words or cunning traps had all of them falling victim to a glamour sooner or later.

All except Juliana.

Everyone had tried—flattery, bribery, trickery… cutting off her necklace in class, trying to break into her room while she slept—all manner of behaviour that went from amusing to cruel painfully fast. It did not seem to matter. Juliana clearly wore more than one ward, and she was not giving up the location of the second.

Hawthorn didn't like that she was winning. He equally didn't like how insidious the rest of his friends were getting, but he refused to lose face in front of them. Faerie friends were hard to come by, mortals were as common as mice. Only one could stand beside you as the centuries turned.

But Hawthorn had never much cared for torturing creatures, so, one afternoon, sparring in the ring, he cornered her.

"Just give up," he advised. "Let me glamour you. I promise it'll be quick and meaningless—I'll compel you to make a cartwheel and we'll be done with it. My companions… I cannot promise what *they* will do, when they win."

Juliana narrowed her eyes. "*If* they win," she said, and then ducked away from him.

A few weeks later, the group finally caught her bathing by herself, her clothes on a pile by the bank. There was the necklace she wore, and they tore the rest of her clothing to shreds, discovering she'd sewn berries into the hems.

The group cackled, hid in the bushes, and waited until she returned.

Hawthorn wasn't having the best of times—he knew mortals were frequently ashamed of their natural bodies, whereas faeries just wore clothes for decoration, and this type of entertainment seemed far from sporting—but he didn't want to call it off for fear of what the others might say if he did so.

Besides which, he'd offered her a way out. She deserved this humiliation. She did.

He gritted his teeth as she slunk from the water, knowing he'd not be able to speak those words.

His friends sprung from the bushes, but not before Juliana had discovered her shredded clothes, sensed a trap, and drawn her sword. They'd not thought to take that from her, assuming they could glamour her into submission.

"Stand down, mortal," said Maize, a particularly cruel boy from Spring, "there's no point. We found your wards. Now..." He stepped forward, black eyes blazing. "*Crawl to me.* Crawl like the insect you are."

Juliana did not crawl. Instead, she kicked him over and slashed the back of his hand. "No," she hissed, her body still dripping with water.

Maize clutched his hand, whimpering. "Witch! I'll see you whipped for this! My father—"

"*My* father is one of the Queen's most trusted knights," Juliana continued. "If you want to play that game. You think he'll let any harm come to me after what you've just done? And in any case... I'm the one holding the blade. I could take off your hand before you could move. Are you willing to risk it?"

Maize's face paled. "You... you wouldn't."

Juliana moved closer. "Wouldn't I? Shall we test it?"

The rest of the group murmured, wondering if they should step in, what they should do. Juliana appeared immune to glamours. What else could she do? They'd never encountered such a mortal before, and most weren't proficient with swords. They stared at her like she was a wildfire they needed to evade.

"Give me your cloak," Juliana demanded.

Maize stared at her incredulously. "What?"

"Your cloak. I require it. Unless you'd like to explain to the entire court what happened to my clothes?"

Reluctantly, Maize obliged.

No one ever found out where Juliana kept her third ward, but they never bothered her again. There were all sorts of rumours—that she swallowed a potion every morning, that she painted her nails with rowan-berries, that she'd made a deal with a forest god or eldritch terror.

Hawthorn, for his money, suspected the truth was far more simple; she had another somewhere about her person.

He searched for it now as she peeled off her layers, but found all thoughts of wards washed from his mind as he saw the scars and bruises dotting her skin and arms.

For some reason—even though he knew he caused a bruise or two of his own when he was younger—the sight of them twisted. He found his fingers twitching towards her skin, as though he hoped to rub them away.

She turned, sensing movement. "What?"

"Don't they hurt?" he asked.

Juliana paused. "I really don't notice them any more."

That didn't answer his question. He turned his gaze to the wooden ceiling, thinking of how different her life had been that pain was like a shadow to her.

He thought of how he'd frozen in battle and she'd drawn a sword, how she'd not complained once about being wounded, or going hungry.

She really was so very different from him.

Silence descended. His eyes turned around the scrap of space that had been hers not so very long ago. On the windowsill sat a line of tiny bones and eggshells—an old remedy to ward off danger. Little patches of faerie in this otherwise mundane hut.

There was nothing else up here but the bed and three trunks. What did they contain? Weapons in one, surely. Clothes in the other. What of the third?

A chipped vase rested on the surface, filled with wilted flowers. Behind it, he saw the faded pattern of leaves stencilled into the wooden walls, then half chipped out with a knife. Why had she done that? Were they not good enough? Had she grown out of them?

Something had happened to Juliana in this hut. Not one thing, but a dozen, a hundred tiny things she probably didn't even remember, but something that had chipped away the smiles she used to wear and the ease she used to flaunt as surely as the blade against the stencilled leaves.

He ought to have been exhausted, but it was still early, and worries churned inside him. He had no idea if his parents were safe, no idea that they wouldn't be tracked here.

Unseelie had never come for him before. They wanted the curse to come to pass. Was it a random attack, or had Ladrien sent them? What was the objective if he had? Just to scare him?

It worked.

Sleep evaded him still.

"If you were a bird, what bird would you be?" he asked, shattering the silence.

"Titania's thorny tits!" Jules seethed. "Do you ever stop talking?"

"I'm sorry, I have a tendency to talk whenever I'm nervous or bored or afraid or in the company of someone I'm trying to impress—"

"And which one are you now?"

Hawthorn went silent, not entirely sure himself.

"I'd be a raven, obviously," he continued. "Dark, handsome... majestic."

"Really? I always thought you were more of a tit."

Hawthorn scowled at her. "For the record, you'd be a sparrow. Small, brown... *common*."

"This sparrow has a knife under her pillow, so watch it."

"Ha..." he said, not believing her for one moment. "Wait a minute..." He tapped her pillow, sliding a hand underneath it. "You *do* have a knife under there!"

"Of course I do. It's foolish to presume I'll be able to stay awake all night. I need to be prepared in case of attack."

"Juliana, I won't have a knife in my bed space. What if I roll over and accidentally impale myself?"

"You roll over onto my side, the knife is the least of your worries."

Hawthorn stilled, finding his words again. "You know it's entirely possible to have a conversation without a threat of violence in it?"

"Oh, shut up."

He lapsed into silence, but it was lighter than before, less tangible. Juliana's warmth spread through the thin, musty blankets between them. His body felt heavier, the bed not nearly so lumpy or uncomfortable.

Slowly, sleep pulled him under.

He dreamt the sluaghs were chasing him through the woods, their claws transformed into arrows. They chased him until he slid into the mud, and then they gathered around him in a circle and twisted into thorns, growing closer and closer around him, coiling like snakes.

Bleed, Prince, bleed, hissed a voice. *You were born to curse them.*

Then a memory, standing outside his parents' room when he was only a boy. They were discussing the curse in hushed, desperate tones. He knew that they'd been talking about it with their advisors earlier that day. That's why he'd come to see them. *Tell me what to do to make it right. Tell me it's all right to be cursed.*

Instead, he heard his father's voice. "Perhaps we should have him taken out of Faerie. Make another to fill his place."

"Another... another child?"

"He's only one child, May. He is not worth dooming a kingdom."

Aspen was right, of course, but his words cut deeper than a dagger.

Hawthorn turned and fled.

The corridor disappeared beneath his feet. He tumbled into the great hall. Snow covered every surface, and still, frozen bodies slept among the snowflakes.

Bones carpeted the floor.

He cried out for Jules, but when he turned, he found a skeleton clutching her sword.

He shuddered awake.

Juliana was already up, sitting in a corner of the loft space on a sack, cleaning her sword. It was still dark outside. She was completing her task by moonlight.

"Juliana," he said, ashamed of the hoarseness of his voice.

"We're all right," she told him. "It's not yet day. Go back to sleep."

"Why are you awake?"

"I don't need much sleep."

He swallowed painfully, the nightmares loosening their hold. He let go of the blankets.

"Are you all right?" she asked.

"Just... dreams," he said, unwilling to say more. He didn't want her ridicule.

Juliana nodded, placed her sword aside, and scurried down the ladder. She returned a few minutes later with a leftover cup of tea.

"You're not the only one to have nightmares, Prince Prickle," she said, handing it over.

He took a slow sip, watching her the entire time, wondering perhaps if he was still dreaming, or she'd been replaced by a shape-shifting demon.

The coldness of the tea suggested otherwise. "What do you dream of?" he asked.

Juliana returned to her sword, voiceless.

"Do I ever feature?" he probed.

"You want to be in my nightmares?"

I want to know that whatever I did to you when we were children doesn't haunt you.

Jules sighed. "Don't flatter yourself," she said, almost as if she could read his mind. "Nothing you did to me was ever terrible enough to warrant a second appearance."

Then what is? He wondered. *Do you dream of assassins in the dark, of coldness, of parents that don't care, of blood seeping onto thorns, of whispers behind your back? What haunts Juliana Ardencourt?*

He knew he should probably use this moment to apologise. A mortal likely would. But if he accepted fault, he would be expected to make amends, and he had no idea how to do that.

"Your bed is likely the cause of all this," he said instead. "Vile, uncomfortable thing. Also, this tea is cold."

Juliana's glare could melt stone. "Then heat it up yourself."

He did so, and lay back down again. A few more minutes ticked by in silence.

"The first attempt happened not long after you left," he said in the quiet. "I was out in the gardens, minding my own business, and someone shot out of the bushes. My guard tackled them to the ground and the next thing I knew I was being whisked back into the castle. I barely understood what was going on. But it seemed frenzied, random. I naively assumed that it was an isolated incident, a one-off, that no one would try anything again. Then, just after my thirteenth birthday, they did. Took an arrow to the shoulder."

He touched his collarbone briefly, an echo of pain hovering beneath his fingertips, though the scar, unlike hers, had long since vanished.

"Wound healed quickly, but I... I could feel it for weeks, months afterwards. And sometimes even when I sleep—" He shook his head. He'd intended to blot out the nightmares, not drag them to the surface. "The time before this, it was poison. Spent the better part of two days in agony, vomiting up my guts while the castle magicians pumped me full of magic to keep me alive whilst they worked out an antidote. That was the worst. I think there have been other attempts I'm not privy to. Haven't asked. Not worth the extra paranoia, right?"

He waited for Juliana to speak, to tell him he was foolish, that she'd been through worse. He doubted she would put him at ease, let him know his fears were unfounded. What he'd do for a mortal lie right now, someone to tell him that it was all right, natural to be scared—

"Why sneak out to the taverns if the threat is so high?" she asked eventually. Typical Juliana response, practical to a fault. "Giving your guards the slip and everything—"

He shrugged. "There's a lot of reasons. The first time I did it, I was rather drunk and it seemed like a great idea. Plus, I hated my guard at the time and I rather wanted to get him in trouble. He didn't notice. Not for hours. It was... freeing. Like telling the world I wasn't scared of it."

Juliana's pause seemed to stretch on for an eternity.

"The other reasons?" she asked, returning to her sword.

He sighed. "The castle isn't that safe, either. All the attacks so far have been organised. Visiting the tavern is random. No one's tried to kill me there... or not for being what I am, anyway. It's fun. I enjoy it."

"Still seems like a big risk to take."

"Risk can be fun."

Another pause followed, and he wondered if she truly believed him.

"I guess there's also a small part of me that invites the chaos," he admitted, his voice slow and quiet. "A part that says, if they're going to kill me, they can do it. But I won't be cowering in fear when they do."

Juliana stilled, her hands against the blade. "You'd rather die in a seedy tavern?"

"Better than dying hurling up my insides in my comfortable castle. Nothing's comfortable when you're dying, anyway."

"Fair point."

"You, I think, would like to die in battle with your sword in your hand."

Juliana snorted. "If I have to die young, sure. But I rather prefer the future where I retire after a full life of adventuring and die peacefully in my own home."

"Hmm. I wouldn't have imagined that for you."

"You? If you could choose how you would die?"

"Hmm. Naked and surrounded by beautiful people?"

She raised her eyebrow.

"Not alone," he said instead. "I just don't want to die alone."

There might have been a healer in the room while he writhed under the poison's influence; he couldn't remember. They hadn't spoken, hadn't come to him other than to administer the antidote. The vines were better company. He remembered them more than anything else, arching over his bed, twisting round the posts, almost as if they understood.

No one in his life had ever understood him, and Hawthorn was almost certain they never would.

No one would sit by his side when that day came.

Curse or no curse, he was doomed to die alone.

11. LADY OF AUTUMN

SIX WEEKS BEFORE THE CURSE AWAKENS

Six weeks before Hawthorn's eighteenth birthday, Lucinda returned to court, unexpectedly and without invitation.

"You could send her away," Juliana suggested, as Hawthorn wrestled himself into a fine velvet doublet in maroon and gold.

"Where would be the fun in that?" He winked, as if this was all a game to him, as if she didn't know him well enough by now to sense a forced smile, to see his fingers twist around his blackthorn ring, to notice the pitch of his voice altering whenever he was caught off guard.

She wondered if he noticed her tells, too, and if she wanted that.

Of course I don't, she thought bitterly. *Why would I ever want anyone to see my weaknesses?*

Someone knocked on the door, and a placid face topped by nut-brown curls appeared in the doorway. Dillon.

"She's waiting in the great hall," he reported.

"Well, it would be rude to keep her waiting..." said Hawthorn, pulling on his gold-tipped boots very slowly indeed.

Dillon bit back a laugh, and held open the door for them. Hawthorn strolled out with all his usual confidence, but Juliana wasn't fooled. His hand was twitching by his side.

Another girl, another person who knew him as well as she did, who was softer and kinder, might have been tempted to take that hand.

But she wasn't kind or soft.

And she was afraid.

Lucinda met them in the great hall in a creamy, layered gown that shook with butterflies. If she'd been beautiful as a girl of fourteen, she was monstrously, hideously beautiful now. Her skin held the radiance of a rosebud draped in morning dew, shimmering beneath the sun. Her red-gold hair was bright as jewels and glittered under the light. A glamour, or a powder, surely, but it didn't matter. It clung to her like stardust. Juliana tried to remind herself of her own worth, fingers tightening on the hilt of her sword as proof. It did not work. She felt like an insect in the shadow of a giant.

Wisely, Lucinda had returned without her mother—only a guard and a couple of ladies' maids, who twittered and fussed as Hawthorn entered the room, sweeping into low bows.

Hawthorn strolled across the room and arranged himself in his throne, legs dangling over the armrest. His mother, already seated, glared but said nothing.

"Lucinda," he drawled. "No doubt you have some fascinating reason for being here."

"Need I have a reason for visiting an old friend?"

Hawthorn's lips pursed. "We did not part as friends."

Lucinda's eyes drifted towards Juliana, standing stiffly beside Hawthorn's throne. Her eyes settled on her face. It occurred to Juliana that she probably hadn't heard who was serving as his guard—it would not be news to the rest of the courts.

"Indeed," she said crisply. "But that was a long time ago."

"Why are you here, Lucinda?"

"I wanted to speak to you," she returned. "To get to know you again. We may not—"

"Opportunities may be thin on the ground for the next a hundred years, or so I hear. Understandable." He glanced around at the meagre congregation. "Well? You are here now. Talk."

Lucinda's eyes darted around the company. "I... I find I am a little on the spot, Your Highness. I had hoped..."

"For what?"

"A more private audience."

"I can understand that," he said, with a cruel smirk, "but alas, I get into all sorts of trouble when I am left alone. I have to take my guard with me almost everywhere." He gestured to Juliana. "You remember dear Jules, I suppose?"

"I have some memory."

"She's really blossomed over the years, wouldn't you agree?"

Juliana's cheeks heated. Why was he bringing her into it?

Lucinda's eyes narrowed, only a fraction. "Yes," she responded, jaw stiff.

"You should see her with a sword. Her skill is unparalleled."

At this, Juliana frowned. How could he say that? Miriam or her father could beat her in an instant. Surely he knew this?

"How lucky for Your Highness to have such a skilled guard."

"Few things I am blessed with, but she is certainly one of them."

Juliana wanted to pull at her collar. Or throttle him. She wasn't sure which.

"Hawthorn," said his mother warningly, "offer our guest some hospitality."

"Fine," he said, like a petulant child being told to eat his greens. "You have journeyed far to our home, sister of the Autumn Court. It would be rude to turn you away. Despite how tempting that may be—"

"Hawthorn—"

"—I will give you the benefit of the doubt. It has been six years, after all. So much can change in that time."

"Your Highness is most gracious."

"You have three days," he said shortly. "You may rest, and return to your own court."

Lucinda buckled. For a journey as long as hers, a week's respite minimum would be the norm. Three days was an insult. "Your Highness—"

"I find this conversation bores me," Hawthorn announced, standing up. "I daresay I'll see you at dinner."

He swept out of the room. Juliana took a moment to bow to the Queen and their guests, and then hurried after him.

In the narrow corridor adjacent to the hall, Hawthorn ran a hand through his curls, breathing hard. "Well, that could have gone worse."

Juliana regarded him carefully for a moment. Every time she thought she knew him, he went and did something that completely threw her off. "Why did you bring me into it?"

Hawthorn smiled, not unkindly. She hated that smile as much as her body loved it. It was a wicked, sinful smile that rippled across her belly in hot, painful waves.

He took a step towards her, the shadow of his head meeting hers. "I wanted her to know you were still here," he said, "and she wasn't."

"Is that it?"

"No." His smile deepened, inching closer. His hand tugged on the end of her braid, hanging over her shoulder. He teased the strands between his fingers. "Would you like to know the other reason?"

Yes, she thought desperately. *No.*

Why was he standing so close? Why was he touching her hair?

Why was she *letting* him?

Before she could think of a suitable response or force a lie to her lips, the door banged open, and Maytree stepped into the passage. Darkness lit her expression.

Hawthorn groaned, moving away from Juliana. "Mother."

"We need to talk."

"Must we?"

"Juliana, please wait upstairs. I assure you my son will be perfectly safe in my presence for a couple of minutes."

Hawthorn turned his head towards Juliana as she eased past him, not taking his eyes off his mother. "Juliana, I am not sure I believe her."

"*Now.*"

Juliana headed upstairs as instructed, waiting for Hawthorn at the top of the staircase. Although there were guards posted outside his door as usual, she wasn't entirely sure of his capacity to make it there without wandering off or inviting trouble.

He didn't wander off. He stormed straight past her, into his room, and uncorked the fresh bottle of wine set by the window.

"Something vexes you?" Juliana asked, hand resting against the pommel of her sword.

Hawthorn poured out a healthy measure, barked at her to close the door, and collapsed in his chair.

"Mother wants me to consider making amends with Lucinda. Having her as my... back-up option."

Juliana's grip on her sword stiffened, but she forced her face into a mask of civility. "Ah, your 'chosen fae bride'."

"We have an arrangement with the Summer Court," he continued, as if Juliana wasn't intimately aware of this. "That ought to be enough."

Eighteen years they'd had to avert the curse, and yet only one plan, one idea remained. One that involved letting it happen. One that Juliana didn't like to think about, and did, far too often.

She took a deep breath. "Does it occur to you that that might not be a terrible idea?"

Hawthorn stared at her. "You want me to marry Lucinda?"

"I want you to be—" *I want you to be safe,* she started, but then quickly shut her mouth. "I don't want to have to quit Faerie. Or, you know, die."

Hawthorn winced. "Understandable." He paused, examining the insides of his goblet, eyes dark and misted. "Do you ever think they might be right?"

"Who?"

"The assassins. The people that want me dead. Do you not think they might be right?"

Juliana blanched, not liking how that made her feel... not liking that *he* felt it. "Do you?"

"The thought has crossed my mind once or twice. I haven't done much to warrant death, at least, I hope not, but I am only one person. You're a knight, or as good as one. Would you not slay one monster to save a village?"

"You're hardly a monster."

"I have my moments," he admitted. "Same as every person in that hypothetical village—and likely more than them. Would it not be easier to just let them finish me off?"

"Keep talking like that," Juliana warned, gripping Briarsong's pommel tightly, "and I'll run you through myself."

"You seem angry."

"I don't... I'm not *overly* fond of the thought of you expiring."

He snorted. "An entirely mutual feeling." He took another long, steady sip. "I'm worried."

"About me running you through? I should hope so. It's been mighty tempting on occasion."

"I am worried," he said slowly, "that our attempts to divert the curse will fail, and that people will get hurt as a result."

"Well, we have a few back-up plans in place—"

"I am worried," he admitted, "that *you* will get hurt as a result."

Juliana froze, as surely as if she'd been rendered in ice. She was aware that he did not detest her as much as he did when they were children—they'd been through much in these three years—but hearing him say it outright...

"I am not easily hurt," she whispered.

"I know, and thank the spirits, or I'd be an anxious ball of nerves all the time."

It was hard to imagine Hawthorn being nervous about much, but the image made her snort. "Now you know how I feel."

"What?" Hawthorn asked, brow furrowed.

"What what?"

"You feel anxious?"

Juliana stared at him incredulously. "For the past three years I've lived under the assumption that we could be attacked at any given moment."

"Ah," said Hawthorn, smiling as he drank again, "for a moment, I thought you were worried about me."

Juliana didn't dignify that statement with a response. "What are you going to do about Lucinda?"

He sighed, slumping back in his chair. "Pretend to entertain her for the next three days. Hopefully she'll do something utterly vile and I can truthfully tell my mother I'd rather die than marry her. Wait," he paused, "*I'd rather die than marry her*. Oh, look, it appears I'm already there."

"You can't be serious."

"Apparently, I am."

Juliana decided not to press it. She crossed the room and lent against the windowsill, staring out at the garden. "I'm usually the melancholy one."

He did not smile. "My turn, for a moment then. I imagine I'll have a few more of these moments before your service is up. Fair warning."

"I shan't complain."

"You will," he said shortly, with a twinge of sadness she couldn't quite pin.

Hawthorn successfully avoided Lucinda all the way until dinner time, where she was seated next to him at the table. Juliana was posted in the shadows, watching her leaning towards him, hating the twist in her gut every time he offered her so much as a smile.

Why should she care? If he forgave her, it was for the best. They'd likely barely see each after his birthday, anyway.

One way or another.

A vine nudged her elbow, and she reached out to pet it. "I just don't think she'd make a good queen, all right?" she whispered.

The vines trembled in their giggling way, and slunk back to the walls.

After dinner was cleared away, dancers were brought into the hall, and after them, music. A few courtiers began to dance.

"Shall we not take a turn about the room?" Lucinda asked, pawing at Hawthorn's arm.

"You are asking me if I wish to dance?"

Lucinda laughed. "I'm asking you if *you'll* ask me."

Hawthorn's jaw twitched, almost imperceptibly. "We may dance, if you so wish."

"I do," she said, dragging him by the hands. "I remember you were a fine dancer."

"I was a boy then."

"Then I'm hoping you'll be even better now."

She placed his hand against her delicate, slender waist, and forced him into a twirl. He *was* a good dancer, but Lucinda moved like a wind nymph, as graceful and fluid as a feather.

Juliana's stomach turned. She could dance as well as any mortal who'd trained in footwork, who'd grown up on a diet of faerie music. But she did not possess this otherworldly elegance. She never would.

I am not one of them. Not one of them.

The vines trembled behind her, no longer giggling, but hissing. They coiled down the walls like snakes, making Juliana panic.

It's the vines, she reminded herself, noting the minute differences in movement that somehow quelled her fears.

They wriggled across the floor.

"Wait—" she whispered. "Stop—"

They slithered across the marble and straight under Lucinda's prancing feet. Only Hawthorn stood any chance of stabilising her, and he didn't.

He let her fall.

She crashed to the ground in a flurry of petticoats, like a cream pie, the music falling away.

Juliana laughed.

Lucinda struggled upright, wheeling around to face her, her expression livid. "*You*!" she seethed. "You tripped me up!"

"The *vines* tripped you," Juliana said swiftly, as they shrank back into place. "And as I am neither faerie or royalty, surely even you know I don't command them?"

"Filthy, lying, mortal!" she hissed, scrambling to her feet. "You used mortal magic on them, or—"

"Or *what?*" Juliana said flatly. "I've no desire to see your petticoats. What have I to gain from such a display?"

"You meant to humiliate me!" She stamped her foot. "You've hated me ever since—"

"Since you tried to manipulate my—" Juliana stopped herself. What was she going to say? "Since you tried to manipulate my prince? Yes. Don't hate me when your actions were the hateful ones."

Lucinda's eyes burned like actual fire. Her skirts started to ripple around her, tugged by an invisible wind. The air turned stony, the vines shrank.

"How dare you," she said, her voice dark and monstrous, "you will pay—"

A loud clatter sounded behind her; Hawthorn had toppled over a chair. He laughed loudly, every eye in the room suddenly on him. "Do you know, I may be rather drunk? Oh dear. I suppose Jules better get me upstairs before I make a complete fool of myself."

Juliana's expression turned as sour as Lucinda's, but the faerie girl's wind died away. "Of course, My Prince," she said, dropping into a bow. "I'd be happy to escort you myself—"

"No need, I'm in no state for company tonight, it would appear."

"Another night then."

"Mayhap." He clambered upright with Juliana's assistance, and let her tug him from the room without another word, not even speaking as they reached his room and he started to undress, which he was suddenly capable of doing without any assistance at all.

He sat on the bed wearing nothing but a black robe, thin as spider's silk and dusted with gold-leaf shoulders. It parted at the waist, showing perfectly sculpted muscles turned bronze in the firelight.

Juliana's traitorous mouth turned dry. He looked like a creature carved from marble, warm and smooth as satin and ember. She bet he tasted like firelight.

Don't, she told herself. *Don't go there.*

"You didn't have to do that," she said instead.

"Do what?"

"You know what. I don't need anyone to fight my battles for me." *I don't need anyone at all.*

"Maybe it was my battle I was fighting."

"What does that mean?"

"Just because I cannot lie, does not mean I can easily explain things."

Juliana sighed, turning to leave the room. His hand reached out and fastened around hers, dragging her back to the bed. She was too shocked to resist when he yanked her a little more and toppled backwards with her in his arms, sprawled against the pillows, holding onto her tightly.

"What are you doing?" she asked, baffled.

"It's a hug, Juliana. I believe you know what those are."

"I think you have me confused with someone else."

"Someone who knows what a hug is? Maybe." His grip tightened, his face buried in her hair. It wasn't entirely unpleasant. Despite her better judgement, she found her hands relaxing against his chest.

"Seriously, why are you doing this?" *Why am I letting him?*

"Maybe I'm just drunk and it seems like a good idea."

"Maybe you're avoiding the question."

Hawthorn sighed, still not loosening his hold. "Are you not enjoying it?"

"I didn't say that."

"*Now* who's avoiding the question?" Finally, he released her, just enough for her to lift her face, for his eyes to catch on hers. "Do you want me to let go?"

Stupidly, ridiculously, she did not. She liked the feel of his warm body beneath hers, the rustle of the silk sheets, the closeness of his skin. His eyelashes were dusted with gold, his aegean gaze brimming in the low light, like the sea at sunset. He smelled of plum wine, sweet and rich, and his mouth looked softer than it had ever done before.

But what she wanted didn't matter.

"I should go to bed," she said, her voice strangely whispery.

His mouth twitched. "There's plenty of space here."

"I—no."

"We've shared before. Rather nice nights, all of them. I can promise to keep my hands to myself…"

And if I don't want you to?

Juliana scooted off the bed, forcing a smile. "Tempting as that is, Prince, I think it's best we keep to our own chambers."

Hawthorn shrugged, as if it were neither here nor there. "What's mine is yours," he said.

A foolish, dangerous thing for a faerie to offer.

He must be more drunk than she thought.

"Goodnight," she said, moving towards the door.

"Goodnight, cherished punishment," he replied, and rolled over in bed. If he was disappointed, he didn't show it.

Juliana closed the door to her bedroom, her chest tight, collar hot. She removed her outer layers and lay down on the bed in nothing but her shirt, fingers tightly coiled in the sheets.

She fought the urge not to go back there, and later, as she drifted off to sleep, she fought the urge not to dream about him.

12. THE ROAD TO ACANTHIA

LESS THAN THREE YEARS UNTIL THE CURSE AWAKENS

The morning after the failed assassination attempt, Hawthorn woke at first light. Juliana was already packed, having found a couple of bags for a few provisions and packed as well as she could. She yanked the blanket off the bed, rolled it tightly, and shoved it into the one she'd prepared for him.

She barely spoke. They guzzled water from the stream, filled their solitary flask, and headed off.

As soon as they found some mushrooms to eat, they stopped to make a fire. Apparently Juliana wasn't too worried about smoke during the day, or perhaps hunger had finally overtaken her. Mushrooms were a staple in the capital, but Hawthorn was used to them being served with butter and herbs, or sliced in a pie. Dry roasted mushrooms were far from appetising.

"Don't pull a face," Juliana hissed at him.

"I was not doing it on purpose." He swallowed another mouthful. "You ate like this for three years?"

"We had a herb garden. Spices, sometimes. It wasn't too bad."

"Juliana, you made food a requirement of your service to me. I am not convinced."

"Just eat your food," she said. "The sooner you're done, the sooner we can leave."

Hawthorn did as instructed, and a few minutes later, they set off again.

To begin with, it was a pleasant hike. He'd never been this far into Autumn before. A myriad of colours shone in the dawn light, reds, greens, browns, golds. The soft, quick breeze was pleasant too, the coppery aromas of earth and sunlight.

It lost its pleasantness after a few hours, when his calves grew sore, his chest tight and breathless. He looked to Juliana, hoping she showed similar signs of strains, but although her cheeks were red and her eyes dark from lack of sleep, she didn't seem to be struggling.

When they were children, he'd hated that about her, hated how she dared to make things look easy she had no right to be the master of. She was mortal, magicless, and yet few could match her in the training ring, few had her stamina or could balance for as long, with such focus.

It still irked him now, but he admired it, too.

He certainly wasn't about to throw stones at her now to throw her off balance.

"I will admit," he said, stirring against the silence, "I was not overly keen on seeing Lucinda again, but this was not precisely how I imagined getting out of it."

Juliana paused, ever-so-briefly. "How *did* you imagine getting out of it?"

"Hmm, good question. Throwing myself from the carriage, perhaps. Creating an injury."

"You could just pretend, you know."

"We are not so good at that. Pretending." He knew that was wrong as soon as he said it, that most of them were skilled at pretending, and that perhaps there were things that he pretended, too.

But faking injuries *was* hard.

"Next time you need me to lie on your behalf to get out of seeing Lucinda, let me know," Juliana said. "Or... I could help you with a real injury. If you like."

"A kind offer," he returned. "But I shall decline."

They headed further into the forest. Around midday, feeling weak from hunger, they stopped beside a stream to hunt for fish. Juliana set Hawthorn the task of starting a fire—one task he felt particularly adept at—while she tried to skewer passing trout with her blade.

He rather enjoyed watching her fail at it.

"I thought you'd be better at fishing."

She looked up from her endeavour to scowl at him. "Usually, I'd have a line, and tackle—"

"There are other ways to fish, Jules."

"Oh? Pray tell me, master of the craft."

Hawthorn leapt up and sauntered towards the water, raising his hands in an arch. With a quick flick of his wrists, he scooped out a chunk of water, fish and all, and sploshed it against the bank.

Jules glared at him.

"Admit it, you're a little impressed."

"You couldn't have done that *before*?"

"You didn't ask."

"Ugh!" She threw her hands up in the air, and then brought one down to skewer the fish. Hawthorn winced at the sight of it wriggling. She lifted it over the fire and drove her hilt into the mud to cook it.

"You have your uses," she admitted, with painful reluctance.

"On a scale of one-to-ten as a travelling companion—"

"Two."

"Two? *Two?* My wit alone is worth at least three—"

"Your wit earns you a minus three. I could list the other minuses, if you like?" She took a swig of their water.

"How many points does my pretty face earn me?"

Juliana spat out her water, and hurled the now empty container at his face.

They didn't rest long, after the fish were eaten and the fire expunged. They packed up again and resumed their journey, eager to make the most of the light they had left. Hawthorn was aware they'd have to camp outside again, and wasn't looking forward to that. He'd passed out in the gardens a couple of times during revels, and woken damp and crumpled at dawn. Doubtless whatever haystack or hollow tree Jules found would be equally unpleasant.

It was almost sunset before they stopped, deciding the best they could do was a fallen oak. Jules murmured under her breath about it being far from ideal, but they were running short of daylight to find anything better.

"We could keep going," he suggested. "There's still plenty of light left—"

Juliana cast her eyes downwards. "No," she said, "there isn't."

He paused, realising what she meant. He had no idea how mortal eyes responded to the dark, but he supposed she must be half-blind by now. A faerie could spit in a mortal's eyes to make them immune to most glamours, at least ones of illusion, but no permanent solution remained to alter their other deficits.

"We can't start a fire, I suppose?"

She shook her head, and he decided to drop it. He felt like he was picking at a scab.

They dined on a handful of berries, a few rubbery mushrooms leftover from breakfast, and a few slices of fish they'd saved. Juliana's stomach rumbled loudly. It was not a sound faeries were capable of, but his own was far from full.

"Why do you think Unseelie attacked the procession?" Hawthorn asked. It had been bothering him for some time. "They've no need to want me dead."

Juliana shrugged. "Sluaghs attack indiscriminately. They might not have been after you."

"And if they were?"

"You didn't hire me for my brains."

Hawthorn had to admit that was true, although Juliana was far from stupid. He searched for something else to banish the silence with.

"Did you like it here in the woods?"

"Parts of it. I liked being close to nature, liked the silence. Lack of decent food and monsters on my doorstep? Less so."

"Did you often have monsters?"

She shook her head. "A few times a year."

"And yet the sluaghs came when they did…"

"I thought we weren't talking about that?"

"Then what *would* you like to talk about?"

"You didn't hire me for my conversation, either."

Hawthorn hesitated. "Do you like Faerie?" he asked. It was a question that had been burning inside him for some years now.

Juliana frowned, as though the answer to this was as simple as the colour of her hair, which, given its tendency to change colour in the light, might not have been so simple. "It's my home."

"But do you like it?"

"Yes," she said quietly. "I do. I don't have anything to compare it to, but the mortal world... it sounds grey and dull. I also hear they have strange views about women wielding the sword, and everything seems... slow."

"Do you know why your mother went back?"

Juliana tensed, and he knew immediately he'd said the wrong thing. She stood up, taking a shaky step forward like she planned to bolt—before realising she couldn't see and she wasn't supposed to leave.

"I'm sorry," he said, offering her a rare apology. "That was—I didn't think."

"I don't know why," she whispered. "I have no idea why anyone would want to leave here, and I'll never be able to ask her."

"Unless you left."

"But I wouldn't be able to come back."

No one knew if that was true, of course, as Juliana had been raised in Faerie and had probably been gifted with truesight within seconds of her birth. He also couldn't imagine her being kept out—could see her banging down the intangible barrier and forcing it to let her back in.

But he wasn't sure he wanted her to know that he thought that about her.

"Wouldn't be attacked by sluaghs all the time, either," he said instead.

At this, she snorted. "I am not afraid of sluaghs."

"What are you afraid of, then?"

A stiff wind whistled through the trees, rustling the branches with its claws. "Right now? Freezing to death."

The cold was seeping into his bones, too, black and bitter. "I'll get out the blanket."

Removing any hard equipment from the packs, they stuffed them with leaves and bracken to resemble pillows, scattering some over the ground to offer some protection from the cold. Juliana pushed Hawthorn next to the fallen tree and lay beside him, facing outwards in case of attack.

"Put your arms around me," she instructed.

Hawthorn tensed, certain he'd misheard, or if he hadn't, that the instruction had some kind of trick to it. "Um—"

"If you want to stay warm, do it. I need my hands by my weapon."

"Right," said Hawthorn, dimly wondering whether or not freezing was a better option.

A sharp breeze blew through the woods, and he decided to chance it, folding one arm under his head and draping the other loosely over her middle, touching nothing.

Juliana relaxed underneath him, scooching closer. Slowly, the warmth of her back bled through her clothes, heating the fraction of space between them. Her hair tickled his nose. He found he quite enjoyed the smell of damp earth and the whispering of embers stirring inside his stomach.

"It's quite nice sharing body warmth, isn't it?" he said eventually, the wind howling outside.

"Please remember that I am armed."

"Oh hush, I don't mean like that! I just mean, well, it's comfortable, isn't it? Cold hard damp earth aside."

"Is this your way of telling me you like snuggling?"

"I imagine almost everyone likes snuggling, and few are comfortable enough to admit it."

"I don't like snuggling," she hissed.

"You can lie."

She muttered something incomprehensible and lapsed once more into silence. Darkness swirled around then, night gaining daggers. He knew she wasn't sleeping, that despite her exhaustion, she'd be awake long after him, and up long before.

He wanted to put his hands in her hair. He didn't know why. It was a tangled mess, couldn't be nearly as soft as he'd like it to be, but it was a fine colour, and it looked thick and not entirely unpleasant.

He wondered what else he'd like to touch, if there wasn't the sword, if this wasn't Juliana, but some soft, warm girl who wanted him to touch her.

It occurred to him that there wasn't much he *didn't* want to touch, so he stomped out those thoughts as surely as embers.

Mostly.

The next morning, they packed up, cold and hungry, and continued on their way. By Juliana's estimation, they could reach the capital by midday. There was little food to be found, nothing but a few nuts and another handful of black, bitter berries. Juliana ate hardly anything at all.

Not long before midday, when glimpses of the Acanthian spires glittered in the distance when the trees moved a certain way, Juliana stopped.

"Do you hear something?" she asked, sword drawn.

Hawthorn hesitated. The wind blew through the trees, the undergrowth murmured—sounds of birds and squirrels scuttling, nothing more.

"No?" he offered.

Juliana nodded, continuing.

A low sound pricked at his eardrums, a slight, whispered hissing.

He stopped, staring at a patch of ferns.

A small green snake slithered through them.

Juliana stiffened.

"It's all right," he told her. "It's just a grass snake—"

Juliana bolted into the trees ahead.

Thinking that they were under attack, that there was an enemy he did not understand, he fled after her. His heart sped in his chest.

The path was abandoned. There was nothing, no one—

"Juliana?"

He couldn't see her, but footsteps showed that she'd passed this way. He followed them until the trees panned out, and found her sitting on a log, panting hard.

"Jules?"

She didn't speak.

Brow furrowed, he dropped down by her side. She was shaking like a leaf, pale and sweating. Was there another snake he hadn't seen—a venomous one which had struck her with its bite?

"Jules, talk. Are you injured?"

She shook her head.

"Then what's wrong?"

"I... I'm..." She swallowed. "Promise not to tell?"

"I'm not making that promise until I know what it is I'm consenting to!"

She took a deep breath, slow and steady. "I'm... I'm terrified of snakes."

"What?"

"Snakes. I can't stand them. Something about the way they move just... I can't."

"You're afraid of snakes."

"*Deathly* afraid," she clarified, voice quavering.

"You lived in a forest."

"One only came inside once. I killed it before my father could come home and see..."

"Does he know about this phobia of yours?"

She nodded, ever so slowly, like a child confessing a secret she was afraid of. "He said I needed to face my fear so he used to catch them and bring them home for me to kill. If... if I know they're coming... I'm not usually too bad. I can prepare myself, put on a mask, but when they sneak up on me..." Her bottom lip quivered.

He had the strangest, most bizarre desire to put his arms around her, even when he was only half-sure she wasn't making the whole thing up. Jules wasn't scared of anything, or certainly not something as simple as a *snake*.

But he knew that she would hate that, that she preferred anger over fear.

He summoned a smile. "This is now my favourite thing that I know about you."

"I will end you—"

"Even if I have a snake around my neck?"

"I'm a very good shot!" She launched forward, grabbing him by the shirt. "Swear. Swear to me. Swear you won't reveal this to anyone."

"It's just a—"

"Swear it, Prince!"

"I swear," he said. "Nothing but the threat of death or pain shall make me reveal your secret fear to anyone."

Jules breathed a horrible, shuddering sigh of relief. "Thank you."

Hawthorn swallowed. There was something about seeing Jules this way—shaking and trembling with fear, raw and vulnerable—that unnerved him. He took no real pleasure in knowing her weakness, when a few years ago he would like to have it pinned and framed like an insect.

"Gratitude doesn't suit you," he said instead.

"I promise never to thank you for anything again."

"Liar."

"No, that one I can keep." She glanced ahead. "Come on. We're not far."

Two hours later, the Autumn Gate finally appeared. Juliana took a moment to pause against a tree, her face pale despite the exercise. She shook slightly on her feet.

"Are you all right?" Hawthorn asked.

"Fine," she said, though her voice wobbled slightly, her grip on the bark tightening.

She'd eaten little more than one complete meal in two days, had barely slept, and been walking for hours. He was struggling to stay upright himself—on more food, more sleep, and the benefits of a faerie body.

He did not want to imagine how Juliana was feeling.

So he didn't.

"We're so close," she said, her voice hoarse as she staggered forward. "Let's not dawdle."

Offer her your arm, said a voice inside him, the one reserved for flirting with beautiful people he was trying to impress.

But he didn't want to impress her. He wanted to help her.

And he was equally sure she'd threaten to cut off his arm if he offered it.

"Of course," he said, adjusting his gait to meet her pace. A few more minutes on the road wouldn't hurt.

Although it was midday, the market seemed oddly subdued, the sun hidden behind a veneer of grey. The capital looked as bleak as the winter gardens and somehow even frostier.

"Something's wrong," remarked Hawthorn.

"Hmm, indeed. If they thought you were dead, there ought to be more celebration."

Hawthorn didn't laugh. The *wrongness* was squirming inside him, like he swallowed a snake. He'd heard his mother talk before about feeling the land, like the earth and trees were an extension of her limbs. She could sense a storm rolling in, an earthquake before it happened, a disaster brewing in the distance—Hawthorn had never felt it.

Not until now.

He broke into a run, hurtling up the road towards the palace, abandoning Juliana, abandoning *everything,* even as she screamed at him to stop. No one else paid the mud-streaked prince any heed until he hit the gates.

They were locked. When were they *ever* locked?

"Halt!" called a guard. "Who goes there?"

"Your prince!" he yelled. "Open up immediately!"

The guard on duty stammered. "Your Highness, we thought—"

"I don't give a shit. Open the gates!"

Dutifully, they obeyed, Hawthorn slipping in the second there was a wide enough gap. He thought Juliana might be following him, but he wasn't sure. He no longer cared.

The vines tumbled down the stone, flat and limp, sucked dry of any energy. They barely moved to greet him. There were no buds, no petals.

For some reason, his mind was stuck on the image of his mother, surrounded by roots as the sluaghs shrieked around her. He remembered the look in her eyes as he hurtled into the undergrowth, the one he couldn't name.

Still couldn't.

But what if that was the last look she was ever going to give him?

He tore through the halls, towards the great hall. The skies above stood stony and black, the room draped in grey, devoid of colour. Courtiers huddled around the throne, quiet and hushed, finery gone, replaced with robes of mourning.

"Your Highness!" gasped one, causing a murmur round the room.

Slowly, the people parted. A coffin stood behind them, glass and gold, covered with a black drape.

"Hawthorn..." His mother stepped forward from the crowd, dressed in a long black veil fringed with crow's feathers. Her pale face was streaked with red. "We feared the worst."

She made a move towards him, to embrace him, or block the view of the coffin, he wasn't sure.

For one moment, he thought it was a joke, that he'd interrupted his own premature funeral, that this was all a mistake. No one was dead. Everyone was fine.

But then the drape fell away, and his father's glassy face stared back.

He didn't have the strength to cry. He didn't have the strength for anything. He remembered tumbling, someone helping him into a seat.

Juliana arrived not long after. Markham rushed forward to embrace her, and then her legs gave out too.

She was hurried out of the room.

That was just as well, because shortly after, Hawthorn lost all sense of reason, and howled.

13. DAGGERS AND DISGUISES

SIX WEEKS BEFORE THE CURSE AWAKENS

It did not surprise Juliana that all of Lucinda's attempts to seduce Hawthorn fell decidedly flat, although it was not for lack of trying. On her last night, she came to his chambers and knocked at his door.

Hawthorn leapt out of bed and skidded into Juliana's room. "Quick," he said, "giggle."

"What?"

"I can't lie and tell her I have company! Giggle for me!"

"I don't understand—"

Unwilling for her to wait any longer, he sprung towards her and attacked her middle, making her squeal as he tickled her towards the bed.

"Stop, stop!" she cried.

He groaned. "Don't say *that*!"

The knocking got harder.

"You'll find I'm otherwise engaged," he called out, his fingers working down Juliana's sides. She *hated* that he knew she was ticklish.

He leant down and whispered in her ear. Somehow, that was worse. His breath sent goosebumps rippling through her, a sensation she felt all the way to her toes. "Moan," he commanded.

"What?"

"Fake a moan of pleasure—"

"I will do no such thing!"

"I will pay you."

Juliana let out a long, warbling moan. Hawthorn clamped a hand to his mouth to hold in the laughter, composing himself just long enough to make a few reciprocal sounds.

The knocking quickly vanished, and footsteps sounded down the corridor.

Hawthorn, still grinning, slowly removed himself from the bed. "What was *that?*"

"What?"

"That sound you made. You sounded like a cat being strangled. Is that what you sound like? Dillon not that great in the bedroom?"

"Dillon was a perfectly satisfactory lover."

"And yet you never invited him back, to my knowledge."

Juliana pursed her lips. "Not that it's any of your business, but no. It has nothing to do with his performance though, I assure you."

"Right." Hawthorn paused. "Has there been anyone besides Dillon, in all these years?"

No. There had been no time—or inclination—for anyone else. "Why do you ask?"

"You know all of my partners. Only seems fair for you to share."

"I only *know* all of your partners because you're not exactly quiet about them and you have me kick them out if they overstay their welcome. I still cannot count them, or name them, or even tell you if you've had them more than once."

"You must remember Barney, surely?"

"Who's Barney?"

"The minotaur?"

"That was the same guy?"

Hawthorn sighed. "I'm beginning to think you're not observant enough to be my guard."

"Hmm. Better dismiss me, then."

"I'd rather not," he said, with the soft smile she despised so much. "Goodnight, fair nemesis. I'll see you anon."

On Juliana's next day off, she readied herself bright and early and handed off Hawthorn to the care of her relief: a stiff, tight-lipped fae knight named Algernon. He stood stoically by the door, as silent as stone, his face almost waxy with indifference.

"Are you all right, Algernon? Oddly quiet today."

"A headache," he said stiffly, barely moving his mouth. "Nothing that will prevent me from performing my duties."

She'd meant it as a joke, but Algernon being fae, she decided not to question it. She'd never known him for his humour anyway.

The gardens were, of course, as fine as ever, the weather mild throughout. It was never hard to find a pleasant plot; the only times when all the seasons were inclimate was when Maytree was having a particularly bad day. When she lost Aspen, Acanthia saw a month of storms, the weather moving from torrential to cloudy depending on the wave of grief.

She remembered Hawthorn watching through the windows as a fog shifted into a gale. "I used to envy that power," he had said. "It would be easier than speaking."

"But would you want the witnesses to it?" She had known that she would not, that she was never more glad of her mortal tongue than when someone asked the dreaded question, *are you all right?*

"No," Hawthorn had said. "I don't much care for people knowing how I feel."

A cold wind shifted through the trees now, as if it too could see inside her memories and shivered at the recollection.

One of these days, you will be able to actually enjoy a day off.

But it was not this day, with thoughts of the dear Prince Prickle still needling through her mind.

Time did pass more slowly without him.

She wandered further into Autumn. It was the quietest of the grounds, the courtiers usually preferring the warm parts that Spring and Summer offered. But Juliana liked the colours here, even if the red of some of the leaves briefly reminded her of Lucinda's hair.

She's gone. He doesn't want her.
Why does that even matter?

There was a rustle in the bushes. Juliana startled, pulling out her sword. But it was only a wealth of vines, trembling under the trees like a frightened shadow.

Juliana paused. "Out a little far, aren't you?"

She extended a hand like one might towards a wounded animal, but the vines shrank away from her, quick as lightning bolts.

Odd. They'd never shrunk from her before.

She moved towards them as they receded, back through the gardens, into the wilder parts beneath the redwood trees—

To a person slumped beneath the roots of one of them, clumsily hidden with leaves and bracken.

No, not a person, a *body*.

It was as still as a statue and pale as ice, a coldness emanating from the limbs even before she reached out to touch them. There was no stiffness, not yet.

They hadn't been dead long.

Death was unusual in Faerie. Juliana had never discovered a body before—not one she hadn't murdered herself. She was unused to the quietness of death.

Her eyes trailed up the body, searching for clues, hoping to find some old, gnarled mortal who had chosen this spot as his final resting place. But the hands were smooth and unlined, and as she pulled apart the bracken, a sticky, red wound blossomed at the chest.

Murder.

She tore through the leaves obscuring his face, and her heart stiffened to lead.

Algernon.

Hawthorn.

She scanned the grass as if expecting to see him somewhere, unconscious, maybe, hurt but alive, because he'd fought off his attacker, or Algernon had died defending him, because he couldn't be dead, he couldn't—

But the front of Algernon's blood-stained tabard had started to crust. She'd skinned enough rabbits in the wild to have an idea of how long he'd been dead. Not long, but not so recently he'd had time to make it down from the castle.

Which meant—

Whoever had come to take over from her this morning, it hadn't been Algernon.

Her pendant started to throb. It was more than a tug, closer to a yank—a hard, desperate pull.

Juliana ran.

Why hadn't she seen it? Algernon hadn't been acting like himself, but she'd not questioned it. Of course she hadn't. *He couldn't lie.*

Mortals could. Somehow, someone or something had taken his place. *Hawthorn, Hawthorn, Hawthorn.*

Was he still in the castle? What if the assassin had already finished the job? *No.*

Hawthorn had said before that the people didn't just want him dead. They wanted to get away with it. They likely wouldn't complete the job until they had the space to escape—

Her pendant throbbed harder, heating to the point of painful.

The gardens. They were in the gardens.

And something was wrong.

Hawthorn disliked Juliana's days off more than he cared to admit, but he disliked more the way she had a habit of wriggling into his thoughts even when she wasn't around. It had been that way for far, far too long. He had a horrible suspicion it would remain that way long after she left.

And she would leave. Soon.

Several times, he'd thought about bargaining more of her time from her. Three years hadn't been enough. Maybe three decades would cure him of the want of her company.

She wouldn't get three centuries, which he hated to think about.

But it was a foolish thought. Besides, he had nothing to bargain with, and *she didn't want to stay.* He respected her enough to not try to make her, and he liked her enough that that thought hurt more than anything else.

She didn't want him.

No one ever had—or not for the right reasons. They wanted him for his body or the power he could provide, and nothing else.

Would it be that way forever? If they side-stepped the curse, if he reigned over Faerie for centuries, would that ever change? Or was he doomed to spend the rest of his immortal life attached to nothing and no one?

Forcing that thought from his mind, he extracted the small leather-bound notebook where he kept his greatest insults for Juliana, and started practising them under his breath while Algernon stared at him from the shadows.

Once upon a time, he'd had no problems calling her hideous. Now, he had trouble remembering why he'd ever thought that at all. *"You're looking as vile as ever"* always worked, for she was not vile, nor ever had been. *"I wish I could say I missed you,"* was also true.

Because he did wish he could say it.

He almost hoped she'd pick up on that one, but she never had.

He whispered out a few more phrases.

A few more weeks, he reminded himself, *only a few more weeks of this*.

This really wasn't working to dispel his mood.

"Fancy a stroll about the gardens, Your Highness?" Algernon suggested. "It is a fine day."

Hawthorn almost jumped. He'd quite forgotten Algernon could speak at all. His voice was utterly unfamiliar to him.

Shock aside, a walk actually sounded far better than moping in his room, and Juliana often frequented the gardens on her day off. They were extensive, true. But there was always a chance he could run into her.

Definitely better than sitting up here all day.

"You know, that sounds like an excellent idea. Fetch me my doublet."

Algernon paused at the dresser, as if he'd forgotten where everything was kept.

"Second drawer," Hawthorn instructed. "Hurry up, man. I haven't got all day."

Algernon selected a fine embroidered doublet in midnight blue. A bit fancy for the day, but Hawthorn didn't complain. It was one of his best colours.

He rehearsed the words in his head. *Why, Juliana, fancy meeting you here! Do you always come here on your day off?*

She'd probably tell him he knew that already, and threaten some mild violence.

He couldn't wait.

He set off with a spring in his step, Algernon trailing behind him. He had no idea where Juliana might be, but he suspected she favoured the wilder parts of the gardens, and probably somewhere not too warm. Some part of the spring wilderness, perhaps? A meadow? She liked pretty things far more than she pretended. The few times he'd seen her genuinely unwind, she'd had ribbons in her hair or fresh blooms on her clothing. He'd seen her buckle beneath beauty on more than one occasion.

He sighed. If only she had the same reaction to him.

Although she had, once. Their visit to the Summer Court, almost a year ago. She'd been drunk and let down her guard, just for a moment, confessing that in terms of appearance, at least, she found him pleasing.

He shook that thought away. It wasn't fair to hold her to a drunken confession.

Something rustled in the bushes. He jolted involuntarily.

"A squirrel, Your Highness," Algernon insisted. "Nothing more."

"Naturally."

He moved onwards through the grounds, ears peeled for any sound of Jules. But there was nothing, nothing at all—

Indeed, the gardens seemed to have turned soundless. No rustling, no birdsong.

Hawthorn turned. "Algernon—"

A dagger flashed. Hawthorn stumbled backwards, the blade catching his middle, just enough to slice the fabric. Algernon moved again as Hawthorn raced towards the undergrowth, flinging fireballs behind him.

There was something wrong with Algernon's face. Not a glamour—any skilled faerie could sense a glamour. Something else, weird and waxy, like it was almost slipping off.

Not Algernon. Not Algernon at all.

Before Hawthorn could land an attack, two more figures sprung from the shadows. Two mortal faces, both unknown to him.

And Juliana wasn't here.

He scrambled over to a large oak, pushing his power into the earth, tearing the roots from the ground. He swung them round like tentacles, catching one of them around the middle and flinging her into the nearby river.

Algernon and the third assassin advanced. One pulled out a crossbow. Hawthorn twisted a root around his ankle, yanking him off his feet as the bolt seared through the air.

It struck the tree behind him, slicing past his ear. Pain crackled at the tip.

"You're outnumbered," not-Algernon said. "Give up, Your Highness."

"If it's all the same to you, I rather think I won't." Hawthorn's voice sounded far steadier than he felt. He *was* outnumbered. The woman in the stream would be back any minute, he was not a skilled fighter and—

Juliana wasn't here.

She'd be so pissed off if he died.

He could almost hear her voice. *"How dare you die. Have you no regard for my efforts these past three years? You promised me knighthood, Prince Prickle!"*

He couldn't die. She wouldn't let him.

Too late, he remembered the damned pendant, hot against his chest. It worked both ways. He could have found her at any point.

He *still* could.

Hurling another fireball towards his attackers, he bolted from the spot. At each footfall, tiny fissures erupted behind him, churning the ground beneath their feet, slowing them down. The tug against his chest pulled him onwards, towards Autumn.

Juliana.

Something snagged at his foot, yanking him to the ground. A rope. Not-Algernon dragged him backwards as he fought for something to cling onto, turning at the last moment as a blade towered above him. He ripped another root out of the earth, wrapping it around his hand.

Not-Algernon was undeterred. He reached for another.

Roots hovered behind Hawthorn, like cobras ready to strike. He knew how to end this.

"Don't," he implored his assailant. "Please—"

The blade moved.

So did Hawthorn's roots.

They tore through the ground, straight through the assassin's chest.

He was dead before he hit the ground.

The second assassin let out a scream, racing towards Hawthorn as the roots twisted out of not-Algernon's chest, leaving a gaping hole in his torso the size of a fist.

This time, Hawthorn didn't plead, or reason.

He said nothing, even as the vines twisted round the attacker's throat, even when the bone and muscle popped and trembled beneath the roots, straining so hard that Hawthorn could feel it in his own hands.

He strangled the man to death.

Faeries avoided saying sorry, but the word raced round inside of him, pulsing with fear.

The man's face had turned an awful, bluish purple.

I killed him. I killed him.

He thought he might be sick.

He breathed, hard and shuddering, thoughts muddled and frozen and everywhere at once.

His pendant throbbed.

Juliana—

He turned, only to find himself face to face with the third assassin, dripping wet from the river.

He didn't see the blade until she'd plunged it into his middle and yanked it back again.

He fell to the floor.

It didn't even seem to hurt. That probably wasn't a good sign. He stared at the wound in his stomach as it pulsed blood.

It looked like a fountain of wine. He almost wanted to laugh.

His killer did not meet him in the eyes. "It's over," she whispered, as if she were the one who had been fighting for her life. "It's all over now."

Juliana hurtled through the gardens, not thinking, hardly breathing, the pendant thumping at her chest like another separate, desperate heartbeat.

There was something wrong with it. The heat continued to rise, but the thrum was weaker than before, lighter than a bumblebee against glass.

She didn't want to think about why. *Couldn't* think about why.

She fled into Spring, running straight into a path of a young woman dressed in dark clothing. She was dripping wet, and holding a dagger stained with blood.

Juliana froze. The girl froze, too.

The pendant throbbed painfully. Hawthorn was somewhere behind her.

"Where is he?" Juliana hissed, unsheathing her sword.

The girl trembled. "Please," she said. "Just let me go. You're one of us. You *know* this is for the best—"

"He hasn't done anything!"

"Neither have we."

Juliana moved towards her. The girl jerked across her path, holding up the dagger. She was no skilled assassin. Just a girl, mortal and alone.

So am I, Juliana thought.

She had killed before. She'd kill again. Always in the name of defence.

It was different from fear.

"Where. Is. He?"

"It's too late," the girl whispered.

But it wasn't. Juliana could feel him. And the girl knew he was still alive, too. Otherwise she wouldn't be trying to stop her.

"Please—" the girl said.

Juliana's gaze darkened. The girl held up her dagger, leaving herself wide open—

Juliana ran her through, moving past her before she could even fall.

Two more bodies littered the path, torn with roots, the ground cracked like a pie crust. One of the bodies had been strangled to death, the other had a huge gaping hole in his chest.

Juliana paused briefly, examining the face. Part of it had peeled away in the fight. Beneath was a mortal man, wearing a mask of wax, ears too. Juliana remembered her father mentioning that she could pass for fae at a glance, and no one would stop to question her words.

These mortals had used a similar tactic.

Fool, fool, foolish girl.

"Hawthorn!" she called out. "Where are you?"

The pendant felt like fire against her throat. He was here, he had to be—

"Juliana," said a faint voice.

Juliana wheeled, spotting a figure slumped beneath the root of a tree, half-covered in vines.

Hawthorn.

She rushed to his side, brushing away the bracken clinging to him. The front of his doublet was sticky with blood.

No, no, no...

"Is it mortal?" he asked, glancing down. His skin was clammy and pale. "There's... there's a lot of blood..."

Juliana swallowed, throat raw. "A flesh wound," she told him, yanking out her handkerchief to press to the wound. "Nothing more. Hold still."

Hawthorn cried out as she pushed down, hoping to force the blood to stay inside him, wishing and praying for magic, the kind he'd once used on her—

But she had no magic, and fae couldn't heal themselves.

"I am growing used to the sound of your lies," he rasped. "You aren't as good at them as you think."

"I'm astonishing."

"No... arguments... here..." His head rolled to the side.

"Don't you dare!" she hissed. "You don't get to die, do you hear me? I don't give you permission. I have not kept you alive all this time for you to die now."

"I knew... I knew you'd say... something like that..."

"Then *listen to me.*"

"A nice... a nice thing..."

"What?"

"I want you to... to say something nice..."

"I don't understand."

"I know you hate me," he said, "but I also think... that of everyone in the world... you might like me best..."

"You aren't making sense!"

But of course he isn't, said a voice inside her. *He's losing too much blood. He's going to die.*

"No!"

"Who... who are you screaming at?"

She let out a long, low whistle, followed by another cry. "Help!" she called. "I need help!"

Her handkerchief was nearly wet through. The vines curled around him, cradling his limbs.

"Help him," she pleaded, like she was the Queen, capable of commanding them, bending them to her will.

The vines criss-crossed over his middle, pinning him in place, plugging up the wound. Juliana pulled her hands back, slick with blood.

She had to go. She had to fetch help.

"Stay," Hawthorn begged. "Please."

"I'm going to fetch help."

"No," he whispered, almost whimpering, "please don't."

"I'll be back," she rushed. "I promise."

14.
Paper Grief

LESS THAN THREE YEARS UNTIL THE CURSE AWAKENS

After his father's funeral, Hawthorn retired to his rooms. The kingdom entered a period of mourning. All revelries and frivolities were cancelled, and a greyness coated the castle. Even the vines seemed muted, sapped of their vibrancy and energy. They shrunk against the walls like wounded tentacles.

The Queen retired to her chambers, and silence reigned in her stead.

For a while, Juliana expected another attack. It would be the perfect opportunity. Everyone was distracted with grief, watching the Queen if they cared, slacking off if they didn't. No one was watching Hawthorn.

No one except Juliana.

For days, Hawthorn sat by his window and stared at the courtyard, watching the people below. Juliana had no idea what he was thinking of or even if he was thinking at all. In body, he seemed fine. He still dressed and ate and drank and slept. He still bathed and washed and breathed. But much like the vines, his actions had lost their lustre.

Eventually, Juliana realised no one was coming. No assassins would dare attack the grieving queen, and anyone who had condolences to offer had already been and gone.

And there *had* been some, particularly at the start. Old friends, distant relatives.

Hawthorn had dismissed them all, and they had followed his orders even when Juliana wasn't sure that's what he really wanted. He reminded her of a wounded animal, the kind liable to lash out rather than accept help, the kind that would rather try and clean its own wounds and die from it.

On the third day, Juliana was close to losing it. She was used to silence living in the woods, but his silence was intolerably loud.

"Would you like to hit something?" she asked.

Hawthorn stared at her as if he'd quite forgotten she was there. "What?"

"When I'm upset, I like to hit something. Or stab. Maybe lightly maim. I could set up the sparring ring for you—"

"I am not—" Hawthorn clenched his jaw— "upset."

"Then what are you?"

For a long while, he remained silent. "I have not the words."

Juliana hesitated. "I lost my mother," she began. "I didn't—"

"You didn't *know* your mother—"

"And you didn't know your father," she retorted, more sharply than she meant to. "And that's the problem, isn't it? Now, you never will. You cannot mourn what you did not love. So you mourn what might have been, instead."

Hawthorn stiffened, jaw tightly set. For a long, trembling moment, he did not speak, reminding Juliana of why she rarely tried to offer anyone words of comfort; she was so ill-adept at the task. She wouldn't blame him if he never spoke again.

"If you had the words, why have you taken so long to speak them?" he asked at last.

"I've been searching for them for three days." She moved closer to him, carefully, the way one might approach a wounded, ravenous dog they were afraid might bite them. *I am not afraid of him*, she reminded herself. And that, at least, was true. It had been a long time since she had been afraid of him.

But she was afraid of how he felt.

"My mother left me," she said, hating the sound of her words. "People have offered me dozens of reasons over the years, dozens of assurances that she cared, that I had nothing to do with why she left... none of them have helped.

None of them have managed to convince me that she loved me. And I'll never know. I'll never know, and I think that hurts worse than losing her."

She did not remember her mother going. She remembered so little about her at all, only that she was there one day, and not the next. She'd been told she cried for days.

She had no memory of that. Nothing to cling to but a legacy of questions and pain she had no place for.

"I prefer breaking things to feeling them," she told him, quiet as a mouse. "That's why I offered."

"And what would you have me break?"

"Anything you wanted," she said. "Within reason."

"And if I wanted to spar with you?"

"I might even let you win."

"All right," he said, with the merest hint of a smirk. "Let's do it."

They went down to one of the training halls, Hawthorn barking at everyone else to remove themselves immediately. Miriam, who was training a couple of squires, looked sharply at Juliana as she left, as if checking for permission.

Juliana nodded. It was fine.

She strode over towards the racks of weapons. "What do you fancy?"

Hawthorn shrugged off his doublet and hung it up with the rest of the equipment. He made no move to pull on any protective gear. "You and I both know I'm no swordsman."

"Then—"

He summoned a fireball into his hand and hurled it towards her, missing only by inches. "Come on," he said, eyes blazing. *"Fight."*

Juliana darted away from another attack, drawing her sword to cut through his onslaught. "You aren't supposed to use magic when fighting mortals—"

Hawthorn's eyes blazed, his face stung with that old, twisted smile, the one he used in front of his friends when he used to torment her.

"Then stop me."

Juliana swerved, slashing through his flames, using them as cover to dive towards him and tackle him to the ground. "If I stop you, I'll hurt you," she said, the hilt of her sword hovering over his palms, threatening to crush them.

He let out another plume of fire, the heat searing against her hand. She staggered back, dropping her sword, stifling a cry.

"Why are you doing this?" she asked, ducking a wild swing.

He'd never attacked her like this before, even when they were children. His acts were tricks, sly and insidious. The occasional shove in the mud, a whispered *you belong there.*

There was no anger. Not like this. Not like she was the enemy to be vanquished.

She kicked his stomach. "Stop," she said. "I didn't kill your father."

"No, *I did*," he hissed. "I did, with the curse and my ineptitude. *I did* by running away."

"You're *alive* because you ran away."

More fire burned beside her face. "Stop trying to make me into something I'm not."

She wasn't sure what he meant by that. When had she ever tried to do that? "Then what are you?"

He flung another fireball, and hesitated. "A coward," he hissed, as if the words pained him. Perhaps they did—or the awful, biting truth of them. He bit his lip, as if more words were threatening to tumble out.

"Hawthorn—" The word sounded wrong on her tongue.

She dodged another move and caught him round the middle, tackling him to the floor and pinning his hands behind his back.

"Don't make me hurt you."

"Maybe I want to be hurt!"

The force of his words slackened her grip, allowing him the needed second to overpower her. He gripped her wrists, pinning her to the floor.

"Hurt me," he begged her.

"Why?"

"Because I deserve it."

Three years ago, she would have agreed with him. Three years ago, she would have hurt him back.

But not right now.

"Let me up," she said. "*Please.*"

The fire in Hawthorn's eyes didn't recede, but slowly, his grip loosened. Juliana scooted into a sitting position as the fire simmered away.

Once again, she didn't have the words.

But she wondered if perhaps she didn't need words, not for this.

If her father had died, and she felt responsible, words wouldn't matter. Words could not plug up that wound.

She inched forward on her knees, and wrapped her arms around him.

For a moment, his arms hung at his sides, as if he had no idea how to use them, so unaccustomed to the action of being held.

Gradually, they lifted up and circled around her back, with all the strength and ferocity of a kitten. He sobbed soundlessly into her shirt.

They said nothing. Juliana had the strangest notion that they *would* say nothing, that this moment of paper grief would be hurled into the fire as soon as they let go, never to be spoken of again.

But not yet.

Not yet.

She did not know which scared her most: that there was a part of him that could still overpower her, a part that wanted to hurt her... or that he could hurt at all.

15. A CALL IN THE DARK

SIX WEEKS BEFORE THE CURSE AWAKENS

Hawthorn didn't remember what happened next. His thoughts turned dark as Juliana disappeared, his vision narrowing on the swing of her tawny braid, a golden flame in the diminishing sunlight.

He would have preferred to see her face.

Mugginess dragged him down. Pain liquified. Someone or something was pulling at his limbs.

Darkness, in and out, like the ebb of a tide.

He swam in the sea once, dived under the surface, went deep, deep down.

Jules was there. There beside him. There to pull him back.

Where was she now?

Voices were all around him, low and rushed. A white face hovered in the doorway, numb, cold, far away.

Mother.

Must be bad.

Vines twisted overhead and light burned in his side, and people were still talking.

Not the right people. Not the right voices.

Jules.

Where are you?

He thought he might have called for her, but he wasn't sure. It was so hard to tell. He was always calling for her now, always wanting her beside him. He's never spoken it, not in so many or so few words, but the truth of it was there.

How long had he felt this way?

Hard to know. Hard to trace a river back to its source. Is it in the mountains or the rain clouds or the air all around you?

He thought it had happened back at the Summer Court, but in his tangled, twisted thoughts, he wondered if it had been earlier, sooner, later, *always.* He may not have been born feeling this way, but he was born *to* feel it—in the way a tree was doomed to know moss and mould and lichen. She'd infected him, diseased him.

And she didn't even care.

Jules, Jules, come.

Maybe he was the moss, and she the tree—he was the one clinging to her, after all. He was the one that wouldn't survive without her.

"Hawthorn." A hand pressed on his cheek, cold and smooth. Not Juliana. His mother. "Hawthorn, stay with us. We have not come so far to lose you now."

"Jules," he murmured, the only sound he was capable of.

Everything else escaped him.

Juliana washed the blood from her hands in the servants' bathroom. She couldn't bear to use the one she shared with Hawthorn, couldn't bear to be anywhere near that room. She'd only get in the way. The healers knew what they were doing.

Slowly, the blood trickled down the basin, like it was never there to begin with.

Only, it had been. She could still feel it.

A hand touched her shoulder, hard and firm.

"Juliana." Dillon's voice, soft and reassuring. "I heard what happened."

"Is he dead?"

He shook his head. "Healers are still working on him."

A strangled sob broke in her throat, and something else dislodged from her heart. The next thing she knew, she was thrown against Dillon's broad chest, tucked tightly into his arms.

He was strong and sturdy. He smelt of the outdoors, of woodsmoke and metal. He was lovely and wonderful and wrong, so wrong.

She wanted to be somewhere else, with someone else.

But she could not go to him.

"It's all right," Dillon told her, stroking her hair. "It'll be all right."

Mortals are so breakable, she thought dimly. *We would not survive without those lies to glue us together.*

Dillon held her until she'd composed herself, pulling enough pieces back to mimic her usual shape. "I'll be all right now," she assured him.

"You're sure?"

She nodded, uncertain as ever, but sure she could keep the mask on.

Better than the one that assassin wore...

She headed back upstairs. The healers were just leaving by the time she arrived. The Queen hovered outside the door, conversing with them in low, hurried voices.

"Thank you," Maytree breathed, as they turned to leave.

Faeries don't say thank you.

Maytree's eyes caught Juliana's. "He will live," she said. "Thanks to you."

The word sneered in Juliana's chest. What had she done to earn such thanks? She shook her head, refusing to accept it. "I should have known something was off with Algernon."

"You were not to blame."

I am. I am, I am, I am. "I won't take any more days off," she assured her. "Not until the day."

"You're entitled to—"

"I expect to be compensated," Juliana said swiftly, knowing this would set her mind at ease. "We won't leave the castle. We'll limit the staff. No more parties or revels or anything."

Maytree bowed her head, almost like Jules was the queen, and she the cowering servant. "He won't like this."

"He doesn't need to like it. He needs to be alive." Aware of the trembling tenor of her voice, she added, "That is what you pay me for, after all."

"Quite." Maytree stiffened, regaining her queenly composure. "Will you sit with him?"

"Will you?"

The Queen looked down, ashamed. "He called for you," she said.

"He was probably confused."

"I think that was the only time he was lucid."

Bowing her head to the Queen, Juliana stepped into the room. The curtains had been drawn, making the faint light grey and dark. Over the bed, the vines wriggled softly, almost humming. Juliana wished for the energy to thank them for leading her to Algernon's body, for giving her the extra minutes that likely made all the difference.

She moved to Hawthorn's side. His midsection was heavily bandaged, far too close to his chest. A little higher and there would have been no point bandaging him. She'd be standing beside a corpse.

The tip of his left ear was sliced. No one had bothered bandaging that. She reached out towards it, but he moved under her shadow, and she bolted back, as if his touch could burn her.

Close, close, too close.

She watched the slow rise and fall of his chest, his slightly laboured breathing crackling against her heart.

She couldn't watch this. She couldn't.

She fled from the room, hurtling into her own and sliding to the floor. Hawthorn let out a sound, almost like a cry, a soft, quiet whimper.

I'm still here, I'm still here, I haven't left, I just can't watch—

But she would leave. She *had* to leave. And one way or another it would hurt just as much as this.

Once, when she was around thirteen or fourteen, not long after Markham had taken her to the woods, he took her out hunting one morning, and they reached a log—more a branch, really—over a stream.

Markham paused, before gesturing for her to continue. It made sense, of course. She weighed less than him. But still, she was sceptical.

"Go on," he urged. "Perfectly safe."

Juliana looked at the log, and back at her father. "Are you sure?"

"Would I ask you to do something dangerous?"

Yes, she thought, *but not without purpose*. She decided to risk it.

Halfway there, the branch gave way beneath her. It was a short drop, but she still sprained her ankle, bruised her elbow, and ended up sopping wet.

She didn't cry. She'd learned long ago to keep those hidden, but she still sulked bitterly as her father helped her hobble home.

"Pain is a good teacher," he remarked. "What did you learn?"

"Not to trust you!"

"To check *yourself*." He paused, waiting for the words to sink in. "You are your own greatest ally, Juliana."

All that Juliana learned that day was that it was better to go alone and trust absolutely no one, but watching Hawthorn from afar now, she felt like perhaps Markham had been right about another thing.

Pain was a good teacher indeed.

Hawthorn dreamed of monsters made of thorns, of vines twisting around him, dragging him down into the dark. He dreamed he was drowning, falling into the earth or away from it.

And nothing, nothing pinned him to the planet.

Nothing ever would.

Juliana.

If he woke at all, it was to darkness and cold. No one was there.

Just under a year ago, he'd fallen sick with faerie fever. She'd stayed with him then. Unwillingly, grudgingly, but she'd stayed.

Come to me, dark angel. Bring me spikes and barbs and irritated whispers. Just come.

But she didn't.

He dreamt she hovered over him at one point, a hand inching over him, but a second later she was gone. A whisper, a ghost of a thought. All he could conjure.

Bring me better dreams.

At one point, he dreamed of music, of an ethereal voice turning over the room, trembling and sighing. A voice he wanted to reach out and touch.

It was gone before he could.

Finally, consciousness returned. He opened his eyes. It was daylight, but the curtains were drawn. Juliana sat in a chair by the window, as far away as she could possibly be, polishing her sword.

Pain crackled in his centre. He reached down a hand, finding his middle padded with bandages. His chest was tight, mouth rusty.

He turned his gaze back to Juliana. He wished he could think of something smart or witty to say, but the words turned to felt on his tongue.

He almost died.

He killed those people.

He *would* have died, if not for her.

Slowly, her eyes lifted, as if feeling his gaze. She blinked, eyes bright. "You're awake."

"I think so."

She put down her sword, crossed the room, and opened the door to speak to the guards outside, asking them to inform the Queen.

"How long was I out?" he asked her, after she shut the door behind her.

"Three days," she said. "I think you've woken before, but not for any length of time."

"You weren't here."

"I was nearby." She paused, heading to the dresser by the side. She poured him a goblet of water and brought it towards him, taking care not to touch him as he shifted up in bed, despite how much he winced. Her free hand remained stubbornly at her side.

"I won't be taking any more days off between now and your birthday," she said, returning to the shadows.

Hawthorn broke his guzzling. "That's a month away."

"Your mother assures me I will be aptly compensated." She stilled, the shadows stiffening around her. "The people that organised this latest attack, they knew about the guard changes, knew that I wouldn't be around. So we need to be more careful, more vigilant. We're restricting the staff, conducting more checks. No more revels, no more strolling into town—nothing."

"Can we go back to death being an option? Because that almost sounds more fun."

Juliana scowled. "We thought about going into hiding, or even faking your death, but with Faeries being unable to lie…"

"You've thought this all through."

"I've had time to."

A cold, hard pause spread out between the two of them. "I killed those people, didn't I?"

Juliana nodded.

"I've never killed anyone before."

She said nothing.

"I didn't like it."

Her eyes stared at the floor. "You were right to kill them. They would have killed you."

"That doesn't help very much."

"I killed the other one. Just... just in case you were worried she escaped. She didn't."

He waited for her to say something else, anything else. It was like something had been stolen from her in the days he'd lost, like she'd reverted to the frost queen she'd been when she first came into his service. "You seem angry."

Juliana sighed. "I am angry at myself."

"For what?"

"For not realising Algernon wasn't himself. For not seeing what I should have, for—*this*," she said, gesturing roughly to his slumped form.

"This isn't your fault."

"I need to be better," she insisted, and crossed to collect her sword. "I *will* be better."

"For another few weeks," he added.

"Yes."

"Juliana?"

"Yes?"

"Will you sit with me?"

Juliana froze. "I've been still for too long," she announced finally. "Your mother will be here soon. I'll be in the next room, training. I'll keep the door open."

"Jules—"

He hardly knew what he was going to say. Would he beg, plead, grovel for her company?

Yes, he realised. He would do anything she asked—anything she wouldn't hate him for.

But a second later, the door opened, and his mother stepped inside.

For a moment, her face flickered with something akin to warmth. A moment later, it had disappeared. "You're awake," she said.

"I am."

"Did Juliana explain—"

"That I'm to be imprisoned here? Yes."

"Not imprisoned," she said, "*watched*."

"Hardly any different."

The Queen stiffened, as if she were thinking of disagreeing with him but couldn't summon the energy. "Are you up for visitors?"

"You're here, aren't you?"

"I'm not talking about me," she continued. "Your fiancée is here."

16. A DANCE AND A DEBUT

TWO YEARS UNTIL THE CURSE AWAKENS

Shortly after Hawthorn's sixteenth birthday, when Juliana was seventeen, she stood next to Hawthorn during a revel on her day off and wondered what on earth she was doing there.

Hawthorn blinked when he turned around and saw her. "Isn't it your day off?"

Juliana frowned, looking down at her clothes. She wasn't dressed for a revel, but at least she wasn't in her uniform. She'd been relaxing in the gardens, she'd come in for food when it got rowdy, and instinctively, irritatingly, she'd just found herself standing beside him.

This job was really starting to get to her.

"Yes," she said slowly, and then stared at the buffet table behind him. At the centre was a magnificent sculpted cake in pitch-black, oozing with berries, glazed to look like shards of rock. "I just came for sustenance."

Hawthorn parted, letting her edge towards the desserts. She started to load her plate, her gaze catching on Dillon on the other side of the spread, also off-duty. He was wearing a slightly smart shirt that parted at the chest, displaying several inches of fine, well-earned muscle.

"Speaking of sustenance," Hawthorn whispered in her ear, "are you ever going to ask dear old Dillon for a dance? Or... more than that?"

Juliana's cheeks heated. "That is absolutely none of your business."

"Only if it happens on duty," he continued. "So, you know, not tonight."

He gave her the strangest wink, like they were old friends, and slunk away to join the rest of the revel. Within minutes he was surrounded by admirers, arms draped over him like necklaces.

Juliana took her plate of sweet treats and sat down in an alcove to eat, determined to completely ignore his advice, if it could be called such a thing, and thoroughly gorge herself on cake.

It didn't taste as delicious as she thought it would.

Meanwhile, Hawthorn had clearly forgotten about the whole exchange. He was in the centre of a group of dancers, twirling and laughing, the gold paint on his face smeared with kisses.

What must it be like? Juliana wondered. Kissing, and sex... the feel of skin on skin.

She'd traded a few kisses with a couple of stablehands and squires before she went away to Autumn. After that, opportunities had been thin on the ground. She'd not had the time since she returned.

But tonight... tonight she had nothing planned.

And Dillon was looking at her.

She put down her plate and marched towards him, courage and nerves like a steaming pot inside her. "Dance with me," she demanded.

Dillon blinked at her as if she'd suddenly sprouted horns and he wasn't sure whether or not it was polite to mention it. "I'm sorry?"

"That was impolite, wasn't it? I meant, 'will you dance with me'?"

"Are you... sure you have the right person?"

Dillon moved clumsily into place, arms slipping tentatively around her waist, as if unsure how to hold her. A rare, simple smile spread over Juliana's face. "Imagine I'm a battleaxe," she suggested. "If it helps."

Dillon's grip on her tightened. "I'm infinitely more familiar with battleaxes..."

"Not scared of me, are you?"

His throat throbbed. "Not scared, exactly, just..."

"Don't be scared," Juliana whispered, and slid her arms around his neck. Her fingers played with his coarse curls, trying not to think of darker, silkier ones. *Don't be scared.*

Juliana had yet to meet a foe she couldn't vanquish, and she felt like she was fighting against something tonight, although what it was she couldn't name. Dillon's breath brushed against her temple, his tight, broad muscles glistened through the shirt, and something stirred inside her, hot and deep.

She leant up and pressed their lips together.

He tasted of blackberry wine and woodsmoke and fresh hay, his mouth hot against hers. His hands trembled on her waist, as if steadying himself against her. His movements turned from clumsy to confident, fingers roaming upwards as her insides turned warm and bubbly. She wanted his hands elsewhere, in other, deeper places.

"Let's skip the dance," she said, parting from the kiss.

Dillon blinked at her as if debating whether or not to question this or do as he was told.

He chose the latter. "All right," he said, a shy grin spreading across his face.

A part of Juliana's haste came from the fact she knew Hawthorn would doubtlessly be shortly returning to his own chambers, and she refused to have him as any kind of audience.

But she also wanted this. Wanted pleasure and knowledge and skin.

They fumbled up the stairs, already unbuckling, dropping belts and weapons to the floor the second the door was closed.

"Are you sure—" Dillon started, as she heaved off her shirt. "Never mind."

She yanked off his trousers, actions clumsy as they both stumbled towards the bed. Dillon was broad, all scars and calluses, velvet hairs over hard muscles. He was human, warm, ripe with sweat, a match for her. No need to be ashamed of her bumps or bruises, the imperfections of her obvious humanity.

His kisses were firm and strong, the rest of him even more so. "Sorry," he said, as she groaned underneath. "I didn't mean to—"

"Don't be gentle," she warned, "don't you dare."

Hawthorn stayed far later at the revel than he intended to, but he made no move to choose a partner or head upstairs. He told himself he was just trying to be polite, giving Juliana privacy for what he was sure was probably her first time.

But it was more than that. Something strange had come over him when he'd seen her kiss Dillon, a vision that had soured the rest of the evening, turning all other kisses stale when they met his mouth.

He lost his appetite for the night, even the wine lacking the bite it usually had.

At last, he stumbled up to bed.

All was quiet on Juliana's side of the door. Normally, when one of these moods hit him—a melancholy born of nothing—he'd go to her and tease her until he quite forgot there was anything wrong with the world.

Not tonight. He didn't dare.

He sunk into a strange, distorted sleep, dreaming of everything and nothing. Black thorns and blood in the snow, lips on his, smears of gold paint on spider silk sheets, and mortal bodies that oozed with impossible warmth.

Things he had no right to dream of.

It was past dawn when he finally rose. Hot light drifted over the floorboards, banishing dark crevices. The vines slunk down his bedsheets, nudging him like a hungry cat. Purple buds sprouted when he reached out to pet them.

Juliana must be up by now. She never slept in. He half doubted she was capable of such a thing.

Certain she would be dressed and ready for the day, he slunk into his robe and barged into her room.

"Jules, my fair vixen, how was your sexual debut—"

He froze immediately. Jules was still in bed, Dillon's arm flung around her, her bare, perfect back littered with fresh bruises.

The rest of the room narrowed. The vines pulsed beneath his fury, screaming down Juliana's bedposts and going straight for Dillon.

He let out a thick cry, springing from the bed as they clawed at his body, thrusting him against the wall, winding towards his throat.

"What did you do to her?" Hawthorn's voice twisted out of him, sounding like another person's entirely.

"Hawthorn!" Juliana hissed, leaping from the bed. She tugged uselessly at the vines surrounding Dillon. "Let him go!"

"He hurt you!"

"What?" Juliana hesitated, and her eyes darted towards the mirror in the corner. "Oh, oh, no... It isn't what it looks like. Put him down, please."

At her steady tone, his anger rescinded, replaced by stark bewilderment. What had just happened? What was he *doing?*

He dropped the vines. Dillon hit the floor, grabbing his clothes and vanishing into the hallway.

Juliana turned back to Hawthorn.

"Did he give you those bruises?" he asked. "If not, tell me who did, so I may have them flayed."

"Um, see..." Juliana's eyes spun everywhere but him. "He *did* give them to me—"

"Then—" He made a move to follow him, but Juliana's hand pressed against his chest. His skin barked underneath hers, his fury tempered.

"I asked him to," she admitted, voice quiet. "Sort of."

"Sort of?"

"So... it turns out I rather like it rough?"

No words escaped Hawthorn in that moment, but his mouth opened in a wide 'o'. He coughed, and Juliana's hand dropped away. She crossed the room to pull on a shirt.

He'd been so angry he'd barely even noticed she was naked.

"I apologise," he said eventually, when she was fully covered, trying to avoid the way the cloth clung to her curves.

"I think Dillon needs the apology more than I." She chewed her lip. "You don't need to fight my battles for me. I'm more than capable of looking out for myself. You think I would have let him stay if he hurt me?"

Honestly, I didn't think at all, was his first response. He was known for being thoughtless, but that—that was something else.

"Well, I am a bit reckless and impulsive, or so they say." He wanted to tell her he'd never do it again, but he knew that would be a lie. That if anyone ever hurt her— "I shall endeavour to take better care in future, and will apologise to Dillon the first chance I get."

"Do so," she hissed. "Now get out. I want to get dressed in peace."

Juliana didn't see Dillon for the rest of the day, which wasn't unusual but felt wrong, somehow, given what had passed between them. She'd wanted it to just be a fun, physical thing, like sparring, but she'd be lying if she said things didn't feel different between them, now. Did she want it to happen again? What did she want *him* to want?

It didn't help that Hawthorn was being disturbingly mute to make up for the embarrassment of the morning. He barely said a word to her all day. Had things altered between them as well? She couldn't shake the strange, dark expression in his eyes when he'd found them together. No cruelty, only a cold fury she'd never once witnessed before.

He reminded her of Maytree, of the power that curled around her like a shadow, the dark radiance that made mortals surrender.

But there was another part that wasn't like Maytree at all, that was so clearly *Hawthorn,* and the colossal echo of the king he would one day be.

All of that was gone, now, thorns replaced by dandelions. He spent the hours either reading or writing at his desk, although he had few people to correspond with.

Just before sunset, Hawthorn declared he had a sudden desire for an evening gallop through the grounds. "It may get dark before I return. It would be dangerous for you to guard me with those weak mortal eyes of yours. I shall take another guard. Please, go down the stables and ready my horse for me."

Juliana knew exactly what he was doing, but she decided not to question it. She followed his commands, slipping silently down to the stables where Dillon was on duty.

"His Highness requires his horse."

Dillon leapt up from the chair where he was resting, a flicker of a smile in his tanned cheeks. "Well, we best not keep His Highness waiting."

Wordlessly, as they had done a hundred times before, the two of them saddled Raven, fingers brushing over feather and fur.

"Did he apologise?" Juliana asked, when the task was almost completed and a runner sent to fetch Hawthorn.

"He did indeed," Dillon said, almost proudly, reaching into his pocket to retrieve a letter. Juliana recognised the elegant scrawl immediately. *"Dear Dillon. Apologies for the misunderstanding this morning. Please accept this coin in recompense."* He produced a shiny gold coin, flipping it in the air.

Juliana groaned. "He was writing all morning. Was that *it?*"

"Probably because he can't lie."

"What does that mean?"

"Well, he can hardly say, 'I don't know what came over me' or other mortal nonsense, can he? He apologised, I've an extra week's wages for some mild panic—I'm not complaining."

Juliana had no idea what had come over Hawthorn, and she decided she didn't want to. Far easier to pretend it never happened.

Dillon's smile wavered. "About last night..." he started.

"It was nice," Juliana admitted. "A shame about this morning."

"Quite." He paused, eyes glancing downwards. "Is there something going on between you and the Prince?"

"What? No! Why would you—"

"He seemed more than a little perturbed to discover me in your bed."

"He encouraged me to—"

"He... encouraged you?" Dillon's brow twisted. "Did you sleep with me because the Prince told you to?"

"No!" Juliana exclaimed, affronted. "I slept with you because after years of seeing faeries going at it at every opportunity, I was curious. And you're nice. I figured my first time should be with someone who wasn't a complete ass."

A stiff silence spread between the two. Juliana hated it. Things had always been easy with Dillon. Had she ruined that?

"It was my first time, too," he said softly.

"I know," she said. "I'm sorry. Did I ruin it for you?"

"No," he said, "not at all. I just... I was curious too. I don't regret it, I just—"

"You don't want to do it again?"

"I rather *would* like to do it again," Dillon admitted. "But, see, the thing is—*holy vines, I can't believe I'm saying this*—I like you more than you like me, and I don't think you're going to change your mind towards me. So if we did... if we continued this... I think I'd just end up getting hurt, and even though I want to, it might be best if we both... pursued other partners." He took a deep, long breath. "Gods, I hope I don't regret that."

Juliana reached across Raven's saddle and took his hand. "You're too good for me anyway."

"I, um, thank you," he said, his thumb brushing over her knuckles ever-so-briefly before releasing. "We're not faeries, you know," he said. "We don't have to act like them. We're allowed to want to be with just one person for the rest of our lives."

"Do you really think they're so different from us?" *I know I do, at times. When I'm watching them be beautiful and perfect, when I watch magic fly from their fingers and charms from their voices.*

But this morning, when Hawthorn flew to her defence—that was the most human she'd ever seen him, fae darkness aside.

"I think we've all been convinced that they are."

17.
THE AGONY OF WANT

ONE MONTH UNTIL THE CURSE AWAKENS

The trip to the Summer Court resulted in many things and many changes, but to a narrow few of Faerie, the greatest and most significant was the decision that Princess Serena, heir to the seat of Summer, should be Hawthorn's 'chosen fae bride' that the curse spoke of.

Their engagement was contingent upon her ending it, and had not been officially announced for fear of making her a target for Ladrien or any other parties keen to allow the curse to come to fruition. Hawthorn had joked, not entirely humorously, that perhaps he ought to announce Lucinda as his intended instead if they wanted a decoy.

Hawthorn was not exactly keen to marry Serena. He hardly knew her, and she seemed hesitant about the whole thing too.

But it would be selfish to refuse.

The plan was simple: Serena would be taken out of Faerie shortly before the day in question, and returned back shortly afterwards, with all manner of precautions in place to ensure she didn't fall victim to the curse. She'd be assigned a small number of guards both mortal and faerie. The mortals would wait for her by the border, unhampered by the curse. The faeries would escort her back again under a series of enchantments.

If it worked, Ladrien would lose.

If it worked, the kingdom would only sleep for a few days.

If it worked, Hawthorn wouldn't have to wake up without Juliana. He wouldn't have to spend the rest of his life wondering what had happened to her.

Even if she left, she'd live, and he'd see her again.

It was for that reason more than any other that he'd consented.

"I'm sorry," said Juliana, helping him into a robe and plumping up his pillows, making him look at least a little bit presentable. Her fingers hovered for a moment beside his head, almost as if she were thinking about touching him. He wished she would, but he knew it was a foolish wish. "We thought it best to bring her here, for her protection."

"You've thought this through."

"I've had a lot of time to."

Once more, her fingers lingered, as if unsure of where to go, but before she could make up her mind, Princess Serena arrived at the door, clad in cerulean and seashells. She was a tiny, nervy looking creature, with enormous doe eyes and the speckled skin of a fawn.

"My Prince," she said, bowing her head. "I am glad to see you well."

"Well, I still have a hole in my middle, but I am conscious, which is likely an improvement to everyone but dear Jules here."

Serena glanced at the floor, stifling a smile. Juliana pouted uncomfortably in the shadows.

"May I come in?"

"Please do. I daresay you're better company than my sour-faced guard."

He'd still, as always, prefer to be alone with her, although there was presently a gloom about her sloughing off in waves. Serena *ought* to be better company, though. And food had been brought up, too. He realised suddenly how hungry he was.

Serena stayed for the better part of an hour, chatting amiably about the journey and how pleasant the palace was. She helped him eat, too, when he found his fingers too weak to hold the spoon.

All actions Jules would have struggled with.

And yet, when Serena departed, and the room fell silent once more, that was when he was happiest.

"Juliana?" he asked.

"Yes?"

"Would you help me into my nightshirt? I find myself tired again."

Juliana nodded, getting up from her spot and moving towards the dresser. Her calloused fingers turned soft against the wood as she pulled open the top drawer and selected his favourite, coming back towards the bed.

She tugged gently on the ties of the robe, sliding it off his shoulders. Her fingertips caught on his skin, sending tiny, pulsing shivers through him. He tried not to buckle beneath that touch, resisting the urge to pull her into bed with him.

Say something, he begged, but she did not, instead levering the shirt over his head and dropping it to his waist.

Her hand rested against his chest, hovering over the bandages. "Someone should change these for you," she said. "I'll send for them."

She got up to leave, and he coiled his fingers into fists to stop them from reaching out to her.

That night, he dreamt Juliana returned to his chambers. He tried to rise towards her, but she pushed him back to the bed, mindful of his wound. She told him not to move as she slid astride his lap, taking his face in her hands.

When she bent her head to his, the proximity turned his thoughts to mush, her kisses hot as fire and yet like water on the leaves of a dying plant. Impossible to exist without them. Easy to crisp away beneath them.

"I'm sorry I wasn't there," she murmured into him.

"You're here now."

"I don't want to leave."

"Then don't. Stay."

"But I must," she whispered. "I must, you see, I must!"

He reached out to steady her, but she had dissolved into shadow and smoke.

The scene shifted. He stood beneath the great boughs of the hall, the branches draped in flowers and ribbons. Serena was beside him, dressed in bridal fashion, a long veil studded with gems and seashells obscuring her face.

"We'll be happy together, won't we?" she asked.

Hawthorn looked out, and realised the congregation was filled with bones. Full skeletons were propped up in seats, scattered with crows that cawed and plucked at ribs. Veils of cobwebs carpeted the room, snakes slithered from empty eye sockets, moss draped over them, parodies of clothing.

In the centre of the room was a skeleton draped in a gown of moths, a veil of spiderwebs reaching across the floor, a flower pendant resting against her ribcage, a sword of thorns in her grip.

Juliana.

He bolted up in bed, seething as he pulled at his wound, pain lashing through him, whip sharp.

In the next room, he heard the sound of Juliana stumbling out of bed, appearing seconds later, sword at her side.

"I'm not under attack," he said swiftly, "just pulled my wound."

Juliana hovered in the doorway. His dream started a little like this, and for a second, he thought she might come to him again, touch him with those hands of hers.

But of course, she didn't.

"Are you all right?" she asked. "Should I fetch someone?"

You, Jules. I just want you. "No."

"Go back to sleep," she whispered. "I am next door if you require assistance."

He did not want her sword, or her help. He wanted her in ways he had no words for.

He found himself bitterly unprepared for the agony of want. He was used to sordid fantasies and sick desires, used to craving flesh and sex. This... this was something else. He wanted to pull her into the bath with him, to stroke that flame-gold hair from her back and kiss every bruise and muscle and scar while she lay slotted against his chest. He wanted to dance with her all night long, body against his, breath on his face. He wanted to wake in her arms, for her stiff face to smile at him, for those lips to speak softness in his ears.

He wanted her body to whisper poetry to his.

He wanted her to want the same things of him.

It was not the first time he had dreamt of kissing Juliana, of doing a hundred other things with her. It was not the first time he had dreamt of watching her die.

He wondered which thought would haunt him longer.

Hawthorn's wound healed within the week, but the stain of the experience clung to Juliana, haunting her nightly.

For the three days he slept, the silence nearly broke her. She'd kept to her chambers, the door open between, unable to look at him, to face him.

My fault. My fault.

His stillness crept into her bones. She wanted to go to him, had strange, foolish fancies of holding his hand, touching his hair.

But what good would any of that have done?

At one point, unable to handle the silence, she'd started to sing. Her voice broke the quiet, but it broke her too.

What was the point? He wasn't listening.

And yet, when he'd woken, she'd wanted nothing more than to throw away her weapon and cling to him like a child.

But she hadn't. She couldn't trust herself not to hurt him, not to scream obscenities—

She couldn't trust herself to let go.

And Princess Serena was in the castle again. It wasn't right.

It was never right to feel this way. It never would be. Not for anyone, and certainly not for him.

Juliana was fine with having friends, friends that could be slotted away neatly in the past, or up on a high shelf, ready to be dusted off whenever she returned to them. Friends like wildflowers who took care of themselves.

She did not want people in her life who grew like roots beneath her, twisting into her, making her something else, making it impossible to leave.

And she needed to be able to leave.

Will he miss me, when I'm gone?

Would she miss him?

What worried her more?

She didn't want to be like her mother, tearing up her roots when she needed to go. She didn't want anyone to bleed on her behalf.

And Hawthorn already had.

Not like that, she reminded herself. *There are worse pains, ones he'll never feel for you.*

The dream she'd had the night he woke burned through her memories.

She'd dreamed she'd gone to Hawthorn's room and apologised for not being there. She'd dreamed she kissed him, that he'd kissed her. In that moment, she'd gone up like a matchbook, and woken scorching in the dark.

Hawthorn had woken seconds after she did, having hurt himself waking from a nightmare. It had taken all her restraint not to go to him, not to ask him if he wanted her to stay.

The boy was quicksand. She had to stay away.

Three more weeks. Just three more weeks and she'd be free of him.

You will never be free of him, whispered a voice in the dark.

"Don't tell me what to do."

Juliana had not yet met a foe she could not vanquish.

She would vanquish this.

She had to.

18. THE ROAD TO SUMMER

ONE YEAR UNTIL THE CURSE AWAKENS

Straight after Hawthorn's seventeenth birthday, the royal party journeyed towards the Summer Court for the sheer purpose of meeting a prospective bride. Time, everyone was intimately aware, was running out, as were the number of willing candidates. There had been a few over the years since Lucinda, but each one had been judged "eminently unsuitable" by Maytree if not Hawthorn himself.

"We are not merely choosing a bride," Maytree reminded all those who would disagree, "but a future queen of Faerie. We cannot have just anyone."

There was a reason she had never married Aspen, naming him only as her consort. There was a reason Ladrien had insisted on a bride rather than any fae creature. And, although fae marriages never swore forever, there was a reason no one was agreeing to become his bride without ensuring some degree of power on their part.

"Let the marriage not be broken until she has known at least ten years as queen," was one stipulation.

"Let her first bear the future king or queen of Faerie," was another.

"Let the marriage not be over until she sees fit," was a third.

Maytree had dismissed them all. "I will not save Faerie to have it ruined."

There were some, Juliana knew, who were not happy with her choice, but Maytree was not to be against said.

Sometimes, Juliana wondered if Maytree didn't have other reasons for dismissing the matches too, if deep down, she didn't want for her son what she had had with his father—love and companionship, the kind that had endured long after death.

Most faeries thought little of sex, but Maytree hadn't taken anyone to her bedchamber since Aspen had been killed, hadn't so much as looked at another man, had barely danced at a revel. There had been a few whispers at court that she grieved too much, but that didn't seem fair to Juliana. It hadn't even been two years. For a faerie as old as Maytree, that must have felt like yesterday.

"You've never been to the Summer Court before, have you?" Maytree asked Juliana, as the carriage trundled down the Summer Road.

Juliana shook her head. "No, but I've been longing to go. I've never seen the sea before."

"We'll have to ensure you get some time off so that you may explore at your leisure. After we've inspected the Summer Palace, of course, and ensured it's safe enough."

Hawthorn groaned. "Am I to be held captive in my rooms until then?"

"You're no prisoner, Hawthorn. Stop acting like you are. Many would be grateful—"

"Ordinarily, Mother, I'm sure many would jump at the chance to live the life of a prince, but people are considerably less excited about the prospect of being murdered every day of their lives. Do you honestly know many who would be happy to be me?"

Maytree remained silent.

"I didn't think so."

The tension in the carriage remained palpable until they at last came to a stop in Merwood, the final respite from their journey before they'd reach the Summer Court. It was a sprawling town carved out of the forest, divided by rivers and waterfalls and humming with firefly light in the warm evening air. Juliana's skin buzzed, dusted by gold. Every time she visited somewhere new in Faerie, she thought it was the most beautiful place she'd ever been. She hoped that feeling never abated. She hoped she never saw *everywhere.*

At the same time, she knew she'd never be happy until she had.

She glanced up at Hawthorn, storming up the winding steps to the inn that Maytree had rented the entirety of for the night.

My cage is bigger than yours, at the moment, she realised. *But one day you may be free of yours.*

That evening, they unwound in the private dining room, the blackness of the skies outside swirling with dizzying light. In the busy streets below, all manner of fae were gathering, dressed in glittering gossamer gowns that sung with starlight. Juliana half-wished Hawthorn was allowed to venture outside; she wanted to experience this place, inhale it.

Hawthorn clicked at one of the serving-girls, a green-skinned beauty with eyes like pearls. "This wine is quite delicious," he said briskly. "Have another bottle sent to my room, will you?"

The serving-girl disappeared, and Hawthorn climbed to his feet.

"Mother, all other respectable company, I bid you goodnight."

He swept towards the chamber he'd been assigned, not even glancing to see if Juliana was following. She did, of course. She always did.

He barged into the room, removing his extra clothing, and slumped down in a seat by the window. The wine arrived shortly afterwards. Hawthorn poured himself a long measure.

"Are you going to lurk at the door all night?" he barked.

"It's as good a place as any."

"Don't you want to inspect the view?"

"For assassins?"

"For the *view*, Jules," he said exasperatedly. "I saw your expression in the dining hall earlier. You looked like you'd found a painting you wanted to fall into."

Juliana was surprised at his power of observation, but she refused to show it. Instead, she walked over to the windows and flung them open, revealing a small balcony. It *was* like stepping into a painting, a living, breathing, glimmering one, filled with music and laughter and the scent of hot wood and honeyblossom.

Rarely did Juliana ever feel like a princess in a story, but in that moment she came close.

Hawthorn turned his head. "I don't suppose I could convince you to sneak out with me, could I?"

"You're lucky I'm even opening the windows. It's like I *want* to make you a target."

"Do you?" He cocked his head.

"What?"

"Do you want me dead?"

Juliana frowned. For two years, she'd been by his side, fending off assassinations and keeping him out of trouble. How could he possibly think she'd want him dead?

"Um, no?" she said. "Not at all."

"I don't suppose you'd care to remove your wards and let me—"

Juliana buckled. "No chance," she said hurriedly.

Hawthorn's wicked smile—the first she'd seen on him since the journey began—flickered.

"Not because I'm not telling the truth, though," she added. "But because..."

Because I can't allow anyone to know where I keep them. I can't afford to let down my guard. I can't afford to let anyone in—

Hawthorn waved his hand, as if it mattered little. "Ah, have a drink with me and we'll call it even."

"I'm on duty."

"You can hold your liquor."

Juliana obliged. It was only one drink, after all, and it wouldn't be the first time she'd bent the rules with him, just a little. During his last birthday, she'd found him wandering the corridors after the festivities had ended, a couple of guests tangled in his bedsheets. He'd consented to return to his chambers only if she drank with him. And she had. Partly because she wanted to relax herself after the day, and partly because even though the ball had been dazzling and beautiful, she sensed that perhaps it was not so much for him.

One year. They had one year.

Tick, tick, tick.

She sipped the wine. It was blackberry, thick and heady. It tasted of pure summer. "It's delicious," she remarked.

"Only the finest for us, my sour-faced vixen."

"Take you a long time to come up with that one?"

Hawthorn went silent. The two turned their gazes back to the busy streets below, piping with music. "You could go out, if you wished," he said eventually. "I'm sure someone else will watch me."

Juliana shook her head. "I'm fine. Besides, you know I'm way more fun to suffer with."

Hawthorn blinked at her. "I *do* know that," he admitted. "I'm surprised that you do."

Juliana, against her better judgement, found herself smiling. She took another sip of her drink. "I think you might quite enjoy my company."

"I don't detest you as much as I used to."

"Feeling's mutual."

They clinked their goblets.

"Should we toast?" he suggested.

"What to?"

"To Summer, to enemies turned *very* reluctant friends, to beauty, to freedom—"

"To not wanting to stab one another in the face?"

Hawthorn laughed. "To not wanting to stab one another in the face," he declared, as they held up their goblets again.

In the middle of the night, Juliana woke. Hawthorn was hovering over her. "I'm going to find a drink," he said. "Is that permitted?"

Juliana was too tired to reply, too tired to remind herself that she ought to fetch it for him, or ask him to call for a servant. She muttered a faint word of affirmation and slipped back into blissful unconsciousness.

Sometime later, there was a soft knock at the door. "Juliana? Are you awake?" Her father's voice.

Juliana groaned. "No."

"Is the prince with you?"

"He's asleep," she said, not checking.

Her father coughed. "Don't let him sneak out," he continued. "There's been an outbreak of faerie fever in the outskirts of town. Maytree is insisting everyone stay inside for the time being."

"Uh-huh." She nodded, not caring that he couldn't see her.

His footsteps shuffled off down the corridor, and the room was left silent once more.

Silent.

She bolted up in bed and stared across at Hawthorn's. Even in the dim light of the room, she could see that it was empty. His boots were gone too, and the clothes he'd left on the chair. What had he said?

I'm going to get a drink.

Unlikely that he'd fully dressed to get a drink from the restaurant below. Unlikely that he'd get it himself at all. She kicked herself inwardly for not waking up enough to question him.

I take it all back. I really, really want to stab him in the face.

Perhaps she would. Not with a knife, or anything that could do any real damage. Maybe a spoon.

Anything's a weapon if you throw it hard enough, her father had told her, more than once.

Juliana was about to throw a spoon really, really hard.

She pulled on her trousers and boots, flinging on a loose shirt over the top. It wouldn't do to be caught in her palace uniform if Maytree had placed them under quarantine—

How had he even gotten out? There were guards posted at the door—

Something banged softly, a light breeze shifting through the room.

The balcony.

Juliana charged out onto it. It was several stories high, and Hawthorn wasn't much of a climber. Had he really slunk down the building?

A building made entirely out of a hollow tree.

Juliana banged her head against the side of the giant redwood. The boy could manipulate plant life. He'd have enchanted a branch to carry him down or moulded himself handholds—

Several of which she now saw in the trunk.

Is he trying to kill himself or me?

She returned to her room to gather Briarsong, and then swiftly climbed down the building.

"You there," she said to a nearby citizen, "where is your closest, seediest tavern?"

Even in an unfamiliar town, it didn't take her long to locate him. Once she'd located Merwood's downtown, she simply found the rowdiest tavern and waltzed right in.

A glass smashed against the wall a few inches from her face as she entered, making half the place roar with laughter. A shard slid across her cheek, but she paid it no heed.

If an assassin doesn't kill him, and I don't, I'm sure his own poor decisions may.

It would be a truly terrible ending to the tale of the Cursed Prince if he died in an unfortunate bar accident, but Juliana was tempted to let that be the conclusion when she discovered him on a table, dancing and breathing fire into his goblet.

"Juliana!" he declared, leaping off the table and misjudging the distance so that he hit the tree trunk in the middle of the room. He cackled with laughter as he righted himself, oblivious to the cut in his eyebrow. "You decided to join me!"

"I came to *retrieve* you, not join you!"

A 'boo' sounded round the room.

"Oh, *please*, Juliana. Stay for just a little bit! It's more fun with you!"

"You really do delight in tormenting me, don't you?"

Hawthorn grinned, thumbing the spot between her eyebrows. "You have just the loveliest scowl. I find myself quite enamoured with it—"

"I find you've had far too much to drink." She grabbed his arm and steered him away from the crowd, lowering her voice. "There's been an outbreak of faerie fever," she told him. "We need to get back to the inn."

Hawthorn's eyes widened, sobering. It had swept through Acanthia once when they were children. It was one of the few illnesses faeries were susceptible to, robbing them of their old, infirm, and their young. The death toll had been mild but significant, and the effects were... unpleasant.

"All right," he said. "I'll come back."

The sobering effect of her words quickly wore off by the time they'd reached the inn, where he became an unhelpful, giggling mess. How was she to sneak him in like this? She'd been hoping to plant him in the downstairs of the inn, sneak up the outside, and slide out again to retrieve him the proper way if he couldn't make his own way up the stairs. She needed to appear not at fault, like she'd had no knowledge of him sneaking out.

But that didn't seem possible, now. Guards were posted at the entrance, and there was no way he could climb up in this state.

"You look worried again, dear Jules. It isn't as fun as your angry face."

"I'm trying to work out how to get us back in."

Hawthorn's eyes gleamed. "I have an idea. I don't think you'll like it, though."

Juliana's eyes narrowed. "I'm all ears."

"Oh! There it is again. Delightful."

Her scowl darkened. *"The idea, Hawthorn!"*

He sighed. "I think I preferred it when you called me Prince Prickle..." He took a step forward, sliding a hand around her waist.

"What are you doing?"

"Relax, sweet viper, I'm not trying to dance with you..." He swished his free hand in an upwards spiral, and a vine twirled down from the boughs above, wrapping itself around them and tugging them off the floor.

Juliana buckled, clutching onto Hawthorn instinctively, hating that the faint smell of sweat and cheap ale only seemed to enhance the scent of apple spice clinging to his skin.

Hawthorn grinned as her fingers dug into the damp silk of his shirt. "Not often I get to be the dashing one."

"If you think being forced to be this close to your disgusting, drunken self is in any way dashing—"

"Ah, Juliana," said Hawthorn as the vine deposited them on the balcony, "but I *do*."

She groaned, freeing herself from his embrace and yanking him back into the bedchamber. He collapsed on the bed as she turned to fetch him some water, forcing it on him whilst she wrestled with his boots.

Hawthorn smiled, setting aside his glass, but not being particularly helpful when she freed him of his shirt, carefully inspecting his neck and chest. "See something you like?"

"Checking for rashes. Faerie fever can come on quickly, or so I hear."

Seeing nothing, she returned to the area set aside for bathing and dampened a cloth to attend to the slight cut on his eyebrow.

"If you get sick," she told him, "I'm not looking after you!"

"Fair enough," he responded, and his fingers drifted to a slight sting in her cheek—the broken tankard must have caught her earlier. Something buzzed at his fingertips, and a warmth spread through her face, the cut healing.

"That wasn't necessary," she said.

"Take it as practice, then," he replied, and sank back against the pillows. "You get hurt too often on my account," he remarked, staring lazily up at the ceiling.

The cut was nothing, and ordinarily, Juliana would have reminded him of such. But not tonight, when he'd lied to her—or the faerie version of it, anyway. "Then stop doing dangerous things!"

"I can't help it," he said, "it's in my nature, playing with fire..." He made flames dance around his fingers.

Juliana wrapped the damp cloth around his hand and extinguished them in an instant. "If you set fire to the bed sheets again, I'm leaving you."

Hawthorn's fingers brushed against hers. "I still detest you sometimes," he said, voice like wine. "And yet I still want you to stay. How strange is that?"

Juliana groaned, rolling her eyes. "Hawthorn, in all seriousness, please stop trying to hurt yourself."

"Hurt myself?" He blinked up at her. "I'm not trying to hurt myself. Other people are trying to hurt me. If other people could just stop trying to do that, that would be great! Although... you'd be out of a job. That would be less great."

"I would cope."

"I might not," he said, sliding further into his pillows. "Jules?"

"Yes?"

"Don't worry about me. I don't want to die, see. I like life too much. Even with the bad bits there's too much enjoyment to be had."

He reached out, and for a second, Juliana thought he might be going for her hair, but instead he flicked her nose and erupted into giggles instead.

Juliana could not think of a response to that, and thankfully, she didn't have to; seconds later he was asleep.

She pulled off her own clothes and slid back into bed.

Very strange, she thought, *very strange indeed.*

19. THE NIGHT BEFORE

The changes to the castle in the lead-up to Hawthorn's eighteenth birthday were both minute and imperceptible and also sudden and all at once.

Whilst rumours surrounding Princess Serena's role in ending the curse were rife, so few knew the truth of it that many were disinclined to believe anything had been put in place at all. Juliana heard all manner of whispers from the servants.

"They don't care about us. They've given into the curse."

"I've heard many say they support Ladrien's claim—"

"They're going to leave us to rot."

Many left, one or two at first, and then whole groups of them, caravans of mortals and their kin fleeing the city.

Maytree said she preferred this. She'd always been a friend to mortals, but the latest incident had shook her. She dismissed many herself, accusing them of plotting or poisoning. Precious few had her ear now—she only seemed to speak to Markham or Miriam. Even Juliana felt the Queen had become more distant towards her. She trusted her enough to have her guard Hawthorn, but she stopped speaking when she walked into the room. She was no longer welcome at meetings.

"I don't suppose you'd tell me—" she asked Hawthorn one night.

He shook his head. "*I* would tell you, if I knew anything," he responded. "You aren't the only one she keeps in the dark."

Juliana tried not to show her disappointment. In all likelihood, it wasn't personal—merely an understanding that Juliana could lie and not be held to her vows, that truth could be tortured from her. It did not matter that she felt like she would never betray Maytree, that she'd sooner die than let harm befall Hawthorn... the fact remained that she could be broken. Rarely did she ever long for the ability to only speak the truth, but she wished she could prove her worthiness through words now, if her actions were not enough. She wished she could make vows that would stay forever.

The castle grew cold and dusty, the food quality dwindling. The marketplace—what little of it Juliana could see on her few excursions from the palace walls—shrank. Only a handful of stalls seemed to remain.

"Your Majesty, perhaps we ought to consider offering the mortals an incentive to stay," one of her advisors suggested. "There is a reason we've invited them into our lands. The economy alone—"

"They are replaceable," she insisted, although her eyes refused to meet Juliana's when she spoke.

"No, they're not," Hawthorn muttered.

Juliana imagined he was probably just annoyed that Owen and his wife were amongst those fleeing the city, the latest in a string of deserters.

The capital turned dark and cold. Cobwebs and moss crept into the crevices. Aoife muttered about her books getting damp, and the vines lapsed into mourning.

"Do you think they miss the citizens?" Juliana asked Hawthorn one evening. "Or... are they just feeding off your mother's energy?"

Hawthorn shrugged. "Hers," he said, "or mine."

The dark silence thickened around him.

Princess Serena stayed with them until almost a week before the day. Juliana guarded them both when they were together. They played board games, walked around the gardens, occasionally showed each other their magic.

Polite. Restrained. As awkward as Hawthorn could be.

There were worse ways to start a relationship, and Juliana could see that he was trying.

Trying, and hating it.

They didn't speak much, either.

Among the humans remaining in the palace were Miriam, Markham, Iona, Aoife, Dillon and Albert. Most did not surprise her, although she asked Aoife one morning when Hawthorn declared he had a sudden desire to visit the library.

"You didn't even think about it?" Juliana asked her, as Hawthorn stuffed his face in a book and pretended not to listen in.

Aoife shrugged. "Did you?"

Juliana tore her eyes away from Hawthorn, which was a foolish action. She was *supposed* to be watching him. "That's different. I have my father here—" *My family, my life.*

"My life is here," Aoife told her, looking upwards at the towering shelves. "I'm not leaving my books for anyone."

Juliana nodded, thinking of the others. Iona and Albert said that they didn't belong in the mortal realm, not anymore. Faerie was their home and their coffin. Miriam and Markham, she knew, were involved in some plan to protect the remaining mortals, hiding them or escorting them out, if worse came to worse. She didn't know the specifics. Few did.

It was safer that way.

The days and nights rushed together, endless and over in an instant. Exhaustion had crept into Juliana's bones, clawing at her mind, stiffening her sinews. She hardly slept, too terrified of shadows in the dark, convinced every sound was an assassin readying to pounce.

One night, just a few days before the main event, she woke up gasping and sweating, desperate for water. The silver jug beside her bed was empty.

Her eyes turned to the door that separated her room from Hawthorn's. It was a long way to replenish the water otherwise. She'd just sneak in, quiet as a mouse...

She tip-toed into the room before she could be accused of over-thinking, silently slinking towards the jug beside the window.

"Juliana?"

Juliana froze. "I'd forgotten you can see in the dark."

"What are you doing?"

"Water," she said, raising her empty glass. "I didn't mean to disturb you."

"Can't sleep?"

She shook her head. "You?"

"No. I think I might have given it up for the time being."

She yawned loudly, pouring herself a measure and taking a long sip. "At least faeries seem capable of functioning on only a few hours…"

"You need to sleep, Jules."

"Can't."

He sighed, the sheets rustling on the bed. "Come over here."

"What, why?"

"Just do it."

Muttering under her breath, Juliana set down her glass and did as commanded. Her knees brushed against the great bed. Hawthorn's hands reached out to help her up, and tugged her into his arms.

"W-what are you doing?"

"Come on. You know this is better than tossing and turning in your own bed. Lie down with me."

Juliana could think of a dozen reasons why that was a terrible idea, but she was sick of the silence between them, sick of sleeplessness. The bed was warm and soft, and she'd be lying if she said she didn't enjoy the feeling of his arms around her.

But she was very, very good at lying…

"Fine," she hissed. "But I'm doing this for your benefit."

"Naturally."

He pulled her down with him, tucking her under his chin, fingers skimming her hair.

They'd huddled together for warmth before. This was just that. Survival.

His throat throbbed against her nose, his heart pressed over hers. She could almost taste his skin; hot chocolate, spice, winter berries.

Survival, she reminded herself. *Sleep.*

That's all it was.

Because it could never be anything else.

The day before the curse, Maytree consented to open up the gates for a precious few, carefully-selected guests, all thoroughly vetted and stripped of all weapons. Unsure of what the next day would bring, faeries did what they did best: they partied.

The great hall was strung with banners. The vines were forced to bloom. Fountains of wine, red, white and purple, spouted in every corner. Golden plates were laden with food, stuffed boars, roasted hogs, a dozen fat birds with crackling skin. Towers of fruit and cheese were spread through the room, piled on tables or floating discs. Music fluttered through the air.

Faeries could not whisper the lie, "everything is fine," but they could put on a display so opulent it would fool even the most cynical of hearts.

Except, apparently, Juliana's.

And Hawthorn's. He was smiling and laughing as usual, but Juliana knew a false one by now, and could see the storminess brewing behind those eyes.

Everyone else was putting on an excellent show of it. Maytree had descended from her throne to twirl about with the courtiers, the vines blooming and twisting above her. Miriam, whilst not drinking, was engaged in an arm wrestling competition at the side with Barney the minotaur. Markham was chatting merrily to the human knights—not about tomorrow, but about old times.

If people were frightened about what tomorrow would bring, they hid it well.

Of course, most of them were promised safety.

Not seeing anyone to talk to at present, Juliana made her way to Hawthorn's side. He was talking to Raife, a fox-haired young man from Autumn they'd gone to school with. Juliana had few fond memories of him, but also few negative ones, which was often as much as she could hope for. He'd grown into a moony, lyrical person with a flair for the dramatic but was otherwise harmless.

Currently, the latest object of his affection was a beautiful young merman with shimmering skin like a kipper and eyes of pure jet. Raife's attempts to court him had progressed little beyond a few sighs and some truly atrocious poetry.

"Do you ever find," he said to Hawthorn, his eyes following the merman about, "that whenever you're around someone you adore, you act like a complete fool?"

Hawthorn's eyes spread across the dancefloor, and Juliana wondered who he was searching for. "Tell me about it," he said.

"You always act like a fool," she interjected.

Hawthorn jumped, but recovered quickly. "Is that so?" he said, not looking at her. "Please don't think too much about that."

Raife laughed, and descended down into the throng of dancers in pursuit of his lover. Juliana sidled up to Hawthorn and leant against his chair. She was half-tempted to sit on the armrest. What did propriety matter now?

"All set for tomorrow?" she asked, trying to sound jovial. "I did try to get you a present."

Hawthorn frowned, turning to face her. "You did?"

"It's not much—just a book. I left it under your pillow. Nothing special, just the last one I read that I enjoyed."

Hawthorn stared at her. She wasn't surprised. It was a silly gift, but he already had *everything* else she could possibly afford and she didn't want to give him nothing.

There was a little note in it too, but she didn't want to mention that right now.

"My birthday is actually the anniversary of when we met," said Hawthorn, in lieu of the 'thank you' a mortal might bestow.

"Is it?" Juliana frowned. "I thought we didn't meet until the naming ceremony."

Hawthorn shook his head. "Your mother was there, you know. When I was born. Supporting my mother."

"I didn't know." She knew her mother had served the Queen, but she hadn't known they'd been so close.

He nodded. "Apparently, after it was all over, your father came to the door with you in his arms. You were screaming for your mother, but before she could leave the room, you'd wriggled out of your father's grip, raced across the room, and bolted over the bed to get to her. Not a care given to the queen or the baby in her arms."

"Screaming aside, that does sound like me."

He smiled. "Apparently, you stopped crying almost immediately, and then became *fascinated* with the baby in the room."

"Hmm. Me, fascinated by you? I suppose I was only a child... didn't know any better."

"Would it be so hard to pretend you like me?"

"It would be easy to pretend..." she said, and nudged his elbow. *It would be much harder to tell the truth.*

Hawthorn shoved her off the armrest. "Go," he said, mouth turning up in the corners. "Your friend is waiting for you."

Juliana turned. Aoife was standing a few feet away, clean and dust-free for once, raven's feathers braided in her hair, her face smeared with shimmering paint, leaves drawn on her bare legs like the ribbons of sandals. Her grin was impish.

"Dance," she said, like she was a faerie casting a glamour, a command that must be followed.

Juliana glanced at Hawthorn, but he was already waving his arm dismissively. She leapt from his side, linking her arm into her friend's, and allowed her to pull her into the throngs of dancers.

The musicians played, their tunes piping hot, gallops and hops, not a sad note amongst them. Juliana flung herself into the revelry, moving from dancer to dancer.

For one fleeting moment, she was one of them. Careless. Free.

For one moment, she belonged.

But she was no faerie. She wasn't even a carefree mortal. She was a creature of shadows and worries not easily discarded.

I wish I could sleep through tomorrow, she thought. *I wish I could awaken when it was all over.*

But she would be there to the end, protecting Hawthorn, protecting the mortals left behind. Waiting for Serena's return.

Lungs bursting, she collapsed with Aoife on a pile of cushions by the side of the room, laughing to dispel the cloud of dark thoughts brewing inside.

"That was fun," Aoife panted.

"Worth leaving your library for?"

"Yes. Every once in a while, it's good to dance."

Juliana nodded, agreeing, but suddenly finding it difficult to speak. Aoife would be here tomorrow. There was no need for a goodbye, and yet…

"Juliana?" Aoife prompted, voice turning serious.

"Yes?"

"We *can* lie. It doesn't mean we have to."

"What does that mean?"

"Ask yourself what you're most afraid of. Then ask yourself why."

I am afraid that too many people I care about are remaining, and that I cannot protect them all. I'm afraid of what tomorrow will bring, how different things will be after then. I'm afraid of people knowing I'm afraid.

I'm afraid I'm not good enough, not as a guard, and not as a—

Her eyes fell towards Hawthorn. *Not as a whatever we are to each other.*

More than prince and guard, that was for sure.

Didn't matter. Couldn't happen. Wasn't worth thinking about.

Didn't dislodge the thought, though.

Dillon appeared in front of the two of them as the music slowed to something softer. He held out his hand to Juliana, which she took eagerly.

She needed the distraction.

He pulled her into his warm, broad arms, as Alia began to sing a song.

"A maiden fell to Faerie, and for Faerie she did fall
A maiden came to Faerie, answering its call.
Lulled by music sweet and fine
Drunk on its heady summer wine,
Faerie grasped her in its snare
The girl no more than a fearful hare—
A maiden came to Faerie, long, long ago.
Where she's buried—no one knows."

"I thought the Queen had banned such melancholy," Dillon remarked.

"I think they're faeries and will soon forget that they were ever sad in a heartbeat."

"Most of them," he said, his eyes glancing towards Hawthorn's throne.

Juliana did not want to think about why his eyes lingered there. "What's your role tomorrow?" she asked, tugging his attention away.

"Guarding the main gate. I expect there will be quite the show."

Juliana's stomach churned with nerves. *No, no, don't think about that.*

"Dillon—" she started, wondering what she was going to say. Take care? Goodbye? Come upstairs with me?

The latter had its plus points...

"Would you like to—"

"If you're asking if I'd like to come upstairs with you, then the answer is yes," he said. "But before I accept, I think you should ask yourself... who do you *really* want to spend tonight with?"

Alia's song had changed now, a soft, slow ballad full of longing, the kind that wriggled into your bones.

Who do I want to spend the night with?

Juliana's gaze fell towards Hawthorn.

"I'm sorry," she said quietly.

Dillon kissed her forehead. "Don't be," he said. "I don't mind."

He was probably lying, but she chose to believe he wasn't.

Hawthorn had disappeared by the time she looked up, the side passage door still open. She glanced at the guard on duty, who nodded, and silently slipped after him.

When she arrived at his room, she found him standing at the window, gazing out over the starlit gardens. A velvet pouch rested on the table in front of him, and he was fiddling with the golden drawstrings.

"What's that?" she asked.

Hawthorn jumped, as if surprised to see her there. He recovered quickly, smoothing down his clothes. "Your payment," he said, "for services rendered in the past three years. Money, jewellery, a few trinkets."

She came towards him, taking the bag from the table. It was incredibly heavy.

Three years ago, she would have counted it.

Now, she didn't want it.

"Shouldn't you be out getting incredibly drunk and piling up your room with lovers?" she teased, putting the pouch back down. "All being well, you'll be basically engaged by tomorrow. Best make the most of it."

"Perhaps I ought to be," he admitted, voice low and quiet, "and yet I find I have not the heart for it." He slid into the seat beside the table, folding his long legs. "What of you, Jules? What will you be doing tomorrow?"

"I agreed to serve you until your eighteenth birthday," she said, even though she had already told Maytree she'd stay throughout. "I suppose that doesn't actually include the day, does it? Want to bargain for a few more hours?"

"What would you do with them?" he asked. "If I made you stay? Would you guard me until the curse took effect? Stand watch by my bedside until dear Princess Serena comes to free me?"

"I could probably be persuaded," she said. "You know. For the right price."

There was no laughter in his voice. "You should go."

"What?"

"Go. Get as far away from here as you can—"

"I appreciate the offer, but I shall be remaining here."

"Gone soft on me after all these years?"

"Something like that."

Juliana sank into the chair opposite, picking the bag back up, just to occupy her fingers. Her lap shifted under the weight of the coins she didn't care to inspect. For a moment, a sharp silence stretched out between them.

"I could do with some barbs right now, Jules," Hawthorn whispered.

"I'm sure I could summon some." She reached forward towards the jug of wine between them, and poured two goblets. "Shall we play a game? I shall say three things, two truths, one lie. If you guess correctly, I'll drink. If not, you have to."

"Drinking on the job?"

"You did just try to dismiss me."

"Then why are you still here?"

Half a smile tugged at her cheeks, but she didn't quite loose it. "One. Because I have nowhere better to be. Two. I am secretly a spy sent to deliver you at midnight. Three. I am here as your friend."

Hawthorn paused. "One?" he queried.

Juliana smiled. "Drink."

Hawthorn obliged, taking a swig from the goblet. "Just checking," he said, "but the right answer *was* three, right?"

Juliana did not reply.

He shook his head. "I wish I could despise you."

I know the feeling.

"Next round," she said, before she could lose herself too much in that thought, "If I wasn't going to be a knight, I would like to be a—"

"Horse trainer," Hawthorn answered, before she could even list her options. "Perhaps a stablemaster. Something with horses. Next."

Juliana blinked. "I don't think I've ever told you that."

"Have you not?" he shrugged, holding up his glass. "I'm right though, aren't I? Drink."

Juliana took a careful sip.

"Your favourite colour is mauve or pale green, your birthday is the 18th Autumn, and your childhood pet was a mouse named Ravenger, before you offer me something equally dull," he said, drinking despite the lack of a loss.

"How do you know all that?"

"I know precisely four pieces of personal information about you, and I've now used them all up," he reported.

"Is that so?" Juliana chewed her lip, thinking. "I didn't always want to be a knight, you know. I used to want to be a bard. I gave up on that dream because one, I hate crowds, two, I can't actually sing, or three, I preferred something more active."

"Oh, I know this one," said Hawthorn eagerly. "You can't actually sing!"

Juliana opened her mouth. *"The maiden cried for the man she loved, and heartbreak echoed around, if you could hear her, you'd cry too, for her voice did fracture sound."*

Hawthorn stared at her. "How did I *not* know you could sing?"

Juliana swallowed a grin, enjoying the amazement in his face. "I'm not exactly a performer."

"But your voice is beautiful. Quite the improvement on your usual barbs." He smiled at her, clearly waiting for a retort. "You've sung to me before, haven't you?"

Juliana's cheeks heated. *More than once.* "I didn't think you remembered."

"I didn't, until now."

"It was just to fill the silence," she added quickly. "Or to drown out your awful moaning."

"Naturally," he said, though he was still smiling. She was amazed he could remember anything about that time with something like joy. "That's the lie, then," he continued. "I think I'm playing this game wrong."

"Do you want to stop?"

"No, but I'd like to suggest some categories, if I may?"

"Go ahead."

"What colours do you think I look best in? Feel free to have 'nude' as an option."

Juliana pursed her lips. "Too obvious a lie."

"No, but that was."

"Fine. You look best in magenta, midnight blue, or forest green."

"Hmm, trick category. I look best in everything."

"Blue," she said quietly, hating the soft betrayal. "You look best in blue."

Hawthorn blinked at her.

"Also, you didn't guess, so you ought to drink."

"Fair enough..." he said, still staring over the rim of his goblet. "First love."

"Haven't got there, yet," she replied swiftly, feeling hot under the collar and too startled to come up with lies. "You?"

Hawthorn took a long drink. "Not Princess Serena, alas."

They sat in silence for a short while. "She's nice, you know," Juliana said eventually. "For a faerie, at least. Asked me once what sort of person you were. It isn't just about money or power for her. You could do worse."

"She could quite likely do better."

Juliana frowned. "Do you honestly think that?"

"I do."

"Rarely have you conceded your own faults. I'm impressed."

"I take great pains to hide my own poor opinion of myself," he admitted, staring at the contents of the bottle. "Hardly seems much point, now, when I'm destined to become the Prince That Cursed All Faerie."

Juliana kicked his chair. "*You* didn't curse anyone."

"Why are you kicking my chair?"

"It's how I show affection," she said, without thinking, and then, "or I think you're being an idiot. Or I'm just aggressive and like hurting you."

Hawthorn stared at her for a long, steady moment, his eyes flickering in the candlelight, beautiful, luminous. "I don't *think* you like hurting me," he said. "I don't think you like hurting anyone."

"Well, you're wrong about that, because sometimes, in the heat of battle or when someone is really, *really* pissing me off, I do like hurting them." She hesitated. "But not you," she added. "Not for a long while."

Something shifted in Hawthorn's gaze. "So you *do* like me."

"I mean, I also think you're an idiot, but—"

"Jules," he said, in that soft, silky way that always made her want to concede, "please."

Tell him you don't hate him as much as you used to, a voice told her. But what came out, in the same, soft voice as his, was, "Yes. I like you."

"How much?" he asked, his smirk wicked.

"More than a hole in the head, less than I love that which I love the most, and as much as you deserve."

He chuckled. "A true faerie answer."

"Drink."

"Why?"

"Because I asked you to."

For the next hour or so, as the moon waned, they traded questions. Jules dealt lies and truths, some outrageous, some silly, some personal. All designed with the purpose to keep him entertained, to keep his mind occupied.

And hers, too.

From time to time, she became conscious of the night propelling onwards, getting later and later, heralding the morning. She wished it was a monster, a tangible thing she could fight.

But she couldn't.

So she drank instead. Tiny, careful sips. Enough to take the edge off but keep her wits about her, enough to ensure Hawthorn drank plenty but didn't think he was drinking alone.

"All right," she declared, "next round. Number one—I didn't put the frog in your bed last Midwinter. Number two—I didn't let you win when we practised sparring last summer. And three... of all the things I'll miss, whatever tomorrow brings... I'll miss your smile most."

For a moment, she swore the ghost of a blush rose in Hawthorn's cheeks, but as quickly as it came, it vanished.

"But those all sound true..." he mused, stroking a long-fingered hand under his chin. "Actually, I refuse to believe my smile is the best thing about me. I have many other admirable qualities."

"Correct. That one is a lie."

Hawthorn pursed his lips, still smiling. "The frog thing was out of order, Jules. Wait. What *will* you miss the most? Did you just agree with me that I have many admirable qualities? What are they? List them all. Don't hold back now, my delicious downfall. I may be as good as dead by tomorrow."

Jules gritted her teeth. "I have no need to list them when you clearly know them all."

"Mayhap," he agreed, "but I should like to hear *you* list them."

This is a mistake, Juliana's head warned. *The object of this game is only to take his mind off things. You don't need to actually tell him the truth. You don't need to tell him you'll miss everything—*

But maybe, just maybe, a little honesty was required, tonight of all nights.

"You're a lot nicer than people think you are," she told him. "A lot nicer than *I* thought you were. You don't like people to know it, and I understand why, because kindness is a weakness to be exploited in this world we live in, but you... you care about other people."

He smiled, dipping into his drink. "Tell absolutely no one."

"Your secret is safe with me."

"And..." His face lit up hopefully.

"And... and you're funny. I know I don't laugh very often, but that doesn't mean I don't find you amusing."

"Amusing?" He arched a black brow. "I'm *hilarious*."

"You're drunk."

He looked across at the empty bottle. "Oh my, so I am. Thanks for that."

Jules downed the sips of her singular small glass. "Faeries aren't supposed to say thank you. It places you in someone's debt. Makes it seem like you owe them."

"I *do* owe you," he said, with surprising seriousness. "Not just for this. For the last three years. For—for everything." He stopped, gaze rising to meet her. "Thank you, Juliana. I don't think I could pay you back. I know I haven't been the easiest charge—"

"I don't know," Juliana replied, hating the faint quality of her voice, hating that she was speaking at all, that she seemed to be drawing closer towards him, that her fingers seemed to be slipping into his, and hating more than anything how fast her heart was beating. "You had your moments."

A smirk dragged across Hawthorn's cheeks, a sickeningly soft one.

Magic, she hissed inwardly. *He's using magic.*

You are immune to faerie glamours.

But not, apparently, to his charms. The smile crashed over her like a wave, dragging her under.

"Care to share any of those?" His fingers were now firmly laced into hers, and she was close enough to smell the wine on his breath. She wondered if it was possible to get drunk by proximity. She felt giddy enough.

"Hawthorn, I—"

His free hand cupped her cheek, grazing her neck, her hair. "You do not have to speak, if you do not want to. I don't want your lies tonight."

"It isn't—I wasn't going to—"

His face lowered towards hers.

She had no idea what she was going to say.

She dimly knew what she wanted to do.

The door banged open, and the Queen appeared on the threshold.

Juliana flew back. The Queen barely batted an eyebrow. "Excellent. You're here too. Collect your weapons. We're leaving Faerie tonight."

20. THE FiRST DROP OF BLOOD

"But we can't," said Juliana, quite forgetting to be polite in the heat of the moment, as Maytree tore into the room, flinging open trunks and wardrobes. "The border is days away—"

There were at least a dozen other impracticalities, but that was the first that sprang to mind.

"I've secured us a solution," Maytree insisted. "Can you—help with packing? I do not know what I am doing."

Juliana stared at her, quite unsure what to make of the situation. Why hadn't she brought servants with her?

Because she can't trust them not to speak, she realised. *And there are hardly any mortals left.*

"Mother," said Hawthorn, stepping forwards quietly, "Juliana can't leave Faerie."

The Queen paused. For one awful moment, Juliana was sure she was about to order her to come with them regardless, but instead, she said, "Will you come with us to the border?"

Juliana chanced a look at Hawthorn. She didn't need to ask.

And if she asked you to follow them in the mortal realm, knowing you might never be able to return? What then?

She didn't want to think about that. She didn't want to think about that because she knew the answer.

"Of course, Your Majesty."

Within a few minutes, clothes had been flung into bags, Juliana's weapons strapped to her body. She took little but a change of clothes, several blades, and the payment Hawthorn had given her.

Wrapped in cloaks, the three of them hurried out into the night, past the revelry, into a deserted part of the garden.

Juliana's dim eyes could just make out a black carriage beside the lake, saddled with four giant winged horses. A couple of guards surrounded them, but Juliana couldn't make out their faces in the dark.

Hawthorn paused, staring. "You've been busy, Mother."

"When you cannot lie, you do not speak," she said by way of explanation.

Juliana knew such mounts existed, but they were rare, difficult to tame. How long had Maytree been planning this? Was this always what she hoped to do—

The words of the curse churned inside her. *When the Prince comes of age, at the first drop of blood spilled from his body...*

It didn't say it had to be tomorrow. Any day after his birthday would count too. Did Maytree honestly hope to keep him safe forever?

But maybe, if they were outside of Faerie when the blood was spilled... the curse wouldn't hold any potency. Faeries tended to lose their magic the further they were away from Faerie, and the longer they were gone. It stood to reason that curses were the same...

"Hurry," said Maytree. "We have not as many hours as I would like."

She pushed Hawthorn into the carriage, climbing in herself afterwards. Juliana hesitated, a hand reaching out to grip her arm.

"Juliana." Markham's tired face looked down at her.

"You're coming with us?"

He nodded. "I'll be escorting them as far as the border. *Only* as far as the border," he added, looking pointedly at her.

"Don't worry," she told him, "I won't leave Faerie."

Her father nodded grimly. "Don't do anything foolish in order to keep him safe," he warned. "Run the first chance you get. He isn't worth it."

Juliana frowned. Not so long ago, she would have agreed with him—or at least, pretended to.

Not now.

"I get to decide who and what is worth it," she said stiffly. "No one else. Not even you."

She yanked her arm away from him and climbed into the carriage, sitting closer to Hawthorn than she'd initially planned. Her hand skimmed the back of his.

"You all right?" he asked.

She blinked at him. "You're about to leave Faerie for an indeterminate amount of time to a land that will drain your magic, and you're asking *me* if *I'm* all right?"

"Of course," he replied, as if this was obvious.

Maytree banged the roof of the carriage, and the whole thing set off at a sudden, horrible, lurching pace. Juliana flung backwards in her seat as the wheels spun from the ground, stomach backflipping as the horses leapt into the air and a horrible, impossible weightlessness branched out beneath them.

Her lungs shuddered, and she half-fell into Hawthorn.

"My, my, snakes and heights, Juliana," he said, smirking. "What other fears are you keeping secret?"

"I'll be fine in a minute," she said, certain that she would be.

"I don't doubt that." And then, in full view of his mother, he linked his fingers into hers and kissed the back of her palm.

Juliana wasn't sure what shocked her more: the action, the audience, or the fact she didn't immediately remove them.

She didn't *want* to remove them.

She chanced a look outside the carriage, the castle vanishing into night, distinguishable only by tiny spots of colour in the sea of ink. All too quickly, colour vanished entirely.

They were alone in a black sky, and everything Juliana had ever known and loved was lost beneath endless, invisible clouds.

To begin with, Maytree attempted to make small talk. That went about as well as could be expected. She'd uttered little but forced pleasantries, instructions and condemnations in Hawthorn's direction for years. In fact, Juliana was inclined to think *she* spoke to the queen more often and at more significant length.

Someone banged against the roof of the carriage. "My Queen," came the voice of Maytree's personal guard, Kieran.

The Queen rose as a hatch opened up in the ceiling. "Stay here," she commanded the two of them, and took Kieran's hand, levering herself onto the roof.

Juliana could see little in the dark, little that wasn't illuminated by the faint crystal lights of the carriage's interior, just enough to display the sharp lines of Hawthorn's face. The carriage gave a strange, shuddering lurch, and faint light crackled along the horizon—not dawn, more like soundless lightning.

Something like a cold fog ripped through them.

"What was that?" Juliana gasped.

"Mother opened a portal," Hawthorn explained, peering outwards. Juliana felt something slump in the seat outside. "Not easy to do—not easy at all. She's transported us several miles. I don't think she can do more."

"Is she all right?"

He nodded. "She'll be fine with rest."

He hovered by the hatch, but she did not rejoin them. Eventually, he closed the opening, and slid back into his seat. Even in the dark she could see how tight his body was, coiled with nerves. She wished she knew how to dispel that, but she was busy battling her own.

She sat down beside him, and waited.

More hours passed. From time to time, Juliana asked Hawthorn if he could spot anything. He'd mumbled a reply, saying he expected they were flying over such-and-such a town, but he had little to offer.

Time, both endless and unstoppable, flooded before them.

"We're not too far away from the border now," Hawthorn remarked.

Juliana glanced out of the window. The inkiness of the sky was starting to recede. Dawn was not far off.

It was Hawthorn's eighteenth birthday.

She turned towards him, wondering if she should make a joke, or whether that was too much, too horrifying.

Hawthorn stared at the carriage floor, twiddling his thumbs. His blackthorn ring had vanished. "Jules, seeing as you can't come with us, it may be that..."

"That what?"

"It may be some time before we'll see each other again, and—"

Or never. It could be never. If Serena didn't make it back, if Maytree didn't have another plan, if Ladrien chased them there—

"I'm not fond of grand goodbyes," she snapped.

"No. I suppose not." His twitching fingers moved towards his pendant, still not looking at her. There was no need for him to wear it now, and yet he'd taken it anyway.

"Why did you give the witch your years?" she asked him. "Truly?"

Hawthorn sighed. "You might not miss a few months, Jules, but I would. If they were your months."

"I don't follow."

"I've always known I would watch you die," he said. "I've liked the idea less and less as the years have gone by. I'd trade many a year to give you an extra month, and still consider I'd got the better end of the deal."

He sighed, running a hand through his hair, grasping at the back. Once done, he reached into the inside pocket of his doublet and retrieved a small, leather-bound notebook. She'd seen him writing in it before and never given it much thought. "I know you don't like goodbyes," he said, "but I'm hoping you'll accept this."

He pressed it into her hands, the leather warmed by his body.

She forced a smile. "What's this? A secret diary? A written declaration of your undying affections?"

"Something like that," he admitted, not smiling. "Or the best I can manage in the time we have left."

Frowning, Juliana moved to open it. Hawthorn's hand shot out, pinning it closed.

"Not here," he insisted. "Only when we're apart, and I never have to face you again."

"Face me? You make me sound like some monster to be vanquished."

"In some ways, you are," he admitted. "In others—"

The carriage gave a sudden lurch. Juliana gripped the side of her seat as Hawthorn toppled against her, the notebook flying out of her hands.

"Sorry," came her father's voice. "We're descending."

Hawthorn didn't speak. He didn't move, either. One hand was braced against the backrest, the other gripping the edge of the seat beneath Juliana.

She didn't speak, either. It was like her voice had been snipped away.

"Juliana," Hawthorn whispered, almost hungrily. Her name sounded strange on his tongue, rough and soft, a serrated blade slicing through silk. The syllables rang painfully, like it cost something to speak them, like he found his voice unworthy of the task.

She had never heard her name uttered in such a fashion, and doubted she ever would again. The years ahead of her were collapsing, folding inwards on this moment, these stolen seconds that would never be theirs again.

She wanted to whisper his name, but sound had vanished from her world.

Everything vanished the moment his mouth fell to hers.

Juliana was sure she'd slipped into a dream. This wasn't happening. There was no way Hawthorn was kissing her, Hawthorn who she used to hate—

But didn't anymore. Hadn't hated for a very long time.

His lips explored hers with expert attention, his breath against her mouth, his hands roaming up her back. Her fingers slid almost unconsciously around his neck, drifting to his thick hair, grabbing at it, at *him*, pulling him closer.

More, more.

He tasted exactly like she'd imagined—ember and woodsmoke, rich wine, velvet given scent. His mouth was soft and hungry and his kisses made her belly rumble. It was like being struck by lightning, sensation everywhere at once, from her claiming fingers to the tips of her toes. With reverence and desperation he kissed her, half saviour, half storm. Did he kiss everyone this way? How were they ever content to release him?

His name whispered up inside her like a prayer. *Hawthorn, Hawthorn.* She used it so rarely, and now she wanted to sing it, but she couldn't bear to break her mouth away from his.

The carriage swept downwards, juddering to a halt, and they sprung away from each other just as Maytree spoke. "We're here," she announced.

Hawthorn's eyes had not left Juliana. She could still feel his hands on her, the press of those perfect lips against her mouth. "Apparently so."

Juliana shifted upright, regaining her composure as the Queen reappeared, dropping into the carriage.

"We shouldn't dally," she rushed, barely glancing at Juliana as she gathered her things. "There's some supplies in the back for you for the return journey... Unless, of course, you wanted to come with us?"

"Mother!" Hawthorn chided. "You can't ask her that! If she comes with us, she won't be able to return—"

"We don't know that! She was born here—she hasn't crossed the boundary before. And she'll be with us. The border will open for its subjects, if she stays with us..." She looked at Juliana, almost imploringly. How much of this plan had she thought out? She had only one guard with her, little in the way of belongings. How much was riding on desperation?

"Juliana?" The pleading in Hawthorn's voice was impossible to ignore.

If she knew she could return, there would be no question. But if Maytree was wrong—

You might be able to find your mother again. To ask her why she left—

But she'd be stranded there, away from everything she knew, everything she loved. It would feel like death to her.

And yet... was she willing to let them face it on their own?

Was she willing to leave *him?*

"Your Majesty—"

Something screeched through the air, a cry that made her bones tremble. Sluaghs.

Juliana dashed outside the carriage, drawing her weapon. Kieran had scrambled out of his seat too. Markham was holding the horses as they strained, sluaghs swarming over them, a black cloud of cries.

Three struck the carriage like a hale of bricks, claws tearing at the roof. Maytree pushed Hawthorn out, shielding his body with hers, roots twisting through the earth, swiping at them. Juliana swung her sword, trying to keep them at bay. There were too many, too many to fight at once—

Black talons flashed in front of her face. A shapeless mouth opened, letting out a long, dreadful scream. Juliana thrust her sword upwards, but a spiral of roots reached the sluagh first, catching the creature round the throat and twisting it towards the ground, branches shooting through its body like bolts.

Juliana swivelled, expecting to see Maytree behind her, but Hawthorn was there instead.

Without speaking, their backs snapped together like magnets. Hawthorn's roots gathered around them, swiping sluaghs out of the sky for Juliana to skewer.

The carriage shot forward, several sluaghs toppling off. A group swooped towards the fleeing horses, clawing at them. Blood flashed in the air like ribbons, along with the sound of braying cut short with a sickening crunch.

Someone—Markham or Kieran, Juliana wasn't sure—cut the remaining horses free. They bolted into the wilderness.

"The border!" Maytree hissed. "Get to the border!"

Roots ripped through the earth, thick as the trees themselves, half whip, half battering ram. The entire wood bent to the might of the seelie queen, the trees blazing like banners.

Juliana seized Hawthorn's hand and hurtled down the path Maytree had cleared for them, towards the fog.

The border between the mortal and faerie realm.

A sluagh made it through Maytree's defence, barreling into Juliana and tackling her to ground. Claws strained against her lightweight armour, her sword thrown loose.

"Go!" she hissed at Hawthorn, struggling for her dagger.

He didn't even look ahead. The roots currently bending to his mother's will alone, he seized Briarsong and sliced the creature through.

He didn't start to run again until she was on her feet, sword returned to her.

Ahead of the border, something was forming, a creature of mist and shadow.

Juliana halted as it emerged: a tall, graceful man, with full horns, long black hair, and two giant leathery wings. He was as straight and pale as moonbeam, his bare chest glistening wetly beneath a feathered robe.

Beautiful and terrifying.

Ladrien. King of the Unseelie.

Maytree's onslaught increased, her roots twisting towards him, but Ladrien merely smiled. He raised his weathered staff and a thousand thorns sprung at his feet, multiplying like ants springing forth from a hill as they raced to meet Maytree's branches.

The forest seemed to explode when they met, a twisting fusion of smooth and sharp, black and brown. Nature cleaved in two.

The noise was unstoppable.

Juliana seized Hawthorn and pressed him to the ground, pulling his cloak over him. A single drop of his blood and it was all over.

Sluaghs still swarmed above, but none made it through the mesh above them. Juliana scanned around, searching for an exit—

A narrow gap of light pierced through the undergrowth, a space beneath the wriggling roots and the ground. She shot up, jamming her sword into the mass, trying to widen it just enough to let someone through.

"Come!" she hissed. "Quickly!"

Hawthorn raced to his feet, sprinting towards her, stopping once he reached the gap.

"What are you waiting for? Go!"

Hawthorn hesitated, mouth open, his face a canvas of unspoken things.

Don't, she prayed. *Don't say anything that might haunt me. Just go. Get out of here. Be safe.*

Something in her expression must have registered, because a second later he squeezed through the gap and vanished.

Juliana turned back to Maytree. The queen was flagging, her knees buckling under the strain. Her powers were not inexhaustible. She was already drained from opening the portal, she'd barely rested—

Ladrien, meanwhile, had been preparing for this day for eighteen years. Everything about his posture and his face sung with power, limitless, unstoppable. His black eyes shone hungrily.

Maytree sank further towards the floor.

No, Juliana thought desperately, knowing it was pointless. *Don't give up, please—*

Boughs cracked and shattered. The earth splintered. Wind screamed. Twigs and leaves sliced through the air like arrows.

Maytree's knees touched the ground.

Stop—

Her shoulders slumped.

No—

Maytree met Juliana's eyes, and seeing Hawthorn was no longer with her, she dropped fully to the floor, her strength depleted.

Her roots and branches shrivelled away, Ladrien's thorns surrounding them. They gathered around Maytree, but before they could fully reach her, Juliana sprung from her spot and leapt into the space between them, sword outstretched.

"Have no fear for your queen, little warrior," Ladrien said, his lips pulled into a tight smirk. "I promised not to harm the fae."

He clicked his fingers, and thorns sprung at Juliana's feet, twisting round her legs like pythons, around her arms, her throat, forcing her to drop her sword as blood blossomed at her wrists.

She couldn't move.

Ladrien moved through the bracken, gliding towards her with the grace of a swan. His cool hands moved to part the hair over her ears. His smile twisted further.

"I said nothing, however, about leaving mortals alone. Quite the opposite, in fact..." His eyes fell to Briarsong, its blade gleaming in the mud. He shook his head. "To grace a filthy mortal with a royal sword... you should be ashamed, Maytree. How the mighty have fallen."

Maytree stared at the ground, panting hard. "I'm sorry," she rasped.

"I knew you would be," said Ladrien. "Too late, I'm afraid."

"I wasn't apologising to you." Her eyes circled to Juliana.

Something flickered in Ladrien's dark eyes, like offering an apology to a mortal was the worst kind of insult. He flung out a hand, and Maytree smashed backwards against a tree, thorns at her throat.

"You dare apologise to *this* thing? You who would not acknowledge your own?"

"You... not... one... of us..." she croaked.

Juliana strained against her bindings. One hand was pinned against her thigh, inches away from her reserve dagger. She twisted her fingers towards it, clasping the hilt even as the thorns bit into her skin.

It barely registered. *Ignore the pain* had been one of Markham's first lessons. *Markham. Father.* Where was he?

"You're right," Ladrien hissed, "I am not one of you. I am stronger, greater. History will forget you, Maytree. You will be no more than a footnote if I let your name survive at all. The Last Queen of Faerie."

Juliana cut through the first of the thorns. They gave way easily beneath her blade; summoned things were never as strong as the real element.

"You... won't win..." Maytree choked.

"Will I not? We shall see."

The thorns crumbled around Juliana. She broke free, springing forward, her dagger raised—

Ladrien wheeled, catching her by the throat and slamming her against the Queen, wrapping them both up in seconds.

"You like this one, don't you Maytree?"

The Queen did not answer.

"I wonder if you will enjoy watching her insides spill."

"*No!*" cried another voice.

Hawthorn. What was he doing here?

"Release her," he said, fists blazing with fire.

Ladrien smiled. "Well, well, well. The Cursed Prince himself. How kind of you to grace us with your presence."

Hawthorn hurled a fireball. It soared past Ladrien's horns. "I will not miss again. Release the mortal. She is not part of this."

"*All* mortals are part of this," Ladrien hissed. "That's part of the problem. But I will bargain for her release, if you submit to me."

Hawthorn's throat bobbed. "You promise me that no harm will come to her? That you'll let her go?"

Ladrien sighed. "No harm shall come to her from my hand, or my instruction, until sunset today, and I shall release her the second your blood spills."

Hawthorn froze, no doubt stung by those last words.

"That's all you'll get from me, Prince, and your blood will spill regardless."

Juliana stared at him, hoping for some last minute reprieve, for her father to appear and run Ladrien through—

Or Hawthorn would think of something. Brutal, clever Hawthorn. He wouldn't willingly give himself up, and certainly not for her.

Ladrien smiled, reading Hawthorn's silence. He summoned a thorn bush to appear at his feet, the spikes sharp as daggers, shiny as patent leather.

Hawthorn raised his hand.

"No—" Juliana struggled against her bindings, but they only tightened around her, cutting off her air.

Hawthorn didn't watch.

This is part of his plan, this is all just part of his plan—

Because there was no way he came back for her, or even his mother. He wasn't that foolish. He was supposed to be selfish—

Be selfish, she begged him. *Just for a minute. Run away. Be the coward I thought you were.*

He pressed his thumb against a thorn. A tiny jewel of blood blossomed at the tip.

He fell to the floor.

Maytree screamed. Juliana thought she might as well, but she wasn't sure. The bonds around her snapped away.

No, no, no—

The winds turned cold and dark. The sluaghs dispersed into the clouds, cawing and screeching, a violent cacophony of noise. Branches, leaves, bracken—all took to the air, like birds of glass.

Stumbling, Juliana dragged herself through the raging storm to Hawthorn's form, slumped beneath the bloody thornbush. His chest was still rising and falling.

She touched his cheek. His eyelids fluttered open, dragged up and down by the force of the spell. "Bet you're regretting coming with us now..." he muttered blearily.

Juliana tried to laugh. "Just a bit."

His fingers found hers, pinning her hands to him with all the force of a kitten. He opened his mouth to speak, but no sound came out. Silver lined his eyes.

"It's all right," Juliana whispered, though the wind stole half her words. "It's all right."

"Liar."

The tempest ripped a fallen log from the floor. It sailed overhead, narrowly missing her. Hawthorn's hands sprung from hers, coming up to cover her head, as though he hoped to shield her from debris with nothing but his fingers.

"You should leave," he told her.

"You're right. I probably should." She caught his eyes, holding his face as consciousness slipped from him. *I'm not sure I will, though.*

"Such touching concern from a loyal guard," crooned a voice behind them.

Juliana turned, dagger in hand. "You won't win," she told him.

Ladrien smirked. "If you're thinking about dear Princess Serena, little mortal, I'm afraid I have some news for you."

Juliana's insides froze. Beneath her fingers, Hawthorn tensed. *How does he know?*

A figure moved through the ferns, blood splattered against his tabard, sword drenched.

Father.

And behind him... Kieran, lying still and unmoving on the ground.

A trick, Juliana told herself. *Only a trick. Kieran isn't dead by his hand. He wouldn't. He couldn't.*

"Markham," Ladrien said, almost as if he were greeting an old friend. "Would you kindly tell our audience where Princess Serena is right now?"

Markham did not share Ladrien's smile. "Princess Serena never left Faerie," he reported. "I intercepted her caravan with your forces, as instructed. She's being held just outside the capital, ready to be taken back whenever you desire."

"No," said Juliana, certain she misheard, that this was all some terrible dream. "You're lying. You'd never... *why?*"

Because Juliana knew her father. And why she'd never had reason to doubt his loyalty to the crown, she knew more than anything else that he would have to have a good reason to break his vows. Something more than money or greed.

But he said nothing.

"For the same reason anyone does anything," Ladrien crooned. "Money, power... *love.*"

Markham walked towards him, still ignoring Juliana's gaze. "My payment," he said. "You promised."

No, Juliana thought desperately. *There's been some mistake.*

Ladrien had been about to kill her. Had he not even thought about that? Granted, he was likely still fighting Kieran, but to not make her protection part of any deal—

She remembered his words before she boarded the carriage.

Don't do anything foolish in order to keep him safe. Run the first chance you get.

He had not expected her to stay and fight. He had told her not to.

No, no, no.

Ladrien smiled. He stepped towards Markham, and whispered in his ear.

Markham's eyes widened. "No," he murmured, and for the first time, his eyes fell to Juliana. "No, no, you're wrong."

"Foolish mortal," Ladrien said, still grinning. "We can be many things, but not liars. I have told you naught but truth. That it is what it is, do not blame me."

Markham shook his head, still mumbling, all his composure lost. Juliana had never seen him this way, his actions painful, deranged.

"I can't... I won't..."

"Then don't," said Ladrien, turning away from him. "Makes no difference to me."

He swiped his hand, and a wall of thorns blazed between them.

Juliana looked down at Hawthorn. His eyes were closed, breathing even. Maytree was staring at the place where Markham stood, utterly disbelieving.

This wasn't happening.

Hawthorn wasn't sleeping. The curse hadn't taken effect. Princess Serena was still coming to save them. Her father hadn't betrayed them.

She looked down at Hawthorn. "Wake up," she whispered. "Please."

If he just woke up, if he spoke to her, if he said anything at all, maybe, just maybe, things would be all right. Somehow.

She didn't know what to do.

Her eyes fell to her sword, resting not far away.

"Oh no, I don't think so," Ladrien said.

"You promised not to hurt me," she whispered, dimly remembering Hawthorn's request.

Why, Hawthorn, why? Why did you come back?

"I did," he said, as his fingers reached for a pouch on his belt. "I said nothing about making you sleep."

Before Juliana could react, he blew a handful of gold dust in her face, fine as sand.

She slumped to Hawthorn's chest.

It's over, was her final thought. *Everything is lost.*

Part Two

The Curse Awakened

FOREST OF DREAMS AND WHISPERS

21. AT THE SUMMER COURT

ONE YEAR UNTIL THE CURSE AWAKENS

After realising he lost most of his coin at the tavern the night before, Hawthorn was in a foul mood when the party readied to resume the journey to the Summer Court. He hardly knew why. It was his own fault, and he'd thoroughly enjoyed himself until he'd been dragged away.

Even that part hadn't been awful. He quite liked it when Jules found him.

But for whatever reason, that thought didn't help abate his mood. Nothing did. It didn't help that the breakfast had been abysmal. It was far too hot, and the carriage was rocking relentlessly.

"Damn roads," he seethed. "Could they *be* any rougher?"

By the time they reached the palace, he was hot and headachy, his skin feeling bruised and sore. He pulled at his collar as though it were choking him.

Juliana stared at him. Not in the way she sometimes did when she didn't realise he could see her, like he was water on a hot day. She stared at him in a blank, unreadable way.

He hated it.

"What?" he barked.

"Nothing."

He'd visited the Summer Court before in his youth, although he could barely remember the young princess he was supposed to marry. The palace he knew to be beautiful, carved out of rock and pearl and seashell, open almost entirely to the elements, but nothing about the beauty reached him then.

He'd forgotten how hot it was there, like being trapped inside an oven.

He wasn't permitted to rest. He and his mother were expected to open the ball that was being thrown in their honour. A quick splash in a basin and a fresh change of clothes was all he was allowed, which was just as well, as his clothes were stained with sweat.

When he joined Juliana out in the corridor, the headache had turned into a fierce pounding. He was regretting drinking the night before. Regretting everything, actually.

He almost tripped on the stairs, recovering less than a second before Juliana's arm reached out to steady him. "Are you all right?" she asked.

"Fine," he muttered, pushing away from her.

He ignored the way the lights were stinging his eyes, ignored the fresh sweat gathering underneath his collar. Faeries rarely got sick, so he wasn't familiar with the sensation. What else was he to think it was, other than drink and a rough journey?

He took his seat beside his mother. Wine was offered, but he refused even that. The thought turned his stomach.

Juliana frowned, but said nothing.

A girl asked to dance. He refused. Food was placed in front of him, but the mere sight made his insides churn. He barked at the server, insulting the offering.

"Curb your temper," his mother hissed.

"How can I?" he spat, "when it's hot enough in here to melt a furnace?"

At this, even his mother frowned. He tried to open his mouth to snap at her, but his tongue felt thick and rubbery. The *air* felt thick, too, like he was wading through cotton.

He stared at the goblet in front of him. He was sure he hadn't drunk anything, and yet...

He felt like he'd been poisoned.

The room span, and he slid from his seat, not even feeling the weight of the fall, barely understanding anything that was happening around him.

He remembered looking up at his mother. He remembered that she shrank away from him, that her only son was falling, and that she let him.

Juliana hurtled towards him. Her duty, of course, nothing more. Screams and gasps echoed around the room as she examined his eyes, forced open his mouth, and sniffed his breath.

"Not poisoned," she announced.

"Well, of course not!" his mother shrieked furiously. "He hasn't touched or eaten anything!"

He watched Juliana's throat bob as her fingers went to his doublet. She peeled it back, along with the sweat-soaked shirt beneath, revealing a black, purplish rash spreading across his chest.

The crowd shrank back further.

Faerie fever. Like Juliana had warned him. Probably not fatal, definitely unpleasant. He groaned; this was not going to be fun.

"Get him to his chambers!" his mother hissed. "Quickly, before he infects the guests!"

Juliana and another mortal servant escorted him back to his chambers. The second disappeared almost as soon as they arrived, leaving Juliana to help him towards the bed.

"You'll be fine," Juliana insisted, as if she wasn't a massive liar and his head didn't feel like she'd thrown an axe at it. He felt like the blade was cleaving his body in two.

He pulled at his clothes. They felt like chains.

Juliana hovered nearby. "How long have you been feeling this way?"

He tugged uselessly at the shirt that seemed welded to his body. "Not sure. Most of the journey, I think."

Juliana tutted, helping him free himself of the clothes. "That'll teach you to visit seedy taverns…"

A hot shaft of pain sliced through him. "I think I'm going to retch."

Juliana handed him the first receptacle she could find—a chamberpot which was, thankfully, empty—and he promptly vomited the contents of his stomach into it. There was little to come up; he hadn't eaten most of the day. Nausea swirled about him nonetheless, incited by pain. He'd never been in so much that he needed to be sick before.

The room was spinning again. Juliana seized the pot from his grip and steered him back to the pillows. A healer arrived seconds later, asking him a series of questions he couldn't answer. Duration of illness, symptoms, level of discomfort.

It hurt too much to talk, and voices sounded more like noise. Juliana answered instead, a few potions were prescribed, and the healer swiftly left.

Hours passed. He tossed in his sheets like oil in a fire, unable to be still. The sheets turned to mush around him. Although there were a few mortal servants at the palace, even those seemed wary of him. A slim ghost of a girl was sent to cool him down, but she shrieked when he flailed beneath her touch and dropped the bucket.

Juliana groaned from the corner of the room. It was the first time he'd really understood that she was still there, and not outside his room or in the adjoining chambers. She seized the bucket from the floor, spat instructions about refilling it, and grabbed Hawthorn by the arms.

He winced at the touch.

"She's trying to help you," Juliana explained.

"Can't. Be. Still."

Jules rolled her eyes. The next thing he knew, a cold towel was pressed against his head.

"Is that... floor water?"

"It is water that has been on the floor which was scrubbed within an inch of its life less than a day ago. It won't kill you. Now, stay still. I need to get you cooled down or else I'll never get to sleep."

"You're sleeping... in here?" he panted.

"Queen's orders. She doesn't want you left alone in this state."

Had his mother visited? He wished he could believe there was some touching motherly concern behind those instructions, and perhaps there was the hint of some—his mother didn't want anything to happen to him, he knew.

But he also knew she wasn't here.

Most likely, she issued those orders out of a sense of duty. And Juliana was obeying them out of a sense of hers. Would anyone ever express any concern for him that wasn't out of some sense of obligation or greed?

"Dear gods, you're disgusting," Juliana remarked, sponging down his chest.

"Not quite... the ministering angel... are you?"

"No one hired me for my healing skills."

The maid returned with a new bucket and fresh sheets. Juliana changed them around him, bathed him with as much diligence as he could really expect of her, and did a half-hearted job of tucking him in again. His chest still felt like a hot iron was resting on top of it, but it was better.

"If you moan in the night, I'm smothering you in your sleep," Juliana said, making herself up a bed on the chaise in the corner.

"I'll do... my best."

For some strange reason, he tried. He tried to focus on how annoyed she'd be, and ignored the pain lancing through every limb, the sodden sheets, the crackling in his chest. He remembered biting his lip to keep it in until he could taste copper in his mouth.

At some point before dawn, he couldn't do it any more. He cried out. And again. And again.

Then Jules was there, hand against him, making it worse and better all at the same time.

"Spirits, Hawthorn, your mouth…"

"Sorry," he murmured, "tried…"

Juliana gave no notion of having understood him. Instead, she was busy wiping the blood from his lips, applying a cold compress to his forehead, force-feeding him the dregs of a potion the healer had brought up earlier. There were no soft words, just lots of remarks about how rubbish he looked and how he was being a baby and mortals got sick all the time.

He curled over into the bedsheets, wishing he could just sink away. In all his life, he had never felt anything like this, like he'd trade anything for relief. He couldn't even remember his poisoning being this bad—or perhaps he'd just been too out of it to remember.

A soft, calloused hand pressed against his back. "Hawthorn," Juliana said, "what can I do?"

He was as unused to the question as he was to hearing his name from her lips. She never spoke it, never sounded… like *that* around him. It was laced with something he couldn't name.

And he had no idea how to answer her question.

Faeries got sick so rarely, he had no experience of being so ill before, no notion of what might ease it, or what others said to help.

But mortals…

"What do mortals do when they're sick?" he asked.

For a moment, Juliana was silent. "Well, *this* mortal never gets sick. Whenever I feel ill, I stop being ill and be my wonderful self instead—"

"Jules," he said, half pleading, "please."

"I… I'm not great with illness," she admitted, as if she was confessing to some great crime. He supposed, for her, it was. Juliana hated being bad at anything.

"But you're here," he said.

"Only because your mother made me."

"Right."

A silence, punctuated only by his heavy breathing, passed between them.

"My mother used to sing to me," she whispered, and he stilled at the mention of her. He wasn't sure Juliana had mentioned her since that journey through Autumn, almost two years ago. "Entertained me, if I was a bit better. Stories. Songs. Shadows on the wall."

"Do I... get a song?"

"I'm no singer," she said, with the same grudging reluctance. "And I have no book to read to you, but..." She sighed, crossing the room, and went to fetch a candle from one of the nightstands. She brought it back to his side, lowered it to the floor, and turned his face roughly to the wall. Her fingers danced in front of the flames, and he watched as the shadows darted and flew across the stone, transformed into birds and dragons and wolves.

A simple trick. Hardly magic. Still beautiful to watch.

And he did watch. He watched until the wax had worn away to a stub, and he too slowly dribbled off into sleep.

He woke in the early hours of the morning feeling like his body had been thrown in a furnace. He wanted to scream, but there wasn't enough breath in his lungs to. So he writhed instead like an insect in fire.

Juliana's face appeared above him.

"Hawthorn, *Hawthorn*! What's wrong?"

But he couldn't answer. The words were turning to ash in his mouth.

Juliana placed a hand against his chest and drew it back as if scalded. "Stop this!" she cried. "Stop it, stop it, stop it!"

He didn't. He couldn't. Even her words seemed wrapped in smoke.

Suddenly, she was screaming for someone else. Doors were opening. Horrified faces appeared in the room, and a healer descended into his chambers. The air was filled with bluish light, and the seizing started to subside...

Replaced with a thin, crackling pain, starting at his feet and climbing up his legs.

He looked down. Ice was encasing his body.

With a strangled cry, he reached out to Juliana, still hovering by his side, and gripped her hand.

"You're all right," she muttered, her eyes lit by fear. "You're all right."

Liar.

"I'm sorry," she whispered, "I'm sorry, I'm sorry."

"Lady Juliana, remove your hand," the healer advised.

"I'm sorry," she kept muttering, as she pried her hand from his. "I'm sorry, I'm sorry."

He wasn't used to this, wasn't used to Jules being scared, or sounding panicked.

That worried him more than anything else.

"Hawthorn," she whispered, in that same awful, strangled voice, "you aren't alone."

But then the ice reached his neck, and blackness dragged him under.

22. UPON A DREAM

Juliana woke to screaming. It was a strange, eerie, distorted sound, like it was happening at the end of a long tunnel, bouncing off the walls, slow and quiet.

She opened her eyes.

She was lying in the middle of the great hall, a hundred guests from the night before slumped in their places. Vines twirled around them, still and quiet.

Nothing else was. Mortal servants screamed across the space, fleeing from the swarms of sluaghs shrieking above them. Some were armed with crude weapons—brooms and pitchforks—others with nothing but their fists.

Three descended on a quivering mortal maid trying to hide beneath the table. Juliana raced forward, drawing her sword—but her blade sliced through nothing.

The mortal screamed as a sluagh grabbed her elbow, but a frying pan swung into the back of her assailant, and another mortal tugged her free.

"This way!" said Dillon, covering her as she fled. "Get to the cellars!"

Juliana called out to him, but he didn't reply. His words lingered in the air afterwards, like a greasy smear.

What is this place?

Was she dead? Ladrien had promised not to harm her, but perhaps something else had. Or perhaps he'd merely kept her alive until sunset and slaughtered her afterwards.

Although it was still dawn here, and the palace didn't look like it had been under attack for long. More likely she was asleep somewhere. Little time had passed, and somehow her consciousness had been flung here.

But why? How?

"Come to torment me?" said a voice behind her, more solid than the others.

Juliana wheeled around, grabbing the speaker by the scruff of their clothes and slamming them against the wall.

Hawthorn.

His eyes widened in shock. "You... you can see me?"

She kept her grip on him, only half-convinced this wasn't a trick of some kind. "You're kind of hard to ignore."

She dropped her hands away from him, only to find them flung around his neck a second later when he launched himself forward and buried himself in her arms.

She let herself hold him and be held. Despite the distortion around them, he felt real, solid. His warmth crackled against her. Just for a minute, a fleeting second that wasn't really theirs, something in the world made sense.

"You're really here," he breathed against her neck.

"So are you."

He shook his head, drawing back. "Not quite."

His face was far too close to hers. The memory of the kiss burned through her, and she dropped away completely, balling her hands into fists as if she didn't trust the traitorous limbs to stay away from him.

"What do you mean?" she asked.

If Hawthorn was offended or confused as to why she'd suddenly dropped away from him, he didn't show it. "I'm still asleep in the tower... or at least my body is. Don't know what *this* is but no one can see me. Where are you?"

"The forest, I think," she said, and bit her thumb. Hard.

Hawthorn's eyes widened. "What are you doing?"

"Trying to see if this is a dream."

"Pinch yourself, you fool. There's no need to cause actual damage—"

"Need to know when I wake up how real this is."

Hawthorn pulled on a smile. "Do I frequently tumble through your dreams?"

"Nightmares, maybe." She glanced up at him, an awkwardness that hadn't existed for a long while brewing between them. "What are you doing here?"

He shrugged. "I could ask you the same thing. I found myself here almost immediately after the curse took effect. Saw Ladrien arrange me on the bed himself. Thought it was some part of the curse—some way to drive me into madness. No one here can see me, and I can't seem to touch anything." He reached out to rub the end of her braid, fingers lingering on the strands of brownish gold. "Apart from you, apparently."

His hand trailed from her hair to the pendant resting against her chest. It throbbed underneath his touch, a dark pulse.

"Interesting," he said under his breath. "Do you think... maybe..."

"You think they connect us?"

"The witch said that they would lead us back to each other..."

"They shouldn't work like this."

"Blood was involved in the bargain," Hawthorn remarked.

"And *dreams,*" said Juliana, with sudden realisation. She had no idea how magic worked, and sometimes even the wielders themselves seemed unprepared for the liveness of it—the way it bent the world to its will, a fickle and changing creature.

"Just checking..." Hawthorn said, playing with her braid again, "but you're definitely not dead, right?"

"You think I'd choose this place to haunt?"

Hawthorn chuckled. "Yes, actually. I think you're rather attached to it. But I also realise now that was a foolish question: death shall have no dominion over Juliana Ardencourt."

Juliana wished she had the same confidence in her immortality as he did.

And she wished he'd stop smiling at her like that.

Is this because of the kiss?

Juliana swallowed, and summoned her words. "Why didn't you run when you had the chance?"

Hawthorn paused, as if he wasn't entirely sure himself. "Well, my chances in the mortal realm were still pretty slim without you or my mother. Ladrien could still have followed me. It wasn't exactly a perfect plan of escape."

"Is that the only reason?"

"What would you like to hear, Jules? That I didn't particularly relish the thought of your death?"

Juliana bit the inside of her cheek. *I do want you to say that,* she realised. *And I don't. I really, really don't.*

Hawthorn raised an eyebrow. "Well?"

Juliana unclenched her jaw. The next question was harder. But she had to ask.

Lie to me, she prayed, even though she knew he couldn't and wasn't even sure of the answer she wanted in the first place.

"Why did you kiss me?" she asked.

Hawthorn tilted his head to one side, smirking. "Why did you kiss back? Quite enthusiastically, I might add."

"Answer the question."

"You first."

"You're a good kisser," she mumbled, looking down. "Not that your ego needed any more inflating."

Hawthorn moved his head, his expression unreadable. For a while, she suspected he wasn't planning to speak at all. "I was about to leave my entire world behind. You'll forgive me for clinging to the constants."

"So, that's it? Just so we're clear? A heat-of-the-moment thing?"

He raised a black brow. "What else would it be?"

Juliana nodded, deciding not to push it. Honestly, that was probably for the best. She'd be lying if she said she didn't find him attractive, but any more than that...

It was stupid to have asked in the first place. There were more pressing matters to attend to.

Her gaze turned instead to the rest of the room. Most of the fighting had moved outside now, although she could still hear the echoey screams reverberating through the stone. She wondered how long those would take to die down, how long this room would be silent for. She imagined it a hundred years from now, overgrown with weeds, the festering feast still laid out, cobwebs strung from the room instead of banners.

Maytree sat slumped in her throne of forest. Juliana imagined Ladrien had placed her there so she could see the ruin of her court when she woke... and so she could watch him take it from her.

At her feet, tastefully arranged on a bed of cushions alongside her maids, was Princess Serena.

"She arrived here not long before you," Hawthorn explained, following her gaze. "He really meant it when he said the fae wouldn't be harmed."

Juliana didn't doubt it, but she also doubted that her entire caravan had been captured without injury. Not with Markham at the helm.

Father.

Her gut stung with the memory.

"Are you all right?" Hawthorn asked.

Juliana shook her thoughts away, instead staring at Serena. *If your chosen fae bride offers a kiss to your sleeping form, you shall awaken immediately.*

"You have your thoughtful face on," Hawthorn remarked. "Possibly scheming face. No, thoughtful. Less malice."

"You say your body is here? In the tower?"

"It is."

"And Serena is here too."

"What of it?"

"What if someone carried her upstairs and, um, made the two of you kiss?"

Hawthorn blinked.

"Look, I know it sounds a little strange, but a tiny kiss in return for saving a kingdom? I think she'd be all right with that. That was the original plan, after all."

Hawthorn continued to stare. "But who would carry her up there?" he said. "No one can see me. Or you."

"Ladrien forced me under a sleeping spell too," she said. "But he only used a powder. That won't keep me asleep forever. If I get back here—"

Hawthorn chewed his lip. "There's a small army between the edge of Faerie and here," he said sceptically. "And you're maybe a week away—"

"You said yourself I'm practically immortal."

"Your sheer stubbornness does not translate to actual immortality, you do realise that?"

"Death hasn't caught me so far."

The stare increased in intensity. "Indeed, dear Jules, but I imagine he's trying damn hard."

"It'll be fine!" Juliana shrugged, patting his shoulder. "Don't worry your pretty little head."

Hawthorn paused, his pursed lips softening into a smirk. "You think my head's pretty?"

"It houses both the worst and best parts of you."

"I am both touched and insulted." He sighed, running a hand through his hair. "This is a terrible plan."

"Got a better one?"

His jaw tensed. "No."

Juliana knew it was risky, knew it was foolish. She'd be better off taking the money that was still hopefully on her person and making a go of it in the mortal world.

But she wouldn't. *Couldn't.*

Everything she cared about was here.

She just couldn't tell anyone that. "I will, of course, be expecting knighthood as previously promised. Maybe a permanent room in the palace. An estate on the banks of the sea."

Hawthorn stepped close to her. "If you survive this, and you free us, I will give you everything you ask for within my power."

Juliana buckled. A wild, dangerous vow. "I won't ask for that much."

The intensity in Hawthorn's eyes sharpened, sea-black, flame-blue. "Everything," he reiterated.

The declaration almost made her buckle under its weight, or maybe it was just that *stare* of his. "I need to wake up," she said, backing away. "How do you think I go about doing that?"

"You could shock yourself out of it, maybe," he suggested. "Or try falling asleep again?"

"After today, what could possibly shock me?"

"Juliana," he said softly, "I'm sorry about your father."

Whether it was the softness of his voice, his choice of words, or just the sudden, overwhelming realisation of *everything* hitting all at once, Juliana started to shake.

Hawthorn's eyes widened. "I didn't mean—"

He reached out a hand towards her, but it was like grasping at smoke. The feeling of falling surrounded her, of sinking, of drowning. Air was pulled from her lungs.

Hawthorn called her name, but she didn't hear it.

She tumbled backwards, through the air, through the floor—

Down,

                         down,

                                                  down.

23. INTO THE WOODS

Juliana shuddered awake in a bed of leaves, unbound, not far from the wreckage of the carriage. Ladrien's thorns had vanished, though the ground remained torn, the trees broken, bent and scarred.

Her own body ached, pulsing with bruises and shallow cuts. Nothing serious. Fine scratches littered her hands—

As well as a small, circular bruise on her thumb, a perfect match for her teeth. Not a dream. Real.

Hawthorn was back at the palace, and waiting for her.

What happened to him now that she was awake? Was he still roaming the corridors, or did he fade into sleep? He seemed to have been there for a little while before she appeared.

She *hoped* he wasn't awake. It seemed a lonely, shapeless existence.

Would she have another chance to speak to him? Perhaps the connection had only worked because Ladrien had thrown her forcefully into sleep. Maybe that was it, and they'd never speak again.

Until she reached the palace, and took Serena to his side to wake him with a kiss. Until she saved him, and the rest of Faerie too.

Iona, Aoife, Dillon, Miriam... all the people still there.

It wasn't like they couldn't handle themselves, but seeing as the plan was to quit Faerie if they couldn't survive there...

They would see Serena had been brought back, if they hadn't already. They would know the plan had failed.

They wouldn't know why.

Father.

Juliana stared around the ruined woods, but he was nowhere to be seen. He hadn't waited for her, hadn't checked to see if she was all right.

Her own father.

Why, Father, why? What did you betray a kingdom for?

She shook it away, not wanting to fall down that hole again. She couldn't give it weight.

She had a job to do.

Unless someone worked out how to end the curse before her. It was the sort of thing Aoife might be capable of.

If she had the chance.

Don't think about that, either.

Shaking, and suddenly cold, she pulled herself to her feet. It was still early morning. If she wanted to return to Acanthia as soon as possible, she needed to make the most of the day.

Never mind that she'd hardly slept. She could push through it. She had to.

She brushed the leaves off her clothes and returned to the ruined carriage. The remains of one of the horses was not far off, the others nowhere to be seen. Juliana hissed in annoyance; she'd have been able to cover lot more ground with one. Maytree had mentioned something about supplies, so she dug through the bags. There were some dried meats and fruits, flasks of wine and water, waxy cheeses, a bit of bread and crackers. Not enough to last more than a few days, and too much for her to easily carry.

She drank some of the wine, forced herself to eat a few mouthfuls of the bread and cheese, and sorted through the rest of her supplies. Weapons, clearly, were a must have—as many as she could comfortably carry. A change of clothes, alas, didn't count as a necessity. Rags and bandages, though? Those never went amiss. The healing supplies she found lacked any needle and thread, but there was some elixir—powerful Faerie healing magic mortals needed to be mindful about using.

Finally, she sat down and opened the pouch that Hawthorn had given her.

It wouldn't hurt to have a few coins to trade with in case she came across any merchants or travellers... even some creatures in the woods would be attracted to gold. But it was far too weighty to take the whole thing with her. Aside from the coins there were beautiful gems and bits of jewellery dripping with precious stones, including one gold, green and purple necklace that she couldn't help but think would really suit her.

At the bottom of the bag was a black, obsidian ring, carved with thorns.

Juliana paused. The blackthorn ring was one of Hawthorn's favourites. He wore it most days. Why had he given it to her? Or... maybe he'd had a copy made? She couldn't remember if he'd been wearing it in the carriage, or the dream...

Each option was baffling.

So was her decision to slide it onto her pendant.

I can ask him about it later, she told herself, and then quickly shook it away. *Or never. Yes, never is better.*

She was remiss to give up the gold she worked so hard for, but it would be foolish to take it with her. Instead, she buried it beneath a nearby tree and marked the trunk with a series of scratches that loosely looked like thorns. The damage would hopefully look unintentional to any passerby.

She drank a little more of the wine, discarded the bottle, and set off.

Despite Juliana's best intentions, after a couple of hours, she found herself lagging, burning with exhaustion and struggling to keep her eyes open. She rested beside a stream, initially hoping that the water would prove restorative enough, but still found she couldn't concentrate. She was using the sun to guide her, but it was hard to see through the trees and she was half-convinced she was going in circles.

If she could find a spot where Autumn seemed to be edging into Summer, or even Winter, she could try to follow that.

But not on so little rest.

Checking her surroundings, she found a quiet spot on the bank and curled up for a quick nap, hand on her hilt.

She slept, but she didn't dream. She couldn't quite go deep enough, too anxious that she might be set upon at any moment. Ladrien had promised an army.

It was likely they would march on the capital first, and they wouldn't come from this direction unless he'd been raising them in the mortal realm. Almost certainly he had some stronghold in Winter they'd been unable to discover.

And now it was coming for them.

At some point just after midday, she roused enough to continue on her journey. She couldn't remember the last time she'd been alone for so long. A few hours was lovely, but this had an endlessness to it—like she was trapped in some kind of void. The rustling of the trees, the whisper of wind and the faint tweeting of birds only served to highlight the piercing silence.

She missed sound, and voices.

One voice.

She bit the inside of her cheek. Less than a day by herself and she was already losing it.

She managed to catch herself a rabbit mid-afternoon and then had to search for somewhere to make camp for the night. She always hated this part of the day, being on the lookout for a decent spot, trying to gauge the safety of the shelter, the provision of water, the direction of the wind, the camouflage from predators—and guess whether or not she could find a better space before light gave out.

Finally exhausted and with little daylight left, Juliana found a spot not far from the river she'd been following that offered decent concealment, and made herself a fire. It took far longer than she would have liked.

Hawthorn could make flames with a click of his fingers, she thought, remembering their journey back through Autumn all that time ago. Considering how out of his element he was, he really hadn't been the worst travelling companion.

While her rabbit was cooking over the fire, she took out Hawthorn's notebook. The first page was a list of insults entirely familiar to her.

Have I told you how awful/rubbish/vile/hideous you look tonight?
You look as vile as ever
Mewling, ill-bred harpy
Gleeking, earth-vexing hedge-pig
Sour-faced vixen

On one page, he'd divided it into three columns, creating a sort of insult-generator. It was almost impressive.

And entirely aimed at her.

It made her smile. She'd always assumed his insults were a spur-of-the-moment thing. She quite enjoyed the effort he'd gone through to craft them. Perhaps she got to him just as much as he got to her.

It was difficult to read by the firelight alone, and her eyes were struggling to stay open as it was. She ate her rabbit in silence (thinking bitterly of herbs and thickly-buttered bread and honey cakes) and stamped out the remains of the fire. She'd be cold, but it wasn't worth alerting anyone or anything to her presence.

She wrapped herself in her cloak, closed her eyes, and prayed for sleep.

And maybe, just maybe, to see him again.

Despite how exhausted she was, sleep did not come easily. She trod the place between dreams for a long time, tossing in the leaves.

She missed her bed, her room. That sounded ridiculous and foolish given the situation—it was just a room after all. But aside from being comfortable, was it even hers anymore?

Say this works, she told herself, *say you get to the capital. Say you free him. What then? He won't need a guard after then. Fae marriages tend to happen quickly. It could happen immediately. Will you be allowed to go back to the room that was once yours? Will you want to?*

She'd endured listening to Hawthorn's countless exploits in the room next to hers over the years. Why was this different?

Because Serena will be his wife. Serena will stay.

Juliana would be the replaceable one.

You are his guard, she reminded herself. *Not a lover. Not a fool. You are meant to be replaceable.*

Sleep was almost upon her when she heard the first howl.

She was tired enough to ignore it at first. After all, one lone wolf was hardly much of a problem. The chance of a wolf attacking anyone they didn't deem a threat was incredibly low. She was safe where she was. No reason to panic.

The howling grew closer.

Juliana raised her head. There was something wrong with the howl. It was too low, too distorted, something more... monstrous.

It took her too long to recognise it.

Not a wolf. A *werewolf.*

Juliana was on her feet in an instant. Shoving her backpack in a cranny under the roots, she grabbed her sword and bolted in the direction of a nearby tree. Thankfully, the full moon offered just enough light to aid her in scrambling up the branches.

She froze, gathering her breath, waiting for the next howl.

This is fine, she assured herself. *Just stay quiet and stay up here. It won't find you. With any luck, it'll move on in a moment and it will be safe to get down.*

She didn't relish the thought of spending all night in a tree. In her haste, she'd left her cloak behind her, and although she was wide awake right now, she knew it would be hard to remain so for the entire night. Maybe she could take off her belt and tie herself to the branch...

The howls increased in volume, something else sliding underneath them.

The sound of panting, low, desperate cries.

The werewolf was chasing someone.

There was a part of Juliana that told her to leave it, that was almost too exhausted to care, that knew it was foolish to take on a werewolf in the dark, to risk her own life when the fate of a kingdom rested on her completing her journey—

But ignoring someone in distress wasn't very knightly.

A hard cry echoed through the forest.

A scream of pain.

Juliana sprung from the tree, sword drawn, and raced towards the noise. In the dim, milky light of the moon she could make out a hunched shape, lurching backwards through the undergrowth, leaving a shimmering trail of blood behind it.

Another larger, shaggier form towered over him.

It was a great, lumbering shape, taller than Juliana by at least a foot, with elongated arms, a pronounced snout and canines the length of her fingers. Its paws ended in sharp talons, and every inch of it was covered in thick grey fur.

Juliana swallowed. She had never fought a werewolf before.

"No," came the man's voice, shredded with fear, "please, don't—"

Juliana launched herself forward, diving into the space between them, sword outstretched. She sliced across the werewolf's chest, making it snarl and hiss.

"No," the man mumbled, "don't—"

"It's all right," Juliana insisted. "I'm here to help."

"Don't... don't hurt her..."

Juliana hesitated. Clearly, the man had lost too much blood. There was no way he was in his right mind, asking her to spare the creature that had just mauled him, not unless—

Unless...

She glanced backwards, catching a momentary glance at his face. "Owen?"

"Juliana?"

The werewolf swiped again, claws narrowly missing Juliana as she darted out of the way, kicking the werewolf in the back when it lunged for Owen.

Not it. *Her.*

Juliana had never seen Owen's wife, Saoirse, in her werewolf form. She was willing to bet she had now.

"Don't—" Owen pleaded again, when Juliana raised her sword towards her.

"I know, I know," Juliana rushed.

This was new territory for her. She was exceptional at killing things. Incapacitating things that wanted to kill *her*, though? That she was less skilled in. Her safest bet was to try and wound her, damaging her severely enough that she'd give up the chase, but not so bad that she'd be dead.

Not that that was easy to do, either. Werewolf healing aside, the creature could scamper off and detransform before anyone found her, dying of her wounds in the meantime. Juliana didn't trust herself to be able to find her in the dark, let alone treat her, without putting herself at more risk.

There was Owen to consider, too. The werewolf had taken a good bite out of his leg. He might bleed to death if she didn't treat him.

Think, think—

The werewolf circled around them, probing, lashing, eyes on the sword.

"Do you have any supplies to hand?" Juliana asked, keeping her back to Owen, blade outstretched.

"Umm, she tore through our food packs..."

"To *hand*," she clarified.

"Oh... um... I've got..." He patted himself down. "Dagger, matches, coins, rope..."

Juliana's ears pricked. "Rope?"

"Aye." He wrestled with something on his belt, pressing a spool of rope into her free hand. She ran it through her fingers, trying to guess the length whilst refusing to take her eyes off the werewolf. Her eyes darted towards the nearby trees, searching for one of the right height. One, maybe two, looked climbable.

But if she ran now, there was a good chance the wolf would decide not to follow, instead returning to finish Owen off, drawn by the scent of his blood.

Thinking quickly, she drew the tip of her blade to the back of her hand and slashed it.

Never your palm, her father had told her once. *Leave fingers and palms free. Elbow or back of the arm is best if you ever want to draw your own blood but not weaken yourself.*

The werewolf's nostrils flared as the blood dripped down Juliana's hand. She ignored the sword and bolted forward. Juliana sprang backwards, sheathing her sword to free her hand and tying the rope in a careful knot. She raced up one of the trees, dropped the rope over a branch, and held out the noose she'd crafted just in time for the wolf to ram her head through it.

Juliana dropped to the other side of the branch, pulling. *Hard.*

"Come on," she said to the wolf, as her back legs skittered along the forest floor. "There's a good girl."

The noose was designed to work against her opponent's weight—if she struggled, it would get tighter, if she relaxed, it would loosen. Juliana only wanted her unconscious, not dead.

Her limbs flailed. Owen moaned in the undergrowth, begging his wife to stop—or maybe begging Juliana.

Slowly, the wolf started to slacken. Juliana released the rope, letting her slide to the floor. She didn't know how long she'd be out, and she needed to bind her so she couldn't escape for the rest of the night, but for now, her attention needed to be on Owen.

She raced back to his side.

"Is she—" he started.

"She's fine," said Juliana, not looking at him. She grabbed his leg. It was a bloody, pulsing mess, at least what little of it she could see by this light. "I'll be right back."

She raced through the woods to where she'd left her pack, returning with the elixir in her grasp and smearing it straight onto Owen's leg. He let out a low moan, the flesh smoking as it knitted back together into something resembling skin. She dared not give him any more, instead binding it tightly and going back to the werewolf to tie her more securely while Owen gathered his composure.

Finally, she returned to his side, ditched the pack, and sank down into the mossy ground.

Minutes ticked by in silence.

"Thank you," said Owen eventually. "For saving me. And also not murdering Saoirse."

"What were the two of you even doing out here?"

"Trying to escape the curse," he said. "Nearly made it too, but got waylaid by some of Ladrien's forces..." He shook his head. "It's definitely happened, then? The curse?"

Juliana nodded.

"What are *you* doing out here? I thought you would have been by the prince's side when—"

"I was," Juliana interrupted. "It's—complicated."

"We've got all night."

"With all due respect, I'm on a mission, and can't afford to be divulging information."

Owen chuckled, eyes weary. "So like your father. Maybe a little of your mother."

The comparison to Markham twisted in Juliana's gut, but for once, no prickle of shame rose at her mother's mention. "You knew her?"

"She was a regular. I liked her. Funny. Or, well, she used to be."

Juliana's voice slipped further away. She had heard the stories, of course. How this once fearless, quick-witted knight turned quiet and withdrawn, *'like her soul was slipping away from her'* Alia had said. Something changed in her, chipping away little by little, until all that was left of her in Faerie was her body... and then that slipped away too.

"You look like her," Owen remarked, as if he thought it might help Juliana to remind her that she looked like someone strong who was broken by Faerie.

But not me, Juliana told herself. *I will not break. I won't even hurt.*

Remembering the minor injury on the back of her hand, she shifted upright, took out the vial of elixir, and used the tiniest smear of it, determined to save it for more significant injuries. She'd used enough on Owen as it was.

"I didn't mean to upset you," Owen added, reading her silence.

"You didn't."

Owen smiled. "Lies don't work as well on us mortal folk, you know. We are prepared for it." He gazed over at where the slumped form of his wife lay beneath the tree. "I take it you have a plan that involves reversing the curse? Saving your bonny prince?"

"Something like that." *And he's not* my *prince.*

"Hmm. Good plan."

"You? Still heading for the border?"

He shrugged. "I'll ask Saoirse what she thinks in the morning."

Juliana yawned, limbs and mind exhausted. "Owen?"

"Yes?"

"The mortal world… is it worth giving up this for?"

"I never stayed for the magic, child. I stayed for her. Wherever she is—that's home to me."

Juliana could feel consciousness slipping from her, but a tiny part of her remained, pinned by Owen's words. *Then where is mine?*

When her eyes opened again, she found herself back in the palace library. Several bookcases had toppled over. Books spilled across the marble like blood. The vines seemed to groan against the walls, sad and lifeless, and when she reached out to touch them, they shrank further away.

"What's wrong?" she asked them. "Tell me."

"They won't speak to me either," came Hawthorn's voice.

Juliana spun round and saw him perched on a pile of books, several open ones sprawled at his feet. He leapt nimbly off the pile and hopped towards her, holding out his hand in a similar fashion.

"I'm not sure if they can hear me, but they've been this way since yesterday. They were fine, at first—even tried to help defend the mortals—but when Ladrien turned up…" His fingers touched the closest of the vines, casting no shadow. "It's like they're sickening for something."

Juliana frowned. "Ladrien came?"

"He flitters in and out. No doubt he's preparing his army elsewhere to march on the mortal kingdoms. I imagine he'll take a few days at least, though. His assault on us, the magic he must have expended… he'll need time to recover. He's hardly in a hurry."

But we are, she knew. They did not have the luxury of time.

"The mortals—Iona, Aoife—"

"Safe, as far as I know. Miriam got them out of the palace, at least. There's a safehouse, somewhere. I haven't located it. Ladrien's forces have taken the gates. They wouldn't have done that if they weren't inside." He paused, jaw twitching, blue eyes dark. "It might be difficult for you to—"

"We'll cross that bridge when we come to it."

"Right. Of course."

A pause echoed between them.

"I wasn't sure I'd be seeing you again," he admitted. "I thought it might be a one-off."

"Me too."

"Disappointed?" He shot her a crooked smile.

It would have been easy to lie; she was so used to it. But she found herself not wanting to. It had been a long, trying day. "No."

His smile widened. "You say such kind things."

She turned her gaze away from him, examining the ruin of the room. Her gaze fell to the open books, and she realised why Hawthorn was here—he was reading them. "Have you worked out how to turn the pages?"

He shook his head. "No. I really do appear to be little more than a dream here."

"Must be dull."

"I cannot disagree." He raised a hand towards her cheek, examining a cut there she hadn't even noticed. "You didn't have this earlier. Trouble in the woods?"

"I handled it."

"I would not expect otherwise." He tilted his head. "Tell me."

With nothing else to do, she did, sitting down with him on the pile of books that didn't move an inch beneath their weight, talking like old friends as the moon waned.

We are old friends, she realised. *For some reason I cannot quite fathom.*

Hawthorn sighed as her story drew to a close. "So, they are gone then? Owen and Saoirse?"

"They will be, soon."

"I suppose I should be glad, but I will miss them. By far my favourite tavern."

"You are easily pleased."

"That is not necessarily true," he remarked. "Not with most things."

He paused, and Juliana was afraid for a moment that he would say something else, but a second later, a yawn broke her silence.

"Sorry," she mumbled. "Although it's strange that I can feel tired in a dream."

"Strange to feel anything at all," he agreed. "But we must be connected to our physical bodies. You're not really sleeping, if you're here. Your consciousness is too awake."

She nodded. "That makes sense. I don't think I want to be shocked out of this one, though. Maybe we should try your other suggestion—falling asleep here."

"We could go up to your room—"

"No!" she said, more harshly than she meant to. She didn't want to be back there and not really there, didn't want to risk seeing his body laid out on his bed. "I'll be fine here, I'm sure. I can't even feel anything, anyway."

"Except me," he remarked.

"Right."

"You can use my lap as a pillow if you—"

"I'm *fine*!"

Hawthorn sighed dramatically, falling back on the pile of books like he was stretching out at the beach. Juliana curled on her side, hugging the hilt of her sword like she'd been doing when she fell asleep, thanking whatever spirit of sleep allowed her to take this with her into the dream.

She closed her eyes.

"Did you ever have a stuffed toy to sleep with when you were a child?" Hawthorn asked. "Or was it always a blade?"

Juliana didn't want to tell him that she'd had a ragdoll she'd worn to pieces but still kept up until her father took her to the woods. He'd not approved of it, and Juliana herself was ashamed of the attachment; her mother had given it to her.

"I might have," she admitted. "Did you?"

"I had a toy horse called Mr Neigh-Neigh," he confessed. "Think I still have him somewhere, actually."

Juliana snorted. "I find that so hard to believe."

"And yet it is the truth." He sighed again, shaking his head. "I think I shall forever envy mortals their ability to lie and pick and choose what they want to believe."

"Really?" She half-opened an eye, unnerved to find him staring down at her, or perhaps glad. She wasn't sure. "I think I shall always envy the fact you can only speak the truth."

Hawthorn lay his head down next to her. She pretended not to notice. "You can speak the truth to me."

But I can't, she whispered inwardly. *Not to anyone, and certainly not to you.*

"Maybe someday I will," she told him instead.

She could feel his smile brimming in the space between them. "I daresay that's probably another lie," he said, in that velvety-smooth voice of his, "but I will take it."

"Goodnight."

The softness in his voice increased. "Sleep well, my knight. Stay safe on your travels. I would prefer you in one piece when you return to me."

FOREST OF DREAMS AND WHISPERS

24. THE SICKNESS AND THE CURE

ONE YEAR UNTIL THE CURSE AWAKENS

The morning after the first, dreadful night of faerie fever, Hawthorn woke hot and exhausted, mouth glued together, headache raging. He tried to sit up, but couldn't.

A hand reached out to steady him, larger and rougher than Juliana's but gentler, too. A vial was placed to his lips. Not caring at this point if it was a poison sent to finish him off, he guzzled the whole thing down.

"Steady on, now, there's a good lad," said a rough, gravelly voice. "You've had a rough night of it. Take it easy."

Hawthorn opened his eyes. A brown-haired, broad-shouldered mortal man was staring down at him. There was something in his face that reminded Hawthorn of another, prettier one, but it was nevertheless somewhat of a disappointment. "Ser Markham."

The knight smiled. "Good morning, Your Highness."

Hawthorn blinked blearily around the room. He couldn't quite see into the next one, but it seemed quiet. "Where's Jules?"

"My daughter, Juliana, is currently enjoying a well-deserved break. I am here to watch over you in the meantime."

Hawthorn could think of nothing to say to that, so he didn't.

"How are you feeling, Your Highness?"

He appreciated the question, although it was unusual to him. Faeries didn't like asking it. There was no room to lie. "Like a barrel of festering apples," he admitted, before trailing off into another coughing fit.

Markham raised a goblet of water to his lips, holding him as he drank.

"Your bedside manner is better than your daughter's."

"Yes, well, I was raised in the mortal realm. Juliana isn't used to illness. Don't judge her too harshly."

The knight looked at him like he expected Hawthorn to say something. He didn't know why. He barely had the energy to drink, let alone partake in conversation. The world seemed fuzzy and insubstantial.

"Pray, Your Highness, what do you think of my daughter?"

It was hardly fair of Markham to ask such a question when Hawthorn barely had the strength to string two sentences together, when he had no energy for tempering the truth in the way that faeries could.

"She is an excellent guard and you have every reason to be proud of her."

"These things I know already," Markham said stoically, "I am asking what you think of *her*."

"Markham, I have no energy for nonsense—"

"Then simply tell me the truth."

Hawthorn exhaled, chest hurting. "I have had worse knights, and do not detest her company as much as I protest."

At this, Markham barked a laugh. "It appears you have more in common with her than I thought."

"Jules? She hates me."

"Juliana can lie."

"I don't think she's lying about that."

"Do you not?" Markham regarded him carefully. "She was worried about you last night, you know."

"She's not here now," Hawthorn said, hating how he sounded like a petulant child. It wasn't that he *wanted* her here, exactly. She was, after all, terrible company.

But he imagined anyone would be awful right now, and at least time was *less* awful, with her around.

"It's not easy to watch the people you care for suffer," Markham remarked, his gaze misty and faraway.

Hawthorn sincerely doubted that Jules cared about him at all. She'd always acted like he was a terrible inconvenience, even when he was upright and capable of breathing properly.

But then... he thought he might have remembered something in her voice last night. Panic and fear.

He was likely misremembering.

Before he could think of a reply, Jules barged back into the room, damp hair around her back and shoulders. It went the colour of burnished gold when wet, a fact Hawthorn knew but wasn't fully aware of until right now. She wore a long night shirt, similarly damp, and it highlighted every muscle and curve of her.

"You look better, daughter," Markham remarked.

"Please," she groaned, blowing a loose hair from her face, "I look almost as rubbish as he does."

"Charming as ever, Jules," Hawthorn uttered, wishing he had the energy to roll his eyes. It was hardly a lie. She was never charming.

"I'm still exhausted," Juliana declared. "Are you all right to watch over His Royal Snottiness while I take a nap, Father?"

"Of course."

She flopped down on the chaise and pulled the blanket up to her head.

"You shouldn't sleep with wet hair," said Markham, at the same time Hawthorn opened his mouth to say something similar.

Jules scowled, lifting up her head and tugging her damp locks free to hang over the armrest in the direction of the fireplace, before lying her back down again. She was asleep within minutes.

"You don't need to stay," Hawthorn told Markham. "I do not require anything. I promise not to disturb her."

"If you're sure..."

"I am."

Markham left the room.

Hawthorn turned back to Juliana. He didn't often get the chance to watch her sleep. It was an oddly peaceful image, when her silence didn't herald an oncoming tongue-lashing or barely concealed contempt.

He found he missed her barbs nonetheless.

Strange.

Soon after, the effects of whatever potion Markham had given him took effect, and he fell back to sleep.

The next time he woke, Jules was beside the window closest to him, staring at him oddly.

"I didn't disturb you, did I?" he asked.

"No, I was just checking you were still alive. You've been oddly still for an hour."

"Sorry to disappoint."

He quickly started to cough again.

"And... there we go again. Oh joy."

"I assure you, I am taking no pleasure in this."

"I assure you, neither am I."

She handed him another draught the healer must have brought, and returned to hovering by the window.

"You look awful," she remarked.

"I *feel* awful, and oddly enough, you reminding me of that fact is not particularly comforting." He paused, wondering what *would* be comforting, and remembered pawing at her hand during the night, scared out of his wits. "Did I nearly die last night?"

Juliana hesitated. "No. Your fever spiked, and the healer encased you in ice to bring it down, but I don't think you were in danger of expiring at any point."

"I see."

"It... it was a bit scary for a moment," she whispered, almost imperceptibly, and her mouth hovered half-open, twitching with thoughts unsaid. "How are you feeling now?"

If he'd had the strength to buckle, he would have then. At most, he managed to blink. "Why are you asking?"

"I don't know," she said. "It all seems a bit pointless. I doubt there's anything I can do anyway, but my father informs me it's a thing mortals will say to express concern."

It was strange to hear her speak like mortals as if she wasn't one, but she'd never known what it was like to live truly amongst them. What must that be like, he wondered, to be neither fully mortal, nor one of the fae?

He decided he didn't like to think about it. "And are you?"

"What?"

"Concerned?"

She could lie, of course. That was the problem with Jules. She could say whatever she wanted, and would, and it was up to everyone else to work out if she was telling the truth.

"Yes," she said, her voice oddly soft. "I mean, I don't think you're about to expire, but yes, I'm a *little* concerned about you. I don't think I've heard you utter a mean word or an order in over twenty-four hours. Most unusual."

"I don't have the strength to," he said. "I can barely lift my own head, everything hurts, it feels like you've finally made good on your threat to throw an axe at my head and I've never felt quite so awful in all my life."

Juliana stared at him, and he waited for the barbs to come, the inevitable teasing.

Instead, she crossed the room, and sat down beside him. "Did it help to speak it?"

"Curiously, it did."

And then in an act that completely surprised him, she leant over, dipped one of the cloths in water, and started to dab at his forehead with curious gentleness.

"And this?" she asked. "Does this help?"

"It doesn't *not* help."

He felt the nausea returning, even though he knew there was nothing to bring up. His fever seemed to have spiked again. His skin felt as flushed as ever, and yet, for a moment, it all felt endurable.

As long as she didn't move away.

The fever didn't break for days. He couldn't tell, looking back, if it got any worse than that night where he had to be iced. He thought it might have done, for many of those days were lost to a burning darkness. He struggled to breathe, his skin felt like it was being flayed, nightmares plagued him awake or asleep. At one point, he imagined Jules was singing to him, but that definitely had to be a fever-addled delirium.

He remembered being utterly mortified when Jules offered to help him get onto a chamberpot, and him ordering her to fetch some male mortal servant to assist him instead. He'd never really been ashamed in front of her before. She'd seen him naked, seen him covered in vomit after a night of drinking, seen him at his absolute worst, and yet now, suddenly, he couldn't bear the indignity of letting her help him take a piss.

All the rest he was fine with. There was even a part, during his better, more lucid moments, when he quite enjoyed letting her bathe him. The healer seemed to have finally made him a concoction that felt like it did something, though it made his head feel woozy and his tongue slippery.

At one point, he remembered Jules leaning over him, hair unbound, and he tugged at the ends of it. He used to pull her braids when they were children, because he liked the colour, although he recalled how much she hated that.

He hoped he was gentler now.

"What are you doing?" she asked.

"Your hair is pretty," he remarked. "Like a flame, in the right light. I've always hated how much I liked it."

"You're delirious."

"Yes, I am. But I still both hate and like it. Much like I've always liked and hated you. You're very attractive, you know. It's most annoying."

"Oh *spirits*," she cursed. "I can't work out if you need more of the sleeping draught or less..."

"Maybe I just need more of *you*, fair Juliana—"

"More," she said swiftly, pressing something to his lips. "Definitely more."

Despite moments of reprieve, most of the time he felt too wretched to enjoy anything. Hours and days were lost to a haze of darkness, a damp fog, searing pain and a coughing made him feel like his lungs were trying to burst out his chest.

"Make it stop," he whispered at one point. "Please."

"I can't," Jules said, with an odd crackle to her voice.

"How do mortals deal with this?" he groaned.

Jules raised a compress to his skin. Everything still felt like fire, inescapable and smothering. "Most mortals don't get as sick as this," she said under her breath.

"What was that?" He'd been listening to her complain about his complaining for days. He hadn't even a suggestion that what he was experiencing was out of the ordinary, or worth his wretchedness.

"I just mean... well... um... *I've* never been this sick before, but I also don't have many mortal friends, or, um, any, so..."

"So..."

"You've got it bad, Hawthorn. You're allowed to feel rotten."

For some reason that he couldn't explain, that thought helped him. "So, what you're saying is... I can do something better than you?"

"No one is saying that."

"I am enduring something that you have never—"

"Right, you're clearly feeling better." She placed down the compress and moved to walk away.

Hawthorn reached out and grabbed her wrist. "I am not," he said, wishing he could lie, wishing that he had even just a fraction of strength not to utter what he was about to. "Or I won't, if you stop. I feel... when you're nearby—even though you have the foulest bedside manner—it... it helps. Stay. If... if you don't mind."

Jules blew a loose strand of hair from her face and rolled her eyes. "Well, since you asked so nicely..."

"You have to hand it to me. Practically on death's door and I'm still managing to charm you."

Jules rolled him roughly onto his side and resumed her dosing, practically soaking him. He couldn't recall why he'd wanted this.

"You are *not* at death's door," she insisted, "and you are *not* charming me."

"As you can lie, you really ought to be humouring me, sick as I am—"

"If you have the strength to joke, you have the strength to do this yourself."

"But *Jules,* you have to let me tease. Who knows how long I have left in this world?"

"I know if you don't stop this, I'll run you through myself."

He groaned into his pillow. "You really are the worst nurse."

"And you're a terrible patient." She put her hand against his forehead. "You're not radiating heat anymore, though. That's got to be good."

Her hand lingered, and his flushness returned in full force. For one ridiculous, delirious second, he felt he'd endure that awful first night all over again if she'd just keep her hand there.

Clearly this fever was affecting his brain.

There was a knock at the door, and in walked the castle herbalist, masked and gloved and smelling of enchantments. She conducted a few routine tests, tutted at the state of the sodden sheets with a harsh look at Jules (which irked Hawthorn a great deal, although he wasn't sure why, as she had clearly done a terrible job and deserved to be reprimanded) and applied a few remedies. She was a lot softer than Juliana, and yet he wished that she'd been the one assisting.

Or that she'd volunteered too.

You are just a job to her, he reminded himself. *A burden. Like you are to everyone. She can't wait to get out of here.*

And yet, aside from that first night, she never left. If she snuck out while he was sleeping, she was always there by the time he awoke. Surely, no one had ordered her to stay with him during his *entire* quarantine. His mother was a fair mistress; rest was mandatory.

Of all the things that helped, knowing he wasn't alone helped the most.

Knowing *Jules* was there helped the most.

He woke one afternoon from a nap to find Juliana in her usual spot by the window, curled up reading a book, a curious, unnatural look resting on her face. It took him a while to realise what it was.

"Are you smiling?" He frowned.

"No."

"Liar. You're smiling. At a *book.*"

"It's a darn sight nicer than your face."

"Rude." He lay back against the pillows. "Have you a pen and paper to hand? I wish to make a note of this occasion. The fourth time Juliana Ardencourt has ever smiled."

"I have smiled more often than four times."

"Not around me, you haven't."

"Strange, that." She turned the page in her book, still ignoring his gaze. "I don't often get the chance to read," she admitted. "It's quite fun."

"What's happening in the book?"

"Oh, nothing that would interest you, I'm sure."

"Why? Some sordid romance?"

Juliana remained silent.

"Is it?" he asked, his interest piqued.

"There may be... some romance in it."

"Read it to me."

"No!"

"Juliana, I demand you read me that book, right now, or else I shall—"

"Do what, talk me to death?"

Hawthorn turned to his bedside table, necked back every available potion and the remainder of a goblet of wine, and cleared his throat. "*What, here, in the carriage?*" he said, in as high a voice as he could manage. "Lady Viola cried. *'Oh no, Sir Bryant, we mustn't! If my father catches us, he'll have your head!' 'He can have my head,'* the gruff knight replied, *'but he cannot have my heart. Nor my—'*"

"Stop, stop!" Jules begged, although her face was creased with laughter. A deeply unusual look on her. Had he ever, *ever* heard Jules laugh before?

He kept speaking until his voice was hoarse, making her cackle, kept going even though his chest hurt to speak and he was coughing every other word.

"Stop," said Jules, "that's enough. I don't care how sick you are. I will throw this book at you."

"Cruel woman," he said, reaching for his goblet. It was empty. He stretched towards the jug, half tumbling out of bed, but Juliana reached out to steady him, holding him as his body raked through another coughing fit.

"You're over-exerting yourself," she told him. "That'll teach you to make me laugh."

"Worth it," he said, through his groaning.

Jules froze.

"What? What is it?"

"Nothing," she said, refilling his goblet and handing it to him. "Don't worry about it."

It was only after he drank he realised that he shouldn't have been able to say that, that pain should not have been worth her laughter.

And yet, for him, it had been.

And now she knew it.

He prayed she put it down to the effects of the fever, that he simply wasn't thinking clearly.

She took away his goblet and forced him back down, then returned to her seat beside the fire. "I will read," she told him, "but don't do that again."

"No such promises," he said.

Despite the lack of his word, she read. She read for hours, her cheeks prickling at certain parts, her eyes jumping over sections where things became a little more heated between Princess Lavinia and the lowly hunter, Reginald.

"You're skipping over the good parts," he remarked at one point.

"This book is too long."

"I'm not going anywhere."

"This book will, if you force me to read those parts."

"Is 'anywhere' my face?"

"Poor, sick, baby prince, the first time you were ever right about anything and only I was here to bear witness."

You are witness enough.

"You are mocking me again."

"Only because you enjoy it."

She was right, of course.

She carried on reading. He carried on listening. Slowly, he drifted into what felt like the most restful sleep he'd had in days.

He dreamed that Jules kissed him on the head and brushed back his hair, perhaps in a way mortals often did to each other. He hardly knew where he'd conjured such a fantasy from.

But conjured it, he had, and it was a dream that would come back to haunt him, night after night, with harder, deeper kisses, that burned through him in a way no fever had ever done.

25. THE LAMENT

Juliana woke on the mossy ground to the smell of meat frying. She looked up and discovered Owen nearby, bent over a campfire, a tall, broad-shouldered woman crouched on a nearby log in a shredded tunic. Her short silver hair was streaked with mud, her feet were bare, her neck red, but she was beaming from ear to ear as she sank her teeth into what looked like a piece of fried squirrel.

"Mornin'," she said, making eye contact with Juliana. "Thanks for your help last night. Want a bit of squirrel?"

Juliana would have preferred pheasant smothered in blackberries and butter, or a hot bread roll stuffed with fruit, or a creamy blue-veined cheese and a slice of honey-apple.

But she was famished, and not about to turn down the offer of a free meal.

"Please."

Saoirse speared a piece from her husband's pan using a nearby twig, and passed it over. Juliana tore into it so fast she barely even noticed the bitter, unsavoury taste.

"Steady on, girl. Don't choke," said Owen, chuckling. "That would be an appalling end to your tale."

Juliana imagined Alia committing it to poetry.

There once was a mortal named Jules
Who turned out to be a bit of a fool
Though she longed to be a knight
She'd didn't turn out all right—
She choked to death on a squirrel.

Alia's would doubtless be much better, if she ever got the chance to compose it.

Suddenly, Juliana didn't feel so hungry any more. She swallowed the last piece with some difficulty.

"There's more where that came from," Saoirse offered.

Juliana knew she'd need more to give her energy on the journey, although the thought soured her stomach. She thought of Aoife in the castle, her inky fingers stained with blood. She imagined Alia singing in a room full of bones, her empty song echoing through the halls.

Saoirse speared her a few more pieces. "Owen says you're on a mission."

"I can't explain what it is."

"Don't trust one of the Unseelie?"

"I don't trust *anyone*," she snapped. "No offence."

Owen chuckled, handing her a few roasted nuts wrapped up in a leaf. "You've seen our clientele. Takes a lot more than that to offend us."

Juliana couldn't think of much to say to that. "And you?" she said instead. "Still going to the mortal realm?"

Saoirse and Owen exchanged glances, shrugging. "If you've a plan, we might stick around here for a bit."

"It'll be dangerous—"

Saoirse raised a thick, silver brow. "I'm a *werewolf*."

"Fair point."

"Don't want any help on your mission, I take it?"

Juliana shook her head. "I—I can't. Sorry."

The two of them dropped it, not seeming remotely put out. They ate the rest of their humble meal in silence, Saoirse licking her fingers clean. Hard to imagine she was the monster that attacked her own husband last night.

"How's the leg?" Juliana asked Owen.

He stretched it out. It had been freshly bandaged, although the shredded trouser leg remained as testament to the damage. "Fairing pretty well, thanks to your elixir. Will probably leave a scar. Won't be the first she's given me." He glanced across at his wife and winked.

Saoirse giggled.

Juliana's desire to get back on the road quickly piqued. "Thank you for breakfast," she said, getting up.

The couple stared at her, exchanging glances. "You're leaving already?" Owen asked.

"Need to make the best use of daylight."

"It's not been light long. You can tarry longer—"

She shook her head. "Thank you for your hospitality. It was a fair exchange for my services last night. I bid you well on your travels."

She collected her things, double-checking her supplies. Everything was in order.

"Juliana—" Owen called out, as she shouldered her pack. "If your plan doesn't work out, we'll be here for the next few days. The mortal world—it isn't anything to fear."

But a cage is. And that was what it was to her—a vast, endless cage, that would keep her away from the closest thing to home she knew.

No matter how curious she was about what it was like, why her mother had chosen it, *she* never could.

Whatever direction her future led, it wasn't there.

She headed north instead.

Juliana walked for most of the morning, only stopping briefly to relieve herself, wash up in a stream, and attempt to clean the inside of her sheath with little success. She cringed at the idea of putting her blood-drenched blade inside it last night, but she'd not had much of a choice. Her father would not be pleased.

Not that she should care about his thoughts. Not anymore.

She shoved Briarsong back into the sheath, anger pulsing under her breath, and marched onwards.

The bronze of the forest gave way to brown and black, and she hit a portion of forest where the leaves vanished altogether, leaving little behind but thin, skeletal trees, so tall their tips vanished beneath a shroud of low-hanging sky.

As she walked, the sky dropped further, until the entire dark forest was swollen with fog.

"Not creepy at all..." said Juliana, as if hoping the sound of her voice would dissolve the prickling of her skin.

If Hawthorn was here, he'd make stupid comments about the clouds or muck about or regale her with silly tales until she was torn between the desire to laugh or hit him.

She'd forget how to be afraid.

You are not afraid, she reminded herself. *And you do not need anyone beside you. Least of all him.*

She tried to repeat a list of old insults for him, but they felt flatter than they did before. Hawthorn's stupid face kept rising out of the mist, alternating between smirking and glaring.

I hate you, Juliana hissed, at the same time as *I miss you.*

It felt like a very long time until nightfall.

She thumbed her pendant. It was ice cold. She had grown used to the warm weight of it against her chest, never really thinking of the magic attached to it, never understanding that it was warm because he was nearby.

It spread through her chest like frost.

Somewhere in the fog, something started to growl.

Juliana drew her sword. She could barely see, which she prayed meant her foe could see little of her. She watched her footsteps, careful not to tread on anything that might give away her position.

A black shape darted in the distance, lower than the werewolf, and larger.

This time, she stilled, waiting. But nothing moved. Not a rustle of wind, or flick of a feather.

The woods were silent once more.

She pressed forwards.

Gradually, the sound of trickling moved through the air, followed by a strange, low hum.

Almost human. Not quite.

Juliana knew better than to call out, to warn the speaker of the dangers in the dark. Besides, there was something unnatural about the noise, something blistery, almost painful—the north wind given voice.

She didn't know why she was drawn to it, but her footsteps seemed to be moving almost of their own accord.

The voice grew louder, into something high and wild.

Another shape darted in the distance, and another—

The voice continued.

Something silvery slithered out of the mist. A river, clear as moonlight. A hunched figure with long, snow-white hair sat beside it, black cloak rolled up at the elbows. Her hands were submerged in the stream, washing something.

She continued to sing in that soft, eerie voice, sharp and shapeless as the wind.

Curiosity got the better of Juliana. "Hello?" she called out quietly.

The woman's face snapped towards her. Despite the whiteness of her face and hair, her skin was unmarred by years. It was smooth as an egg, as ancient and new as the forest.

But she was not human. Juliana realised what she was the second her eyes met hers. They were blood-red, her cheeks stained with tears.

A banshee.

Which meant the clothes she was washing...

Juliana forced her eyes away. Banshees were benign, a creature classed neither as seelie or unseelie, but they could see death in a person's future, and washed the clothes of the dying in the stream, as if trying to scrub out fate.

Anyone Juliana loved, or even her own self... the banshee's vision would show her.

Don't look, don't look—

Something darted amongst the trees.

The banshee was not the only thing in the forest.

"Stop singing," Juliana whispered. "Please."

The banshee shook her head, and held up one of the items of clothes she was washing—a copy of her own cloak.

The shadow in the distance crept forwards. It was a fearful mix of bear, wolf and hedgehog, with broad shoulders, a thin body, and a back and tail covered with quills. Claws like knives padded across the ground, its monstrous, twisted jaws drooling.

A barghest. A goblin dog.

The banshee rose to meet it.

"Don't—" Juliana whispered.

The banshee turned to Juliana and half smiled. It was not a nice smile—neither was it cruel. It was more like Juliana was the one about to meet her fate, and the banshee the one powerless to stop her.

The barghest lunged, sinking its teeth into the banshee's shoulder. She let out the tiniest of cries, more like surprise than shock.

Juliana stumbled backwards, something rushing past her shoulder.

The barghest wasn't alone.

Claws sliced through the air. She scrambled backwards, tumbling into the undergrowth, pulling up her sword just in time to meet the fangs and slashing across the roof of its mouth. It reared, hissing, blood littering the ground beneath. Juliana stumbled upright, regaining her balance, searching for higher ground, a better angle.

Another set of claws flashed from behind.

A third barghest.

She ducked out of range, sprinting downstream, hoping to find something, a tree maybe, to climb up. If she just had a few seconds to ready her bow...

Jaws snapped behind her.

The trees were too narrow, too tall, to support her weight. Shelter was limited, the fog impassable. She lost her footing, sliding down the bank, hitting the stream with a splash.

Righting herself, she squeezed against the sides of the bank as one barghest sailed overhead, thrusting her blade upwards into its soft underbelly. The weight of the beast wrenched the sword from her hand as it fell, the second creature dropping into the space between them before she could snatch it free.

She drew her dagger. The remaining barghest swiped.

The dagger didn't have the reach that Briarsong did. She drew her second.

You are not the only one with claws...

But the barghest had three on each paw and a mouth full of fangs, and moved easily through the water while Juliana stumbled, slipping on the rocks.

Backwards she went, pushing upstream, eyes still rooted on the monster, all too aware that there was another not far behind her, still munching on the banshee. She could hear the distant crunching of bone.

Her fingers grazed the water behind her, curling around something thick and heavy.

The banshee's cloak.

She wrapped it around her fist and flung it in the barghest's face, catching one of its paws and blinding it just long enough for her to get a clean shot at its chest and drive in her dagger, hilt deep.

The creature flailed and struggled as she twisted the blade, jumping free before the claws could strike again, scrambling up the bank.

Something was twisted about her ankles. Without thinking, she leaned over to remove it—

A knight's tabard, the gold thorns and white thread stained with banshee's blood.

Juliana dropped it, not searching the size, the shape. It could belong to anyone.

One of the knights was going to die.

"It's all right," she told herself. Knights were built for battle. They were defending the capital as she spoke, ready to lay down their lives, it wasn't like—

Something brushed against the bank. A fine silken shirt. More clothes drifted down the stream, rough browns, muted greens—

They could belong to anyone. Anyone at all—

But too many for one person. Far too many.

Forgetting the other barghest and leaving the remains of the banshee behind, Juliana fled downstream to retrieve Briarsong, and bolted into the fog.

It was almost dark by the time Juliana stopped again, hunger replacing fear and desperation, exhaustion padding every footfall. She might have forgotten to stop entirely, merely walking until she fell, if she hadn't wandered into a tiny hamlet.

It was a mewling cat that jolted her back into existence. Juliana had forgotten that such sounds existed in the woods, that something as normal as a cat could be found.

It mewled again, demanding to be stroked, and then, seeing that Juliana came without food, quickly slunk away to the lap of a fae woman sleeping propped-up on a bench nearby.

Juliana swallowed at the image, wondering what would happen if she failed, and if this woman would awake in a hundred years to find a pile of dust and bones in her lap in place of her beloved pet.

"Sorry, little kitty," she said, stroking its ear. "You'll have to find your own food for a while."

It occurred to her that although the fae had fallen under the curse, their animals seem to have been spared, at least the more mortal ones. It had been two days—what about Cercis? Would someone have freed her, or would she get so hungry soon she'd break out of her stall?

If the sluaghs hadn't got to her first.

That thought in her head, she hurried to the hamlet's stable. There were three fae horses there, fast asleep, all bright green manes and golden hooves.

The only creature awake was a small brown pony that barely reached her waist. Too small to ride.

Juliana freed it, refilling the trough and giving it a good pat. She didn't much fancy its chances in a wood filled with barghests, but it was better than staying here. With any luck, it would stick around for a few days, eating the food Juliana had left, and would still be here after Juliana broke the curse.

Because she had to break the curse. *She had to.*

Brushing off her clothes and trying not to think of the ones swirling in the stream, she stepped inside the first of the houses. She ought to be savouring the closest thing she'd had to luxury in a few days, but she couldn't. The incident with the banshee still chilled her.

Aoife has a green shirt like that. The knight's tabard—was it broad enough for Miriam? Dillon was wearing a brown doublet at the feast... did any of them look like a doublet?

She circled through other friends, ones she hadn't spoken to that last night, old school friends that didn't live in the palace, the countless servants who did.

Her thoughts clung to her the way she used to cling to Iona's aprons, before she learned not to show her fear.

That did not make its claws any less sharp.

She forced herself to eat the last of the perishable goods she could find, hung up her still-damp clothes, and made herself a bed by the hearth. With the door locked, she trusted herself to build a fire for tonight. She needed it if she was to get warm and dry again.

Even when the cold felt like an infection, like warmth had been stolen from her reality.

She cleaned her blades, packed everything away and fell exhausted into her make-shift bed. She tried not to fixate on the clothes, or the delicate lace on the shirt bubbling in her memory... like the one Hawthorn had once torn to bind her wounds with.

Not him, she prayed, to whatever forces might be listening. *Please. Anyone but him.*

She woke in the palace gardens, robed in moonlight.

"Well, well," came Hawthorn's voice, "the wandering knight returns."

Not thinking, hardly breathing, Juliana spun around and launched herself into his arms. All his quips and smiles faded. After a moment of shock, his arms circled around her, clutching onto her securely.

"What happened?" he whispered into her hair.

"I had a run in with a banshee."

He stiffened. "What did you see?"

"I don't want to talk about it."

"All right," he said, voice soft. His hands brushed her back. She tried not to think about the fact she was wearing nothing but a shift. He'd seen her in far less over the years. "You're cold."

"I fell into a river. I set up a fire. I won't be cold for long."

His hold on her only tightened. "This can be just for warmth, if you want," he said. "It doesn't have to be anything else."

And if I want it to be? What if she wanted to crawl out of her clothes and peel him out of his and save him from the banshee's prophecy by marking his flesh with hers? The thought sank in its teeth, convincing her that all she had to do to save him was bury him under her skin.

You can't do that, a voice reminded her. *It doesn't work that way. He isn't worth what you would lose in the process. Don't let him in any further.*

She pulled away from him, carefully, slowly. "Distract me," she begged. "Talk, recite poetry, sing—whatever. Only banish the silence."

Hawthorn paused, and then that old familiar smirk spread across his cheeks. "Hmm, I can't seem to think of any poetry right now. I'll happily reel off a list of insults for you, though?"

It was silly and forced and exactly what she needed. Laughter and their usual barbs, nothing serious.

A list of insults.

The notebook.

"I started reading your notebook."

Hawthorn tensed, almost imperceptibly. "I see."

"What's the meaning of it?"

"Insults," he admitted. "I got into the habit of collecting ones for you."

"What? Why?"

"To practise them."

"Practise?"

"Because I struggled to find ones that were true." He paused, as if waiting for Juliana to comment, bracing himself for the strike that didn't come. "Have you read all of it?"

"No, not yet."

"You may wish to ignore the later entries. Or maybe just burn them."

"That juicy? Can't wait."

Hawthorn did not smile.

"I'm sorry," she said. "I remember you said not to read it if we still had to face each other, but I wasn't sure if this was going to happen again and I..."

"You don't have to explain yourself," he said, tilting his head, "although I *am* curious."

"I may have been at a loss for company the other night, was all."

His eyes gleamed. "You *missed* me."

"I didn't say that."

"You didn't have to."

She elbowed him in the stomach, he pretended she'd been too rough, and they sat down together on the ground, Juliana tucking her feet underneath her. She waited for Hawthorn to make a joke about her attire, but he didn't. "Still cold?" was all he said.

Juliana nodded, and Hawthorn unbuckled his doublet and draped it over her shoulders, still warm from his body. For some reason, it made her skin prickle more, the pendant heating between her breasts.

How is it I can still feel you? she wondered. *Why is your warmth different?*

Hawthorn caught her gaze, almost as if he could read her thoughts, and she waited for another barb that didn't come. Instead, he spoke to her of nothing—tales of their childhood, shared teachers they'd disliked, books they'd been made to read, old friends and enemies and what they hoped they'd been doing when the curse took effect.

"I hope Raife finally spoke to that merrow he was mooning over."

"I hope Lucinda was halfway through eating something and wakes up with rotten food in her mouth."

Hawthorn snorted. "I enjoy hating things together. We should do so more often."

Something about his words, or perhaps the setting, reminded her of an evening she'd spent with her father years ago, before they'd left for Autumn. She had asked for tales of her mother, and he'd given her the usual—brave knight, excellent swordswoman, beautiful voice—but she had begged him for *more.* Earlier in the day, she'd watched a couple curled up together beside the bank, whispering to each other. She had not been sure of the words, only that something about the image seemed to trickle inside her, like imbibing a hot drink.

"What did you like doing with her?" she'd asked her father.

Markham had paused, as if the answer was a hard one to collect. Perhaps it was; he so seldom spoke about her Juliana sometimes wondered if she were half a dream, a creature summoned only when thought of.

"Everything," he said finally. "Or rather... nothing. I liked doing nothing with her but being."

Juliana frowned, her fingers stroking her ragdoll, its felt hands turned threadbare. "I don't understand."

"You will, one day."

Juliana hadn't believed him, but now, sitting here in the dark, she felt something familiar to that sensation she'd experienced watching that couple on the bank, the warm, whispery, hot-drink feeling.

And for once she was too tired to fight it.

"What are you thinking of?" Hawthorn asked, glancing down at her.

She realised she was resting on the ground. "My mother," she answered, unwilling to admit the full truth.

Hawthorn folded an arm beneath his head and sank to the floor beside her. "Do you really not remember her?"

Juliana paused. She liked to pretend she didn't remember her. Partly for her father's sake, partly for her own, and partly because she could never be sure how much of what she remembered was real and what parts she'd conjured based on wishes or the recollections of others.

"I remember her," she admitted, her voice quiet, like the truth might shatter the world. She had never told anyone before. "In tiny things and bits and pieces I've stitched together. I don't know how much of it is real though, how much I've made up, how much other people have told me."

Hawthorn's free hand reached across, then stopped. "I wish I could remember her for you." He paused. "What *do* you remember?"

"Her songs," she admitted. "The colour of her hair in the firelight. The way she smelled of elderflower and citrus and baking hay... sometimes all at once." She stopped, her throat tight. "Mostly, I remember that I loved her, that she made everything better, and I have never, ever understood why she left."

The day before, she'd sliced the back of her hand with a blade. This was worse, more visceral, more exposed, and to *Hawthorn* of all people, who was far more frightening than any element.

"Why she left *you*, you mean?" he asked.

She could only nod.

Hawthorn's gaze circled back to the sky, as though he were aware of the intensity of it, how it made her buckle. "Do you not like to sing because that's what she did?"

Juliana stiffened. How did he see right through her? "Yes. Also, because I'm not perfect at it, and I don't like performing anything to anyone unless I'm perfect at it."

"This," he said, "I already knew. But... well, your voice is... not unpleasant, and... and as for that other thing... much as I may have complained about your presence once or twice, why anyone would leave you is... somewhat baffling. To say the least. To me, that is. And possibly a few other people you haven't managed to irk yet."

It was, oddly enough, the perfect thing to say, which made it all the more strange how he'd stumbled through it. Juliana could count the number of times Hawthorn had slurred his sentences on a single hand, outside of alcohol consumption. He was usually far more eloquent and far less serious.

Tease me, she begged him, *be cruel, be horrible. Make me regret telling you.*

Because she needed to regret it. She needed to be reminded that he was detestable, that she hated him. Because the alternative—

She froze.

The alternative wasn't natural.

Her gaze turned to Hawthorn's pendant, resting on the ground, the leather cord around his neck. Her own buzzed pleasantly.

There may be side effects, the witch's words rang in her head. *Other ways you find yourself bound.*

26. THE GIRL BY THE SEA

ONE YEAR UNTIL THE CURSE AWAKENS

Hawthorn's fever broke a few days later, replaced by equally violent shivering. He was lucid enough to be aware of how awful he looked, to see the swollen rash over his body and the pale clamminess of his body. He dreaded seeing his reflection in the mirror.

He wondered what Juliana thought of his disgusting appearance.

Jules ordered the fires made up, and he was piled high with blankets. They barely seemed to reach him.

"How much longer must this go on for?" he hissed through gritted teeth.

Juliana lurked by the window, open a tiny crack. "You're telling me."

"Would it kill you to say something nice for once?"

"Would it kill you to quit complaining?"

He sunk further under the covers.

At lunch time, a servant brought him some broth and a diluted wine. As usual, he didn't manage to get much down. Juliana conversed with the healer when she came to check on him, too quiet for him to hear. Afterwards, she came to sit on the bed.

"You need to eat more," she said. "Healer says you should be on the mend by now. You're as gross and weak as a newborn kitten."

He turned over in his blankets. "Can't."

Juliana ground her teeth. He could practically hear her contemplating. Eventually, a hand pressed against his shoulder. "I told you I'm no good at this," she said. "I don't know what to say to make it better or easier, so if you could go back to being your usual self and making unreasonable demands, that would be best."

He disliked this soft side of Jules almost as much as he hated how wretched he was feeling, and yet a part of him clung to the warmth in her tone.

"Warmth," he murmured.

"Come again?"

"I can't... I can't get warm... I want..."

"Right," said Juliana, audibly chewing her lip.

A moment later, the sheets rustled, and she pulled herself under the covers. The sudden warmth was liquifying. He felt worse and better than ever.

"Sharing body heat," Juliana explained. "Like we did before."

"Uh-huh..."

"If you tell *anyone* about this—"

"Murder. Unspeakable acts. Entrails for sausages. I understand."

"As long as we're clear."

He started to cough, hard, lung-crunching coughs. He thought Juliana might be glaring at him, but she seized him roughly and propped him into a sitting position, slapping him on the back as if trying to dislodge his spine from his skin.

"Lie down on your side," she commanded, "here."

She slid an arm around him and pulled him back against the pillows, cocooning herself around him in an action he was almost certain she had *not* learnt during her training. The warmth was helping, though, as was the position.

"I'm so glad you're finally wearing a night-shirt again..." she said.

"Am I that disgusting?"

"Vile."

And yet, he thought he might have detected a squeeze. It was possible he was mistaken. His heart was thumping very loudly and everything felt a little like it was under pressure.

This was the nice kind, though.

"Will you tell me a story?" he asked. "I don't want... quiet."

"I'm not a great storyteller."

"I find it likely you're a better storyteller than a nurse."

"I will leave this bed."

"There's many a woman who would be delighted to find themselves in my bed…"

"Only the ones who don't know you."

Hawthorn stiffened.

"I'm sorry," she said, still not moving from her spot. "That was… that was too harsh."

"I don't think I've ever heard you say sorry before."

Apart from that night the fever spiked, and I'm not sure I understand why.

"That's because I've never had to. But that… that was too far. And for all my barbs, I don't find you *completely* detestable."

"You're so charming, Jules."

She hesitated. "How can you say that?"

"What?"

"Isn't that a lie?"

"I—"

"Oh my, you actually *do* find me charming!"

"You… get out of my bed."

"As you wish…"

"No," he said, grabbing her arm before she could slip away, "stay. Please."

And then, with a raw softness he feared he'd never be used to, "all right."

Hawthorn had shared his bed with women before—even the occasional man—but not one had stayed the night. He'd never had anyone put their arms around him, never crawled into the warmth they emitted, never dreaded crawling out of it.

He really must be sick.

He wrapped his arms around Jules' middle and rested his head against her chest, his heart hammering like a demented creature.

Don't go, he wanted to whisper. *Don't go, don't go, don't go.*

Of course, by morning, she'd slunk off, and didn't say one word to him about it.

He didn't mention anything, either.

Little by little, his strength returned. The days and hours came back to him, not lost to fever or drug-induced sleep. He couldn't believe how badly the fever had knocked him, how his limbs had turned numb and wobbly. The first day he tried to stand unassisted, he almost fell flat on his face.

Jules pitched him back towards the bed.

"This is embarrassing," he mumbled.

He wasn't sure what response he was expecting, but the one she gave surprised him. "I don't think you *should* be embarrassed," she said, "given how sick you've been. Of course it's going to take a while for you to build your strength up again. But I think I'd be embarrassed too. I'm not exactly great at relying on other people."

It was a small admission, but for Jules she might as well have been stripping naked. He let her help him get dressed.

Numerous times she'd assisted him in dressing or undressing when he was too drunk or hungover to do it himself. He'd never cared before, but now he found himself conscious of her brushing his skin, how scrawny he'd become during his illness.

"Are you all right?" she asked. "Your face looks red."

"Well, I have been very ill..."

"Sure," she said, buttoning up his shirt. "I'm going to see why breakfast is taking so long."

Finally, Hawthorn was considered well enough to leave his rooms. He was assigned another guard and Jules was granted a much-deserved break. She disappeared for two days. He couldn't remember the last time he hadn't seen her in so long. Even on her days off she was usually still... around.

He didn't like it.

Princess Serena, his possible future bride, had been removed from the palace the minute he'd fallen ill. Her mothers were very precious about her like that. He had the dimmest recollection of seeing her the first night, but he couldn't recall. In any case, there was nothing to do whilst she was absent still.

He still didn't have the strength for revels and formal events, so he retired to his chambers outside of meal times, and sat in the spot Juliana had occupied by the window. It afforded an excellent view of the sea.

The sea.

She'd spoken about it before, how much she longed to visit it. Yet never once in the past two weeks had she ever complained about only being able to see it.

Where else would she have gone?

Certain he knew how to find her—and in an innocent fashion that would not look like he'd been seeking her out—he gave his guard the slip and hurried down to the beach. Fine golden sands stretched towards an azure sea, glistening below a sequined sunset. The tide was low, the waves silken soft, hushed as whispers.

No one was around.

No one except Juliana.

She emerged from the sea like a goddess of stories, as beautiful and fierce as any monster of the deep, her hair a dark flame beneath the dusky sun. Water clung to her slip, illuminating every sharp curve of her. He'd always liked mortal bodies, rounder and less reed-slim than the average faerie woman.

He enjoyed the curves vastly more on Jules.

It wasn't that he hadn't noticed before, he'd have to have been blind not to, but there was something about this moment that threw it into stark relief, highlighting every wonderful, awful, distracting inch of her.

He'd heard it said that mortals were frequently struck dumb by the splendour of Faerie, but now he found he was the one rendered speechless by the beautiful mortal creature before him.

"What?" said Jules, stopping in front of him.

It took a painful few seconds for him to find his voice. "The sea suits you," he managed.

Jules groaned, dropping to the sand where she'd left her clothes, towelling herself dry. "My first day off in two weeks, and you spoil it with your presence."

"I gave you two days..."

"Are they over already?"

Her barbs prickled in a way they hadn't before, and he wasn't sure what to make of that. "How was the sea? Everything you hoped for?"

Jules could only smile, in a way she didn't very often. He wanted to put his finger against the slight dimple in her cheek, or between the slight lines on her forehead she had from frowning so often, but he did neither, tugging off his shirt instead.

"What are you doing?" asked Juliana.

"Going for a swim. Need to build this muscle back up after all."

"Hmm..." said Juliana, not looking at him.

He stripped to his underwear and barrelled into the water in a fashion most inelegant, kicking up water beneath his feet. It was a warm day, and the water felt cool against his skin. He glanced back to see if Jules was watching, but discovered she'd managed to slip past him and was already leagues ahead, dividing the water in swift, easy strokes.

He followed her, splashing, disturbing her calm movements until she splashed him back, and they found themselves giggling like the schoolchildren they never quite were.

Further and further they went, until the rocks eased and vanished beneath the sea.

Jules stopped abruptly.

"What?" he said. "What is it?"

"I'm not sure how much further I can go," she admitted.

"Come again?"

She stared at the horizon. "The border to Faerie. Is it invisible? I can't remember..."

Suddenly, he realised what she meant, what she was afraid of. "It looks like a mist, if I recall," he said.

"And it doesn't move?"

He shook his head.

Jules relaxed, her shoulders slackening. "Of all the entrances and exits to Faerie, this would be the worst one to be stranded in."

He could only imagine. If she passed through the veil, a wall of fog would spring behind her, impossible to pass. It would spit her outside of Faerie and never let her return. If she was stranded here, an entire sea between her and the mortal lands...

He shuddered at the thought.

I wouldn't let you be stranded. He was sure, if he had a choice in it, that he absolutely would follow through with that promise.

He just wasn't quite sure why.

She's a fine guard, he came up with, even though he doubted he'd be able to offer that as the real reason if someone asked.

"Prince Hawthorn!" a voice called from the beach.

Hawthorn shuddered. His relief guard.

Juliana scowled. He couldn't believe it had taken her this long to notice he'd come unaccompanied.

"I was with you!" he said, holding up his hands before she could say anything. "What was the worst that could happen?"

"Right now? Drowning. Drowning is the worst thing that could happen, and I'm thinking of giving the sea a helping hand."

"YOUR HIGHNESS!" shrieked the guard.

Hawthorn groaned. "I'm coming…"

He started back towards the shore.

"Hurry up!" the guard uttered. "Princess Serena has just arrived. Your mother demands an audience."

27. RIVERS AND GRINDYLOWS

The weather when Juliana rose had turned sharp and cold, a mist like ice settled across the forest outside. She wondered where exactly she was, if she'd strayed too close to winter or if this was just a side-effect of the curse, the absence of Maytree's emotions.

Or even perhaps Hawthorn's tumultuous ones. The vines might not be listening to him, but maybe the land was. He was all smiles whenever they spoke, but he wouldn't be smiling now.

The thought iced her more than the weather.

There was no way to tell either way, but she pilfered some gloves and a piece of fur from her unwitting hosts to guard against the cold, leaving a coin in return. She ate a meagre breakfast, stroked the cat, enjoyed what was left of the little warmth she'd likely experience for the next few days, and resumed her journey on high alert.

The incident yesterday with the banshee and the barghests had unsettled her, still scratching beneath her skin. When she'd finally fallen back asleep, the clothes kept bubbling up again, stained with blood, sometimes with people inside them.

They aren't dead yet, she reminded herself. *You can still save them. You can still save everyone.*

She couldn't remember much about banshees from her school books, if the predictions were absolute or avoidable, and, in any case, she didn't *know* who the clothes belonged to. Could have been anyone.

The worst thing about walking, especially through decent terrain, was that there was nothing to distract herself with. Her mind could not choose but to wander. It was so hard to stay focused that several times she took a slightly harder path just to give her something to concentrate on.

It was almost a relief, when, not long after midday, she reached a river.

She hovered at the edge and looked both up and down, searching for a crossing or a shallower spot. The river wasn't too deep, or too treacherous. She could wade across, but it would mean getting wet or undressing, neither great options on a cold day like today. It was more than just discomfort; she could be risking her life if the chill set into her bones. Even just getting a cold would hamper her ability to journey and defend herself.

She walked a little further downstream, finding a spot dotted with stepping stones, where the gap was short enough for her to throw most of her equipment to the other side; she didn't want to risk losing her balance or damaging any of her supplies if she did fall in.

She kept her sword on, though. Habit. If anything, it helped her balance better.

She leapt onto the first stone, a wide, flat thing, barely slippery at all.

The second was harder, her boots hitting water. She almost lost her footing there.

One more stone, just one more and then the bank.

Her pack seemed to wink at her from the other side, urging her on.

Not far now.

She hit the third stone, one heel treading air. Something gurgled at her ankles.

Juliana paused just a second too long, staring into the river.

Something green moved through the water, slippery and scaled as a fish. For a brief, hopeful second, Juliana convinced herself that's all it was. Just a large fish. Nothing more—

A long, wiry arm reached out and fastened itself to her ankle, another sloppy body launching onto the rock and sinking its teeth into her boot. The weight threw her off. She slammed against the water, claws grabbing at her flesh.

Grindylows.

One on its own wouldn't be a problem. They were small, spindly things, but two of them, in the water where they had the advantage—

And there were bound to be more. Grindylows hunted in packs.

She kicked one, the other latching onto her sheath, pulling her down. She tried to claw her way to the surface, snatching fistfuls of air before water shot into her mouth again. Weighted blackness dragged her down, teeth pierced her skin—

She couldn't get free.

Acting on instinct, she unbuckled her belt, the weight falling away from her. The grindylows dived after it, giving her time to scramble towards the bank and haul herself upwards, coughing and hacking on the cold, sodden ground.

She only realised what she'd lost when she had a second to breathe.

Briarsong. They had Briarsong.

She scurried back to the water's edge, hoping they'd give up when they realised their prize wasn't made of flesh, but the two snatched and clawed at the blade, fighting over it like a couple of feral dogs. One slashed the other across the face and chomped down on the sheath, sliding away downstream.

No, no, not Briarsong!

Juliana flung on her quiver and grabbed her bow before she could even think. She still had a dagger strapped to her thigh, but reason should have told her that arrows and single short blade would be of little use against a pack of grindylows.

Don't let it turn into a pack, warned another voice.

She nocked an arrow and aimed it at the twisting shape, but it hit the water beside it. She fired another, and another, each one smacking rock or water. This was pointless, a waste of her arrows. She chased the grindylow downriver, the other not far behind it, watching Briarsong flash in the silvery stream.

The cold had started to settle, but she refused to give weight to it, ignoring the voice in her ear that sounded suspiciously like Hawthorn that told her it was just a sword—

Not *just* a sword. Her sword.

She wasn't leaving it.

The two grindylows arched and dived through the water, and Juliana followed. She would not be stopped, not be swayed. The earthy bank started to dwindle, replaced instead by rock. The stream cut through the remains of a mountain, a stony mound cleaved in two.

The grindylows slowed. Ahead of them was a dam stretching between the two sides of the craggy mountain. Juliana, nearly out of bank, slowed too.

The grindylow shoved Briarsong into the dam. Several other floppy bodies crawled out to inspect it.

Not a dam—a nest.

Juliana scanned her surroundings, counting, anticipating, planning. She could possibly use her equipment to start a fire, although whether it would take in such damp conditions seemed unlikely. She'd also have to climb onto a fiery mound to take Briarsong back.

Not the best plan.

What else could she do? The grindylows were easier targets in the dam, but she didn't have enough arrows to realistically take all of them out. She only had her daggers now, none of which had the reach she'd need to fight so many. And she'd been fighting them on their grounds, where they had the upper hand. It wouldn't take much to topple her, bring her into the freezing waters, and hold her till she drowned.

Just leave it! said the voice again that sounded like Hawthorn's. *You can get another sword!*

But it wouldn't be this one.

Her eyes drew to the rocky ledge over the stream. Several large boulders toed the edge, none wobbling...

At least, not yet.

Fighting against the cold that was now progressing to numbness, Juliana clambered up to the top of rocks, peering over the ledge, testing the weight of the rocks. At least two were immovable, but a couple of them, with the right leverage...

She grumbled inwardly. Her sword would actually be perfect here. As it was, she had to scuttle back down and find a branch that looked about right, testing its weight and praying it wouldn't snap under the pressure.

It nearly did. Irritated, she turned to one of the smaller rocks, prying it loose, muscles straining.

This is good, she told herself. *I can't freeze while I keep moving.*

The first boulder toppled over the ledge, taking out a portion of the nest and squishing at least one grindylow. Three dived away, hissing and spitting.

Juliana heaved a second rock over the edge. This one struck down the middle, catching another two. The branches of the dam heaved against the strain.

Sensing another boulder might collapse the thing entirely, Juliana sprung down the cliff face and raced onto the dam, boots squelching and slipping against the wet branches. Remaining grindylows snapped at her heels, but she paid them no heed until her fingers clasped the hilt of her beloved blade.

She drew it out. It gleamed in greeting.

A grindylow shot towards her, but Juliana sliced it straight through, blood spraying. One bit at her calf, but a quick stab and a kick later, it fell to the stream.

That didn't stop the others. They crawled out of the dam like enormous ants, hissing and spitting, claws sinking into her calves, her thighs, her hands—

Her balance threatened to desert her. Her legs sank beneath the woven branches. Water hammered against the construction.

Juliana refused to fall. She kicked and slashed, stabbing and swinging, hacking off spindly arms, fins, clawed paws, slicing through scaled bodies till the river ran with blood and all fell still and quiet.

The dam sagged again. Juliana grabbed her belt and sheath, leapt off it, and waded towards the bank.

Her skin was littered with scratches and punctures, but she was alive.

And she had Briarsong.

She cleaned the blade in the water, resisting the urge to hug it, and slid it back into its sheath.

The urge to fall back against the bank and curl up was overwhelming, but she knew that meant the need to get up was pressing. She'd progressed beyond cold, beyond discomfort. Forcing herself to walk quickly, she traipsed to her pack, shouldered it, and walked back to the rocks where she found a shallow alcove that almost passed as a cave. It would do.

She made herself up a fire, stripped herself of her clothes, and hung them up as well as she could. Next thing to deal with was her wounds. Most of them were superficial and not worth wasting the elixir, so she used it sparingly, only on the wounds deeper than scratches likely to hinder her movement.

She glanced up at the sky, and then back at her dripping clothes, and sighed. There was still plenty of daylight left, but she'd be foolish to force herself back into damp clothing and continue onwards. She'd help no one by sickening for something and dying in the cold. A terrible end to her story.

Juliana had no choice but to wait out the rest of the day here, turning her clothes, slowly folding back into them whenever they were dry.

It was a dull, boring way to pass the time. She was almost glad when sleep came.

Juliana woke in the cave, nearly toppling over when she discovered that she was sitting next to another version of herself.

I'm still dreaming, she realised. *I must be.*

Indeed, she couldn't feel anything—but her mind seemed alert and awake.

Why wasn't she at the palace?

"Nice of you to finally join me," sneered a voice from outside.

Juliana turned. Hawthorn sat besides the remains of her campfire, arms folded, glaring in the shadows. "What are you—" she started.

"A *sword*, Juliana?" he hissed, leaping to his feet until he was towering over her. "You risked your life for a *sword?*"

"Wait—what are you doing here?"

"Don't change the subject!"

"Oh, I'm changing the subject!" Juliana said, rising to her feet and whipping out the smallest of her blades. "How are you here? Have you been watching me the entire day?"

Hawthorn stared down the end of her dagger, his anger going nowhere. "I grew bored at the palace," he said flatly. "I wondered, if the pendant could draw you to me, it could work in reverse. Apparently it does."

Juliana flushed. She'd undressed. She'd sat by the fire naked for hours—

"Were. You. Here. The. Entire. Time?"

"Most of the afternoon," he admitted. "I turned away when you undressed."

"You spied on me!"

"Do you have any idea what it's like to just sit there and have no idea what…"

"*What?*" she prompted. "Go on. Finish your sentence."

"To have no idea what's happening to you," he finished, as if the truth were an arrow being yanked from his flesh. "It's maddening, the waiting. Hoping to see you again. Worried I won't." He shook his head. "You act like your death is a thing you don't fear. But *I* do. If you die, and I'm trapped there, I will go out of my mind, Juliana." He took a deep breath, barreling onwards before she could formulate a reply. "So, I repeat, you risked your life *for a sword?*"

Juliana dropped her blade, dissecting his words. *He only said the waiting is maddening,* she reasoned. *Which of course it is. And of course he'd want to see me again when he's been alone all day. Of course he fears my death. He needs me alive.*

Or maybe... he did like her. Maybe the pendant was messing with him, too.

"It's really useful to have a sword in these parts—" she said.

"You and I both know that you are far from unarmed and are just as deadly with a dagger."

"It doesn't have the reach—"

"Juliana," he sighed, exasperated, "you know how you can usually tell when I'm dodging the truth? I can tell with you, too. Most of the time, anyway. What is it about this sword?"

"I..." She threw up her hands. "It was the first proof I had that I belonged, all right? That I was just as much a part of your court as any faerie... as any knight."

Hawthorn blinked, as if he never couple have imagined a more ludicrous answer. "It meant that much to you?"

"Yes." She pursed her lips. "Why did you request the thorns on it?"

"Because you're prickly?" he suggested. "Or... or because I knew you'd like them. Because you *deserved* them."

Juliana wasn't quite sure she knew what to say in response to that. "I hate it when you're thoughtful," she settled on.

"I hate it when you risk your life for weaponry, but there we go." He paused. "It always seems odd to me, the idea that you don't think you belong in Acanthia. Sometimes I've thought you belonged there far more than me. If I ever made you feel otherwise—"

"It wasn't you," she said quickly, and then hesitated. "It wasn't *just* you. It's everything. It's our short lives and limited power and the way we have to train twice as hard to be half as good."

"You made it look easy," Hawthorn continued, voice steady. "Everything you've ever done, you make it look easy."

She didn't know what to say to that. Because it wasn't. Nothing in her life had ever been easy, and for years, she'd assumed that his life *was,* that he was a fool for squandering it, but somewhere in the past three years she'd come to understand that his life was just another kind of difficult.

"Do you really think you don't belong?" she asked instead.

He shrugged, as if it mattered little. "Sometimes. I've been somewhat of a disappointment since I was born and I gave up rather young trying to be something else. Too much hard work. Easier not to try."

"Must be hard though, if you still care."

The brush of a smile passed his lips. "Must be."

It was as close as she would get to an admission. "How does it feel?" she asked a moment later. "The curse actually coming to pass?"

"Terrifying and almost liberating," he surrendered. "I've less to fear now. Apart from, you know, the obvious."

"Me failing?"

"You *dying*, you silly fool." He shook his head, waves of silken hair brushing across his brow. His eyes fell to the sword in Juliana's grip. "Do you really hate me being thoughtful?"

"It... confuses me. Especially back then. Buying me the sword was the first nice thing I'd ever seen you do for anyone." She sighed, loosing a long breath and leaning back against the rock. "I prefer hating you, you know. It's easier to hate you."

"I prefer hating you, too," he admitted. "But I haven't, you know. Not for a long time."

I think I hate you more now than I have ever done, but for entirely different reasons.

She wanted to ask him how long, but did she really want the answer? If he told her it was only a few weeks, or a few months, she'd know it was because of the pendants. And if he said longer...

If he said longer...

No, she told herself, shoving it aside. *There are different kinds of like. And you do like each other, at least a little. As much as you're allowed to.*

And no more. No more.

Hawthorn stared at her as if waiting for a question, one that she couldn't ask.

"I don't care how bored you are," she said, thumping him on the arm, "you can't follow me. It's disconcerting."

Something flickered in Hawthorn's eyes, disappointment, maybe, or something else. "All right," he said slowly.

She'd been expecting a fight, an argument, some light whining. "You can check in on me at midday," she told him. "For an hour. No more." She could be mindful of her actions for an hour or so, at least she hoped. "And after dark. You can come after dark." She hated that time anyway, alone while the night grew around her, isolating her in the blackness. Even if she couldn't see him until she fell asleep, knowing he was there might be a comfort.

"All right," he said, eyes now lit. "And... when you're sleeping? Can I stay when you're sleeping?"

Juliana's throat felt tight. "Yes," she said. "You can stay when I'm sleeping."

28. THE WAY TO WINTER

Juliana fell asleep beside him, but woke on her own in the cold, translucent air, shuddering at the stiff breeze that had fastened around her in the night. She hugged her cloak tightly around her, ate a little breakfast, and rubbed her hands by the remains of the fire.

"Are you still here?" she whispered, receiving nothing in reply. "You can stay for breakfast too, if you like. But please don't follow me on the journey."

A shaft of wind blew through the cave. No way of knowing if it was him, but she chose to believe it was.

She set off.

She regretted telling him he couldn't follow less than an hour later, when the loneliness set in. She'd been annoyed at the invasion of privacy, but truth be told, even voiceless company would be better than none. Plus, there were so many threats and insults she could hurl his way, and he'd be powerless to defend himself.

Although, the lack of reaction would make it all rather boring. She enjoyed sparring with him—there was no victory otherwise.

She touched her pendant, but it was ice cold.

Everything was ice cold, come to think of it. Frost was thickening on the ground, her breath eeked out in icy spurts, and icicles had started to form on the trees.

Damn.

Unless it was the work of frost spirits, it seemed likely she'd lost her bearings and was halfway to Winter.

Never mind. If she followed this path, it should eventually lead her back to the Autumn Gate.

The one Hawthorn said was heavily guarded.

They hadn't yet come up with a plan for getting her through. All three gates were taken, according to him.

There's a way around everything, her father had told her once. *If you stay alive long enough to figure it out.*

Juliana paused. *A way around.*

Because there was one way into Acanthia that wouldn't be guarded. The way through Winter.

Juliana sat down for a moment to consider the geography, drawing a crude map on the floor. It was true the terrain was rough, but so was taking on an entire army by herself. What was the safest route?

Sure, many people never returned from the depths of Winter, but she wasn't going to the *deep*. She'd tread the border the entire way. Maybe Hawthorn could chart a path for her while she slept...

Actually, he'd love that. Something to do that was useful, that he could boast about later, lording over her head that she couldn't have done it without him.

She thought about making camp, trying to sleep, talking it over with him. But there was still a lot of daylight left and she wasn't tired enough to sleep whilst battling the brittle cold. She didn't want to waste hours.

She'd risk it. Snow could hardly be worse than what she'd faced already, after all.

She set off into the cold. The trees began to thin, bushes of holly springing up in their place, the leaves as black and shiny as patent leather. Frost turned to snow, soft and powdery at first, then hard as iron. The chill gnawed at her chest.

She should have taken more from the hamlet than the fur and gloves, but there was nothing for it now.

Stopping to rest briefly beneath the flimsy shelter of a tree, she stared back at the white, endless plain behind her, undisrupted aside from her tracks, each footprint a giant hole.

She frowned, staring down at them. Some of the footprints further down the mountain seemed bigger than the ones closer to her, and, unless her eyes were deceiving her, seemed to split around a cluster of rocks, like someone or something had purposefully used it to disguise their ascent.

She was being followed.

She drew her sword, sliding down the slope, maintaining the higher ground. "Reveal yourself," she commanded.

When nothing happened, she dug into the snow and hurled a fistful in the direction of the rocks, hurling projectile after projectile as if she hoped to bury them if they didn't come out.

"Hold!" barked a voice. "I yield."

Juliana recognised the voice before the figure slunk into view, his white cloak and uniform now muddied and grey, the gold thorns sucked of colour.

Father.

Juliana's grip on Briarsong tightened. "What are you doing here?"

"I could ask you the same thing," he returned. "Winter is not a safe place for anyone. Come back to Autumn."

"As if you care!" she hissed. *As if I have any intention of listening to you ever again.*

Markham's face hardened. "Never make the mistake of thinking I don't care for you, Julie," he said.

"You're hardly one to talk of mistakes."

Markham stared at his boots, and did not reply.

"Why?" she asked finally. "Why did you do it?"

"For the same reason I've done everything in life," he said. "For *us*. To keep you safe, to bring your mother back to us—"

Juliana chilled. "What do you mean?"

He shook his head, sighing. "It doesn't matter now. What Ladrien promised... it was not the answer I sought. Not a price I could pay."

"A price *you* could pay?" Juliana screeched, stepping forward, blade extended. She jabbed it at her father's throat. "People are *dead*! People are dying! I might never... *You* aren't paying the price! Everyone else is. You may have destroyed Faerie, damned the entire mortal world, and for what?"

Markham stared down the end of her blade. "For love," he said, with a sincerity that buckled against her, scraping at her bones. "Always, everything, for love."

Juliana wasn't sure if she wanted to scream at him or stab him. This was his fault, all his fault. If not for him, Serena would be back in the castle by now, or almost there. Juliana wouldn't be alone on the frozen mountain, trying to take on the world, to fix this, knowing no prize in the end would be worth it. She'd have everything she ever thought she wanted and nothing, nothing at all.

Because of him, *everything* because of him.

In the end, she let out a frustrated howl, and plunged her sword into the snow beside him.

The wind burned around them, snow cutting her skin like a thousand tiny daggers. She stared at her polished blade and debated thrusting it into his ribcage. It was no less than he deserved.

Maybe she'd be able to forgive him if he was dead.

"How long?" she asked him finally. "How long have you been in league with Ladrien? The whole time, or—"

"A few years," he admitted.

"Is that why you took me to Autumn?" It was a question that had burnt against her chest for years. "The truth, this time."

"It was why I returned," he said. "I couldn't do his bidding outside the court. It was where I met him. Out here... searching."

"For a way to find Mother?"

"Something like that."

"Then, taking me from the palace—"

"You were growing too soft there. Too complacent. I knew there was a good chance Ladrien would win even without any help. If you were to survive, I needed to teach you how to rely on no one but yourself."

The cold around her was a poor reflection of the ice inside. Because he had done that. And for years—so, so many years—she'd been so proud of herself for being all that he'd made her. Strong, self-sufficient, independent to a fault.

She was a polished shield he'd wielded, a lump of hard, cold iron.

And for the first time, she hated him for it.

"And you?" she asked.

"What of me?"

"Did you honestly care for none of them? Were you not growing *complacent* there too?"

To this, Markham had no response, and only silence whispered between the two of them.

"It wasn't just me you were trying to toughen, then." She paused, gathering another onslaught of thoughts. "Making me Hawthorn's guard. That was all part of your bargain with Ladrien, wasn't it?"

"Ladrien had heard of the attempts on the prince's life. He needed him alive. I couldn't watch the boy myself, not with my commitments to him, but you... you were the next best thing. I knew I could trust you to guard him."

"Did you never once think what that would do to me—"

"Of course I did!" Markham snapped. "You don't think I wondered if I'd gone too far, every time I saw you together? But you promised me you hated him, that it was all just duty—"

"You're a fool!" she screamed. *And so am I, in so many ways.*

Markham sighed. "Would it make a difference if I was sorry?"

Maybe. Yes. No. This is still all your fault, and I am what I am because of what you have made me.

Did she even like this version of herself, cold and tempered? Would she like the other version of herself better?

No way of knowing. She had to live with the person she'd become—or grow into a better version of it.

"Come away with me," Markham suggested, when she said nothing. "We can go to the mortal world, far away from all this. We can be a family, Juliana. That path isn't lost to us."

Juliana shook her head. She wasn't sure that path had ever been open to her. "I am what you made me," she whispered, though the wind stole half her words. "I break or bend for no one, and certainly not you."

Markham bowed his head, and turned to leave.

"I hate you," she hissed to the back of his head.

Markham paused. "But you don't, do you?" he said. "And that, I bet, hurts worst of all."

29. A Fighting Dance

ONE YEAR UNTIL THE CURSE AWAKENS

The summer court was ruled over by two ladies, Yasha and Lahoime. Yasha was tall and muscular, as lithe and strong as a panther. Her dark skin was unblemished, her hair orange, and her arms adorned with black runic markings.

Her wife was small and round, with tawny skin, golden eyes, and blue hair like the sea. She was as pretty and curved as a pearl.

The couple had a daughter, Serena, one of the few royal children not educated at court. From what Hawthorn could tell, some form of magic had been used to conceive her, and even though he suspected a man might have been involved at some point, she carried characteristics of both her female parents.

She was as speckled as a fawn, doe-eyed, petite, with hair like the sunset over water. He knew the girl must be at least fifteen, but her big eyes and tiny stature gave her the impression of a child.

She looked far too young to be contemplating marriage, and far too young to have the fate of a kingdom resting on her shoulders.

"Prince Hawthorn," she said, dipping into a bow, blue skirts swishing beneath her, "I am glad to see you've recovered. I was worried about you."

He paused, surprised at the concern, examining the words for another meaning. "I was worried *for* you" was a more Faerie turn-of-phrase. Worried *for* gave more leeway.

"I appreciate your concern. I hope you were not too troubled to be removed from your home whilst I was quarantined."

"Oh no," she shook her head. "Not at all. My other lodgings were delightful. And my mothers worry too much."

"On the contrary," said Yasha, with a cool glare, "we worry precisely the right amount."

Hawthorn glanced at his own mother. He'd barely spoken to her since his recovery. Her glance was cool too, but with frosty indifference.

He returned to Serena. She seemed nice. He wasn't used to that.

She joined him at the table, and they tried to remember when they had met before, not to much avail. They spoke of the weather and courtly politics, predictions of what might occur if Yasha drank any more wine, and who would win in a fight between her and Miriam.

It was not an unpleasant conversation.

"I do declare, this is the best company we've had since Maytree's post-coronation visit," Yasha announced loudly, a bold claim indeed given that Maytree's reign spanned over six centuries. "What say you, wife?"

Lahoime paused, stirring the wine in her goblet with a lazy twist of a finger. "I don't know, there was that summer that mortal playwright visited and we spent weeks watching those bizarre comedies with all the mistaken identities and innuendos and girls pretending to be boys. What was his name again? Wigglesword? Wobblyblade?"

Yasha laughed. "He was very amusing, I'll give you that. But I've never been as fond of poetry as you, my darling."

They started to kiss at the table, and Hawthorn turned his gaze away, searching for Juliana. Although she wasn't on duty, she wasn't present at the table, even though the company would have welcomed her. Summer prided itself on its hospitality and Maytree had always treated Juliana as if she were the adored daughter of a fine noble.

"Are you looking for someone?" Serena asked.

"My guard," he said. "It is very unlike her to miss a meal."

"Is she the beautiful mortal girl with a gaze like stone and a face like fire?"

"Ah! You do know her! But if you could find a way of making that more insulting, I'd be obliged."

Serena blinked. "More insulting?"

"We have a tendency to insult one another," he said. "It's difficult to explain. Largely done in jest. I think. Hard to tell with mortals. Damned liars."

Serena giggled. "It sounds like you're friends."

He turned to face her, but he was distracted by the arrival of a woman in a long sea-foam dress, cut at the centre for movement and created from layers of soft, floating fabric. The bodice was embellished with gold, the sheer sleeves parting at the elbow. It was a faerie dress so perfect, so ethereal, it seemed impossible that it shouldn't belong to some creature of air or water, a nymph of sea or sky.

Instead, it belonged to Jules.

Jules, who was all earth and fire, Jules who he rarely saw out of her uniform or covered in mud.

Jules who had absolutely no right to walk into a room looking like she belonged at the head of the table.

No one else seemed to mind. No one else was staring.

"What?" Juliana barked, taking a seat.

Hawthorn picked up his jaw. "I didn't recognise you there for a moment," he admitted. "It's hard to recognise you when you're not covered in mud. I'm not entirely sure it's an improvement, however. Seeing your face so clearly is... disturbing."

What was definitely disturbing was his reaction to it. For years, Jules had just looked like *Jules* to him. First the moment on the beach, and now *this*. She had no right to suddenly look so... otherworldly.

"Well, I have to put up with your face daily, and I never complain about it," she said, reaching across to select a bread roll. Her hair slipped over her bare shoulder, darker and more red than usual. It looked threaded with gold.

"You must be his guard," said Serena, beaming. "A pleasure to meet you."

Juliana bowed her head. "Juliana. I am honoured, Princess."

"You're never so formal with me," said Hawthorn, doing his best not to pout.

She raised a disbelieving eyebrow. "Do you want me to be?"

No. Yes. I wouldn't be adverse to the occasional nice word... maybe a bit of reverence...

He wanted to make her look at him the way he was certain he was looking at her.

It was a relief when the meal finally ended and revelry began. Yasha did indeed challenge Miriam to a fight. As was standard when fighting mortals, she was forbidden from using magic, and the amount of wine she'd imbibed by this point made it an easy win for Miriam. Yasha didn't seem the least embarrassed;

she invited Miriam to spar with her the next day and even half-jokingly suggested inviting her to join her in bed with her wife.

Neither Lahoime nor her daughter seemed to mind this brazen request.

"You have quite the reputation in the bedroom yourself, or so I hear," Princess Serena remarked to Hawthorn.

"I cannot lie to you," Hawthorn replied. "Nor shall I attempt to hide the truth. If you have a question, I'd encourage you to ask it."

Serena nodded, not looking at him. "When and if you marry, do you suspect you shall continue your pursuits?"

Hawthorn paused. It was a fair question. "It would depend on my partner," he responded delicately.

"What they wanted? What they were happy with—or *who* they were?"

His second pause was longer. He was not known for his long term lovers. That was not exactly his choice, however, whatever the rest of Faerie might think. Truth be told, he could see himself being content with a singular person... if they could be content with him. He suspected this was a desire shared by many: merely to want and be wanted in equal amounts.

He also suspected that such a luxury was probably beyond him.

"I would prefer monogamy, to be honest," he admitted, surprised by the words. "Yourself?"

"I've had little experience in romance to know precisely what I prefer," she told him. "But my heart tends towards that way. I suppose it would depend on my partner too... and my reasons for marrying."

"Naturally."

She paused again. "If there's someone else—"

A juggler crashed into a fountain of wine, splashing Serena's dress. She laughed it off, assuring her there was no harm done, and excused herself from the party to freshen up.

Hawthorn's eyes found Juliana in the room, finishing off a dance with a man who appeared to be part stag. She excused herself at the end of the dance to slide towards a table of refreshments, eyeing the freshly-iced cakes.

Hawthorn sauntered over towards her. "One day, I would like to find someone who looks at me the way you look at cake."

Juliana blinked. "No one wants to eat *you*."

"And yet I am so delicious." He glanced at the tower of desserts. "Made up your mind yet?"

"I—no."

"Good," he said, and slipped an arm around her waist.

"What are you doing?" she asked.

"Trying to dance. I am succeeding. You are not."

"We're... dancing?"

"Can you think of a good reason why we shouldn't?"

"Several," she said sharply.

"You can always leave. I won't—" Suddenly, he realised he *would* be offended if she left, and the words stuck to his tongue.

Troubling.

"I won't hold it against you," he finished instead, and then his fingers drifted unconsciously to the rounded edges of Jules' strange mortal ears.

She glared at him. "What are you doing?"

"Your ears fascinate me. I can't help it."

Jules whisked a tiny dagger out of nowhere. "Help it."

"I—*where were you keeping that?*"

"I am never unprepared."

"Apparently so..."

He watched as she folded away the blade beneath her skirts.

"It's a lovely dress," he remarked. "Where did you get it?"

"Payment," she said, "for watching your sorry ass these past two weeks. Almost worth it."

"Your concern is, as ever, touching..." He whisked her out of the way as a couple of drunken mermen, stomping on their borrowed legs, came barreling past. "I thought you'd be better at dancing."

Juliana's grip on him tightened, and she twisted him round in three circles and stopped shortly. "I *am* good at dancing," she said. "I am just not so good at being led."

Hawthorn grinned, flinging her in and out of his arms in a sharp, fluid movement, and dipping her towards the floor. Juliana stomped on his foot with the heel of her gold sandal, twisting him over and jerking them back together.

"I can't tell if we're dancing or fighting," he said, his grin widening. "I like it."

Juliana's scowl darkened, her chest heaving against his. Her legs marched them across the dancefloor. "I hate it."

"Then stop." He twirled her under his arm. "There're no winners in a dance."

Evidently, this was not a statement Juliana agreed with. Her movement grew slicker, sharper, faster, as if she were trying to trip him up. It didn't work. Hawthorn had put almost as many hours into dance practise as she'd put in with a blade. His balance was unparalleled.

"Give up?" he asked.

"*Never,*" she snarled.

A shadow cut across them both. "My, my, my son. Do save some of that energy for your fianceé."

Hawthorn dropped away from Juliana. "With all due respect, Mother, Serena and I have yet to come to any kind of understanding, seeing as we just met."

"Then perhaps you better invest a little more time in getting to know one another." Her curt look disappeared the minute her eyes settled on Juliana. "The dress becomes you, child. I knew the colour would suit. Your mother wore a very similar one when she was here."

Juliana froze. "Thank you, Your Majesty."

The Queen swept away.

"My mother bought you the dress?"

She nodded.

Hawthorn didn't know what to make of that. He found himself strangely irked by the idea.

A second later, he saw that Serena had returned, and swept away to join her.

The evening wore on. He tried not to think any more about Jules or the dress, but both thrummed in his mind all night. Even in the glistening sea palace, the warm mint of her dress seemed to blaze.

It didn't matter that Serena was a fine partner, as light as air, soft as a moonbeam.

He wanted the cold fire back.

He lost sight of Juliana at one point, which was just as well. But his eyes did catch on a couple of merrows by the punch bowl, stirring something white and creamy into the concoction and giggling.

He stopped his dance, pointed out what was happening to Serena, and marched towards them. "What are you doing?"

The merrows laughed. "A little harmless fun for our mortal guests," explained one.

Hawthorn had no sword to draw, but he came close to summoning fire. "I require further explanation."

"It's a truth serum," giggled the other. "Makes them instantly drunk and bypasses any wards they're wearing. Completely harmless."

Hawthorn doubted that. Making someone defenceless was rarely harmless, and the mortals needed those lies. They weren't able to side-step the truth like the fae.

Without any further deliberation, he pushed over the punch bowl. It shattered against the marble.

"Oh dear. It fell over."

The merrows gasped.

Serena hovered by Hawthorn's elbow, brow furrowed. "Have someone round up your mortal guests and servants and see that they're safe," he instructed.

Serena nodded, shooting off without another word.

Hawthorn scanned across the crowds for Juliana. He spotted her by the side of the room, talking to an attractive young merman.

"Apologies," he said, tugging at her elbow, "but I must have a word with my guard."

Juliana pouted, an unusual expression. "I was enjoying myself."

"I am sure you will forgive me." He steadied her, holding onto her shoulders, trying to glean whether or not there was something different in her eyes. Mortals' pupils tended to dilate when they were glamoured, but drugged was another matter.

"Did you drink the punch?"

"Yes. It was delicious. Very sweet. Perfect texture."

Hawthorn's stomach dropped. "How long ago?"

"I'm not sure..."

"Tell me something I don't know."

"Your mouth is very troublesome."

"Oh, is it now?" he said, arching an eyebrow. "How so? I thought I was well aware of how troublesome my mouth could be..."

Juliana groaned. "But are you aware of how attractive I find it, despite of all the nonsense that comes out of it? You have this really squishable, stupidly kissable-looking mouth. It's very annoying."

Hawthorn blinked.

She had *definitely* drunk the punch.

And was that really what she thought?

"We need to get you to bed."

Juliana stamped her foot. "I'm not a child."

"No, but you have been drugged. A couple of merrows tampered with the punch. You can't lie."

"Yes I can!" she insisted.

"Tell me that the sun is green."

"The sun is..." She stopped, mouth moving, words not forming. Her eyes widened. "This is *so weird*. It's like there's a cork in my mouth! *Four plus four equals... My father is... My favourite colour is...* whoa."

"Yes, it's very intriguing for you I'm sure, but let's get you out of here before you say something you'll regret."

She nodded, suddenly understanding. "All right."

He steered her away from the crowd. No one stopped them. Why would they? He was the crown prince and she was his guard. There was nowhere that was supposed to be forbidden to them.

Juliana tripped on the stairs halfway up, skirts sprawling everywhere. She laughed in a highly un-Jules like fashion.

"These stairs are proving most problematic. Where's my sword?"

"You can't vanquish stairs, Juliana."

"Have you ever tried?"

Hawthorn sighed. "Come, my wicked wench, let's conquer these stairs together."

Jules barely managed two before falling flat on her face. The disconcerting giggles continued. "They're conquering *us.*"

"They're conquering *you*, certainly." He shook his head. "Come here." He looped her arm over his shoulder and swept her against his body, groaning under her weight. "You are much heavier than you look."

"I'm pure muscle!"

His eyes drifted down to the warm, soft slope of her breasts, pushing against the fabric of her dress. "Not quite *pure* muscle..." he muttered, entirely against his will.

"Are you looking at me?"

"I'm always looking at you," he admitted glumly. He really hoped she didn't remember that particular admission in the morning.

They stumbled into their chambers. Hawthorn swept her into her adjoining room, depositing her on the bed. He wasn't used to Jules being this way. He wasn't entirely sure what to do.

But whenever she'd dragged him back to his chambers, drunk out of his mind, he always remembered she removed his shoes.

He stooped down to unlace her sandals, quite sure he'd never been this close to her before, never touched this part of her body.

Why am I thinking about where I've touched her before?

"Hawthorn," said Juliana, her tone now devoid of giggling. "Don't tell anyone what happened. Don't let them see what a fool I was."

Hawthorn exhaled, as if too deep a breath would shatter the thinness of the night. "It really matters to you, doesn't it? Keeping your weaknesses hidden?"

"That matters to *everyone*," she insisted. "I just have more weaknesses than most."

He frowned. "What do you mean?"

Without another word Juliana dropped the sleeves off her shoulders and peeled down the dress to her waist, displaying every glorious naked inch of her chest.

"Holy vines," Hawthorn uttered, desperately trying to look away and somewhat failing in this endeavour.

Juliana had no notion of his distress. She picked up his fingers and placed them against a long, silvery wound, which curved down her chest. Her torso was littered with them. "I am mortal," she reminded him, and he really did need the reminder, because he often thought of Jules as cut from something else entirely. "My body breaks more easily than yours, and I have to find ways of making it stronger. And my heart too, carries mortal scars. Mortal weaknesses."

"You have a heart of steel, Jules."

"Then why does it hurt all the time?" she asked, and to his alarm, tears sprouted in her eyes. "I have too many. Too many fears. Too many weaknesses. Mother, Father, snakes, failure... you."

"Me?" His brow furrowed further. "How am I one of your weaknesses?"

"I don't know," she said, a tear sliding down her cheek. "And it isn't fair. Because I *hate* you, Hawthorn. I really, really hate you..."

Her head started to lull, and he realised, with a heavy heart, how ashamed she'd be to know what she'd just told him in the morning.

Also, she stripped in front of him. He fancied she might claw out his eyes tomorrow if she remembered.

"Juliana," he whispered, "can you remove your wards?"

Obediently, Juliana did. Off came the ribbon tied to her ankle, the clasp on her dress, her necklace of berries. More impressively, she took out a strand of hair at the back of her head and yanked out the three berries she'd threaded there.

Ah, so that was where she kept them. Her usual braid was so thick he doubted anyone had ever noticed.

He really hoped she didn't ask him how those had come loose the next morning.

He sighed, pulled the blanket up to her shoulders, and clasped her face. "Jules, repeat after me: you had a most excellent evening of dancing and revelry," he told her. "You danced, you ate, and you drank far too much. But you got back to bed by yourself. We never spoke."

Later, Hawthorn would wonder at the magnificent unfairness that he could only ever speak a lie if he was spilling it into a mortal's ear, and how Jules made a poor receptacle for the only lies he had ever uttered.

30. THE WINTER QUARRY

Juliana plodded onward through the thick, heavy snow. Several times, she thought about turning back, or at least finding shelter, making a fire, speaking to Hawthorn, weighing her options. But she didn't want to admit this wasn't the best of ideas, and at the end of the day, she still had no way of getting through the gates to Acanthia.

This *was* the best way. She could do it. She had to.

Distracted, her foot slipped on a patch of ice and she tumbled down a slope, hitting a dense, flattened part of snow on something that looked almost like a road.

Juliana surveyed her surroundings. She had landed on a footprint almost as large as she was tall.

A giant had come past here.

She examined the rest of the trail. By the looks of things, it hadn't come alone. Dozens, maybe hundreds of other tracks ran alongside it. Narrow, thin lines, claws and paws... a dark myriad of patterns and footprints.

Her father would have been able to name all of them, to give a precise number.

All Juliana could guess was that it was a *lot*.

Don't follow, warned a voice inside. *Stick to the path.*

The trail led deeper than she'd planned to go. She ought to stick west, moving towards Acanthia. She shouldn't allow herself to be sidetracked—

But she was also acutely aware of Ladrien's plans to invade the mortal realm, and she had to—*had to*—find out if this had anything to do with that. If she saved Faerie but doomed the rest of the world in the process, she wasn't sure she could live with that.

Just find out what you're dealing with, she told herself. *Don't do anything stupid. That's Hawthorn's area.*

But even as she thought it, she knew that wasn't true. Hawthorn was cunning and calculated, at least when it came to things like this. He never rushed into a fight. He thought about everything he said and did.

She really should have waited to talk to him.

Too late now.

She crept forwards, footsteps sinking deeper and deeper into the snow. If anyone caught her trail now, she'd never lose them.

A thick, dense wall of thorns appeared ahead of her, obsidian-black and shining against the snow. It parted where the tracks lead. Juliana inched forward, remembering the thorns Ladrien had summoned, expecting these to be like the vines at home, alive and whispering.

But they were silent. If these were conjured by Ladrien, there was no life to them. Perhaps that was the difference between Seelie magic and Unseelie—one life, one death.

A short while later, smoke appeared in the distance, followed by a faint red glow. Rocks emerged, the snow sloped away. A quarry opened up ahead of her.

Juliana took a moment to gather her breath, forgoing the path down into the centre, and instead climbed up to a ledge to peer over the side.

Her stomach leapt from her body.

Inside the pit were hundreds of Unseelie. Giants and goblins, all kitted out in armour; sluaghs shrieking overhead; viscous red-caps, painted in blood; fanged, grey-skinned nixies with hair like pondweed; barghests all collared and harnessed, with dozens of other brutish beasts she couldn't name or see clearly enough to hazard a guess at their origins.

A force like this could flatten a mortal town. Devour it, liquify it, drain the souls to feed their ranks and carry on to the next.

And the next, and the—

She shouldn't have come. What could she even do? There was no way she could take on an army and no one she could turn to. She just had to reach Acanthia as soon as she could and try and convince Maytree to lend aid—

A shadow fell across her. Instinctively, her hand flew to her dagger, whipping round in an instant and toppling her opponent to the floor, blade against his chin.

"Juliana?" he breathed, voice ragged.

Dillon.

Juliana dropped her knife and catapulted into his arms, ignoring the stinging cold around them, the brush of snow against her skin. Dillon. Dillon was here, and *safe*, and for a split second the darkness inside and out seemed to recede.

"I feared you might be dead," he whispered, clutching her tightly.

"I feared the same for you." She pulled back, brushing her damp cheeks, hoping he didn't notice. "What are you *doing* here?"

"Recon mission. Miriam sent me." He pointed to the doublet beneath his cloak; white and gold, stitched with thorns, splattered slightly with blood and at least a size too small for him. "I received a temporary promotion. There was an opening. I'm an unofficial knight."

He didn't seem thrilled by the prospect, but of course he didn't. His uniform belonged to someone else.

She didn't want to ask who.

"What are *you* doing here?" he pressed.

Juliana sighed. "It's a long story."

"Simplify it."

She took a deep breath, and filled him in on the details—how she and Hawthorn had fled, how they were connected through their dreams, how they'd come up with a plan to break the curse.

Dillon paused when they got to the bit about Serena's role, and thumped his head with his fist.

"What?" said Juliana, brows knitting together. "It's a decent plan."

"It's a perfect plan," Dillon hissed, teeth gritted. "If we can get back into the palace... Vines and spirits, she was *right there*. Any one of us could have... Miriam is going to be so annoyed when she hears about this."

Juliana smiled. "Then let's make sure she does."

Dillon nodded, but then his gaze cast out to the quarry behind them. "We just going to leave all these guys here?"

"Not sure we have a choice."

"If they get to the mortal world—"

"I know," said Juliana swiftly. "But taking out an entire army? I'm not sure that's in my skillset."

"Hmm," Dillon nodded. "Agreed. Shame though. The way they're all gathered together. We could flood the place if we had the power to melt things."

Juliana snorted. "I think even dear Prince Prickle would struggle with that kind of firepower…"

She imagined him trying, though. He'd been a formidable force against the sluaghs, even when outnumbered and they had the benefit of flight. How much damage could he cause here before the forces reached him? He had a sound tactical mind. If he took out some of those levels with a few well-aimed fireballs, cut off the escape routes, maybe set off those explosives being loaded into carts…

Juliana paused.

They were putting explosives into carts.

"Juliana?" Dillon nudged her elbow. "You have scheming face."

"I do *not.*"

"I've known you your entire life. You *definitely* have scheming face. That's the exact face you pulled when you were working out how to sneak inside Prince Hawthorn's room and tie his hair to the bedpost."

At that, Juliana's smile widened, her confidence strengthening.

As a child, you snuck into a highly guarded location, committed a crime against royalty, and got out. You can do this.

"Dillon," she asked, "how good are you with explosives?"

"Pretty good," he returned. "Why?"

She returned to surveying the quarry. The explosives were just one element. They wouldn't do much good against flying foes, or the larger enemies—there were at least six giants. Most of them could brush off an explosion like a scratch. Dillon was right when he suggested a flood—but she knew of no lakes nearby, nothing they could drain quickly enough for the Unseelie to be taken out in one fell swoop…

Her eyes settled on the dense, powdery snow of the mountains nearby.

"How's your maths?" she asked him.

"Also sharp. Why?"

"We don't need water to flood this place," she told him, pointing. "We have snow."

"For the record," Dillon said, face tightly set, "I still think this is insane."

"You said the numbers added up."

"The numbers adding up and this being insane are not contradictory points."

"What's the worst that can happen?"

"Do you really want me to answer that? Because I have a list. A *long* one."

Juliana was already aware of the dozens of things that could go wrong with this plan. Death by capture. Torture. Accidentally blowing themselves up. Deciding to blow themselves up to take some others out with them. Being crushed to death by snow. Freezing to death. Dying of wounds.

The mortal lands being invaded.

No one coming to save Acanthia.

Ladrien ruling.

Hawthorn waking up alone.

If she perished, would the connection between them snap? Or would Hawthorn find himself appearing next to her corpse when night finally fell? What if he never found her body at all, buried beneath the snow, and assumed she'd discarded the pendant and fled?

Her gut churned with the awful thought that she'd never given him enough reason to doubt that was something she was capable of.

I'm not going to die, she told herself, double-checking all her weapons. She and Dillon had taken refuge in a cave not far from the quarry. It was a good place to plan their attack and store their supplies, and Dillon estimated it would be out of the way of the trajectory once they set off the explosives.

"Ready?" Dillon asked, patting her shoulder.

"Born ready!" she declared.

Dillon sighed, rolling his eyes. "Born a liar, more like." He yanked her into a brief, tight hug, holding on a little longer than he should have. "Be safe."

She held him back, savouring the broad, sturdy weight of another human being against her. "I'll do my best."

Juliana fled outside of the cave, Dillon not far behind her, stringing a bow. He admitted he wasn't the greatest of archers, but as Juliana was the far smaller target, who could creep around rocks like a wraith, it made far more sense for her to steal the explosives than him.

"I'll try not to shoot it whilst I'm covering you," he'd said as they'd planned.

"If you do," she'd returned, "just make it quick."

She walked down the path, keeping to the shadows, ducking under awnings, carts, flimsy structures. Ladrien must have used all manner of charms to keep this place hidden—the thorn wall itself must have been enchanted and riddled with spells. He'd only let the glamour drop now because he was moving out his army—and he wasn't expecting anyone to be here.

She wondered, not entirely for the first time, if her father had merely been tracking her when she'd discovered him. Was he coming back here? And if so, was it to help or to hinder?

No way of knowing now, and no time to waste. He *wasn't* here. He hadn't stayed.

Taking short, quick looks to make sure eyes were averted, she moved swiftly behind the next obstruction. There was so much movement, few would notice her if she didn't draw attention, but she hugged her cloak regardless. Luckily, Ladrien had foregone any kind of uniform in the place of rough armour—leather, wood, the occasional bit of metal. As long as her black cloak hid her palace uniform and her human features, most would assume she was one of them.

Most.

She ducked into an alcove behind a cart being loaded by a couple of trolls, and glanced down at where the explosives were. There was a limit as to what she could carry, and a specific number they would need. Dillon had recommended taking several trips. Juliana wasn't sure how much to press her luck.

She did a quick calculation of how far away the explosives were from the ledge hanging over them, did a cursory glance to make sure no one was watching, then locked her legs around one of the poles, dipped down and swiped a projectile from the top of the cart.

Seconds. It took seconds.

Spurred by her success, Juliana concealed her prize beneath her cloak and started back up the path, the force of gravity making the return trip much longer, making her calves and lungs burn. In and out of the crowds she wove, past armoured ogres and saddled barghests.

I am a shadow. I am without form.

She reached the top of the quarry and slid back to Dillon's side, panting hard. "You got it," he said, taking it from her.

"One down, three to go."

Dillon hesitated, his face stony as he appraised the explosive. "I can't cover you while I position this."

Juliana waved it away. "I'll be fine."

She took a few minutes to gather her breath, and slid back down into the quarry, her heart lurching when she realised that the cart carrying the explosives had been moved away... further into the quarry. Juliana was skilled, but she didn't fancy her chances getting all the way into the centre of the pit and out again without anyone noticing... at least not looking like this.

A proper disguise. She needed one.

She scanned around, noticing that parts of the quarry had been hollowed out, fashioned into tunnels. Clearly, this army had been here for a long time. They'd had barracks and stores—somewhere where clothing and armour was kept.

Was she really going to walk inside?

She didn't see what choice she had, but as an added precaution, she picked up some of the red dust littering the floor and smeared her features with it, obscuring her face.

She dipped inside the first tunnel.

It was poorly lit. Of course it was—Unseelie eyes were far sharper than hers. She stumbled on in the dark until she came across a torch, and used it to wind further down the passageway. She passed a mess hall and a kitchen, squirming with the noise of banging pots and the smell of roasting meat, mingling with the dark, earthy scent of the halls.

Eventually, she came to a crude dormitory, not much more than a dozen poorly-constructed cots and a few trunks for belongings. She set down the torch and began to rifle through the trunks, searching for anything her size. She found some black face paint which she used to further disguise her face, but any clothes she came across were far too big.

The banging of the pots echoed down the hall. Juliana had a sinking suspicion that dinner was not far off, that soon these halls would be packed with Unseelie warriors and her luck would permanently run out.

Finally, her fingers fell across some rough armour that worked just enough to hide her uniform, to allow her to move more freely without holding the cape around her all the time. She buckled it on and readjusted her weapons. There were no mirrors; she had to hope this did the trick.

She pulled her hair down over her ears, lifted up her hood, and dissolved back into shadows.

Mercifully, the explosives cart had yet to move. With her disguise adding to her confidence, Juliana slunk down to the lowest level, weaving through the crowds towards her target. Could she honestly just lift them out of there and back again? Wouldn't that look suspicious?

She approached the front of the cart. No one was yet sitting in the seat behind the giant toad. She offered it an affectionate pat out of habit, eyes still on the prize.

"You, louse, what are you doing?" barked a cold, hard voice.

Juliana stilled, blood turning cold. She knew that voice. She'd heard it speak only once before, but she knew it, in the way one remembered the feel of a blade that stabbed them.

She turned carefully, keeping her face down, not daring to look up.

Ladrien towered over her, skin gleaming wetly in the faint light. His wings and horns shone like the thorns surrounding the quarry, the feathers of his black robes now replaced with fur.

For some reason, her father's words came back to her—the echo of some old storyteller.

He never liked the cold.

"I asked you a question, creature," Ladrien continued, voice dark. "I will have your answer."

Juliana coughed, adopting a raspy voice she hoped matched whatever creature she was pretending to be. "Just getting the cart ready, Your Majesty, as instructed."

"I thought Merryweather was in charge of these supplies?"

"I don't rightly know who gave me the instructions," Juliana continued, still not daring to look up. "I didn't want to ask. I just do as I'm told, me…"

Ladrien remained in front of her, still as stone. For one horrible moment, Juliana was sure she'd been rumbled.

But Ladrien merely tapped the side of the cart with his staff. "Be careful with this," he warned.

"I assure you, Sire, I will be."

He swept off without another word.

Juliana took a deep, steadying breath. That had been far too close. But of course—he did not expect her to be able to lie. He thought all the mortals were fleeing for the border or trapped inside Acanthia. He had doubtless not spared one thought for the mortal guard he'd met a few days beforehand, probably assuming she'd fled.

He did not expect them to resist.

Still steadying her breathing, Juliana clambered up into the seat of the cart and shook the reins. She was driving these explosives out of here.

She expected some resistance, someone to run forward and ask her what she was doing, but although someone double-checked her supplies before the road out of the quarry, no one else said a thing.

It was a long, slow ascent up the mountain, her heart hammering in her chest the entire time. She could still feel Ladrien's gaze on her, like a plate of iron. She hadn't even failed yet, but all her earlier confidence had been stripped away, replaced with cold, dark dread.

She barely breathed until she reached the top, and even then, following the convoy on the road to the border, she knew she couldn't relax. She needed to find a way to slip out of the procession.

Thinking swiftly, she took her smaller dagger from her belt and slashed through the traces linking the mount to the cart. With a sharp yank of the reins (and a murmur of apology under her breath) the toad lurched off over the snow. She let out a frustrating cry as it barrelled past another supply cart, causing just enough of a fuss that no one noticed her scrambling out of her seat with an armful of explosives, heading for a copse of trees.

Waiting until the majority of the carts had passed, she slunk away to join Dillon at the designated meeting place. His eyes widened when he saw her, and he drew his sword.

"Steady on! It's me," she said, dropping to the floor and picking up handfuls of snow to try and sponge the dirt and paint away.

"Juliana?"

"Who else?"

"Good point." He turned to the explosives she'd set aside. "You actually did it. How did you get all of that—never mind. We need to work quickly. It'll be dark soon and we do *not* want to be traipsing around in the dark and the snow…"

Juliana groaned. "Too right. Here, you take these ones. I'll do the last."

She took a moment to double-check the rudimentary map they'd drawn into the ground, and then set off without another word, setting her charge as Dillon had instructed and trying not to count the minutes before his return. Sometimes, she could make him out in the snow, but other times he was invisible. The pit, meanwhile, swarmed with energy… and her cart still sat abandoned beside the road. How long until someone questioned it?

Come on, Dillon, come on…

After an age, he reached her side, breathless and ruddy faced. He held out two crystals, connected to the explosives by magic Juliana couldn't fathom, as she positioned her rocket towards the mountain peak.

"So, I guess that's it then," he remarked, as she dithered with the rocket.

"What is?"

"We get Serena to wake up Hawthorn, and they marry."

"That was always what was supposed to happen."

"Was it?"

"What other ending could this possibly have?"

Dillon sighed. "You're not very romantic, are you?"

"Being romantic isn't very useful," she said pointedly, not sure what he was getting at.

At this, Dillon chuckled. "I spoke to him, you know. About how he felt marrying Serena. I expected him to be casual about it, like it meant nothing, like he had no plans to change after the event. He said he thought he should try and make it work with her, that he had no plans to take on lovers or continue his old ways. He's loyal, you know."

Juliana bit her lip. "I know."

"Doesn't that bother you?"

"Should it?"

Another sigh, deeper than the first. "You're so stubborn."

"One of my best qualities." She looked down at the rocket, still unsure if it was pointing in the right direction. This was vastly different to aiming an arrow and far more terrifying. "You sure this will work?"

Dillon grinned. "Not pointed like that, it won't." He set the crystals down carefully and readjusted her rocket, large, calloused hands brushing over hers. "Where'd the confidence go?"

"I can't be perfect all the time, Dillon. It would exhaust me."

She took a match from her belt as he smiled at her again, stepping back to pick up his ignition crystals. "Ready?" he asked.

"Born ready."

He clicked the crystals together.

For a long, unflinching moment, there was nothing but silence. Then, in the distance, there came a rumble, a fierce, dark purr. The mountains began to tremble and shake. Slowly, chunks peeled away from the rock. The rumble mounted, sounds and sensations tripping over each other like thunder. The snow turned into a white, twisted sea, waves of ice tearing down the slopes, a freezing, trembling flood—

"Now, Juliana!" Dillon yelled.

She struck her match and lit the rocket. They scrambled backwards as it soared into the air, a blaze of red and fire. It smashed against the mountainside in a crowd of smoke.

The trembling increased. Huge shafts of snow like powdery icebergs charged down the mountain, racing towards the quarry.

Shouts and cries pierced the air, along with the braying of mounts trying to race up the path, out of the range on the oncoming avalanche. Wheels churned against rock. In the pit, one of the giants bolted for the road winding up the quarry, the pounding of his footsteps lost behind the roar of snow.

The shaking was like nothing Juliana had ever felt, like the entire earth was being split apart. There was no room for triumph inside her, no amazement at the fact their plan was working, only sheer disbelief at the devastation unfolding before them, horror at the unquestionable, unstoppable power of nature.

Not even the Unseelie King could stop an avalanche. It was overwhelming, indestructible.

The avalanche reached the edge of the quarry, ving over the lip, crashing to the rocky bottom, sweeping away everything in its path. It caught the fleeing giant by the ankles and wrenched him backwards. He struggled against the tide, gaining nothing, losing much. A hundred, a thousand dark shapes vanished beneath the endless white.

Any flighted creatures took to the skies, screeching and wailing, the convoy clattering onwards, refusing to look back or stop or try to help.

A magnificent dark shape rose above it all, letting out a horrible, blood-curdling cry.

Ladrien, wings extending, horns silhouetted against the moonlight—the only still white thing in the entire scene.

It was too much to hope that he'd be caught in the onslaught, but it didn't matter. His army was lost.

Ladrien seemed to realise it too. He took a long, sweeping look over the quarry, and with a strange, juddering motion, he vanished into mist.

The avalanche raged on. The constructs bolted to the sides of the quarry washed away. *Everything* washed away, until all that was left of the quarry were a few bits of red rock protruding from a sea of snow.

Finally, everything went still and quiet.

Juliana turned to Dillon, standing a few feet away. "We did it," she said, with a kind of breathless wonder. "We actually did it. Dillon—"

But Dillon didn't answer. He turned towards her in a slow, endless fashion, clutching the front of his white doublet, rapidly staining with red.

Before she could even scream, he was falling to the floor, and Ladrien stood behind him with a knife.

31.
HOLLOW

"Mortals!" Ladrien bellowed, in a voice half a scream, half a fearsome, desperate hiss. "Filthy, lying mortals! How dare you! How dare—"

His body seized, like his anger was a violent power trying to break out of him, some great swarm of poisonous insects. He gave a terrific roar and vanished from the spot, his body misting. Juliana ran forward, racing towards Dillon—

And straight into the blade of the re-forming Ladrien.

A pain both hot and cold spread through her middle as she fell backwards. Ladrien yanked the blade out of her, expression livid. Blood streamed through her fingertips as she clutched at her stomach. Dillon groaned in the snow nearby, and she raised one hand towards him, trying to move, realising she couldn't.

This is bad, bad, very bad.

Ladrien took a deep breath, sliding the knife away. The violence seemed to have soothed him, though anger still peppered his voice. "Die here, you filthy rodents," he hissed. "Freeze, bleed... I do not care. You may have destroyed most of my army, but I have decades to rebuild. You haven't won..." He glared down at Juliana's face, at the crude armour she'd attached to herself. He ripped off a piece of it, making her cry out. "Palace guard," he said, seeing the blood-stained uniform beneath. "*Juliana.* I should have killed you when I had the chance."

Juliana knew there was something she could hiss back, some retort, some venom she had stored somewhere... but she couldn't find it. Her mind was collapsing. She was reminded of one time Aoife accidentally knocked over a bookcase in the great library, the way the books had spilled out, one by one, before crashing against the floor.

Aoife, Aoife.

The memory fell silent.

Ladrien spat on the ground, and then with a hiss and a groan, like he was fighting against the cold, he vanished in a trembling mist.

Dillon was lying not far away, eyes blinking upwards, circling. Blood stained the snow around him, and he was otherwise completely still.

Dillon.

She tried to roll, but pain split down her centre. She couldn't reach him like this, and her thoughts were mush, spilling away from her.

Steady, steady. Think, think.

Fighting for a fragment of consciousness, her hands trembled as she plucked the vial of elixir from her pocket. There was so little of it left after her fight with the grindylows. She tried to measure it as she poured a few droplets on her wound, but her fingers were shaking too much to count.

She rolled onto her front, pain still lancing up her side, and crawled towards him.

"Dillon," she whispered, reaching his side.

His face moved towards her, just a fraction, and she chanced a look at his wound. Parts of him were spilling out of his stomach, held in place only by his clothes.

It was probably beyond the elixir even if she had more of it.

"It's bad, isn't it?" he asked, his voice sounding gummy. He tried to move his head. "It feels bad. Jules, it feels really bad—"

"Ssh, ssh, don't look—" Her voice caught on the word.

Once, when she was a child, she'd fallen from the rafters in the stable and had broken her arm. It was Dillon who raced towards her, Dillon who covered the protruding bone, who told her it was fine, who tugged her towards the healer's before she could pass out, before she could realise the extent of her injury.

Dillon, who only ever lied to help people.

She took his face in her hands. "Look at me," she whispered. "*Listen* to me. You're going to be fine. I have some more elixir. I just need to go back and get it..."

Dillon's throat bobbed. Shaking fingers reached out to clasp hers, still glued tightly to his face. "Not fae," he whispered.

"What?"

"I know... know a lie... when I hear one..."

"It's not... it's not that bad. I can fix it, I can..."

Dillon drew something on the back of her hand, daubed in his own blood. "Tunnel," he said.

"What?"

"There's a tunnel. A tunnel you need to..." His face turned pale and still, and for a second, Juliana thought he'd already slipped away.

"My father—"

"I'll find him," Juliana promised, quite forgetting to lie. "I'll see he's looked after. I'll tell him you were brave and strong and true to the end, that you died a hero, that your last thoughts were of him—"

"You," he murmured.

"What?"

"My last thoughts... you." His eyes started to circle. "I liked you," he whispered, voice ragged. "I could have..."

She waited for him to finish, but slowly, as the world groaned around them, she realised that he wouldn't. Dillon would never finish that sentence. He would never finish anything again.

Tears stung her eyes. Her chest surged. Her entire body shook, rattling, numb. Hardly hers at all. Her hand was scrunched in his and she didn't want to let go.

How could she let go? Dillon was threaded to her story. He'd been there at the beginning, chasing her through the stables when they could barely walk. Dillon couldn't be gone. She wouldn't *let* him be gone. Not Dillon who had dragged her to the healer's the countless times she'd hurt herself, Dillon who spoke to horses like they could speak back, Dillon who'd kissed her and looked at her like she was beautiful and had been her friend before and afterwards and should have been her friend forever—

And he would be. Because she wasn't letting go.

His hand started to grow cold, the only warmth in his palm her own, echoing back. Dillon's warmth, Dillon's soul, whatever made him, *him*, wasn't here anymore.

Nothing was.

"I liked you too," she whispered, placing a kiss against his still, inert forehead. She wanted to whisper other lies to him, other wishes of what could have been in another life, a different time.

But she did not want to lie to him.

"You were one of the kindest people I knew," she said instead. "Faerie didn't deserve you. *I* certainly didn't. But I'm glad you liked me. I'm glad I knew you. I'm sorry if I ever caused you pain."

With trembling fingers, she reached up to close his eyes. She drew the faerie symbol of peace on his forehead, and spoke the words given to knights of Acanthia.

"Rest easy, knight of the realm. You have served your country well. The earth is your blood now, the trees your bones. Wherever your spirit goes, a part will remain with us still. Farewell, brother-in-arms..." Her voice stalled on the next words, throat tight and aching. "Farewell, my friend."

32.
SHADOWS AND EMBER

She didn't have the strength to bury him. She didn't have any other choice but to leave him there in the freezing snow, sprinkling what remained of the elixir on her own wound, and crawling away to the cave where she'd stashed the rest of her supplies.

She could have tried to use it on him. She could have tried to do *something.*

But she hadn't, and although she knew it was because it wouldn't have helped, the thought didn't comfort her.

I shouldn't have gone after the grindylows. If I hadn't, maybe, maybe I would have had enough...

Juliana doubted that was true, that Dillon could have been saved by something small enough to fit in her pocket, but the thought refused to leave.

As did the pain crackling through her body.

She crawled into the back of the cave, too weak to move, thoughts turning mushy. How much blood had she lost?

Dillon had set up a fire earlier, thinking ahead, thinking that they would come back together at the end of the day and sit here together and laugh and toast to their victory—

But there would be no more toasts with Dillon. No more laughter.

No more *anything*.

Her thoughts turned ragged again, like they were being torn against a bread knife. She hadn't examined her wound since she'd splashed it with the remains of the elixir. She wasn't sure she wanted to.

At the back of the cave were a few vine-like roots, like the ones from back home in the palace. She moved towards them, pretending they were trembling around her, like they could offer her some comfort in this cold, dark place, where even the light of the fire couldn't reach her.

Juliana shut her eyes tight and prayed for sleep or something heavier to take her.

Someone was shaking her awake, rough and hard. "Jules! *Jules!* Open your eyes!"

"Don't shout..." she whispered hoarsely, curling into her wound. She wasn't bleeding anymore, she didn't think, but that might be the result of whatever strange spell she was under. She was dimly aware of her real body somewhere nearby, but she couldn't turn to examine it.

Hawthorn exhaled, just a fraction. "You're hurt."

"Don't worry, I won't let it slow me down."

"I'm not worried about it slowing you down, I'm worried about it—" He stopped, hand sliding to her middle, covering the wound with his hand. His face screwed up in concentration, and the vines around her shuddered and bent. Light splayed from his fingertips, but the wound didn't heal.

"Dammit..." he hissed.

"There's no land for you to draw from," Jules whispered. "We're not really here."

"Or perhaps I'm just desperately poor at magic and ought to have paid more attention in class."

"Going to rip your shirt again?"

"This is finest spider silk, Jules."

"Doesn't answer my question." A soft moan eased passed Juliana's lips. How dare she try to joke with him. How dare she be finding anything funny, when—
"Dillon's dead," she told him.

Hawthorn tensed. "What?"

"Dillon, he... he..." Slowly, carefully, she told him everything that had happened, leaving out nothing but what she and Dillon had spoken about. She couldn't bring herself to believe that those were the last words they'd ever share.

Hawthorn listened quietly and attentively, not speaking until the very end. "You took out his army?"

"Most of it, I think."

"You never cease to amaze me."

"I didn't do it alone."

"No," he said, "I know." He stroked her hair over her shoulder. "I can't make this right. I can't bring him back. But I will find some way to honour him when this is over. Some way to..."

His voice lost all quality, and tears prickled at Juliana's eyes. She didn't have the energy to be ashamed, she was too tired and too hurt to care about anything other than the fact that Dillon was *gone*.

Hawthorn stroked her hair, and let her cry.

"I just left him there. Left his body exposed—"

"You didn't have a choice."

"I wasn't careful enough. I thought we'd won. I wasn't paying enough attention—"

"*Ladrien* killed him, Juliana. Not you. And when you rescue me, we'll make him pay."

"Death is too good for him," she whispered. "I want it to hurt."

"We'll find a fitting punishment for him, I swear it."

"Good," she said, and sobbed some more, pain still fracturing through her. She turned her head numbly towards her sleeping body. She was still bleeding, her face pale and clammy. "Dillon... Dillon wanted me to speak to his father..." she told Hawthorn, hoping he understood.

"You will. Or *we* will. We'll go together."

"But if... if I can't..."

"Don't," he said sharply, and then, more softly. "Please. Don't."

"I need someone to know..." she said, because she knew it was fruitless to get him to promise. Albert would be dead long before he woke. "But if you see my father again, I want you to stab him in the face."

Hawthorn laughed. "Duly noted."

"Aoife was a good friend," she continued. "And Miriam a good mentor... and Iona a good aunt..."

"You don't need to tell me this—"

"But I do," she said, "I do, because someone needs to know, because I never told them, I never told them how much they meant to me and—"

"Jules."

She blinked out tears, swallowing hard. "I don't hate you as much as I pretend."

Hawthorn slid his fingers to her face and cupped her cheeks. "I know you don't."

"Sometimes, actually, I think you might just be my favourite of all the beings." She punched his thigh with all the strength that she could muster. "But bear in mind I hate almost everyone, so don't be flattered by my depraved tastes."

"Favourite being, hmm?"

"Oh, shut up. It's momentary."

"And now?"

"I'm sorry?"

"Where do I stand on your scale right now?"

She wanted to joke, but the energy to do so was slipping away from her. Everything was slipping away from her, like the walls of consciousness were coated with honey.

"I like you now," she said, and glanced up at him. Hawthorn was staring down at her, face milky smooth and pale as moonlight. His eyes shone like pools of lakewater, intense and wondrous, ice-fierce and ember-soft. He had no business looking at her like that, his silken mouth dripping with concern. "I really, really like you now..."

But that was the pendant talking, not her, and she had liked Dillon too, Dillon whose eyes would never twinkle at her again, whose mouth would never smile, whose body lay frozen somewhere in the snow outside—

She'd not liked him like this, but she thought he might have felt something more for her. Could she have felt more for him, if it weren't for these infernal pendants?

"I want to sleep now..." she said.

"Sleep then," Hawthorn whispered. "Just make sure you wake up."

Tears came again, and she closed her eyes, ashamed of feeling anything for anyone.

Hawthorn sang her mother's song until he was hoarse, and then used magic to make shadows dance along the cave walls until she fell asleep.

33. BENEATH THE SEA

ONE YEAR UNTIL THE CURSE AWAKENS

"What happened last night?" Juliana asked, barging into Hawthorn's chambers in the early hours of the morning in nothing but a robe. Her wards were clutched in her hand, strands of hair and all.

Hawthorn's neck suddenly felt rather hot. He unclenched the blanket, trying to appear calm. "Do you not remember?" he said placidly. "There was rather a lot of drinking and dancing…"

She frowned, rubbing her head. "Did I do something embarrassing?"

"You're asking me? Don't assume I was paying you any attention last night. You got to bed safely, and I haven't heard any scandalous rumours. All in all, a rather fun night."

He'd be rather pleased with that clever bit of manipulation if he wasn't so terrified of her seeing through his not-quite-lies.

Parts of it really were rather fun... he thought wickedly, trying to keep his eyes away from where her robe parted at the chest. *I saw you naked.*

Juliana's scowl did not abate. "You'd tell me if I had reason to be worried?"

"Your reputation is intact, Jules, I promise you."

"Right," she said, eyebrow finally dropping. "I'll... go back to my room, then and... get dressed for the day."

"You can guard me in that," he said, grinning with the thought, "I have no problems with that."

"You might not," Juliana responded, walking away from him, "but I imagine your fiancée would."

"She isn't my fiancée!" Hawthorn yelled after her, but she was already gone.

Unsurprisingly, Hawthorn was assigned the task of spending the entire day with Princess Serena, forcibly enjoying endless walks through the town and gardens. Most of the buildings were carved from rock or shell, with endless waterfalls and streams cascading down to the shore. The citizens used the rivers like roads, darting through the currents, waving to their friends as they passed. Several storefronts opened directly onto the water, and a strange aroma filled the air—sweet salt and baking rosemary.

It was truly a delight to experience, and yet he had found more pleasure in it yesterday evening down on the beach.

"You seem once more distracted, Your Highness," Serena remarked.

"The beach," he declared, in lieu of saying anything that might be considered offensive—an admission that he found her company less desirable than someone else's. "I was wondering if we might go down to it?"

Serena's eyes brightened. "You are fond of the sea?"

Not as much as others, he thought, eyes searching for Jules, who'd been traipsing behind them all morning, painfully silent. "I like it," he responded.

Serena glowed. She clapped her hands together and started to run, her flurry of blue-white skirts trailing behind her like a cape of cloud. Hawthorn followed, picking up the pace. They seemed to reach the shores in seconds, whereupon Serena dropped her dress entirely and dived into the water like a mermaid.

It occurred to him she probably *was* part mermaid. Most of the Summer Court seemed to be.

He yanked off his boots, unbuckled his belt, and stopped when he was down to his underwear. Faeries were notoriously bold with their bodies—especially in this part of the country—but he knew Juliana was slightly less comfortable and she was the one guarding them. He kept on his breeches as he dived into the foam, even when Serena reappeared and gave them a curious glance.

Juliana stopped by the waves. "How far are you going to go in?"

Serena twirled in the water. "As far as we can!"

"I think my mortal guard is slightly concerned about accidentally straying beyond the borders of Faerie," Hawthorn explained.

Serena shook her head, kicking up seafoam with a small, dainty foot. "The border is far beyond our shores—not until way past the Under Sea Court."

Hawthorn shivered. He'd heard tales of the Under Sea Court, one of the handful of unofficial courts within Faerie, a mix of Seelie and Unseelie, and the dark creatures that lived there.

"Scared, Prince?" Serena asked, with unusual coyness. He quite liked it.

"I fear my guard might be," he said instead.

Juliana huffed, removing her outer layers and stripping to her short, thin petticoat. She restrapped two daggers directly onto her legs. Half naked and covered in weapons was a decidedly good look for her.

"Sea monsters, wrecks, the great unknown?" she said boldly, strolling into the waters. "Sign me up."

"I stand corrected," Hawthorn said, trying not to smile. "Although I'm not sure we'll be going quite far enough for sea monsters..."

"I don't know," said Serena. "We'll see."

She disappeared beneath the waves.

Hawthorn and Juliana stared at one another, searching her words for meaning and coming up short. "After you," Juliana insisted.

"Try not to stare at my rear as we descend," said Hawthorn, taking a deep breath, and diving down before she could form her displeasure into words.

A deep, murky world rose to greet him, a land of sand and rock. Serena drifted in a current ahead of them, smiling as they approached, summoning two giant bubbles and fixing them over their heads to allow them to breathe. She, apparently, needed no such measures, and when she moved again, Hawthorn noticed something iridescent shining between her fingers and around her toes.

Webs. She had webbed hands and feet.

Juliana's fears had long since vanished. She glided through the water with ease, deeper and deeper, till the sands dropped away and another world opened before them, miles of ink-black coral swirling with silver fish.

Serena slithered into sunbeams, rolling under the ripples, chasing lines on the sand. Juliana moved with her, eyes alight, and he found it difficult for his eyes to move elsewhere, like there was something more wondrous about watching her experience the world than seeing it for himself.

Once upon a time, he hated to see her happy, his gut turned nauseous by her enjoyment.

Now he felt like he'd cut off a limb to see her look that way at him.

He followed them through the current. They swam through reefs and wrecks, ancient boats more barnacle than bark. Although everything was covered with a veneer of blue, he found himself amazed by the colour blossoming here, corals alight with red and orange, like a sunset emerging from the rock. Sunlight blazed in ribbons along the sandy floor, huge rays cutting through the shoals of fish.

Eventually, the sea turned dark, a bank of cloud drifted overhead, and coldness that hadn't been there before stung through the water.

Something white glared in the seabed beneath, an enormous, still thing, like a colossal centipede.

Jules buckled beside him, her eyes going from awed to panicked in a second. *Snake,* they seemed to say. *Snake, snake!*

She spluttered to the surface, Serena and Hawthorn hurrying behind her.

"What's wrong?" Serena asked, the second they met air.

Juliana's face was white as bone. "I... um..."

"Perhaps she went a little too deep," Hawthorn suggested. "I've heard mortal's lungs and heads aren't best designed for it."

"Are you all right?" Serena asked softly. "We can go back—"

"I'm fine," Juliana breathed, looking gratefully at Hawthorn. "What was that... I thought I saw..."

Serena grinned. "You asked for a sea monster."

"A... a giant sea snake?" Hawthorn guessed.

Serena shook her head. "A sea *dragon.* Couldn't you see the wings? It's an oilliphéist—the last of its kind. Have you not heard the stories?"

Hawthorn shook his head. Juliana still seemed to be recovering from the shock. "I have not. Pray, tell us."

Serena lay back in the sea, basking in the warm glow of the sun, though the water beneath her still seemed dark and murky.

"His name was Caoránach," she told them. "And he was the great lord of the sea. Centuries ago, when Faerie was still new, it is said that one of Titania's granddaughters came down to shore and heard the creature singing. The two met for the first time, and, whether then or in a hundred years—the two fell in love. He planned to give her the Breath of the Sea so she could come with him beneath the waves, but a jealous knight saw the two of them together, and slew him."

"Oh, that's sad," said Hawthorn.

Juliana, revived from her shock by the opportunity to tease him, raised an eyebrow. "I never knew you were romantic."

"I can be romantic."

She raised her eyebrow further.

"I couldn't say it if it wasn't true! I just prefer a happy ending, all right?"

"I don't mind a sad ending," Juliana admitted. "As long as it's suitably epic. Tell me, Princess, was the battle glorious?"

"They say that Caoránach cleaved the Summer Isles from the cliffs with his struggle, and that Fiona's cries cracked the very earth."

Juliana's eyes gleamed. "What happened to her? After the fight?"

Serena glided backwards, pushing through the water. "No one knows. Some say she flung herself from the cliffs to join her beloved in death, others that she flayed the knight alive before vanishing from Faerie. Some say her love was so strong that she became an oilliphéist herself, and swam away, never to return." She paused in the story, gaze drifting out the thin, blue horizon. "They say you can still hear her voice during the storm, begging them to stop."

Hawthorn's skin prickled. "Slightly morbid."

"I think it's beautiful—a love so strong it shaped the world."

"I still prefer happy endings," he said, stopping short of pouting. "Also, I find myself famished. Shall we return to the shore?"

Another feast was arranged for the evening; fried scallops, seaweed bread, oysters on golden plates, pastries stuffed with crabs, buttery haddock stews—all accompanied by fine music and bards that spoke of storms and monsters, lost loves and sun-kissed shores.

Juliana was decked out in another gown, a diaphanous, lavender creation that made her look soft and lovely. He was surprised no one had told her it was unfair to look like that next to Princess Serena. She was, of course, quite lovely too—amber wrapped in silk. But she didn't have that strange, steely fire in her that Juliana possessed.

She's pretty enough to pass for fae, her father had said of her once.

She was more than pretty now. Her beauty was as deadly as her skill with a knife.

When the dancing began, he was careful to give her a wide berth, dancing the first three with Serena and then excusing himself for refreshment. When he returned, Serena had vanished.

He couldn't see Jules anywhere, either.

Curious, he stopped a passing servant and asked her if she'd seen either. She pointed to a nearby alcove, a small silver enclosure stuffed with purple cushions. Serena and Juliana were reclined inside it, eating tiny slices of sugared fruit.

They did not appear to have noticed him.

"So tell me," Serena asked, topping up Juliana's goblet. "What kind of person is he, really?"

Hawthorn paused. He knew he should walk away or announce his presence, but it occurred to him that this might be a good opportunity to learn what kind of person *Serena* was—who she was when she wasn't with him. He didn't want another Lucinda.

And, if he was honest, he was curious how Juliana would answer.

To begin with, she didn't. She stared at Serena with her mouth open, like she was working out some complicated problem.

"You must think me foolish," Serena continued. "What does it matter who he is, correct? If he is Prince of Faerie? Who would not give anything to be queen?"

Juliana was quiet again, staring at the bottom of her glass.

Speak, he begged her. *Please.*

"Us mortals have a saying," she said finally. "*'We're only human.'* There seems to be no Faerie equivalent, but it's meant to say that we are capable of feeling, that we're *meant* to. I do not think you foolish. I think you are a creature capable of worry. And I understand why. The prince has a reputation. In his youth he was prone to cruelty."

Hawthorn's stomach dropped, a dozen hateful memories rushing back to haunt him, a hundred things he wished he'd done differently.

Especially with her.

"But he isn't that person anymore."

His heart lifted, ears hanging onto her every word.

"He can be insufferable, but he isn't unkind. He can be very thoughtful at times, though he tries to hide it. He has many redeemable qualities. I am not sure if he will 'honour' you, but... but the possibility is there."

Serena nodded, and Hawthorn, hearing all he needed to, silently slunk away.

Juliana found him on the balcony a short while later, staring out at the dark, ink-blue sea. The stars here seemed sharper than in the capital, the nebulous spray glittering in the quiet depths, like a mirror of diamonds.

"Did you mean what you told Serena?" he asked. "I overheard; don't be cross."

Juliana paused, her fingers brushing against the balustrade. She did not meet his eyes. "I did."

"You think I should marry her, don't you?"

"I think we ought to have something in place, and that she's a fine option."

"*A fine option*," he repeated, running his hands through his curls. "She isn't a meal, or a business proposition. She's a person. A person that I could be bound to—"

"It need not be forever. Faerie marriages seldom are."

He groaned. Faerie marriages could come with all sorts of stipulations and recompenses should the couple ever decide to break their vows. He could not imagine her mothers agreeing to the match without some sacrifice on his part, some promise of decades. It ought not to feel like a long time when he'd have close to forever, but he was seventeen and decades felt like centuries to him.

Juliana wouldn't be around for that long, although he knew that shouldn't factor into anything.

"She *is* nice," he admitted, with some reluctance. "I'm just not sure she's my type."

"You have a type?" Juliana turned around, leaning against the balustrade a little too casually. "Other than 'attractive' and 'there'?"

"I am not particularly fussy with who I bring to my bedchamber, it's true... but for a partner, a *queen*..." He shook his head, unable to speak it.

Juliana stared at the floor. "You've never had any long-term lovers, have you?"

"I have not."

"Never found anyone who can stomach you for that long?"

"Partly. But I am starting to understand that I do, in fact, have a certain type that it would be somewhat hard for most to measure up to."

"Are you going to share?"

"I am not," he said shortly, aware of what or who his list of desirable traits would sound like. "What of you? You've never taken on a lover for any length of time, as far as I'm aware."

"Your Highness keeps me far too busy."

"You have time enough for a dalliance, I'm sure."

"Maybe," she said, playing with her necklace of berries, "if I really wanted it."

"You do not?"

"There's other things I want more than companionship."

"Knighthood? Freedom? Adventure?"

"All of those things," she whispered, her gaze turning once more to the sea. "And more."

"And if you had them? What sort of person would accompany you? Some broad-shouldered knight, loyal, brave and true?"

"Not qualities to be sniffed at," she added, pursing her lips, "but, well, I'd rather like someone intelligent. Someone... someone I could speak to. Someone who can make me laugh."

"Is your mouth even capable of such an action?"

She glared at him. "You *know* it is."

"I know it's hard to earn."

He remembered the sound of her laughter like one remembered a fine drink they'd had one summer and never quite forgotten the taste or found its like again.

Juliana's cheeks flushed. "I don't often find much worth laughing at."

"Even with me?"

"Oh, you I laugh at all the time."

At this, he snorted. She half-laughed too. "You did not have much laughter during your childhood," he remarked, "and I apologise for any part I might have played in that."

Juliana blinked at him as if he'd suddenly grown antlers. In fact, she might have looked less surprised if he had. "You are not to blame for my troubles," she told him.

"Who is, then?"

To this, Juliana would not respond. "We should go back inside," she told him. "It's growing cold. Wouldn't want you to catch a chill, or anything, being so newly-recovered."

Now did not seem like the time to remind her that Faeries were immune to such things. For once, she did not sound like she was teasing. She almost sounded concerned, and he didn't know why the thought reached him so, soft as the brush of a feather. He wanted to say something else, to stay with her there a little longer, but before he could find the words, she moved back towards the party, and he knew the moment had whispered away from them.

A few days later, having come to an agreement with Serena and her mothers, the royal party departed for the capital. All the softness he'd experienced with Jules during the trip departed also. He'd thought something had changed between them, but nothing had. She snapped back to her usual ambitious, prickly self, as if the past two weeks hadn't happened at all.

Eventually, he convinced himself they hadn't either, that whatever stirrings of something he might have felt was just some side-effect of the fever, induced by delirium.

Most of the time, it worked.

But Jules entered his dreams in ways she never had before, and as much as he tried to ignore it, as much as he knew she didn't feel the same, and that nothing had *really* changed between them, he knew that *he* had.

A lifetime affliction.

34. THE WITCH RETURNS

Someone was screaming Juliana's name, but the voice kept disappearing, snapping off mid-syllable, only to rise again, fog-like and indistinct. She knew she should clutch at that voice, *wanted* to clutch at it, but her limbs had turned to lead.

Get up, said a voice inside. *Move.*
I can't.
It was too hot, too cold, too hard. Consciousness felt like syrup.
"Jules!"
Come back, don't leave me, stay, I'm coming, I'm going, I'm lost, I'm nowhere. Nowhere, nowhere, nowhere.

Time was stripped away, minutes and hours mashed to meaninglessness. She no longer knew where she was or who she was with. Fragments of pain spilled against her.

She thought she might be moving, but she wasn't sure. She thought someone might be pulling off her clothes, examining her wound, but she wasn't sure of that, either.

She was only sure that sometimes, sometimes there was a warmth beside her, a pressure, a light, something touching her that she wanted to touch back.

Stay with me, she wanted to say, but she couldn't.

She couldn't do anything at all.

When Juliana at last returned to consciousness, she was warm and dry, lying on a bunk in a hut so cluttered with objects—both mundane and arcane—that you could barely see the floors or walls or windows. Plants hung from the ceiling or lined the shelves, leaves in every hue of green, spiky, spindly, long, short, fat, thin. Books were piled everywhere, crammed into bookcases or stacked so tall they were used as side tables. Surfaces dripped with wax, and everywhere else was stuffed with jars—bits of bone, shrivelled herbs, withered organs that looked suspiciously like hearts.

She bolted upright at the sight, making pain split through her side. She winced and fell back to the rough canvas mattress, piled high with furs.

"Steady now," said a voice beside the roaring fire. "You're out of the woods, but you still went through them. You'll be sore for a little while yet."

Juliana angled her head towards the voice, and found herself face to face with a wrinkled old woman.

"You," she said, as her features slotted into her memory, "the witch from the market. Mabel, wasn't it?"

"My friends call me Mab," she said, cackling for some reason. "But Mabel will do just fine. How are you feeling, dearie?"

Juliana pressed a hand to her middle. It was thickly bandaged, skin and muscles tight behind it. Her head felt light and woozy. "How long have I been out?"

The witch shrugged. "A couple of days. That prince of yours was most distressed."

"That... wait." She paused, gathering her thoughts. "How did you find me? How do you know about him? Is he here—"

"Steady, steady," said the witch, coming forward to offer her a bowl of piping hot stew. Juliana dug in hungrily, not caring if it was laced with something. She was ravenous. "Your prince is still condemned to a dream world. Luckily for you both, I've some experience with the place, and can sense when others are in it... at least when they're as loud as your prince fellow. Good grief. There I was, idly out picking herbs, when he came shrieking into the glade a couple of days ago, demanding my assistance. Had to trek up a mountain to find you, girlie."

Juliana swallowed down a lump of potato. She could not imagine the witch hadn't demanded some sort of payment. "What did you get for your troubles?"

"A favour," she said, "unspecified, to be extracted whenever I see fit."

Juliana gritted her teeth. It was dangerous to make that kind of promise, especially with a witch.

"I did specify it would not be that which he could not bear to part with," said Mabel hastily. "I'll not be asking for his firstborn child or the heart of his true love, you'll be happy to hear."

That was not a great deal of comfort. There was still plenty of damage a promise like that could do.

"Is he... is he here now?" she asked.

The witch shook her head. "He came in and out whilst you were out of it, but I haven't sensed him in a while."

"I should..." Juliana swung her legs out of the bed. "I should get moving again."

Mabel shoved her back into the bed. "You'll do no such thing. Even with my magic, you'll need at least another day to recover."

"I can't afford any more delays—"

"You're outside the borders of the Whispering Woods," Mabel informed her. "Two or three days away from the capital. A week away if you leave in this state. You'll be crawling there. Don't see you taking on Ladrien's forces like that, do you?"

Juliana blanched. She'd taken out most of the army, but there were doubtless still plenty inside Acanthia. Would he divert the avalanche survivors back there, with his mortal invasion on hold?

"Why are you so eager to reach the castle?" Mabel asked.

Juliana paused. "My knighthood."

The old lady shook her head. "I feel sorry for that poor princeling of yours, to be saddled with such a liar..."

"It's not a lie!"

"You keep telling yourself that, dearie. Won't make it any more true. Eat up."

Juliana drained the dregs of the bowl, examining the rest of her body. She could move, despite the hot, dense pain in her middle, but her limbs were tired and weak. She hoped Mabel had some serious potions to bolster her strength, and wondered if they'd been included in the bargain she'd made with Hawthorn, or if Juliana would have to trade with her herself.

Her fingers skimmed against the pendant, still resting against her chest, cool and smooth.

"This charm you made for us…" she started, only half-sure of her words. "It's what allows us to speak to one another?"

The witch nodded. "A rather useful side-effect I did not foresee."

"Does… does it do anything else?"

"Like what?"

"It's supposed to connect us, right? To allow us to find one another. But is there any chance it could have created another kind of connection?"

The witch raised an eyebrow. "Like what?"

Juliana's chest felt tight, her breath stilted. "He's definitely not here?"

Mabel shook her head.

"I feel… different towards him," she admitted, each word painful. "I hate it when he's not here and I'm terrified I won't be able to save him but I'm terrified of succeeding, too because I don't want to watch him marry Serena when I…" She looked up at Mabel imploringly. "Please, tell me that it's just another side effect, that I don't feel this way, that it's all a result of this stupid pendant…"

Mabel regarded her stonily from her seat. "If you thought that, why haven't you taken it off?"

Juliana paused. "Because I want him to find me," she whispered. "I want it. I want… I want *him*." Sobs banged against her chest. "I need the connection to be something I can break when this is over, something I can control—something that can't break *me*." She sniffed into her shirt. "Please," she whispered. "Tell me it's the pendants. Tell me I don't feel anything for him. Because I can't. I can't—"

Mabel sighed, patting her shoulder. "The pendants can't have forced affection on you, child. Indeed, I suspect the dreams are caused by a connection that was already there. What you feel is real, and should not be feared."

But I can fear being without him. I can fear what will happen when this is all over.

A hard lump snagged at Juliana's throat, a weight against her chest both tightening and lifting. This was what she was afraid of, and at the same time… a part of her welcomed it. A part of her knew it couldn't be anything else. These feelings hadn't sprung up in the last few weeks. They'd been there for a long, long while, no matter how much she'd tried to bury them.

Tears started to fall—for Hawthorn, for Dillon, for this situation, she wasn't sure. Silent, guttural sobs, as hard and unstoppable as the avalanche had been.

"Rest, child," Mabel suggested, handing her another vial. "The world is not yet hopeless."

When Juliana woke, darkness had fallen over the little hut. Mabel sat in the chair by the fire, knitting. She did not appear to hear her when she called out.

Someone was stroking Juliana's face, their touch feather-soft. "Hey," Hawthorn said, when her eyes met his. He was crouched on the floor beside her, the rest of the bed being taken up by her sleeping form behind her. It ought to have been weird, but she was too tired to care. "I hope you don't mind me sneaking in here. I haven't been watching you all day, I promise. Just leaning in every now and again to check in on you."

"You weren't here earlier," she said. "Mabel said she could sense you."

He nodded. "Quite useful, that witch."

"She said you made a bargain with her."

His thumb brushed her cheek. "I didn't have a choice."

That shouldn't have been true, but Juliana didn't press it. "No more making bargains with witches for my sake."

"No such promises," he said, still smiling at her. "Besides, you made one for my sake first."

"What makes you think it was for you and not my knighthood?"

He snorted. "A faerie answer if there ever was one, you delicious liar." All traces of smiles dropped away. "I went back to the mountainside," he said, "while you were resting. I found Dillon. I buried him."

A knot in Juliana's chest heaved and then loosened. It was a small but important comfort to know that his earthly remains no longer sat upon the lonely snow, waiting to be picked at.

"Thank you," she breathed. And then, "How?"

"How what?"

"How did you bury his body when you can't..."

"Touch anything?" He smirked, but she could see him trying to contain it, to seem less pleased than he was. He raised his hands and flicked his wrists, making the branches outside shake against the window. The old witch startled in her chair, but then carried on knitting.

"I've been practising," he told her. "Little else to do. Hoped that maybe I could try and get a message to Miriam if I mastered it, or even tug Serena up the stairs myself... but no such luck yet. Did manage to free the horses, though. Cercis was making a frightful racket."

"That's actually quite smart." *And kind, too.*

"I did pay attention in *some* of our lessons, you know."

"Oh? Which ones?"

Hawthorn pursed his lips, as if trying to resist the impulse to answer. "The ones you were merely mediocre at," he admitted. "I found myself too overwhelmed with jealousy in the classes you excelled in... and too boastful in the ones you didn't." He paused again, harder than before. "I don't think I ever apologised for—"

"You don't have to. I gave as good as I got."

"I had power, and you had none," he continued. "It was inexcusable for me to treat you as I did, and quite honestly, I'm surprised you agreed to be my guard." He swallowed. "I wasn't particularly good to you in those early days, either. I deserve no praise for 'not being as bad as I was' but... I hope, in your eyes at least, I have improved."

Juliana swallowed, because of course he had, and it shocked her to realise that he didn't know it, or needed to hear her say it. "Immeasurably."

Hawthorn looked decidedly more pleased at this than he did his command over the trees.

"And I?" she asked him.

"You what?"

"Have I improved, in your estimation? Or am I still the same lying, filthy mortal I once was?"

"You *know* I don't think that," he said, coming closer. "You know I have nothing but the highest admiration for you. Annoyingly high, actually. Frustratingly. *Distractingly.* Every day, I am more and more impressed by you and..."

"And?"

His hands returned to her side, skimming against the blackthorn ring she'd threaded next to her pendant, now lying on the mattress beside her. "Why are you wearing this?" he asked her.

"Why did you give it to me?"

"I suppose I wanted you to have something of mine," he admitted.

"Then I suppose I wanted something to keep you close."

At this stark confession, his eyes widened, as if certain he'd misheard. He bent his head towards her, breath brushing her face. "I'd really like to kiss you again now."

Juliana's throat tightened. No longer could she convince herself that it was a side-effect of the pendants, that some other force drew them together... and even though she knew that it would hurt, that she was sharpening a sword destined for her own chest... she no longer cared to resist.

Her fingers unfurled around his face, tugging him gently towards her, his dark lashes fanning shut. "Just a kiss?" she questioned.

Hawthorn paused, eyes flickering open. "If you wish it."

Juliana closed the gap between them, conscious in a heady, light-headed way of the chappedness of her lips next to the smoothness of his, but hardly caring. His mouth pressed hers, soft, sweet, hard, lingering against her like the first sip of wine.

It was never going to be just a kiss, and despite the bruised form of her body, her insides ached for him.

"Hawthorn?"

"Yes?"

A silly request. A foolish one. It wasn't like he had anywhere else to be, and besides, she wouldn't be able to feel him when she was asleep anyway—

And yet, as much as she loathed to admit it, she wanted him there. Wanted it with a pain that felt like need, like his presence was sustenance she fed from.

"Will you stay?" she asked. "Even after... even after I fall asleep?"

Hawthorn brushed back her hair. "I would stay with you forever, if you wished it."

A strange statement. Perhaps she'd misheard, or there was some lie in it she couldn't quite decipher. She was tired, after all, so tired...

She'd deconstruct it in the morning, when her wounds were healed, when she wasn't so woozy, when the world made sense again.

In the meantime, words blossomed on her tongue, unbidden. "I do wish it," she told him. "That's rather the problem, really."

The next day, plied with potions and with nothing else to do but rest, Juliana picked up Hawthorn's notebook and read. Luckily, the witch had brought Juliana's belongings with her.

And Dillon's, which would have to be returned to his father in time.

Juliana couldn't bring herself to look through his pack, too afraid of the *nothingness* that it would contain, the supplies and equipment that contained nothing of who *Dillon* was.

She shelved the rawness in her chest, refusing to give weight to it. If she fell apart now, it might drag her under.

She focused on the notebook instead. It was better than dwelling on the pain, on her grief, on the slow, restless task of healing, a monster of necessity and one she could not fight.

"You're sure Hawthorn isn't here?" she asked, fingers tracing the pages.

"Sure," the witch replied. "He disappeared just after you woke up."

Juliana's chest heated with the thought of his proximity beside her all night long. She hoped she hadn't done anything embarrassing like whisper his name in her sleep. It would be hard to find a lie to cover that one up.

The witch returned to watering her plants. There were a few blood-red ones she seemed particularly fond of, examining their leaves and humming to them as she watered.

"What do those ones do?" Juliana asked, almost reluctant now to read.

"They're curse-catchers," Mabel explained. "Designed to wither and die in place of myself if someone tries to put a curse on me."

Juliana counted them. She had almost a dozen. "You have a lot of enemies?"

Mabel shrugged. "I did, once. Never grew out of the habit." She pointed to a bigger one, larger than any of the others and so old that the pot was now held together with thick, gnarled roots. "Now if *that* one ever starts to wilt, I'll know I'm in trouble."

"It looks ancient."

"So am I."

Juliana frowned, but didn't press it. Witches might live longer than mortals, but they never grew ancient by faerie standards.

Mabel turned back to her other plants, and Juliana finally cracked open the notebook. She flicked through insults, some scribbled out and some so over-the-top she couldn't even try to decipher his meaning.

After far too many pages of this and a few more entries of no matter, her eyes came across a longer entry dated almost a year after she'd started her service.

> When Juliana doesn't scowl her eyes are actually really pretty. I've heard it said that mortals' eyes are plain and boring—that they mimic the skies, the earth, the grass—devoid of the multitude of colours that sing within the eyes of the fae.

> Jules' eyes are forest-green and full of fire and yet sometimes, when she's petting her horse or staring out the window or biting back a smile, they're as soft as meadows.
>
> I hate that I've noticed that. I may need to seal this notebook with magic.
>
> Or maybe burn it.

Juliana paused in her reading, the thought both warming and delighting her. Regardless of the witch's insistence that their feelings weren't conjured by the pendants, a part of Juliana had still doubted this. But Hawthorn had made this entry over two years ago.

Two years. Had he felt something for so long? Did he *still* feel it? If last night's kiss was anything to go by—

It doesn't matter if he does, she reminded herself. *He's still not yours to fall for.*

But it was nice, just for a moment, to indulge the sensation.

She moved through the rest of the pages, indulging in similar entries, comments about her hair, her walk, the way she sliced her apples or her eyes lit up at the delicacies placed in front of her. A tally of the number of times she'd smiled. How had he noticed all this about her over the years? Why did he even care?

Why did every other page offer up insults?

Towards the end of the available extracts were a few pages of appalling poetry, mostly scribbled out or reduced to a few clumsy lines.

He was a smooth talker, but he was no poet.

But there was a short limerick she rather enjoyed.

My lady walks with beauty,
My lady walks with grace,
But if she ever saw these words,
She'd stab me in the face.

Juliana snorted with laughter.

"Something amusing?" remarked Mabel.

"Nothing I care to share."

The witch came over and checked her wound, liberally applying more cream and forcing more potion down her throat in an effort to speed up her healing. It made her groggy, and it became difficult to read after that.

"Will I owe you? For the potions?"

Mabel shook her head. "I'll take it out of your prince's payment... unless you want to take on his favour for him?"

Juliana bit her lip, because the truth was, she *would* take it. And not out of some sense of debt, or because it was less dangerous for the witch to hold a favour from her. She'd take it purely to keep him safe.

"I doubt you'd want a favour from me."

Mabel smiled, her aged cheeks crinkling like paper. "I don't know. A favour from you might hold similar weight... one day."

Juliana's thoughts muddled. She wasn't quite sure what that meant, but before she could collect her words into some semblance of order, a fresh bowl of steaming stew was pressed into her lap.

"Eat," the witch instructed. "You can be out of here in another day if you get your strength up."

Juliana did what she was told, but she hated every minute of it. She hadn't been bed-bound since she was a child. The blankets might well have been chains. Hawthorn had been a poor patient when he was sick with faerie fever, but she was fairly sure she would have been worse.

Hawthorn.

From time-to-time, she thought she felt someone's eyes on her, but she couldn't give weight to that feeling. At one point, one of Mabel's wards went off outside, but nothing seemed to have been disturbed but a few branches snapped over in the wind.

He was practising, Juliana realised. He was growing stronger while she couldn't.

Night came, and with it, Hawthorn. Juliana had spent most of the day dozing under the influence of the witch's brew, recovering her strength and trying not to die of boredom. When she finally lay down to sleep, a strange giddiness plagued her insides. She *wanted* to sleep. Longed for it.

But not for rest.

She wanted to see him.

Thank the stars he could not read minds, and for the shield her lies offered her.

"Miss me?" Hawthorn grinned at her from the floor, looking something a little like an energetic puppy.

She groaned, largely out of habit. "You wish. It's been lovely and quiet."

He rolled over, folding his arms underneath his chin on the mattress, inches away from her face. The endless smirking continued. "You're lying."

"Maybe."

"I refuse to believe I'm not better company than the mean old witch."

Mabel, who'd been snoring by the fire, startled in her sleep, as if she knew she'd just been insulted.

"She can't hear us," Hawthorn reminded her, sensing Juliana's thoughts. "More... she can just sense us. I had to use branches to gain her attention before."

He paused for a moment, reaching out to stroke a loose lock from her face, and then pulled his hand back suddenly, like the action was too intimate now she was so lucid.

I kissed him, she remembered. *I let him kiss me.*

I want to do it again.

She swallowed, biting back her impulses.

"So, how was your day?" Hawthorn asked brightly.

Juliana scowled.

"Right, yes, trapped in a bed with just a mean old witch for company, silly question." He waited a moment. "How do you feel?"

"Like I'd like to get out and go murder something."

"Ha!" Hawthorn laughed. "That certainly sounds like my dear guard." His eyes fell over her form, drifting down to her middle. "Does it hurt?"

"A bit."

"You can tell me."

"It won't change anything."

"Right," he said, "of course." He rolled away again, staring into the embers of the fire. The wind howled outside, making the branches scrap against the windows.

"*I've* had a fascinating day in the library, making pages move with my powers. Read some stuff about the oilliphéist and the beginning of the Unseelie Court."

There was something wrong about that statement, something she couldn't put her finger on, but the niggling feeling of uncertainty was glossed over next to his words. "The off-east what?"

"*Oilliphéist,*" Hawthorn repeated exasperatedly, with the kind of perfect diction found only among the ruling classes. "Giant sea-monster? We saw the bones of the last one at the Summer Court—"

"Oh, was *that* what it was called?" Juliana said. "I wasn't paying too much attention. My brain was still screaming 'snake!' at that point."

Hawthorn chuckled.

"Why were you reading about the oilliphéist?"

"Uncertain. It was in a book about the Unseelie, though. I'd never questioned the two courts that much growing up, you know? I'd just accepted that that was the way things had always been—Seelie and Unseelie since the dawn of time."

"It wasn't?"

He shook his head. "There was just one court at first—the Faerie Court, ruled over by Titania and her husband Oberon. There was some faerie rebellion led by a courtier called Maeve—"

Juliana had heard parts of this, but the story was so old that even faeries had trouble deciding what precisely had happened.

"Anyway, a bunch of creatures were rounded up as having sympathised with Maeve, and they were branded 'Unseelie' and exiled from Acanthia. There've been some tentative alliances over the years, but not many, and never for long by faerie means."

Like before Ladrien cursed you.

Before Hawthorn's name day, the Seelie had lived in relative peace with their Unseelie brethren, though tentative and uneasy. Most would not be seen within its walls, but they were not forbidden. Some—like Owen's wife, for example—had been embraced.

But not many.

"What else did you read about?" she asked.

"Teleportation, mainly."

"Teleportation? Why?"

"Because, as far as I can tell, no one can just *vanish*. They transform, or they open a portal. Both are very tricky magic. Even my own mother struggles with it. Ladrien is, of course, supposed to be very old, but even he shouldn't be capable of bending the laws like that."

"Is it possible he's stolen the magic from someone else?" Juliana knew such a thing was possible—only a few very powerful fae were capable of it, but she'd heard stories, and once even seen it. Maytree had done it to a faerie accused of treason. Juliana had only been eight, forbidden both by Iona and her father from attending the trial, but she'd snuck in through the servants' quarters. She thought, like most magic, it would be quick, beautiful to watch.

It wasn't either, and the faerie had screamed like Maytree was cutting her out of her skin.

Hawthorn shook his head. "No. I've no doubt he's stolen magic before, but he still shouldn't be able to do that. I can't explain it."

Juliana wished she had the energy to offer up an explanation or even just to think, but the words once more turned slippery on her tongue. She let out a yawn.

"Sorry," said Hawthorn, "I know you're tired, and I'm just here wittering on about nothing."

Juliana pinched the back of his collar, tugging lightly, drawing him ever-so-slightly towards her. "I don't mind," she said. "I imagine your day has been a little boring without me to bother."

Hawthorn leaned further against the bed. "Do I really bother you?"

"Not today," she whispered. "Not *most* days, actually. Not really." She yanked back on his collar. "Don't tell anyone!"

Hawthorn laughed. "I'm the only person that needs to know that anyway. Sleep, Juliana. I have time to bother you yet."

But not much, she realised. Soon she'd need to resume her journey. Soon she'd be at the palace. Soon, one way or another, they would run out of time.

She fell asleep gripping the back of his shirt, as if she had the power to hold him there.

35. THE VALLEY OF MEMORiES

The next day, Juliana was released from her bed and set a few tasks to build up her strength. She had no objection to the tasks in principle—indeed, she welcomed the chance to test her mobility—but she did object to how thoroughly *bad* she was at most tasks, especially laundry. She hadn't had to do her own for three years, and it really showed.

She was better at chopping wood, even if her side still stung. She hated how weak her muscles had become in just a few days, like she'd borrowed someone else's body.

"Your strength will return," Mabel assured her, without Juliana having to mention a single thing. Swinging the axe into the nearby stump had apparently been communicating her frustration as perfectly as words. "You could be dead, you know. Or laid up for weeks. Most mortals would be without a bit of magic."

She spoke as if she wasn't one of them, or perhaps she'd just been a witch so long she'd forgotten what mortality was like.

Then again, Juliana didn't always count herself as fully mortal either. She'd grown up too close to faerie, caught it like a childhood illness she'd never fully shaken.

Or maybe it was Hawthorn who'd infected her.

She tried to shake the thought away, and battled through her list of tasks. Something else was bothering her, separate from her wound and her ineptitude. It wasn't until later in the day she realised what it was.

If Hawthorn had spent all of yesterday in the library, who had set off Mabel's wards?

If he hadn't been there, who had she felt was watching her?

She shared her concerns with the witch, but she merely shrugged. "If anyone was wishing us ill, they'd be dead," she assured her.

Juliana was not fully convinced.

Finally, she slunk exhausted into bed, her pack all ready for the journey home.

Hawthorn was there when she woke again.

"All set?" he asked.

"You know I am. How's the capital looking?"

"Ladrien's forces are still prowling it, but they've not found any of the mortals. Miriam has hidden them well."

"Do you think they're still there?"

He nodded, twirling his fingers, itching for the blackthorn ring he no longer wore. "I can sense them."

"I would have thought Miriam would have quit the place once Serena appeared."

"Maybe she knows something we don't. Or maybe she's just a stubborn mortal who refuses to give up even when she's lost. Perhaps you have more experience in that regard than I do..."

"You're so funny."

"You know, I rather am. I wouldn't be able to say it if it wasn't true."

"You wouldn't be able to say it if you *thought* it wasn't true," Juliana insisted.

"You try saying it then."

"I can lie."

"You can. And sometimes well. But not about things like that." He poked her middle. "Juliana, tell me I'm funny."

"You're *hilarious*," she told him, gritting her teeth.

"Tell me I'm pretty—"

"You're very pretty, Haw—"

His mouth slammed against hers, cutting her off. His fingers tangled into the bedclothes as he arched over her, mouth hard, lips silken. Her hands slid to his neck, stunned into softness.

Hawthorn pulled back, sliding off her. "Sorry," he said. "Got—carried away. Wanted to... never mind."

He climbed to his feet, and she had the strongest sense that he was going to vanish.

"Hawthorn—" she called out, grabbing his wrist.

He turned around, hope lingering in his features. "Yes?"

She hated the way she could make him look like that... hated it, and longed for it. "Tomorrow, when I resume my journey... would you come with me?"

A smile ghosted his cheeks. "I'll be here at sunrise."

He blinked away, vanishing into a dream.

Juliana sighed. That wasn't quite what she wanted to tell him. But what *did* she want to tell him? What was there to tell?

So much. So much, and nothing at all.

She sighed, lying back down and staring up at the ceiling. She wished she could blink out like he did, blink away to sleep, to nothingness. Of course, he couldn't do that, either. He'd just gone back to the castle. What was he thinking there, alone in the dark?

She thought about trying to follow him, but her courage thinned by the second. Never mind how much they needed to talk; she was far from skilled with words. Why wasn't *he* saying anything?

Tomorrow, she promised herself. *Tomorrow night, we'll talk.*

At first light, her pack brimming with potions and food from the witch, Juliana set off into the forest.

"I'd thank you," she told Mabel at the door, "but..."

"You have no debt with me, child. Be on your way. Take care. I'll likely not get that favour from your prince if you fail."

She'd certainly have to wait a long time for it otherwise, and if Ladrien took over, there would likely be little Hawthorn could offer her.

Juliana tried not to think too much about what Mabel wanted. It wasn't worth worrying about today, not with an army between her and her prize.

He isn't a prize, a voice reminded her.

I meant my knighthood! she shot back.

Mabel's words taunted her above the own voice in her head, telling her she was sorry for Hawthorn to be saddled with such a liar.

It was easier to battle with her thoughts than to think about the challenges that awaited her, or to fall back into thinking about Dillon, although he was still there in the back of her mind. He would be for some time yet.

He deserves to be.

She walked onwards, taking him with her.

The sparse trees soon gave way to deep crimsons, and Juliana realised she'd strayed into the Redwood, the largest of the forests in Autumn. She knew it well, her old hut being nestled on the borders of it. The Autumn Court wasn't far away, not that she had any inclination to visit it. The temptation to go spit on Lucinda's sleeping form was mildly tempting, however, which she announced to the air, hoping Hawthorn was listening. The trees rustled in response, and she smiled.

"You know," she said breezily, "I think you make a much better travelling companion this way. Much more agreeable when you're silent."

The trees rustled harder.

She shook her head, scrambling over a fallen tree and ducking under a low branch. A path opened up shortly afterwards. "I'm starting to understand why you feel the need to fill the silence all the time. No, that is *not* me saying I miss the sound of your voice."

Even if she did. He didn't have to know that.

The trees seemed to cackle.

Onwards she walked, Juliana filling the silence every so often by remarking on the different flora and fauna, or the pleasant weather, or some old memory she had of this particular part of the wood. "Took down a direwolf, there." "Fought my first bear in that glade." "Nearly froze to death in that lake after I fell in while fishing."

She avoided talking about any memory that took her too close to her father.

It occurred to Juliana that the hut she'd shared with him was on the route back, and it would be sensible to stop there for the night, regardless of how much the thought pained her. He had tarnished the walls with his betrayal. She didn't think she'd reach it by tonight; her side was giving her more grief than she cared to admit and the terrain was far from easy.

Something snapped behind her.

Juliana wheeled round, not drawing her sword. The woods were filled with noises. No one was close by. Any number of critters could have caused the noise, and yet—

There was something *heavy* about the sound, not easily dispelled or attributed to a small, light-footed creature.

She could ask Hawthorn to check, of course, but she didn't want him to think she was paranoid.

She moved onwards, deeper into the woods, the sun turning the blood-red leaves orange and gold in the fading light. She quickened her gait, knowing what was ahead of her—and still not entirely convinced she wasn't being followed—but an hour later, she slowed down again. The sun had almost set, she was losing light, and there was no point trying to make it through the valley before nightfall.

Between the Redwood and her old home was a rocky valley that seemed completely benign in the daylight. Only when the moonlight reached it did it become something else. The Valley of Memories, a place that conjured perfect illusions of memories, both good and ill—although it tended to be the latter.

The ones you'd rather forget.

Her father had taken her there for training a few times before, although he'd never entered it with her after dark. He'd pointed out the bones of the people driven mad there, lost to their memories, their dreams of yesterday so potent that they'd starved waiting for them to return.

There were all sorts of stories about how the valley came to be—stories of grief-stricken faeries searching for a way to see their loved ones again, or vengeful spirits who'd never passed over, or that it was the graveyard of an ancient and powerful race, or even that it simply *was*. A thing that had always been, old as magic itself.

Juliana didn't need to know the story. She just needed to know to avoid it.

She set up camp before the entrance, trying to enjoy the sunset, ignoring the dark chill creeping into her bones and the strange, wriggling sensation that she was being watched. She ate some of the food Mabel had given her and sipped at a potion that would help her sleep.

She debated not using it. She didn't want to be defenceless. But she had been informed the potion was also a restorative, and she had no desire to sit in silence any longer. Besides, she or Hawthorn could watch her sleeping form.

She drifted off to sleep.

Hawthorn was right beside her when she woke.

"Evening," he said, staring up at the sky. "It's a beautiful night."

Juliana stared up at the sky. She could make out little but the inky blackness and a fragile handful of stars, the moon hidden behind a cluster of trees. "Describe it to me," she said.

"I'm no astrologer," he admitted, "or a poet."

"So I noted," she said, grinning.

Hawthorn paused, as if unsure of her meaning, before his eyes widened with realisation. "You read my notebook."

"Haven't quite finished it," she admitted, "although I think I've committed one of your poems to memory. How did it go again? *My lady walks with beauty—*"

"Please don't," he said, covering his face with his long-fingered hands. "Unless you plan to stab me afterwards."

"And prove you correct? No chance."

He shook his head. "I am entirely unused to you laughing and I really wish I wasn't the target of it."

"Don't be embarrassed. I liked it. It made me laugh. Quite the feat."

Hawthorn dropped his hands and lay back against a nearby log. "Yes, I think that might only be the sixth time I've heard you laugh."

"You've actually been counting?"

"I have," he said. "The first time was when I tried to charge Count Ulfred and ended up falling flat on my face in the mud. Don't think I didn't notice that."

"I'm surprised you noticed anything, with all that mud…"

Hawthorn smiled, listing the rest, little moments she'd long since forgotten that he'd clung to, folded away like a summer flower in a scrapbook. "And that's number six," he said, his voice oddly whispery as his hand brushed her cheek. "That smile…"

"What about it?"

"It's as much of a weapon as that blade of yours. I feel like it cuts a bit of me away every time you use it."

Juliana startled, stunned once more by the intensity of his words. She remembered her decision earlier to talk to him—to *actually* talk, before any of this went too far—but she couldn't quite remember what she wanted to say, or even if she meant to stop him.

Hawthorn tilted his head. "Have I alarmed you?"

"No," she said quickly, and then sighed. "Yes." Her fingers tied themselves in knots as she struggled with the words. She felt she'd rather break them than speak, that that was likely to happen far before the words formed.

Hawthorn put a hand over hers, stilling them instantly. "Take as long as you need," he told her. "But do not worry yourself on my account. If that's a concern."

"You are," she said, barely breathing. "You *are* a concern of mine. Not... not in a 'you constantly irk me' way, either... although you do do that. A lot. I mean... what I mean to say is that... *spirits.*" She yanked her hands back, curling her fingers into fists and hitting her head.

"My, my, Jules, you sound almost nervous..."

"Oh, shut up, I—"

Something rustled in the bushes behind her. Hawthorn stiffened, eyes widening. She turned her head, but she could make out nothing in the gloom.

"Can you see something?"

"Someone," he said, "Human, I think. They're heading towards the valley."

Juliana stilled. Few would be so foolish, but maybe the person was injured and not thinking straight, or a human that had walked across the border and didn't know any better.

"We should stop them," Juliana announced. "If I wake myself up—"

"Too late," Hawthorn announced. He climbed to his feet. "They've almost reached the entrance. I'll go after them and I'll see if I can block up the path with my powers, or spook them out enough that they turn back."

Juliana nodded. "I'll come with you."

"Oh, I was so hoping you would say that. My powers have really grown some. It's impressive. Dashing, even."

Juliana groaned. "We won't be affected by the valley ourselves, will we?" The last thing she needed was for her memories to start spouting out in front of him.

Hawthorn shrugged. "Seems doubtful, in this state, but we'll see. Quickly, now, before we lose him."

He held out his hand, fingers inching towards hers. He looked at her expectantly. "So we don't get lost."

Juliana doubted that was the only reason, but she didn't complain. Partly because the trees were so thick and dark here that they looked like shards of shadow, and partly because she enjoyed the feel of his hand in hers.

He probably enjoyed it more, alone in the sensationless dream all day. Maybe that was why he clung so tightly.

She clung tightly back.

They moved up the embankment to the narrow gap in the rocks that served as the entrance to the valley. A sharp, sudden path rolled ahead, silver in the moonlight. Mist covered the valley floor. In the daytime, it was all trees and streams, glassy ponds and lush growth, but under the veil of night, every tree turned to shadow, the mist swamped the plantlife, and the valley held all the pleasant wonder of a graveyard.

A figure moved through the swirling fog, darting along the path.

"There," said Hawthorn, following it.

Juliana allowed herself to be tugged forward, but the mist rose up, smothering the vestiges of light.

She heard a child laughing.

Not ominous at all.

A small girl stepped onto the path, two tiny light-brown plaits behind her rounded ears. A plump, jolly woman ran after her.

Iona.

Juliana knew this was her memory, that somehow they'd not been spared, but she couldn't quite place when it was.

Her father stepped out of the fog, face dark and grim. Iona paused in her chasing. "Ser Markham!" she cried out. "We weren't expecting you back until—where's Ser Cerridwen?"

Markham shook his head. "Gone," he said.

"Gone?" the colour drained from Iona's face. "You don't mean—"

"She left," he said. "She finally did it. She's gone to the mortal realm."

Iona's hands shook against her apron. Though the vision was a pale, translucent copy, Juliana could still make out the flour on her hands. "No," the woman replied, voice wavering. "No, she would never—Juliana. How do we—"

Hawthorn's fingers dug into hers.

"I don't want to see the next bit," she whispered.

She barely remembered it, barely remembered the moment she'd been told her mother wasn't coming home, because she knew the conversation had happened a dozen, a hundred times over. How do you explain such a thing to a child?

"When is Mama coming home?"

"Have you seen Mama today?"

"Where's Mama?"

"I want my mama! I want her, I want her, I want her!"

And although she had stopped her screaming eventually, Juliana was sure she'd never stopped wanting her to come home.

She paused on the path.

"Hawthorn, if we're seeing memories—maybe we shouldn't go in."

"We're dreams ourselves, Juliana," he answered. "What's the biggest danger? Our physical bodies can't be lured here."

Juliana wasn't so sure in the harmlessness, not when there was so much more she didn't want him to see.

The next memory was his, some moment of waiting outside his parents' door to be let in, only they never came. The vision faded before anyone noticed he was there.

Another laugh, another memory of hers, her father teaching her how to hold a sword while Hawthorn watched nearby. She was five years old. Markham swept her up in his broad arms as she practised her first steps, grinning from ear to ear.

He boasted to one of his friends nearby, and then Hawthorn threw mud at her face the minute Markham stepped away.

Adult Hawthorn cringed. "Sorry," he said. "For that, and... anything else."

Child Juliana threw her wooden sword at his face. "Same to you."

They moved through memory after memory, more training, more schooling, more pranks that no longer seemed funny. Hawthorn witnessed her crying over one that left her with blisters on her fingers. She saw him scream in the memory of waking up with his hair tied to the bedpost.

Years, years walked by.

There were good memories, too. Picnics and hikes, night-time strolls, dances.

More of her father being there.

More of his parents not.

I hate that I can't hate you, she whispered to her father's ghost. *I hate that I know you love me.*

Why, her entire life, was it so much easier to hate than love?

The memories caught up with her departure to Autumn, a hundred painful lessons interspersed with Hawthorn's. She saw each of the assassination attempts, the awful, wretched poisoning, Hawthorn writhing in bed, body breaking, drenched with sweat.

"Sorry," he said, when she turned her head away. "I should have warned you about that one."

I hope your mother killed whoever did that. I hope it hurt.

She witnessed her triumphant return to court, and her painful defeat at the hands of her own father. She watched Hawthorn watching her throughout the tournament, watched the crescent-marks he made in the armrest whenever she was in danger, his face cool and placid throughout.

She watched herself pledge her service to him.

"Oh good, one fine memory," Hawthorn said, smirking. "One of my favourites, in fact."

The scene swirled until they were being attacked on the way to Autumn.

"Another good one!"

Juliana frowned. "How is an assassination attempt a good memory?"

The vision landed on an image of the two of them curled up together in the hut. Hawthorn raised an eyebrow, still grinning. "Need I say more?"

She scowled, and he kissed the hand that still held his. She was fairly sure she blushed in response, which only made her scowl more.

Memories blurred together until they were at the Summer Court, and she was watching him fall. *No, no, not this again.*

"Yours or mine?" Hawthorn asked.

Juliana watched him on the bed, cheeks flushed, wheezing and gasping while she looked on like a piece of flotsam in the path of a shark. "Mine," she said. "Definitely mine."

Memory-Juliana watched as his body was encased in ice, and fled from the room—

Straight to Maytree's chambers.

She didn't knock, she didn't wait. She ducked under the guards, fighting them when they tried to stop her.

"Juliana!" Maytree rose from her seat, dismissing the guards with a wave of her hand. "What is the meaning of this—"

"You need to go to him," she rushed, half crying. "You need to go to him and just be there because I can't. I can't, I can't, I can't—"

Maytree didn't argue. She didn't say anything at all until they were back in Hawthorn's chambers, and the mage had broken him out of the ice. She looked down at Hawthorn with a similar expression she'd worn at Aspen's funeral, and did not move for a long, long time.

Finally, her words came. "I know it cannot be easy to watch—"

"No, you don't know," Memory-Juliana insisted, "because you have never even cared about him!"

Present-day Hawthorn jolted at the next action—when his mother struck Memory-Juliana clean across the cheek.

"You've watched over him for a few hours and you think it's tough to watch him?" Maytree hissed, her words venomous. "He is my *son*. How many centuries do you think I waited for him, only to be told within a few days of his birth I would lose him a few years later? Eighteen years is nothing for a faerie. I thought if I just... if I didn't watch... it wouldn't hurt as much. Blink and it would be over..." She squared up to Juliana. "You know *nothing* of my pain."

Memory-Juliana watched her leave, but then her eyes drifted back to Hawthorn, pale and still on the sheets. "And you know nothing of his."

For a moment, the entire valley seemed to still.

Hawthorn turned to her. "You did that for me?"

"I don't know. I think I did it for me. I was so desperate to get out of there, so angry at the world... I had to put it somewhere."

"Was I that disgusting?"

"Not disgusting. Hurting. I couldn't bear it. That was... that was when I realised you were more than a job to me. A lot more."

Hawthorn squeezed her fingers, and looked like he was about to say something, only another vision cut between them.

A woman running.

For a second, Juliana thought it was herself. The woman had hair almost the exact same shade as hers, fashioned in an almost identical braid. They had the same weather-tanned skin, similar features, a steeliness to their expressions.

But it wasn't her. It was like someone was painting her from memory.

"Cerridwen!" Markham's voice called. "Come back! Let's talk about this!"

Mother.

Cerridwen wheeled around, leaves blazing around her. Juliana tried to place where they were—only to realise they were here. They were somewhere just outside the valley, toeing the edge of the cliff face. "I *have* been talking, Markham! You are not listening—"

"Just give it some more time—"

"How much longer, Markham? Long enough that she grows to love this place? That it becomes her world? That she hates us for taking her from it? *She isn't safe here.* No mortal is."

"But you love Faerie, Cerridwen."

"I did," she whispered, her voice hoarse. "I do. I think I always will. But I miss home, Markham. The missing is scraping away at me, more and more... and I can feel Ladrien's presence here."

"We will find a way out of the curse."

"And if we can't?" Cerridwen's eyes blazed.

"You swore an oath. You're a *knight.* You have the queen's favour—"

"The Queen has given me her blessing."

Markham paused. "What?"

"She knows. She knows what it's like to love someone more than anything in the world, to forsake any and all things to want to keep them safe... there's nothing, *nothing* I will not do to protect my daughter. No monster I will not fight, no limit to the evils I will commit. I would sell my heart to Ladrien itself to keep her safe. I would prefer not to. So *come with me.* We'll go back to the palace and pick her up."

"No," Markham said, shaking his head as if the world was crumbling around him. "No, no, you cannot mean that. This is our *life*. We aren't mortal enough to survive out there, not anymore. We made vows, we made vows—"

"To each other!" Cerridwen insisted. "To *her.*"

"I can't leave," he murmured, "*you* can't leave."

Cerridwen's expression turned dark. "I'm leaving with or without you. But I'm taking her."

"No," Markham mumbled, his words desperate, "*No!*"

He drew his sword, as if his own wife were something to be vanquished.

And Cerridwen did what most people would do when presented with a blade, particularly when they had no wish to harm the person wielding it.

She moved backwards.

Straight over the edge of the cliff.

Juliana screamed.

Hawthorn yanked her into his arms, trying to whisper something of comfort, but his words never reached her. She pulled against him, fighting.

This was not her memory. She'd been safely back at the palace. It couldn't be Hawthorn's, either.

Which meant—

The figure they'd been chasing through the fog cut across them.

Markham. Markham was here.

"Jules—" Hawthorn started.

But his voice didn't reach her. Her vision went black, and she bolted awake in the glade a second later.

36. THE SACRIFICE

Cerridwen Ardencourt had never left Faerie. She had not abandoned her daughter, she was not still alive somewhere in the mortal realm.

She had fallen off a cliff sixteen years ago. Her husband had gone back to court and told everyone she'd left.

And they'd believed him.

Why wouldn't they? Cerridwen had been upset for months, years, even. She told several people she wanted to leave. They'd seen her grow quieter and more withdrawn.

And they were not used to lies.

Juliana ran through the valley, ignoring the swirling memories that raced up to greet her. What hold could they have over her now, when the present was her nightmare?

She's gone, she's gone, she's dead.

Had Markham killed her? It was difficult to say, exactly. He certainly held himself responsible.

But why lie? Why say she'd run away? Why not say she'd just fallen? Why lead Juliana to believe her mother had left her, to grow her life around that lie, to let it fester at the heart of her?

Markham had been wrong that day on the mountain. She could hate him. She did right now.

It didn't take long to reach him, not at the speed he was taking, slow and dawdling, almost like he was savouring the visions that were conjured.

Or maybe he wasn't. Maybe it was some form of punishment.

She caught up with him at the end of the valley, childish images of herself swirling around the path. Days she laughed with him. Days when they were still a family.

Gone, gone forever. Smoke from a fire that had long since gone out.

He must have known she was following by this point, but he did not stop. He continued out of the valley and down the slope, disappearing into the trees, down towards a series of caves beside a short waterfall.

Juliana had never come here before. She dimly remembered some tale of horrors beyond the valley, horrors she'd never pressed.

She didn't think of them now. She followed him down to the water's edge, to a cave behind the sheet of water.

Crystals lined the walls, casting faint blue light along the stone, like memories of moonlight. Something glowed in the back of the cave, glassy and white. Another crystal? It was the size of—

Of a coffin.

Something lay suspended in the watery glass, someone with light brown hair tinged with red, with a face painfully like Juliana's own.

Mother.

Markham stood over her still, inert form, his fingers brushing the surface of the crystal. Around the coffin were markings on the floor, candles worn to stubs, bowls of herbs, strange effigies—bones and wood all etched with runes.

What had he been doing here?

He did not look up when Juliana approached, but walked around the room instead, relighting candles.

"You saw, didn't you?" he said, voice soft. "In the valley. Somehow. You saw what happened to her. What... what I did."

Juliana's words stuck to the roof of her mouth. She couldn't speak.

"I didn't want to hurt her," he continued. "I never would have hurt her."

"You drew your sword."

He sighed, turning to stare at Cerridwen's face. "I did," he admitted. "That's what we do, isn't it? You and I? We fight. We turn to the blade when we cannot think."

"I do that because I learned it from you," Juliana whispered. "I don't know another way to be."

"It's who we are, Juliana. Warriors. Fighters."

But we're fighting ourselves, Juliana realised. *My entire life, I've made an enemy of my own heart.*

Not anymore.

"Why?" she asked. "Why keep her here—why tell everyone she'd left? Why let me think…"

Markham exhaled, still not meeting her eyes. "I am sorry about that, or at least sorry about what it did to you. I tried to make you understand it wasn't you she was abandoning, but I failed in that regard."

Oh, Father, you have failed in so many more ways than that.

"I needed her to be alive, see. So that she could come back."

Juliana's insides iced. "What?" Her gaze fell once more to the markings around the coffin, the herbs, the candles— "What have you done?"

"She was still alive when I found her," he explained. "Still clinging onto life. A witch came upon us quite by accident, and I traded a few of my years to keep her in this shell, her last breath preserved. She's not dead, not truly. Neither is she fully alive. For years, I searched for a way to bring her back from the brink, all to no avail. And then… then I found Ladrien."

Cold, hard realisation dawned on Juliana. "Your bargain. That was what he promised you. What he gave you. A way to bring her back."

Markham nodded.

"But the answer—it wasn't what you wanted?"

He nodded again, movements slow. "I knew a sacrifice would be required," he continued, and Juliana noticed a number of dark stains on the floor, small… and large. "I just wasn't sure what."

"And?" Juliana sucked in her trembling. "What was it?"

For the first time, Markham's eyes rose to meet hers. "The heart's blood of the one I loved most in the world."

Juliana's veins chilled. She wanted to move back, but her feet remained stuck in position. Something rocked against the stone, dark and powerful.

Hawthorn.

Markham glanced around him, but said nothing. Not even when he drew his sword.

"No," Juliana managed.

"I'm sorry, my dearheart," he said. "There is only one way to make this right."

He wouldn't. He couldn't. He won't!

His blade lunged for her, and she drew Briarsong to meet it, not trusting her instincts over her steel.

His attack drove into her, knocking her back to the wall. The cave trembled more, but there were no vines here to help her. Nothing for Hawthorn to manipulate. The stone stood strong.

"Come, daughter!" Markham hissed. "Fight back like I taught you!"

"You don't want to do this!"

"Of course I don't," he said, his eyes ghosting over, "but I must."

"What will you tell her when she wakes?"

To this, he had no answer. His sword struck the stone above her head, biting into the rock, the terrific blade gleaming like a shard of moonlight.

He wasn't holding back. He was trying to kill her.

But if there was one thing Juliana was good at, it was fighting back.

She kicked him in the stomach. He wavered backwards, winded but grinning. Juliana lashed out again, sword aiming for his middle. He kept smiling, darting out of reach, moving closer and closer towards the coffin.

"I've taught you well," he said. "You'll be the greatest swordsman in Faerie one day. The finest knight."

Juliana barely heard him. She barely heard *anything*. She didn't stop to think or process what he was saying, her mind narrowed on the blade, the goal. *Swipe. Stab. Move. Stay alive. Hurt him. Left. Right. Duck.*

He was stronger than her. He always had been.

But not faster.

Her sword jabbed towards his side. His blade caught hers, hilts grinding together. He didn't try to shuck her off, not even when he had the advantage of strength. He buckled beneath her weight, moving her blade not out of range, but further towards his chest.

If she wondered what he was doing, she didn't falter, didn't pull back, didn't stop pressing.

Didn't think about anything until he dropped away his blade and let gravity drive her own straight through his heart.

Juliana screamed. Briarsong slid from her grip as Markham stumbled backwards, hilt protruding from his chest.

It seemed to take an age for him to fall.

He smiled the entire way down.

His body crashed against the coffin with a thud, blood pooling into the circle beneath, crimson against brown.

He stared at the blade in his chest like he'd won a great victory, and then stared at Juliana the same way. His hand went to her cheek.

He couldn't speak. No one could with a blade through their heart, but she swore she heard his words anyway—some sickening mix of pride and joy.

Well done, daughter.

The candles flickered. The circle glowed with golden light. The life in Markham's eyes flickered and finally extinguished. The crystal seemed to heave and sigh, but as soon as Markham stilled, so did everything else.

There is only one way to make this right.

But sitting in that cavern on the cold hard floor, Juliana wondered if anything would ever be right again.

37. THE LAST WORDS

This body Juliana could bury. This one she could lay to rest. As a weak sun rose over the woods, Juliana tugged her father's remains into the shade of a tree, closed his eyes, washed the blood from his hands, and started to dig with her fingers.

The roots of a nearby tree trembled around Markham's body, hesitantly, carefully, as if they were waiting for an instruction, permission to help.

Juliana looked at her hands, and the tiny patch of earth she'd managed to scoop away with them. It would take hours to make even the shallowest of graves.

"Please," she said, "thank you."

The roots dug into the earth, clearing a space, criss-crossing around Markham's body. Then, with a reverence she wasn't prepared for, they pulled him gently into the ground.

Juliana watched as he vanished from sight, and set his sword in place of a headstone.

She couldn't find the strength to utter the words she'd given Dillon. Couldn't find the words to do much at all.

She placed a hand against the mound, tentatively, almost as if it had no right to be there.

"If I forgive you, I'll come back," she told him. "Perhaps I'll have some words then."

She kneeled by the graveside for a long time, the sun thickening in the sky.

Slowly, carefully, the roots cocooned themselves around her, the tip of one reaching up to brush away the one tear that had dared to form.

It jerked her from the numbness of thought.

"I can't," she said, standing clear of the roots. "Not yet, not right now."

She wanted to scream and cry and wail and break in his arms. But she couldn't imagine sleeping right now, and she didn't want this imitation. She had ground to cover.

She had to move.

Unable to stomach a proper meal, she drank the dregs of the last of Mabel's potions, chewed on some dried fruit, and kept walking.

She kept walking until she'd lost all sensation in her feet, until her body and mind had turned to rubber, until there was nothing in her but the dull, desperate need to place one foot in front of the other and just keep moving. She thought of nothing else. Her mind wasn't capable of thought, wasn't conscious of anything.

It still wasn't thinking when she arrived back at the hut she had once shared with her father, now a nest of dust and cobwebs.

A part of her had missed it over the years, a part of her longing to return. It was simpler, here. Nothing to be frightened of.

Because whatever her father's flaws, whatever hard lessons he had taught her, she had always felt safe with him. No matter what peril she'd faced, dimly in the back of her mind she'd known that if she couldn't get herself out of trouble, he would.

And he had.

But not anymore. Or ever again.

She set herself up a bed and made up a fire, forcing a little more food down.

On the counter top were two crisp letters, waxed-sealed and undisturbed. One was addressed to her mother, the other to her.

Markham must have known what he was going to do almost as soon as Ladrien told him, and he'd come back here to prepare. Perhaps he'd taken one of the winged mounts Maytree had used, picked up Juliana's trail and followed her to Winter, and afterwards, watched over her at Mabel's.

The presence she'd felt had been his.

Juliana picked up her letter. She held it for a long time before cracking it open. A part of her didn't want to. She wanted to lock those words away, unread, unheard, unspoken. If she never read them, his last words were still out there. She'd never have *nothing*.

But she had to read. She had to know.

> My Dearest Juliana,
>
> I have not the time to sit and write something perfect, and in either way, words were never my forte—a trait I fear we share. I will be as brief as I can be.
>
> Even if I lived a life as long as a faerie's, I would never love anything as much as I love you. You have been my greatest pride, my greatest joy. I have failed you in so many ways, and I hope returning your mother to you makes up for at least some of them. I pray you can forgive me one day, and if you cannot, I understand that, too. I have never forgiven myself.
>
> History, if it remembers me at all, will remember me as a monster. I hope you remember me as a father. A man who loved not wisely, but too much, and never in quite the right way.
>
> I have no advice to offer you, no words of wisdom, only this, my dear girl: may you be yourself, and far better than I ever was. May you listen and love in ways that I could not. May you never place duty over that which you love.
>
> Be happy, Juliana.
>
> Your ever-loving father,
>
> Markham Ardencourt, formerly Markham of Kent

Exhaustion took over grief, and somehow, Juliana slept. She woke up with Hawthorn beside her, and within a shard of a second had launched herself into his arms so hard she felt she could have broken his ribs.

She said nothing. She just sobbed, breaking occasionally to mumble awful, guttural words that made no sense.

Hawthorn held her and stroked her hair as she clung to him like a raft in a storm, and held her until the worst of the tempest was past.

"It didn't even work," she wailed into his chest. "All that and it didn't even work."

All that, and she was parentless, all that and she was completely alone.

She gripped onto the front of Hawthorn's shirt.

No, she realised, *not alone. Don't forget that.*

"I know," Hawthorn said, kissing her forehead. "I'm sorry. I don't know why it didn't. Ladrien can't lie, the spell looked flawless—perhaps some of the ingredients weren't potent enough?"

Juliana knew as soon as he spoke that that had nothing to do with it.

The heart's blood of the one I loved most in the world. But Markham had not loved himself more than he had loved his daughter, and Juliana didn't love him as much as she loved—

Not him. Please. Anyone but him, she'd prayed once. Awful as this loss was, there was another, worse one. One that would cleave her in two.

And one she could never speak, no matter how much she felt it.

"Because I hated him," she whispered in the dark. "I hated him. It wasn't a sacrifice."

"It was," replied Hawthorn, "and you didn't hate him. Not completely. Not always. But it's all right to hate him for now, if you need to. I know that's easier."

She'd lost Dillon. That loss still fractured against her, and would for some time, when she was allowed to feel it fully. If she had to lose another person she loved, another person who had loved her, truly and completely, however wrongly, however poorly—

"I can't," she choked instead. "I can't, I can't, I can't—"

Hawthorn's arms tightened around her, showing no indication that he would ever let go. She cried for what felt like hours. "I feel like he had me under a glamour my entire life," she said, finally drying her eyes. "He didn't need any magic to glamour me, but I still only saw what he wanted me to see." She didn't know what to do with that knowledge, that feeling, didn't know who or what she was supposed to fight to make it go away. And perhaps that was the point—she shouldn't want to fight anything. She'd been made to feel that way and no ward or pendant would free her from that spell. She needed time.

She took a deep breath, and shook her head. *No more, not now. Later.* "At least I can be assured that *you've* never glamoured me," she whispered, clinging to the certainties she had, assurances that no one but him could give her.

Hawthorn went silent.

"Hawthorn?"

"I have something to tell you," he confessed. "I fear your reaction, but I shall tell you nonetheless. I'm not sure now is the best time, but—"

Juliana's eyes narrowed. "Go on."

"Remember our trip to the Summer Court? One of the last nights we had there. You drank some punch laced with something."

"I think I'd remember—" Realisation dawned. She remembered waking up and finding all her wards flung off nearby, and no clear memories of the night before, only Hawthorn's assurances that everything was fine. "Oh. *Oh.*"

"You didn't do anything embarrassing!" he added hastily. "At least, not publicly. I steered you out there the second I realised something was amiss."

"What do you mean, not *publicly?*"

Hawthorn's throat bobbed, as if he'd been hoping she wouldn't pick up on that. "You said a few things... stripped naked... I was slightly worried you might gouge my eyes out the next day, but I also knew how mortified you'd be, so... I glamoured you to forget." He paused. "You can be angry now, if you like."

Juliana hesitated. She felt more embarrassed than angry. Perhaps she should have found it a violation, but the truth was, she was actually rather thankful. She *would* have been mortified. And her anger at him for helping her back then would have been unwarranted the morning after.

"I'm not angry," she told him, voice steady. She waited another second. "What sort of things did I say?"

Hawthorn pulled a face, like he wasn't sure whether or not to smirk or cringe. "You may have told me how attractive you found me."

"*May* have?"

"Um, you did. You did say that."

"Oh *lords*. What did I say? Did I mention your eyes? I bet I mentioned your eyes."

"My eyes?" Hawthorn frowned.

"I'm obsessed with them," Juliana admitted through her fingers. "Have been for years. Hated that I didn't know the word for the precise colour."

"Really?" The disbelief on Hawthorn's face was as stark as raven in winter. "Please do go on. I've never found my eyes to be my best feature. My rear, perhaps. My sinfully sharp cheekbones or kissably soft mouth. My surprisingly lithe muscular form..."

"I don't need to compliment you, you're doing an excellent job yourself."

"It isn't the same. Observe." He took her hand in his. "Juliana, for all that you seem to be perpetually covered in mud and your scowl is a permanent fixture of your face—"

"You're not very good at this complimenting business, are you?"

"—and you have a tendency to interrupt me, for all your many, many flaws, both physical and otherwise, I find you to be a person of exceptional beauty." He paused. "In fact, I find you to be the greatest beauty I have ever beheld. I fear that I may spend the rest of my immortal life searching for a fraction of beauty I find in you in a sliver of something else." He kissed her hand. "See? Works better than when you tell yourself, doesn't it?"

Juliana paused, hanging onto his words. It was like a chasm had been opened up beneath her. Being with Hawthorn was often like that—like toeing the edge of a cliff, like one wrong move would be her downfall.

But maybe, just maybe, for a moment, for tonight, she wanted to fall, wanted to dive into that pit, to be consumed by him.

"Hawthorn," she whispered, knowing what he uttered next would forever change the shape of things between the two of them. This wouldn't be like how it was with Dillon, a friendship easy to fall back into. This would alter her irrevocably. "Do you like me?"

Hawthorn blinked at her. "Has it honestly taken you so long to figure that out?"

"You aren't answering."

His fingers dropped away from her. "Yes," he said, "I like you. Immeasurably."

Now it was Juliana's turn to blink, as if the words were alien to her. "For... for my personality?"

"I know, I'm rather shocked too."

"But I'm awful to you."

"I happen to think you're one of the kindest souls in my acquaintance... which admittedly says more about the rest of them."

He stared at her as if waiting for a reply, but her words had vanished, half her mind with them. She'd suspected, deep down, but to *hear* them, to know...

"I don't expect you to share my affliction. Indeed, the whole business would be a lot simpler if you didn't. But I... I should like, I think, to know your thoughts anyway. You've often spoken of hating me. I suspect that you do not, not really. But if you could..."

He turned to move away from her, as though he meant to disappear. The action alone was enough to jolt Juliana back to her senses, because she couldn't, *wouldn't* let him leave. Not tonight.

She grabbed his wrist, making him half-turn towards her. He kept his gaze cast down, as if he couldn't bear to face her.

You make me sound like a monster to be vanquished.

In some ways, you are.

"I don't hate you," she whispered. "I know at one point, I must have, but I don't remember why. Or when. When that changed. When I stopped hating you. When I..." her words trailed off. "I don't hate you," she reiterated.

And then, when words failed her, she kissed him instead.

Hawthorn stood there for a moment, as shocked and numb as she had been that day he kissed her in the carriage, as if this were a dream inside a dream, one he expected to be yanked from. But suddenly he was kissing her back, crushing her against the wall, his weight hard against her, kisses desperate, like he was trying to win a battle.

"Tell me that you despise me," he moaned into her. "That you detest everything about me—"

"But why?"

"I need you to hate me. I need you to *crush* me. Convince me I am without hope. If you do not, I'm afraid..." His fingers traced her neck. "Make me hate you."

"I can't." *I can't hate you either.*

"Make me stop wanting you."

"I can't do that, either."

"Cruel, vicious creature..."

"It's revenge."

"What for?"

"For making me want you too."

It's all right to want him, she told herself. *It's all right to have him. Sex is just sex. Perhaps it'll go away if you give in. If you let go, just this once...*

But his kisses were like drops of alcohol on the tongue of an addict, like rain after a drought, like a river breaking down a dam. Impossible to resist. Impossible not to be dragged under.

You will destroy me, she realised, *and I will let you.*

Her skin quivered beneath his touch as they slid beneath her tunic, his soft palms brushing her scars, her bruises, examining them like artwork, lowering his lips to her middle like the shrine of a saint.

"Jules," he breathed. "Tell me what to do, and I will do it."

"Lie to me," she whispered. "Tell me that you hate me, too."

"You know I cannot." His tongue found her mouth, slowly teasing at her lips, nibbling softly. "I hate you as much as I detest the sun, as much as I loathe velvet, as much as I adore the worst of all the shadows."

"That's not hate."

"Worse than hate," he whispered against her breath. "Intolerable. Insufferable."

"What would you say to me, if you could lie?"

He kissed down her throat. "If I could lie, I'd tell you I despise you, that I never think of you, that I have no need of your kindness, that there is nothing I want from you. That you could never make me beg or plead or grovel. I would lie to you until I believed the lies myself."

His kisses trailed down her collar bones as his hands moved to part her clothes. He let out a hard, tight breath as his palm graced her breast, shivering under her warmth. It lingered there, unmoving, as if he didn't quite dare claim it.

"Give me your truths," he begged. "Tell me anything real."

"I want you," she murmured. "I've wanted you for so long—and I hate it, but it's true."

His lips hovered at her hips, brushing the scars he found there. "And in what ways do you want me, Jules?"

Too many, all of them—but it was too much, too much like lying down on a bed of knives. If she balanced, she'd be fine, but one weight in the wrong place—

She peeled off his shirt. "This is a good place to start."

She craved more than his flesh. She craved the scent of him inside her, his honeyed words against her heart. She wanted to bottle him, have him, consume him, be consumed by him. She wanted the courage to turn misshapen feelings into words, to craft him sweet, soft phrases, promises she could be held to.

It was foolish and stupid to want to make him happy, this person she'd spent so long hating.

And yet, she wanted it.

More than honour and glory and riches and freedom.

She wanted him to be happy.

They fell back against the floor, fumbling once more for their clothes.

"It's a bit strange, not being able to feel anything but you," Juliana breathed, and then found the thought vanishing. "But I don't think I need to."

Hawthorn moaned into her mouth, as if her words were honey after a feast. He arched her back against the floor, kisses descending down her neck, across her collarbones, chest, the flat, scarred panes of her stomach... "It's just as well we can't touch anything," he told her. "I think I'd break the hut."

Juliana hooked her legs around his waist and flipped him underneath her in one fluid motion, pinning him to the floor. "Or I would." Her hands glided up his chest, hard, firm, claiming. "Or perhaps I'd break you..." Her mouth fell to his throat, nipping and teasing.

Hawthorn's hands braced against her hips. "You have already broken me," he whispered in her ear, "and I give you full permission to do so again..."

Juliana kissed him again, hard, rough, claiming. She thought about biting him. She wanted him, wanted more, more, *more* of him than she had ever wanted anything else and she needed to kiss him, to devour him, to press their bodies together until there was not a fragment of space between them.

She shoved him back against the floor and scrambled upright, hauling off what remained of her clothes. She opened her mouth to command he do the same, but before she could, he came towards her, braced on his knees, eyes wide.

For a second, the room fell silent.

He stared at her like a creature to be worshipped. A god of the forests. An eldritch terror. Something to be feared, adored, respected.

"You're magnificent."

"You've seen me naked before."

"Yes, but I wasn't really supposed to be looking..." He trailed a hand down her naked flesh. "I have never seen you like this before."

He marvelled at every scar, kissed every freckle, worshipped every imperfection, his blue eyes turned black with desire. This was a softness she hadn't expected, made her feel far more exposed than the nakedness.

"You destroy me, obliterate me, unravel me," he murmured.

Juliana's thoughts turned dizzy. "Take off the rest of your clothes."

Hawthorn laughed against her flesh, his kisses moving upwards as he climbed to his feet, pulling off his remaining garments and letting them fall to the floor, until they both stood naked before one another, inches apart, not touching.

He felt tall in front of her. She swallowed, trying to keep her eyes level with his. He'd been tall for years, but she'd never once felt it.

Hawthorn grinned, as if sensing her wandering eyes. "Still up for this?"

"Do I look unsure?"

"Fair point." He took her by the arms and backed her into a beam, hiking her legs up around his waist. "I seem to recall something about you liking it rough?"

"Maybe," she said, before wrapping her arms around the pillar and flipping him onto the floor, her on top. "A little rough... but maybe not with you. Not right now."

"Afraid I can't take it?"

"I want to savour it," she told him, "I want to savour *you*."

It was those words or the careful rocking movement that elicited a moan of him, deep and desperate, almost painful. Juliana still couldn't believe that this was happening, that she was doing this with *Hawthorn*. Hawthorn who she always pretended to hate.

Pretended. It was only ever pretend.

This—this was real.

Never mind that their bodies were smoke and dreams, she could feel him and herself and nothing else. The steady shake of his body beneath hers, his breath against her skin, his hands, touching and stroking—that was real.

She wanted to whisper things to him, lies and truths, promises that he was hers, declarations of undying affection.

Her words wouldn't come.

She touched him instead, writing words with her body she couldn't form with her tongue, manoeuvring herself into the right position, holding him to the floor—

And suddenly Hawthorn was inside her, rocking against her, locked together in a way that had no right to feel this good, this permanent.

She half-expected him to say something ridiculous, some comment about finally seducing her, a foolish joke, a command that she screamed his name.

He said nothing. He seemed beyond all words. Instead, he took her face in his hands, his eyes open, as if he needed help convincing himself that this was real.

He stayed looking at her even as they rocked together, bodies colliding like stardust, swaying in perfect tandem, thoughts and sensation turned nebulous under the soft, teasing pressure of their flesh. Heat trembled between them, one blissful moment sliding into the next, over and over and over until they exploded together.

Together.

This is it, she thought afterwards, as they lay together, a tangle of limbs. *This is how we were always meant to be.*

38. THE ROAD HOME

She woke alone, reaching out for the warmth she fell asleep to, but of course, Hawthorn had vanished. At least from her eyes.

"Are you still here?" she asked.

Branches knocked against the windows, and she smiled. She felt his eyes on her as she dressed.

"Enjoy the sight whilst you can, Prince."

The banging branches assured her that he was.

She got dressed very slowly.

Savour this, she reminded herself—or both of them, she wasn't sure—because by tomorrow, all being well, she'd reach the capital.

Tomorrow, all being well, Hawthorn would be awake.

And engaged to someone else.

She tried not to think of that. It was definitely future Juliana's problem. This Juliana needed to work out how to get into a heavily-guarded city and free him, first. Maybe she'd die in the attempt. At least then she'd never have to watch him marry someone else.

She wondered, if she was a faerie, what words she could speak, what truths she could utter. Could she say, *I'd rather die than watch him marry Serena?* What utter insanity would it be to admit such a thing?

She shook it away. No point dwelling on that.

She finished getting ready and headed off.

A quietness had settled over both the wood and the two of them, but it was not uncomfortable. She had a feeling she was smiling as she walked, the memories of the night before swirling through her, tempering her grief.

She'd been unable to read the letter Markham had written for her mother. She wasn't sure it was right to. They weren't her words.

She'd left it under the floorboards in the hut, a place she was sure she would never return to.

Much like Markham never would.

He'd never make amends, never apologise for his misdeeds, never live to see the consequences of his actions or her triumphs over them.

And she would triumph. She had to.

A root twisted from a nearby tree and prodded her in the side.

"I'm all right," she assured Hawthorn. "I promise."

And somehow, she felt that was the truth. She was all right, or would be, because he was beside her.

For a little while longer.

Night came again eventually, and Juliana was forced to make camp. She was almost certain it was the same fallen tree that had been their shelter three years ago, but she couldn't be certain. The woods largely looked the same here.

But she knew where she was. Half a day from the Autumn Gate.

She lay down and struggled to sleep. Tomorrow, tomorrow. It could all be over tomorrow. This might be their last night together. She couldn't stomach the thought, and yet she wanted sleep to come more than ever, to bring them together.

One last night.

Still unable to sleep, and desperately aware of the dwindling hours, Juliana sat up. "Hawthorn," she said, "if you're waiting for me, would you mind just disappearing for a little while? Maybe half an hour?"

There was a rustle in the bushes, which she took to mean a yes, and after a moment she reached into her pack and brought out his notebook.

There were still a few pages she'd not read.

If she couldn't be with him in the dream, she'd have his words instead.

FOREST OF DREAMS AND WHISPERS

She worked her way through the remaining entries, savouring every line of dire poetry, every scribbled insult, every minute entry mocking and praising her physical attributes.

Only two pages left.

At the penultimate page, her heart stuttered, and she was glad she'd sent Hawthorn away so that he couldn't witness her reading it.

> My eighteenth birthday is just around the corner, and among all the fears it brings is the one regarding you.
>
> I am afraid of you leaving. I am afraid of never seeing you again. I'm afraid that you'll slink away the morning of the day and that I shall be alone once more.
>
> I'm afraid of waking to a world without you in it.
>
> I'll never know what happened to you. If you slunk back to the mortal realm, if you lived a decent life, if you were happy.
>
> I'm afraid of you staying, too. I'm afraid of you dying.
>
> I'm afraid, Jules. For you, of you, of everything.

He'd never addressed any of the entries to her before, but this one shunted along her bones, warming and chilling to her heart in the same breath. How well she knew these thoughts, felt them too. Felt them for him.

The final page was somehow worse.

Over and over, in a scrawled hand, Hawthorn had written:

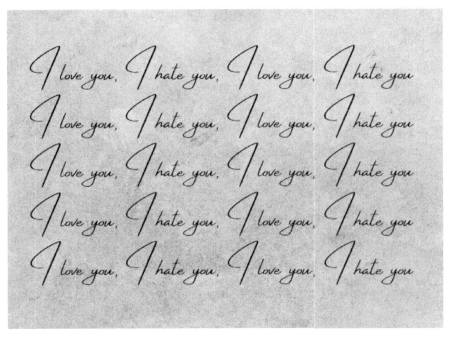

He'd almost torn through the paper.

Juliana found herself wondering which was the lie, which one he could speak, and once more what words she could utter if she too were banned from lies.

Silently, softly, Juliana closed the notebook and put it away, curling up on the hard ground, her thoughts louder than ever.

Finally, exhaustion overruled nerves, and she woke in Hawthorn's arms.

"Good evening," he said, with his same stupid, sinful smirk.

Juliana leapt up and kissed him, as if she hoped to wipe it away with her lips. It worked—for a few short seconds.

"Nice to see you too..." he responded, arms around her, still smiling. She really didn't hate it as much as she pretended.

"Don't speak," Juliana insisted. "Just... not yet."

Talking would break the spell, would unravel them both, would sacrifice this night to the morning. And she would have this night. She would have *him*.

Just once more. Just once.

After, they lay together in the steady glow of the fire, golden and naked, no need of any coverings, staring at each other the way one gazed at paintings in a gallery.

No, she thought, *better than that.*

It ought to hurt to admit it, but she'd never stared at anything the way she stared at him. Puzzle, marvel, masterpiece—the sea she had craved most of her life and would die craving still.

Hawthorn's fingers stroked the bare skin of her arm, the other in her hair. One of her hands was tucked against his chest, the other wrapped around his back. She adored this body, the smooth, perfect shape of it. For a moment it was slightly baffling he'd decided to share it with her.

"I have never liked your silence," Hawthorn admitted. "I often find it very hard to know what you're thinking."

Juliana smirked. "You talk enough for the both of us."

"I talk a lot when I'm nervous, which I have a habit of being around you. I talk to fill the silence." He stroked her arm again. "I would have one of your thoughts, if I may. A truth from your mind."

Juliana paused. "I finished reading your notebook."

Hawthorn stilled, all traces of smiles vanishing. "I see."

"I won't waste time asking you if you meant it all, because..." She shook her head, sighing. "Why give it to me? Really?"

"I wasn't going to," he said. "I wanted to keep it. I wanted it close to me when I woke, so that even when you were gone, even if I lived for centuries... I'd remember."

"Remember what?"

"You," he said. "Every detail. Every time I cursed your name and cursed my feelings. I wanted to remember it all. I never wanted to forget."

"And yet you gave it to me."

He swallowed. "I couldn't tell you how I felt. Not to your face. Even at the end, I was still too terrified. But... I wanted you to know."

Ask him about the last page, her mind begged. *Ask him what it meant!*

"I'll leave it under the roots of that tree over there," she told him, pointing to a large oak. "I'll mark it with something. You can fetch it in a hundred years if I fail tomorrow. If... if you still want to."

"I'll always want to, Jules. That's the problem. I'll always want *you.*"

"How can you say that? How can that possibly be true?"

"I don't know," he said. "But it is. I have spoken of it often enough in shadows. I want you. I always will. I—"

His words drifted away as he claimed her mouth with his, or perhaps they never existed in the first place. Her thoughts spiralled beneath his lips, drunk and dizzying. How was she supposed to return to normal after this, to be with someone—anyone—else?

She ought to hate him for this, or hate herself, hate how her body was betraying her to emotion.

But she didn't, she couldn't.

She refused to let the sorrow of tomorrow slay this moment.

Perhaps it is the future I want to vanquish, not him, not us. Perhaps impossibility itself. He was never my enemy. Never could be.

She kissed him harder at the thought, hands grasping at him again, dragging her mouth to his neck, his breath against her ear, gasping into them. He pulled her back to him, hands sinking into her hair. He drank her like wine, soft and savouring.

When his eyes met hers, they were wide and wonderful. "I don't suppose there's any chance I could convince you to break our deal and run away, is there?"

Juliana froze. How could he go from confessing his feelings to asking her to abandon him? "What, leave you to rot and damn a kingdom?"

"Yes."

Juliana pulled away. "Why would you want me to do that?"

"The kingdom will be fine, eventually, according to Ladrien's curse. We won't die. But if you go there tomorrow... you might."

Juliana stilled, uncertain, shocked by his words. If Faerie remained sleeping, the realm would not be theirs when they woke. Ladrien would take it and twist it into something else, a land of shadows and thorns. "I'm not worth a kingdom, Hawthorn."

"You are to me."

Juliana buckled. He'd said he *liked* her. It was all right to like each other, to indulge... but saying something like that...

It was dangerous, deadly. They couldn't. He wouldn't.

Hawthorn sighed, turning up to face the skies. "You look surprised, yet you read my words, my desperate attempts to work out which was the lie, and learn what wasn't. I suppose I've done a rather good job, this past year, of hiding how

I feel for you. It's been a wretched kind of agony, I'll have you know. But I'd promised you knighthood, and I didn't want to make things too awkward or unbearable for you to stay. And, selfishly, I *wanted* you to stay. As awful as it was to be beside you, the idea of you leaving was far, far worse."

A pause thumped around the glade, loud as a heartbeat, soft as thunder.

"I love you, Jules, in case that wasn't clear. I fear I may always love you."

She would have been less shocked if he'd struck her with lightning. It wasn't that he felt that way, because really, deep down, she ought to have known. *Did* know. But that he'd said them—said the words that could never be taken back—

It was all right to sleep together, to want each other.

But they weren't allowed to love.

But you do love him, a voice reminded her. *You have for a long while.*

She could not pin it on a moment, could not trace that river back to its source. It was a thousand raindrops, a storm. A tempest of days spread out over years.

Say something, her mind whispered, or perhaps it was him, desperate for a response that wasn't coming.

She couldn't speak.

She could face monsters and death and betrayal, but not this.

Hawthorn sighed, shaking his head, as if this was all he could expect. "I just wanted you to know."

He vanished in the blink of an eye.

"Hawthorn!" she screamed, finally finding her voice. Because how dare he leave, how dare he go before she could—

They had so little time left—

No. She wouldn't let it end that way. She seized her tunic, looped it over her head, and followed that *tug*, that hard pull that snapped her back towards the palace. She landed somewhere that gave the vague sensation of being cold and hard: the throne room, she suspected.

It was hard to tell. Darkness swamped the room. She was almost blind.

"Hawthorn!" she called out.

He didn't answer.

It occurred to her she didn't need to worry about bumping into things. She was non-corporeal. She ran, straight through tables, through sleeping bodies, through walls and rooms, screaming his name.

Where are you, where are you, where are you?

He didn't answer.

She kept going, kept searching, out of the palace, into the streets, the town, the gardens. Into a vast, palpable darkness where nothing existed but the sound of his name.

And still no reply.

Her pendant felt cold, a hard rock against her chest.

He didn't want to be found.

39. THE AUTUMN GATE

Juliana trudged through the forest alongside the Autumn Road, covered just enough from the sight of any prying eyes. Acanthia loomed in the distance, great and grey.

"If I die today before I get the chance to kick your ass, I'm going to be so mad at you," she murmured under her breath.

His words from last night rose in voiceless response.

I love you, Jules, in case that wasn't clear. I fear I may always love you.

For a year. She remembered that part correctly, right? He'd said he'd been hiding it from her for a *year.* Her own recent struggles paled in comparison to that. Why hadn't he said anything?

You didn't say anything either.
You didn't know!

She thought about telling him she loved him now, just in case he was listening, but she didn't. Partly because she wanted to see his reaction and partly because she was furious.

Plus she didn't want to utter the words out loud to thin air. She felt ridiculous.

"I really did prefer hating you," she muttered instead, unsure of the truth of her words. *It was much, much easier to hate you.*

At last, the end of the Autumn Road appeared in sight. Knowing it would be dangerous to approach directly, Juliana scoured the forest for a tree that towered over the rest, and climbed as high as she could go. As she suspected, the gate was heavily guarded. Two minotaurs and a stout ogre patrolled the gate itself, with a series of archers up on the battlements. No sluaghs or anything else airborne.

Juliana calculated her next move. With the element of surprise, she could *possibly* take on the minotaurs and the ogre—providing her first attack took one of them out and only left her with two foes to deal with. She had the benefit of speed, but that wouldn't help her a great deal if she was hit by an arrow, and who knew what else might be alerted if, by some miracle, she managed to make it past the gate? Speed would only protect her for so long, and dragging Serena up the stairs would be impossible without stealth.

No, getting in through the gate was not the best option.

Scaling the wall would be safer. It was so thick with vines that it wouldn't be hard to climb, although time-consuming. Not to mention she had no idea what awaited her on the other side.

I'm just one person, she realised. It was a ridiculous feat for one person.

Her best bet, she decided, was to find a safe place to sleep and at least explore what was going on in Acanthia from the dream side of things. With any luck, she'd find Hawthorn there, and he could help her with his control over the vines.

Yes, that was definitely her best shot.

If he let himself be found.

Determined, she shimmied down the tree and crept into a deeper part of the woodlands, searching for somewhere concealed and far away from the gates. Deeper and deeper she went, through copses and glades. She couldn't be too close to the patrol, couldn't risk leaving her body so defenceless.

It felt wrong to be moving away from the city. She was so close—

Her eyes fell across a mark on one of the trees, a circular symbol. No way it was made by accident, and it appeared to have been etched recently. It looked familiar to her, yet, at the same time, she couldn't place it. It wasn't a rune, nothing she'd learnt at school—

She crept closer, examining the carving. It had been made with a blade, and not particularly well.

She peered harder into the forest. The symbol appeared on other trunks too. Almost... almost like signposts.

Juliana followed the line, the overgrowth twisting beneath her feet before flattening into something that resembled a path. Someone—a group of people—had moved through here recently.

Juliana pressed her hand against one of the markings, and a memory jolted through her.

Dillon. He'd drawn this symbol on the back of her hand before he died. She'd never stopped to recall it before because Mabel must have cleaned it off as she slept. What had he said to her?

Think, think—

"Halt!"

Juliana stilled, fingers inching for her sword. The voice sounded Unseelie—deep, thunderous, slightly animal. But why wouldn't an Unseelie simply cut her down?

"Identify yourself!" the voice called again.

The depth of the voice sounded loosely familiar to her, wavering slightly, as if unused to giving orders. She decided to tell the truth.

"Juliana Ardencourt," she responded.

"Juliana?" The voice turned into something else, and before Juliana could turn, there came a rustling in the bushes. Half a dozen faces peered out of the leaves, streaked with mud, loaded with bows and sticks.

Juliana recognised almost every face. Servants of the castle, mortal subjects—and Barney the Minotaur, dressed in the same muddy armour, a ring of daisies tied to one of his horns.

"Julie!" A round-faced woman with nut-brown hair tumbled out from behind a tree trunk, launching herself at Juliana with such ferocity she was almost knocked off her feet. "We thought... we were sure—"

"Iona." Juliana breathed her in. Gone from her clothes was the smell of bread and vanilla, replaced by earth and sweat. It hardly mattered. She still felt like home. "What are you doing here?"

"What does it look like, lass?" said a cheery voice.

Juliana wheeled around, and found herself face-to-face with Dillon's father. He carried an axe in one hand and wore a smile on his face.

Her stomach dropped. *He didn't know.*

Albert Woodfern continued to grin, shouldering his axe. "We're the Resistance!"

It was considered far too dangerous to chat for long out in the open, so Albert and Iona left the younger ones still on patrol and took Juliana towards a thick oak in the centre of the wood. They pressed on a concealed knot between one of the branches, and a tunnel opened up in its roots.

Tunnel. That's what Dillon had been trying to tell her. There was a secret tunnel under the gate. It was how he'd gotten out of Acanthia to begin with.

"What is this place?" Juliana asked, as they descended beneath the earth, the dank walls lit with crystal.

"Maytree built them," Albert explained. "And pretty much by herself, over the years. A way to get the mortals out if the curse came to pass. She told precious few they existed until the day before, when she…"

When she left. Had that always been part of her plan? That part seemed done in haste and desperation. When the end was nigh, she'd chosen to abandon her people to try and save her son.

Like Juliana's own mother had planned to do.

The Queen has given me her blessing.

"But you didn't escape," she said, the tunnel widening. "You stayed. Why not—"

"We sent off the children, the elderly and infirm," Iona said, "those that couldn't fight or shouldn't have to. But the mortal world won't be safe from Ladrien either. We had to do something. We caught wind of an army mobilising in Winter—"

"We sent Dillon on a scouting mission," Albert said, voice quiet. "He didn't return."

Juliana stopped, knowing this moment could not be put off any longer. "You don't need to worry about the army," she said, insides frozen. "At least, not most of them. Dillon and I found them, and we took them out."

For a while, the tunnels turned silent, the walls shrinking around them. There was no joy in Juliana's voice. There could be no mistake.

"Then, my boy—" Albert started.

Juliana cast her eyes downwards, wondering how much she should say, what mix of truths and lies she should utter. "He was brave, and it was quick," she told him. "I could not have done it alone. We took out most of Ladrien's army together, before Ladrien himself discovered us. Dillon wasn't alone at the end," she added, for that seemed like the most important part. "Hawthorn himself buried him."

All this time, Albert had remained quiet, as if the news were hardly news to him at all. He must have suspected it, when he didn't return, but to know beyond a doubt...

Slowly, he nodded his head, turned on his heels and moved onwards down the tunnel. His eyes were cast downwards with such finality Juliana wondered if he would ever raise his head again.

He will grieve later, Juliana knew. *We all will.*

Iona patted Juliana's hand, her own eyes filled with tears. "Come, love," she said.

Juliana appreciated the lack of useless words, and followed after her. The tunnel diverged into something like a warren, a series of hollow chambers of earth and roots.

"You say Hawthorn buried him?" Iona asked, brow furrowed. "But how can that be when—"

"An excellent question," said a cool, steely voice, "and one I will have answered."

Juliana looked up and found Miriam of Bath staring down at her, her eyes ice. She was still in full armour, her hand upon her sword as if she intended to draw it at any second.

"You've a tale to tell, girl, and I will hear it," Miriam declared. "Someone betrayed Princess Serena to Ladrien, and precious few knew about her role or whereabouts. I do not wish to believe it was you, but I'd be a fool to trust in that."

Juliana buckled. She should have been expecting this. "It was my father," she said, voice hoarse. "My father betrayed us."

A collective gasp went up among the audience. More crept forward out of the other tunnels, eager to hear the tale. Even Albert returned, although his eyes were misty and faraway.

Carefully, Juliana recounted the events as well as she was able, explaining her father's role—although not his motives—her connection to Hawthorn through the dreamscape, and their plan to awaken him using Serena.

At this, Miriam punched a wall, so hard that earth fell from the ceiling.

"Ser Miriam!" Iona shrieked.

"It's so simple," she said, rubbing her temples. "Why didn't I see it? She was right there when we were evacuating the castle—"

"Ladrien placed her there, and he's had eighteen years to think this through," Albert told her. "I would not be too hard on yourself."

Miriam sighed, turning round to face the rest of the congregation. There were some two dozen people in attendance, crammed in around the sides, more backed up through the tunnels. Miriam seemed to look at them all.

Her eyes fell over the knights. "You," she said, and then jabbed a finger at Juliana. "And you. Follow me."

She swept down one of the wider paths, people hurrying out of her way, and marched into a small chamber away from the rest. A table had been set up in the centre full of maps and a curiously accurate model of the city. A war room.

Miriam rested her fists against the table. Juliana understood what was going through her mind. A strange, guilty kind of relief. She was angry at herself for not seeing a solution before, but equally so, she'd been anticipating a war.

Now, this could all be over by nightfall.

If they could get back into the city. If they could get to Serena—

Miriam stared at the model of the city, and then back to the knights. "Send out the best scouts," she said to one of them. "As many as you dare. I want to know *exactly* what we're facing out there. Chart me a path to the castle."

The knight nodded, and swiftly left the room.

"The rest of you"— Miriam surveyed them carefully— "give me every worst-case scenario you can think of. And then give me five more."

Juliana was not given a scrap of a moment for reflection for the next three hours. Every fraction of a second was dedicated to planning and organising. When they weren't actively strategising, they were checking equipment or polishing swords, as if a single blunted blade could mean the difference between victory and defeat.

She wanted to pause, to rest, to speak to Hawthorn. It seemed ridiculous to be afraid now, to be pausing here when she'd fought so hard to get to this point.

"Please," she said to Miriam at one point. "Let me rest for a moment. Let me see if I can scout in the dreamscape. Talk to Hawthorn. He might be able to help."

Miriam nodded, clicking at a sentry to escort her to the rudimentary dorms. "It's a good idea," she said, as Juliana was halfway out the door. "We should all take some time to rest and reflect. Just..."

Don't be too long.

The longer this went on, the greater the chances of discovery or death. The remains of Ladrien's army could march on the city. Ladrien could realise the flaw in his plan and remove Princess Serena himself.

They had lost people already. Juliana could see that much from the thinning numbers, the absent faces. She'd asked about Aoife, earlier. No one had seen her since she fled the palace.

It was difficult to imagine an Acanthia without her. Difficult to imagine one without Dillon. Difficult to imagine a future without her father.

Enough death, enough loss.

It had to end.

She didn't think she'd sleep easily when she finally crept into a bunk, but exhaustion overruled trepidation, and after a few minutes of sitting in the still and quiet, she began to drift.

She woke in the throne room, but the air seemed thunderous, distorted far worse than it had been that first day, like she was trapped in a storm. Sound crackled at her eardrums.

"Hawthorn!" she called. "Hawthorn, where are you?"

He did not answer.

Juliana forced herself to move, but every step was like pushing against a tide, expecting each step to rip her under. She pressed onward, towards the castle doors, trying to take note of everything she saw but finding it hard, her vision plugged up with darkness.

She called his name again. Still nothing.

Panic increasing, she flitted through the palace, out into the gardens, searching, calling, crying—reaching for that tug. The pendant wasn't cold, it felt... empty. Like something was stopping it, or there had never been anything in it to begin with.

"Hawthorn!" she called, amazed at her voice's capacity for wretchedness, how it stumbled and crackled on his name. Her throat was raw from shouting.

How much could he love her if he wasn't willing to set his pride aside and speak to her now, when her very life—his, even—depended upon it?

Perhaps he didn't love her as much as he thought, or perhaps the merest hint of rejection had broken it. He rarely took the same lover twice. Perhaps he was already done with her.

It didn't feel right. The logic didn't match what she felt in her bones. But what other explanation was there?

Unless something was wrong.

It might not be him. It might be something she'd done, some default in herself—

"Please come," she whispered, still struggling against the tide.

But a second later, she lost her footing, and was wrenched away from the dream.

Miriam was standing over her when she woke again, face pale, expression severe. "Any luck?" she said. "You were thrashing a lot."

"I couldn't reach him."

Miriam raised an eyebrow. "Did you see anything?"

Juliana shook her head. Nothing helpful had made its way past the grainy, streaming air.

Miriam sighed. "Have you ever not been able to reach him before?"

"Once," Juliana admitted. "When he didn't want to be found."

"Do you think he's ignoring you now?"

Juliana hesitated. She didn't know *what* to think. It was possible one or both of them had caused this subconsciously. She certainly didn't want to believe he was ignoring her…

But the alternative was that something was wrong. That he was in danger.

I'd rather have him furious with me than hurt.

Slowly, she shook her head. "I don't think he'd ignore me, not at the moment. Which means…"

"Something might be wrong?" Miriam shook her head. "No matter. This doesn't change anything. Do you need more rest?"

Juliana couldn't rest if she wanted to. "No."

"Collect your gear," Miriam said, voice hard. "We move out as soon as you're ready."

40. CITY OF THORNS

In no time at all, Juliana was moving through the dense, dark tunnels, deep under Acanthia. Roots studded the ceiling, still and lifeless. Everything above her seemed solid, immovable, and yet she still felt a distant rumble, like a giant stomping over her grave.

"Where does the tunnel end?" Juliana asked Miriam.

"A public garden," she replied. "There's only the one entrance. Maytree didn't want anything too close to the place, or too hard to guard. Only one way in and out."

Juliana swallowed. No wonder they were worried about being found. If they were, they'd be ducks in a barrel. A few sluaghs down here was all it would take.

Gradually, the tunnel curved upwards. A small, slight soldier went on ahead, knocking along the walls until he reached wood. A sharp click echoed down the tunnel, and light swung inside.

The group crept out, one by one, all scurrying into the small building on the corner just outside the tunnel and ducking down in the centre of the main room. Two knights drew their swords, standing by the door. One person kept watch outside.

Miriam went through the plan again, and the group split apart.

No one had been left behind. No one really wanted to be. They would need as many as they could get.

Every person knew the end goal—get Serena, inside of the throne room, to Hawthorn in his chamber. Anyone could pick up the gauntlet if the first mission failed.

As long as reinforcements didn't arrive. As long as the enemy didn't realise what they were planning and remove Serena from the picture. As long as—

As long as a dozen things didn't go wrong.

Breathe, Juliana reminded herself. *Just keep doing that.*

Someone whistled overhead.

"That's the signal," Miriam whispered, counting down. *Three, two, one—*

Something exploded beside the palace gate. The trolls on duty lumbered down to investigate, leaving only two behind. An arrow from a rooftop lodged itself in the temple of the first, and Miriam raced forward to dispatch the remaining one, cutting him down before he could even look in her direction.

She tugged his body out of sight, two more soldiers doing the same with the first troll.

Barney the minotaur stripped off his armour and pulled on the rough leather waistcoat of the troll guard, taking their place. "Do you think it suits me?" he asked, wrestling into the helmet.

Miriam looked at him blankly, and picked the daisy chain off his horn. "You've never looked better."

Barney chuckled, shouldering his spear, and returned to keep a lookout. Juliana forced herself not to look back at the explosion and check on their team. She had to trust them.

She'd never been very good at that.

The group crept forward under the second gate, sticking to shadows where they could, pressing against walls and under bushes when they couldn't. A few more unseelie blocked the way, but each was dispatched as silently as an arrow.

The doors were close. So close.

Just a little more. Just a few more steps, a few more feet—

Something screeched overhead, like the caw of a crow, only louder, more ragged—as if someone had stitched a dozen calls together, torn them up, and shoved roughly back into the body of a bird.

Shadows flickered across the lawns.

Just birds, just birds, just—

"Sluaghs!" someone hissed. "Take cover!"

People hit the floor, diving behind trees, running back towards the gate. Juliana glanced upwards as the flock descended.

Dozens of them.

Too many. Far too many.

Only Miriam and a few others stayed to fight. "Get to the princess!" the knight called.

Juliana looked at the sluaghs, looked at the doors, looked at every obstacle between—and ran.

Sword outstretched, she skidded under one enemy, slicing it across the torso and not stopping to watch it fall. Arrows covered her as she flew over the lawn, feet sliding, lungs breaking.

She didn't stop. She couldn't. She was so close—

She vaulted over an ogre in her path and kept up the charge, hoping and praying those behind her were following, that someone would keep them at bay and give her the time to get Serena up the stairs.

She would wake Hawthorn. This would all be over.

A monstrous roar sounded from behind, and a huge chunk of stone raced overhead. For the first time, Juliana froze, unable to gauge its trajectory, to move at all—

A series of vines launched from the side of the castle, catching the stone and circling over her head like a whip, flinging it back towards the sender.

Hawthorn.

A smile slipped out of her.

It was him. She knew it was him. The rest of the vines, sapped dry by Maytree's sleep, hung limp around the castle. This wasn't them acting by themselves, this was someone controlling them.

He'd come for her. However angry, however hurt—he'd come when she needed him, his actions speaking of a promise he'd never made and yet she heard nonetheless.

I will always come for you.

She felt the words against her bones, the vow that whatever happened between them, he would be there for her for the rest of her life.

And she would be there for him.

"Juliana!" Miriam hissed. "Go!"

Ashamed of her hesitation, Juliana bolted, leaping up the stairs and into the throne room. She spotted Serena on the dais at the end—

And a cool, blue cloud gathering at the centre of the room.

A shadow formed before she skidded to a halt. A wave of his black staff sent her flying back to the doors, shock pouncing through her bones as she hit the floor. Vines reached out to protect her, but thorns tore through them, snaking down the steps, tearing through the grounds, wrenching weapons from her allies, gripping their ankles, twisting around their throats—

Miriam struggled, yanking and pulling, slashing and hissing. Her armour and strength protected her from most of the attacks, but the thorns grew tighter and more monstrous until she was more black than white, until they'd almost covered her eyes and blood streamed down her cheeks. Everyone else had stopped moving.

"Stop!" Juliana screamed, as Ladrien approached her. "Stop! Please!"

Ladrien's icy eyes screamed at her. "You again," he hissed. "I was a fool to let you live. I will not make the mistake again. I will wipe you and your infernal kind from the Earth—"

"I'll help you!" she shrieked, desperate, unthinking. "I can help you do it if you let them live!"

Ladrien scoffed. "What have you to bargain with, little mortal? You have nothing I cannot take from you."

She could offer him years of service. She'd seen mortals pledge their troth to many a creature before, in return for wishes or riches. Her own father had bargained with him. But skilled as she was, she knew that Ladrien would likely laugh in the face of such an offer. He would not want a mortal servant, not now. Not one who had obliterated most of his army.

What he wanted was power. And there was only one thing she had left to give.

"My mortal soul," she said. "And my human heart. That you cannot drag from my corpse. But I offer it to you freely if you beat me in single combat. No magic."

It would be too much to ask him to break the curse. He would never agree to it. But a freely given mortal soul... it was a tempting offer.

She could see him mulling it over. It was a potent thing, an ingredient he could enact numerous spells with. A part of her shuddered at the thought of being reduced to an *ingredient*, at the evils her soul could be used to create. Would she be conscious of it? She had no idea how such magic worked.

Could she even beat him?

The quick answer that came to her was *no*. He was an ancient faerie, and even without his magic, he would be a formidable foe.

She couldn't beat him. She was just buying time. Time for someone to come up with something better, time for the others to escape, maybe even get Serena upstairs—

"I will let your comrades live," Ladrien interrupted her thoughts, "if you beat me, but no more than that. *If* you beat me, fragile child."

"No magic?"

"I will not use magic against you," he promised. "If anyone else tries to intervene—"

Juliana nodded. She would not get a better offer.

"Then it is done," he declared.

He snapped his fingers together, and the flock of sluaghs spiralled closer to Miriam's forces. "In case anyone gets any ideas."

He threw off his cloak, his white skin glistening, as pale and watery as ice. His wings widened, growing to ridiculous lengths.

She'd not banned him from using those, or his horns, which seemed to be growing longer and longer by the minute.

Ladrien dropped to the floor, wings spasming. His back rippled, like some creature was trying to break out of it. Juliana flinched, extending her sword. "We agreed no magic!"

"No magic?" came Ladrien's voice, but it was a deep, twisted version of it. "This is not magic, *girl.* This is who I am!"

His nose stretched into a long snout. Blue scales ruptured at the tip, coursing over his muscles, to the tail sprouting at the base of his spine. Fangs blossomed in his gums, a forked tongue slithering out between them.

Snake, said Juliana's mind, going blank with fear, before being reminded that snakes did not have wings, nor the monstrous black talons sprouting at Ladrien's fingers.

His limbs grew longer and wider, his body stretching, growing hideously, grotesquely, until it seemed he could have wrapped himself twice around the entire castle and his wings were large enough to block out the sun.

His skin, now shimmering and blue, dripped with moisture.

Not a snake. A water dragon.

Juliana ran.

She hit the inside of one of the turrets and bolted up the stairs. Ladrien slammed into the door behind her, making the very stone shudder and shake.

She had only two—maybe three—advantages. Her speed and size, her knowledge of the castle, and her mortal lies.

Technically, she could run from this. If Ladrien never beat her, her soul would never be his. But how could she outrun a *dragon?*

By staying in small, confined spaces. By remaining hidden. By being very, very careful.

But not for long. He'd find her eventually.

Think think think think think—

She bolted up the stairs, her heart in her chest, windows showing flashes of his enormous scaled body as she climbed.

"Shall I tell you a fairytale, Juliana Ardencourt?" came his deep, snarling voice. A second later, his fist smashed through a window ahead of her, followed by his massive head. Juliana dived underneath it, slashing upright, but he jerked upwards before she could get in another attack, taking half the wall with him.

Juliana reached the top door and burst into the corridor, Ladrien snaking behind her, the stone bursting at the seams under his gigantic size.

"Once upon a time, a beautiful faerie princess fell in love with a handsome sea monster"— stone fell overhead, making Juliana swerve— "but a knight grew jealous of their love, and slayed the beast. The princess in turn slayed *him*, and, for her transgressions, was banished from the faerie court, all whilst a child grew in her belly."

More stone trembled. Juliana ducked, half falling, half rolling, skidding through the library doors at the end of the corridor. She dived behind a bookcase as Ladrien burst in behind her, finally able to move freely in the colossal space.

He shot into the air, wings cutting across the light. She twisted into another aisle of books, desperately trying to keep out of his line of sight, clinging to stacks and shadows.

"The Seelie said her child would be a monster, an abomination... but there were plenty of creatures called that. And the princess found them all. Every beast, every faerie deemed too vicious or too dangerous to live in the glittering court... she sought them out. Gave them a home. A princess of Faerie became the first Queen of the Unseelie. And her child its beautiful prince."

You? Juliana realised. But the birth of the Unseelie Court was millenia ago. Unspeakably ancient.

Was Ladrien truly that old?

"I have seen the rise and fall of the fae," Ladrien continued, flicking his tail and toppling over a shelf. Books went flying, wood reduced to splinters. "I have seen its worst and best. I have seen it fail and flourish. I have seen its *end.*"

Another bookcase toppled. Juliana threw herself out of the way, accidentally diving into his line of sight. He lunged for her. She slammed against another bookcase. It crashed into his body, allowing her a chance to ram her sword into the side of his neck.

Not deep enough, not by half. She withdrew the blade as he reared and shot off down another aisle.

"But have you *actually* seen it, or are you just... you know, guessing? Because it's kind of extreme to exterminate an entire species based on a hunch."

"When you live to be my age, you *know* things, girl! You don't need to see them to believe them!"

His jaws plunged through a bookcase, snapping and snarling. Juliana stabbed his nostril and kicked over another shelf.

No one should live as long as he had. There was a reason most faeries didn't, why they 'returned themselves to the earth' when the centuries grew too heavy. A madness would take over otherwise.

A madness had.

Ladrien reared. A bookcase fell, catching Juliana's legs as it crashed to the floor. She wasn't hurt—at least, not badly—but she couldn't move. Her legs were trapped, and Ladrien's huge jaws rose above her.

This couldn't be it. She couldn't die here, alone, trapped, her sword out of reach—

A book flew out of nowhere and hit the dragon squarely in the eye.

"Stay away from my books!" called a voice.

Juliana glanced upwards. On a balcony far above her was a small, barefooted figure, looking wilder and fiercer than ever.

Even Ladrien looked taken aback.

"And my friend," Aoife continued. "You stay away from her too."

Ladrien lunged for the librarian, but his massive head struck the small door behind her. Aoife flung herself off the side, scurrying down the ladder while he strained against the frame, and the vines around him tightened.

Aoife raced towards Juliana, grabbing a loose plank from one of the shelves and shoving it under the bookcase to lever it up, just enough for Juliana to free herself. She seized Briarsong and followed Aoife as she opened a hole in the wall, a dense, dark tunnel between shelves.

The door closed, and they both sank to the floor, panting hard.

"Aoife!" Juliana said, when she'd gathered enough breath, "You just threw a book at the Unseelie King!"

FOREST OF DREAMS AND WHISPERS

"I know. Don't worry. It was Egberd's encyclopaedia, though. Monstrously out of date and wholly inaccurate. Not worth the paper it's printed on."

Juliana stared at her.

"What?"

Juliana laughed, and yanked her friend into her arms. "It's good to see you again."

"You too," said Aoife, relaxing into the embrace. "When Hawthorn came back and you didn't... I feared the worst. Should have known better."

The tunnel shuddered and shook. A terrific roar indicated Ladrien had freed himself.

"What now?" Aoife asked. "I'm not fond of the idea of abandoning my library, but if the alternative is being eaten—"

"I'm thinking, I'm thinking!"

Something collapsed outside. "Think quickly!"

Juliana tried to calculate the likelihood of getting back down to the throne room, retrieving Serena, and getting her upstairs without Ladrien noticing. The odds didn't sit well.

She would need to defeat him first.

But how did one defeat a dragon?

People have, a voice reminded her. *The storybooks are filled with them.*

Most tended to be nonspecific on the details, though. And it wasn't like she could crack out a textbook now...

You don't need to.

Juliana hit her head. Of course she didn't. She had the entire library right next to her.

"Aoife," she started, "have you ever heard of an oilliphéist?"

Aoife fixed her with an incredulous glare. "Oh, you mean like the giant water dragon currently attacking us?"

"Yes, but I'm thinking specifically of the last one—"

"Caoránach," Aoife muttered, as if this were a bedtime story she'd read every night. "Defeated in battle by Ser Gallioch on the—"

"But *how?* How did one man take down a dragon—"

Aoife rolled her eyes. "The same way one *man* does *anything*," she said exasperatedly. "With the help of a woman."

Juliana blinked. "A woman?"

"A witch, to be exact. She froze the seas for him."

"Froze the seas?"

"Oilliphéists don't like ice."

"They're water dragons."

"They like *water*. Warm water, to be precise. The cold weakens them. The dragon couldn't move through the icy air..."

Aoife was still speaking, but Juliana's mind was back in Winter, watching Ladrien shudder in the cold, watching him try to teleport as if the cold hurt him.

Because it did.

And he wasn't teleporting—he was transforming.

Transforming into water.

"Not that that's much use to us here," Aoife continued. "Neither of us are witches. I have some theoretical knowledge, of course, but anything of great magnitude—"

"We don't need a witch," Juliana rushed. "We've got the Winter gardens."

And a pile of snow waiting on the mountain tops.

It was time for another avalanche.

"Get back to Miriam and the others," she said. "They're being held outside the palace gates. Free them, however you can—" She paused, thinking swiftly. "Hawthorn, can you hear me?"

A vine shot through the wall, making Aoife jump.

"Go with her. Get them up. Bring them to Winter. Make it snow."

For a moment, she felt something brush her cheek, but a second later it was gone, so swiftly it might have been the wind.

"Go," she told Aoife, when the vines fell limp around them. "Go!"

"What are you going to do?"

"What else?" she said, climbing to her feet. "I'm going to take on a dragon."

Juliana could never quite remember how she got out of the palace, only she did, somehow, with the benefit of a head start. She recalled feeling Ladrien shatter through the library ceiling and spill out into the darkening air, roaring her name.

"JULIANA ARDENCOURT!" he howled, his body blackening the clouds. "I WILL HAVE YOUR HEART. I WILL HAVE YOUR SOUL. I WILL MAKE YOU WATCH AS I DESTROY EVERYTHING YOU LOVE."

Juliana didn't watch him, didn't turn back. She streamed through the gardens, weaving in and out of sight. The lawns turned white and glassy, the trees crisp with frost.

Not much further.

Her feet sunk into snow. She kept to the dense pines, woven so thickly Ladrien couldn't enter. Any further, she wouldn't be able to move herself. Ladrien paused at the wooded entrance, and then swung his huge tail straight though the trunks, cutting several of them down like butter.

How long could she hide here? How long would she need before Hawthorn and Aoife freed the others?

If they even could. Two against all of his forces… what had she been thinking?

She waited as long as she dared, until half the trees were demolished, and then sprinted for the mountains. She'd cause an avalanche herself if she needed to.

It took Ladrien a while to realise what she was doing, by which point she'd already reached the path up the side, carved out of the rock, half-hidden. He was slower than he was in the library, his breath wheezing. When he rammed into the side, the mountain rammed back.

"Come on, come on…"

She struggled up the rocky incline, lungs burning. Ladrien took a second to gather his breath, and Juliana took a moment to glance out over the grounds—

A small force was heading towards them, a shining white figure at the head.

Miriam. Miriam was coming, and one of the soldiers behind her carried a rocket in his arms.

But overhead, the sluaghs were gathering again.

No.

Ladrien shot through the rock, slicing away the path in front of her. He trailed up the mountainside and then sagged like a weighted feather, dribbling down the slopes.

Her way up was completely destroyed.

Before she could panic—or think of a solution—a vine wrapped around her middle and flung her ahead. All around her, vines launched from the stone, closing gaps, offering her platforms, helping her up.

Ladrien landed on a rocky ledge, barring her path, wings cutting through the air.

"Juliana Ardencourt…" he snarled again, like her name was the gravest of insults. "Yield, and I may yet let your comrades live."

"Like I believe that," she said, gripping her sword tighter.

Hawthorn's vines sprung towards him, but she could see they were losing their strength, buckling under the cold like everyone else. Ladrien cut through them with a single swipe.

She could no longer see Miriam or any of the others, and it was growing dark.

Snow glistened atop the mountain as she slid under Ladrien's body. So close, too far.

"Hawthorn," she whispered, hoping he could hear her, "can you reach the top?"

The vines trembled in response. She took that to be a yes.

"Get up there," she said. "Set it off."

The vines shook and trembled. Ladrien reeled, shaking and unsteady. Juliana slashed his paw, but one of his claws caught her shoulder. She hissed, low and painful, stabbing him in the knuckle and diving into a crevice out of reach. Just. Not for long.

"Do it!" she screamed, clutching her shoulder.

She could almost see him shaking his head, almost hear his voice, like he was trying to burst through the dream to get to her. She knew why. She was in the direct path of the avalanche.

"Hawthorn, I'm not going to die," she whispered. *And even if I was, this would be worth it.* If she could take out Ladrien, Faerie would be safe. Someone else could break the curse. It didn't have to be her.

It seemed a poor end to the tale, crushed to death beneath the ice, Hawthorn alone, marrying Serena—

But Faerie would survive. *Hawthorn* would.

Aoife could spin the tale better.

And she would.

"Do it," she told Hawthorn, as Ladrien's claws streaked past her face. "*Do it!*"

The vines trembled again, but this time, it was like they were gathering energy, or sucking in a breath before a scream. They sprung together, racing up the mountainside, and ripped away a chunk of snow.

It was like pulling a plug on an overflowing dam. Snow churned over the edge, gushing like water, a cascade of ice. Ladrien glanced upwards and tried to launch out of the way, but Juliana leapt from her spot and vaulted onto his back.

Oh no. You don't get away from this.

She sprinted along his spine, drove her sword into his membranous wing, and sliced it through.

Ladrien began to sink, screaming and cursing.

Juliana slid. She plunged Briarsong into his back, holding herself in place as he flapped desperately, sagging against the piling weight of the snow and his own mangled wing. The world turned upside down. Juliana glanced desperately through the fallen debris, searching for way out, a passage to safety—

A ledge opened up ahead of her.

She pulled out her sword and ran, hurtling along the length of Ladrien's body, flinging herself into the air—

She missed by a few short inches, and the entire world narrowed as she fell, weightless and weighty, down, down—

Something wrapped around her, slowing her descent. A dozen warm vines, cushioning her fall, hugging her limbs, pulling her out of the way of the snowfall, down the mountain, slowly, carefully, all the way to the quiet, undisturbed gardens as the snow slowed and steadied.

Juliana's heart took an age to still. The grounds took even longer. Ladrien's massive body twitched beneath the avalanche, his shredded wing bent and broken. As she watched, it shrank away entirely.

The vines pressed Briarsong into her hand, and hovered there, like a hand helping her up.

She climbed shakily to her feet, as the King of Unseelie crawled out of the snow.

One of his horns was missing. His left wing looked broken beyond any repair. He was breathing hard, his chest bruised—ribs likely broken.

He made no motion to move as Juliana approached, and raised her sword to his neck. "Call off your forces, or I will run you through."

"The curse won't end with my death, girl. It will still stand for a hundred years."

Juliana was still sure she could wake Hawthorn, but if she couldn't, if there was even a chance... "Then yield, faerie," she warned, "before I take my chances."

Ladrien raised his hand, wincing, and clicked his fingers. The sluaghs circling overhead stopped their assault on Miriam and the others, and slid away into shadows. The trolls and ogres looked up, awaiting instruction. "Stand down," he told them. "Stand down."

Juliana glanced at her allies, all relatively unscathed, and nodded at Miriam, who immediately started giving orders to round up Ladrien's forces. Weapons were thrown down, but Juliana didn't care to watch.

"It's over," she told Ladrien.

The Unseelie King shrugged. "As you say."

KATHERINE MACDONALD

Juliana began to run.

41. TOWER OF THORNS

It wasn't until Juliana reached Hawthorn's side that she realised, in her haste, she'd forgotten to bring Serena. No matter, perhaps it might even be easier to tug him down than bring her up.

Even though she didn't want to. Even though she was tempted to go back to Ladrien right now and demand he find another way to break the spell, because how was it fair that she had gone through all that not to be with him now?

Not all fairytales are fair, a voice reminded her, and she had to quash it for fear that it would mention tales cut short too soon, names she couldn't bear to hear... not right now.

Hawthorn lay on the bed, looking as perfect as she had ever seen him, arranged on the pillows, the vines twirling round him. She approached him slowly, carefully, as if she expected him to flicker away like candlelight.

She sat down on the mattress, sagging beneath her weight, and caressed his pale, beautiful cheek.

It should not be ending this way, but she did not know what else to do.

"Hawthorn," she whispered, "can you hear me?"

She waited for a rustle of the vines, but it didn't come. No matter, time was short. Her courage would wane before long, or Ladrien would figure out some new plan of attack.

"I don't know what will happen after I wake you. I know that things cannot be as they were before, that it would not be fair to anyone. But I want you to know that whatever lies I've told you, and for however long you live... you were mine, once. And you will forever own a piece of this lying mortal heart of mine."

She bent down, and placed a kiss to his still, frozen lips.

The last time, she told herself. *Don't entertain the idea again.*

With poisonous reluctance, she stood up again, trying to calculate what to do now, all the endless, painful roads opening up ahead of her, free and consuming all at once.

"Juliana?" called a weak voice.

She glanced down. Two brilliant aegean eyes stared back at her, bright and blinking. "What—what happened? Where's Serena?"

Juliana's knees gave out. She sunk back to the bed. "You... you're awake."

"Apparently?" Hawthorn sat up groggily. "I don't... I don't understand. The curse said—"

Only his chosen fae bride.

And she wasn't fae.

And they weren't engaged.

But she'd woken him. Somehow—she'd done it.

Juliana felt a smile ripping through her, a warmth unlike anything she'd known, quiet and tentative. She was afraid to give it weight, and at the same time—she didn't care. She wasn't afraid anymore. He was awake, he wasn't engaged to Serena, they were here, together... what could she possibly fear? "It doesn't matter," she told him, stroking a lock of hair behind his ear. "You're free. We're *all* free."

"I don't..." He shivered under her touch. "I don't... feel right."

He fell back against the pillows, eyes circling in his head. Colour ran from his cheeks.

"Hawthorn!" Juliana grabbed his face. He was as cold as ice. Her hands slid to his chest, finding his heart beating rapidly. Too rapidly.

A laugh sounded from the door.

"I was so, *so* hoping you'd do something like that."

Juliana wheeled around, drawing her sword. Ladrien stood in the doorway, still bruised, still hurt, but upright and alive and *laughing*.

"Worry not, girl, I've broken no vows. You won, fair and square. Your mortal friends are free. But the curse isn't broken. Only a kiss from his chosen fae bride could do that. And you... you are neither. What did you think? That true love's kiss would win the day?"

Juliana glanced down at Hawthorn, his breathing sharp and shallow. She raised her blade to Ladrien. "Heal him," she demanded.

Ladrien laughed. "Even if I could, I wouldn't. I prefer this ending much more. Go on, girl. Run me through. My curse will still stand. In a hundred years Maytree will wake and find her only son dead... you won't be alive to tell your side of the story. Who's to say she won't assume *you* did it? Or some other filthy mortal, hoping to end the curse. Maybe she'll follow in my footsteps, decide you mortals are pests to be eradicated—"

Juliana stepped forward, ready to stop his words with her blade—

"Juliana," Hawthorn called.

The word dragged her from her quest, dragged her from everything, had her snapping back towards him like a magnet.

She gathered him in her arms. Ladrien could wait. She'd deal with him in a minute, once she'd worked out how to fix this, how to...

He couldn't die. He couldn't. Not after all this. Not at all.

I prefer happy endings, he'd told her once.

Me too, she realised now. *Me too, me too, me too.*

"You look... worried..." he panted, each pained word slicing into her.

Juliana's throat tightened. "I might be. Just a bit. Trying to work out a few things." She found his fingers and wound them into hers.

"You... have to... hand it to me..." he whispered, "at death's door and... I'm still... managing to charm you."

"You're not charming me."

"Liar." He coughed, hard and brittle. "At least I won't have to watch you die, now. I was always so afraid of that. This... this is better for me..."

Juliana ran her fingers over his mouth, thumbing his lips. "You are not going to die," she told him. "I forbid it."

"I'm not sure even you have that power, my sweet enemy." His gasping worsened, sounding hard and painful. "But this is what I would have chosen. Your arms, your face..."

"Hawthorn," she whispered, mind spinning, "You're not allowed to die, remember? And your heart isn't failing. *What's mine is yours.*" She took his hand, placing it over her breast. The last, desperate thing she could think of. A mortal heart, freely given. "You have my heart. Take it."

Hawthorn's eyes widened, realising what she was suggesting. "No..."

"Hawthorn—"

"You'll die."

She squeezed his fingers. "Trust me. Death shall have no dominion over Juliana Ardencourt."

Tears rimmed Hawthorn's eyes, but his hand pressed against her chest. "If this is another lie of yours, I'll hate you for as long as I love you."

Juliana hardly knew whether she was lying or not. All she knew was that she couldn't watch him die, and that she couldn't imagine herself quitting a world with him still in it.

More than the pendants connected them. Something else tighter than thread and tougher than wire had threaded between them long ago and would not let go.

Yours, mine, always.

Hawthorn's fingers radiated light. Warm, at first, followed by a hard, sharp pain crackled over her chest, like being speared with fire. She let out a gasp, and then, terrified he'd stop, that this might be it, that it was all over, she seized his face and kissed him.

The room trembled, the vines shook. Air gathered around them. Juliana ignored it all, ignored the room, ignored the dense, hard pain spreading through her limbs. She focused on the press of his lips, the silken feeling of his hair between her fingers, anything that kept her tethered to him, that tempered fear.

Take it, take it, it's yours!

Elements swirled about them in a mad, frantic haze. Juliana was conscious of things knitting and unknitting, like she could see the very fabric of Faerie, a thousand, a million golden threads that bound everything together. Light speared through her, a line connecting between the two of them, blinding and brilliant, a blistering, beautiful agony that made her feel like she was unravelling into fragments and atoms before gathering again, whole, and new, and different.

And still her.

Still *his*.

Slowly, gradually, the wind rescinded. The pain dissipated, every cut shutting, every bruise melting away. The wound in her shoulder sealed. A light feathered against her bones, tracing every muscle until she felt weightless enough to float.

And yet she was still tethered to the ground, to the weight against her lips still, to the arms around her.

She inched back and opened her eyes.

Hawthorn stared back at her. "You're still here."

Juliana wanted to smile, but she wasn't sure she could. Her whole body seemed devoid of feeling, hardly hers apart from the parts he was touching. But she wanted to smile. She wanted to smile and laugh and cry.

"Yes," she said, "and so are you."

42. THE SENTENCE OF THE UNSEELIE KING

Slowly, gingerly, Hawthorn climbed to his feet, sticking close to Juliana. Ladrien stood slumped in the doorway still, expression livid.

"Beyond words?" Hawthorn said, arching an eyebrow. "Juliana often has that effect on me too. In a vastly different way, I imagine." There was no joy in his voice. It was as flat and cold as when he used to torment her as children, worse even, as a kind of power trembled underneath it that she had never heard before. "I do recall there were some words about surrendering to immediate judgement should the curse be broken. Do you remember?"

Ladrien's jaw tightened. "I remember."

"Excellent. I hereby strip you of your title, Ladrien of the Unseelie, and all magic you have accumulated. You are to be banished to the northern mountains of Winter. You will raise no armies, hurt no mortals. You will not transform. You will not set foot outside of your prison for one hundred years… after which point I may just kill you. But death is a gift you have yet to earn, given to others far more deserving."

Ladrien stared at him, his eyes stone. "A hundred years is nothing to me," he snarled.

"Perhaps, but I do rather like the poetic justice of it. You ought to be glad of my mercy; you'll be able to see if your predictions come true. You might get a delightful, 'I told you so' at the end of your imprisonment. You get to see what *we* are able to accomplish in that time."

"You have doomed your own realm."

Hawthorn shrugged. "Not really for you to decide, is it?" He surveyed Ladrien carefully for a moment. "I suppose I should offer you the same courtesy you gave me—a loophole, a way out. Let it be known that if you ever learn to love someone, and earn their love in return, your sentence will end. Only your sentence. You will have earned nothing more. Do you hear?"

"I hear."

"Good. Then hear this too: you will never earn another's heart. You are beyond that. But the choice is yours nonetheless. You had an opportunity for salvation, but I believe it already squandered." He turned back to Juliana. "Anything to add, my dear?"

Juliana came forward, blade extended. "His name was Dillon Woodfern," she told him.

"What?"

"There will come a time when you regret what you have done, if only because you will wish we'd killed you now. When you wish for death, remember him. The man you killed. The reason you live. I want you to remember his name."

Ladrien said nothing.

Juliana pressed the blade deeper. "Swear it," she hissed.

Ladrien's throat bobbed, blood bubbling at the tip of Juliana's sword. "I will remember his name."

"Say it."

"Dillon," he whispered. "His name was Dillon Woodfern."

Hawthorn's eyes caught Juliana's, and he nodded in approval, before turning back to Ladrien. He extended his long, elegant fingers, holding them over his chest.

Juliana did not look away when the light began to tug out of Ladrien and into Hawthorn's fingertips, even when it brightened and boiled to the point of pure, harsh white, even when Ladrien began to twitch, when his broken wing twisted, when his entire body bent backwards, magic being ripped from every pore.

Even when he started to scream.

She wanted it to hurt, although she found no joy in the pain, no joy in watching him cower. She felt nothing except for a mild, dizzying kind of relief. He deserved this. This was better than death, even if a part of her blade still itched for his blood.

She suspected it always would.

Finally, it was over. Hawthorn's skin hummed with a golden glow, radiating with power. He clicked his fingers, and a shimmering portal opened in his room, displaying the snowy mountains and the rocky ruins of the old Winter Court.

Bare, barren and empty. Ladrien's home for the next a hundred years.

The former king stared at it. For all he had said the time meant nothing to him, he did not seem willing to go.

Hawthorn swished his hands, like a wave of indifference, and the portal swept forward and swallowed Ladrien whole. He let out a scream, but it cut short when the portal vanished.

The last Juliana saw of Ladrien, he was standing in the frigid cold, bruised and bleeding.

And utterly alone.

Hawthorn slumped the second the portal disappeared. For all the magic he'd just absorbed, portal-making was no easy feat, and he had just nearly died.

He'd nearly died. She'd nearly lost him.

"Careful," Juliana warned, arms around him.

Hawthorn grinned, his smile very close to her. "Worried, my dear Jules?"

"A bit," she admitted, still feeling slightly dizzy herself, like she expected the world to be ripped away from her again. Like she expected *him* to be ripped away. "You probably shouldn't use any more magic for a while."

"But I look so dashing when I do it..." He stepped away from her, swirling his fingers. Through the open door, Juliana spied the damage to the castle being knitted back together, stone snapping back into place, torn tapestries mending, vines curling along the walls.

Hawthorn sighed, the power stuttering through him. Sounds turned around them, shouts and cries, tentative cheers.

"We... should probably go downstairs," she said. "We have some explaining to do."

"That we certainly do," he said, still grinning irrepressibly. "I don't have to marry Serena."

"I know."

"I don't imagine she's too disappointed."

"I'm sure she's thrilled."

"You rescued me."

"Don't make me regret it," she said, pressing against his chest.

"You wouldn't."

Before she could open her mouth to confirm that she would, indeed, never regret it, there came a thundering of feet along the corridor. Seconds later, Maytree burst into the room. She took one look at the two of them and immediately flung herself at Hawthorn, muttering incomprehensible sounds and words of relief.

"*Thank you*," she mouthed at Juliana. "*Thank you, thank you.*"

When she finally parted from her son's arms, her cheeks were very wet. Hawthorn looked little better.

She touched his face. "You're all right?"

"Honestly, Mother, I'm not sure I've ever been better."

"Ladrien?"

"Stripped of his magic, forbidden from forming another army, and banished to Winter for the next one hundred years. We shall not be hearing from him again."

"I would have executed him."

"This felt more poetic."

Maytree shrugged, as if it was neither here nor there. "Come," she said instead. "We need to address our subjects."

Everywhere they walked, vines blossomed. The castle sung with golden lights. Stones knitted back together, floors and walls reformed, stronger than ever. Any trace of battle faded. When they reached the throne room, banners blazed. Trumpets sounded.

Hawthorn parted from Juliana's side to take his place beside his mother. Juliana, meanwhile, spotted the mortal forces, Aoife amongst them. She ran forward to embrace her and was offered a firm pat by Miriam. "You did good, girl," she said. "Your mother would have been proud." She paused, lips thin, face taut. "Your father, too, for all his failings. He'd be proud as well."

Juliana bowed her head, unwilling to think of him today, or her mother—her mother whose body still rested in the forest. That was tomorrow's problem. Today's—

Wait, did today even have a problem?

Did she actually have anything in the world to worry about?

Hawthorn's gaze caught hers, and the smile she'd been fighting poured across her cheeks. There was maybe *one* thing to worry about, and even that... she knew exactly how to handle.

Maytree stood, waving her hand. The room fell quiet.

"Loyal subjects," she began, "that which we have feared for so long has come to pass; the curse is broken at last."

A cheer went up from the crowd, hoots and jeers. The trumpets burst into a short chorus.

"We owe our release to a loyal group of mortals," Maytree continued, "who did not abandon us to Ladrien's rule, even at the cost of many of their own lives."

A quietness fell over the group, and Juliana's eyes darted to Albert. No amount of celebration could bring Dillon back, no recompense would ease his loss.

"I cannot bring back the dead," Maytree carried on, reading the room. "All I can do is honour them. Posthumous knighthood for anyone who perished serving the kingdom, compensation for their families, statues raised in pure gold—and my personal promise to never forget their names. Let them be added to our books and our memories, heroes of this dark time."

A moment's reverence was afforded, the clouds even darkening at Maytree's unconscious behest. After a minute, they brightened again.

"We shall mourn, but not today. Today we celebrate what is, and give thanks to those that made it through. Miriam, step forth please."

Miriam did as she was bid, kneeling before her queen.

"You already have knighthood," Maytree said. "What would you have in addition?"

"To be honest, Your Majesty, I really fancy a holiday."

A laugh went up from the crowd. "Then you shall have it, Miriam of Bath, as well as a house here in our grounds and one wherever else you desire. Your soldiers, too, shall be justly rewarded."

"The day could not have been won without them," Miriam agreed. "Although we owe most, if not all of our fortune to Juliana."

All eyes turned towards Juliana, who now wished she'd been afforded a few moments to freshen up. She was absolutely filthy.

Maytree smiled. "I suspected as much. Come forward, Juliana."

Hawthorn leant across. "I have already promised her knighthood and riches for her assistance," he explained.

Maytree nodded. "Then I offer you another boon of your choosing," she proclaimed. "Anything within our power. Title, lands, magic, a geas—anything you wish for will be yours. You need only speak it."

Juliana hoped she wasn't trembling. The weight of Maytree's words swam above her, heavy as stone, twinkling like starlight.

Anything. She could have *anything*.

How many things had she wished for as a girl? Fine things, wealth no one could take from her, power she had earned.

All now within her grasp.

And yet there was only one thing she wanted.

She bowed, and then righted herself. A thousand fairytales had ended this way, why should hers be any different?

She wished she wasn't sweating so hard as she raised her eyes to Hawthorn. "Him," she said. "I want him."

The whole room startled, sucking in a collective breath. None looked more surprised than Hawthorn, whose face went white. It was impossible to tell if he was appalled or overjoyed.

The Queen stared at him, and then back towards Juliana. "Be more specific."

"For freeing the kingdom from Ladrien's control, I would like Prince Hawthorn's hand in marriage."

The crowd murmured again.

The Queen looked around uncertainly. "I promised you anything within our power," she continued, after the longest of pauses. "But this—"

"I accept," Hawthorn declared, leaning forward in his throne. "I shall marry you, Juliana Ardencourt. Right here, right now, if you wish it."

The gasps escalated into a frenzy. Juliana's own breath stuttered in her chest. She could hardly believe this was happening.

"How long for?" she asked hesitantly, for faerie marriages could be brief and fleeting. No one promised forever, for such a thing could not be undone. Not even those in the deepest of love proclaimed such a thing.

"Careful, son," Maytree advised.

But he did not appear to hear her. His eyes were still rooted on Juliana. "For as long as you wish it."

"And if I want you for the rest of my life?"

"I will be yours until death, if that is what you want."

"And what do *you* want?"

"You," he replied. "I just want you."

Hawthorn rose from his seat and strolled down the dais, stopping shortly in front of her. He gazed at her like he had that day in the carriage, before everything changed or solidified or liquified—she was never really sure.

She still wasn't fully sure when he reached out and kissed her, his lips casting the rest of the room into shadow.

She was dimly aware of yet more gasps and exclamations, but she no longer cared for them. She no longer cared about anything but the fact that Hawthorn was kissing her as if he never planned to let go.

Eventually, of course, he had to.

The world carried on spinning around them.

"Well," said Maytree, now smiling through her shock, "now that's settled..."

She clicked her fingers, and the boughs overhead burst into flowers, sending a shower of petals over the entire room. The banners shimmered, the thorns of the castle crest adjusting themselves around a golden oak—a symbol that honoured Juliana's own name. The great hall brimmed with life and colour, white and gold, sunset and dawn.

Most wonderful of all was when the petals started to spin around her, dissolving her of dust and grime, pulling at her braid, twirling it into perfect curls. A crown of some sort blossomed at her temple, something fine and laced brushed her ears. Her mud-streaked uniform disappeared, replaced instead by a gown of white and gold, stitched with thorns.

Her sword still gleamed at her side, but in a polished golden sheath; she was a knight and princess both.

Juliana looked up at Hawthorn and smiled.

And his. More than anything else, she was that.

His wife, his equal—a true creature of Faerie.

43.

A HEART SHARED, A HEART BARED

Juliana was quite sure that even if she lived for centuries, she would never again experience the revelry that she did the night of her wedding. It seemed the entirety of Faerie somehow miraculously appeared, their humours elevated to the point of divine. She felt different, too, quivering with a strange kind of energy, the way she always expected magic to feel, like her blood was filled with champagne.

She tried to trace the feeling back. Was it after she brought Hawthorn back, or after the ceremony? Was it just a result of celebrations, or something... *more?*

"I don't have to marry Hawthorn!" cried Serena, twirling about the room. "Um, no offence."

"None taken," replied Hawthorn, who had barely taken his eyes off Juliana since they exchanged vows. "I rather think this arrangement has worked out better for everyone."

Serena beamed, and a short while later, Hawthorn was finally tugged away to repeat the tale of the past week or so to another group of latecomers.

Juliana seized the moment to rush to the buffet table and stuff some food in her mouth. She was *ravenous*, and yet every time she'd approached it the last couple of hours, someone had swept in, eager to hear her story or gush about the wedding, which was lovely but so was the food which had been eyeing her all night.

"I never get tired of palace delicacies," said a gravelly voice. "The chefs here are utter magic."

Juliana turned. Mabel stood in a nearby alcove, her dark robes blending into shadow. Juliana was quite sure she had not been there a moment ago.

"Any point in asking how you got here so quickly?"

Mabel smirked. "I have my ways."

"If you've come to claim your favour, witch, I beg you do so tomorrow. I'm having really quite the delightful day."

Mabel snorted. "Fear not. Today is not the day. I'm not even quite sure what it is I plan to claim… only I *will* claim it. Of that, you have my word."

Juliana nodded. "But no first-born children?"

"No first born, or second-born, or anything after. The Guild of Witches actually banned fathers promising their children in the year of Briar 314."

Juliana raised an eyebrow. "But not mothers?"

"Of course not! They do all the hard work. They want to bargain off their newborns? Fine. Can't say I really blame them. Loud, horrible things, children. Tough on my teeth, too."

"What?"

"I'm teasing, dearie. I don't eat children. Not anymore."

She waited for yet another reaction, but Juliana refused to give it. "What do you want?" she asked instead.

"Revenge," said the witch.

Juliana's blood ran cold.

"Or perhaps… satisfaction. They often collide but aren't always one in the same."

Juliana had no idea what to say to that. Mabel didn't appear to be in a mood to elaborate, either, instead loading up one of the golden plates with a very large slice of cake and cream. She sat down to eat it, licking her lips.

"Don't worry yourself too much," the old woman said. "I've no desire to cause any harm to you or him. I actually quite like you both."

"That is not as comforting as it ought to be."

Mabel shrugged. "Suit yourself, but I mean what I say."

Juliana bit her lip. "I woke Hawthorn," she said. "It didn't quite work—he was dying—but I did wake him from the curse. And then I shared my heart with him, but I didn't die. Do you know why?"

Mabel smiled. "For the same reason those pendants tied you in ways we didn't expect. Because you were *already* tied. How could you die when his heart still beat? He'd already given it to you, I expect."

Juliana couldn't disagree, but neither could she find her voice.

"But enough of that. Enjoy tonight. Your mother-in-law wishes to speak to you."

Juliana turned, and found Maytree coming towards her. She swivelled back briefly to Mabel, but she'd vanished into thin air.

"Who were you talking to?" Maytree asked.

"Some old witch, I wouldn't worry about it," Juliana answered, glancing briefly at the cake to ensure a piece was missing and that she hadn't imagined the entire conversation.

"Hawthorn has been filling me in on the entire story. It seems I have missed quite a bit."

Juliana watched Hawthorn dancing, with a strange lightness to his face she'd never noticed before. "I think we all have."

Maytree looked down, only slightly, before regaining her queenly composure. "I was wrong to keep my distance from him," she admitted.

"I know why you did."

"But I also know you never approved." Her gaze shrank again. "Your mother was a great help to me when I first had him. She understood motherhood in ways I think that Faeries cannot... the fear. The way that even something you've wanted for so long can feel... not as you expected. She never expected me to perform."

"You were close to her, weren't you?"

"I loved her," said Maytree simply. "Which is why—"

"You let her go."

Maytree bowed her head. "Hawthorn told me what your father—"

"Your Majesty, with all due respect, I am in no mood to talk about that. Not today."

The Queen nodded. "I understand." She placed a hand against her cheek, gazing into her eyes with a look Juliana barely remembered from the snippet of childhood she had spent with Cerridwen. "I gave you your truesight, you know," she whispered. "I was honoured when your mother asked me. Most knights wouldn't have dreamed of doing so... but that was her. And us, back then."

Juliana wasn't sure what to say to that, so she turned the conversation back to a much more comfortable topic. "Why did you assign me to be Hawthorn's guard? Was it just because of the boon, or—"

"Your father raised a good point, I must admit," Maytree explained. "But I like to think I would have agreed to it without the boon. Hawthorn was always trying to escape from his previous ones, whereas you... for whatever reason, he gravitated towards you. Maybe for the wrong ones, when he was younger, but you'd always been able to handle him. And for all that you'd never seemed to care for him, you reported Lucinda when you didn't have to. You'd looked out for him at the expense of yourself. A true knight, even then. Perhaps, I thought, you could be something like a friend."

She paused for a moment, glancing over the festivities, her smiling son, Juliana's gown.

"I can't say I planned *this*, though..."

"Did you know?" Juliana asked. "About the two of us? It appears that most people did."

Maytree's smile widened. "I knew he liked you. Infatuation, perhaps. A little more as the years went by. It was clear he enjoyed your company, and that he cared about you. You... I was less sure of. You've always been so guarded. When he was injured, I suspected a little more, but duty and love can often be confused."

"Of that, I am now quite aware."

Maytree looked over towards her son, smiling and laughing among his subjects. "You deserve each other," she declared. "He has grown into a man worthy of you. All that is left to do now is for *me* to become a mother worthy of *him*." She stopped, smiling downwards. "I've the better part of forever to work with, I suppose."

The better part of forever.

Juliana wondered how long she'd live, now that she'd shared her heart with Hawthorn and *married* him—become a princess of faerie. Mortal girls never did this. There was likely no way of telling how she'd been altered.

Time would tell.

Hawthorn came back over to her, still grinning. "Mother," he said, "I'd like a word with my wife, if I may?"

Wife.

"By all means," she said, patting his cheek as she passed.

Hawthorn stood in front of Juliana for a moment, as if startled by her presence. "Enjoying the party, wife?"

Juliana grinned, an action that had become more natural to her these last few hours. "Actually, I think the party might be getting a little dull. I was thinking of retiring to bed."

Hawthorn's smirk widened. "Would you like company?"

"Only if it's yours."

Hawthorn linked his fingers into hers, and tugged her away up one of the concealed staircases. There were no guards on duty, no one at all. People had abandoned fear.

They snuck away to his chamber like they were being chased, giggling like schoolchildren as they locked the door behind them. The vines trailed round the bedposts and curled around Juliana's fingers, blooming at her touch.

They had never done that before.

"The vines seem to like you," Hawthorn remarked, appearing behind her. "They already seem to know you're their future queen."

Queen. *Queen.* She would be queen one day. She hadn't even thought of that.

"I doubt you'll be considered exactly human anymore," Hawthorn continued. "The vines alone seem proof. You may never be quite Fae, but you may well live forever, and... and you'll be able to leave Faerie, and find it again. The borders shall open for their queen."

Juliana could say nothing to this. The thrill of freedom paled beneath the chance to be with him, but to have both...

Something was still niggling at her. "You ran away," she said. "After you... after your confession. I can't exactly blame you, but you didn't come when I ran after you. Or... or the next day, when I really, really needed to talk to you—"

Hawthorn frowned. "You came after me?"

"You didn't hear?"

He shook his head. "I didn't hear you the day after, either. I just... sat there in the dark, not thinking or listening or doing much at all. Not until I saw you were in danger."

Juliana bit her cheek. He hadn't abandoned her, not at all. The connection between them... he must have put up a wall, subconsciously, not thinking. He had never meant to ignore her.

A smile twitched in his cheeks. "Why did you come after me?"

"You're an idiot if you don't know why."

"Well," he said, finally closing the door behind them, "you have often called me an idiot before..."

"I don't imagine that will change."

He chuckled. "So... we just got married."

Juliana snorted softly. "That we did."

"A week or two ago I was certain you felt little for me other than disdain."

"Maybe a *little* more than disdain..."

"Juliana," he said softly, "I'm loath to ruin a potentially wonderful day, but... I would know your reasons for marrying me. For coming after me. You've made no secret of your desire for knighthood over the years, but I think what you craved most was power. I understand that. Who doesn't want an element of control, especially in a place like Faerie?"

"You think I married you because I wanted power?"

"Or acceptance, perhaps. Somewhere to belong. No one will argue you are not one of us now—"

"I didn't marry you for power," Juliana replied, shocked. "Or for a place to belong... although I rather hope I have that anyway. I married you because I thought that's the only time I might get to claim you. And because... because there was nothing I wanted more. Nothing I'll *ever* want more."

Hawthorn stared at her, eyes wide, unblinking. "I'm sorry," he said eventually, "but would you mind saying that again?"

Juliana rolled her eyes, and punched him on the arm. "You really are an idiot, Hawthorn!" she hissed, gathering all her courage, all her nerves. "I've been in love with you the entire time!"

His eyes widened further. "The... the entire..."

"Well, maybe not the *entire* time," she clarified. "But for far longer than I want to admit it. Too long. *Painfully* long."

Hawthorn stared at her. "*Why didn't you say anything?*"

"Because I hate you!" she hissed. "Or I thought I did. I think mostly I hated feeling for you. I... I don't like being out of control. You know this. And..."

"I am not the easiest person to love," Hawthorn admitted.

"You are," she corrected. "I'm not. And yet you do..."

He stepped closer towards her. "I do," he whispered. "Tremendously. Voluminously. *Painfully.* I love you, Juliana Ardencourt." He kissed her neck. "Say it again, please..."

Juliana pushed back. "Don't make me repeat it!"

"I think you're supposed to repeat after you say it, that's rather the point."

"Right," she said. "I probably won't. Much. Maybe for special occasions. I'll show my affection in other ways. Threatening to cut off your head and so forth."

Hawthorn smiled. "I wouldn't have it any other way." His grin widened. "But you love me."

"I love you," she said, hesitant at the sound. It was too loud, too much. "I gave you my *heart*, Hawthorn!"

"Yes, I remember that much, but I thought that maybe there were political reasons for that, too. Or you thought that I'd be able to bring you back. Or—"

"I *married* you, you silly fool! You said yes!"

"Because I wanted to keep you," he admitted. "By whatever willing means. That seemed a good way. I never thought... I didn't dare hope that you..." He shook his head. "When? When did you fall in love with me?"

"I can't pin it to a moment," she admitted. "Things changed, much like they did for you, at the Summer Court. I think after that I fought with myself a great deal not to care about you any more than I did. A battle I have been losing for a long time." She paused. "I didn't know until recently. Didn't let myself acknowledge it until I almost lost you, but I... I would have come for you regardless of the bargain we struck. I would have found a way to save you. I will *always* find a way to save you."

He grinned. "Because you love me."

"I do."

"And you want to be with me."

"I do."

Hawthorn rushed at her, sweeping her up in his arms and flinging them both down to the bed. Juliana let out a laugh, breathless and giddy.

"This is your bed now too, wife," he said, "although I fully understand if you want to keep a room of your own for whatever purposes. We may have to lay out some ground rules."

"Ground rules?" she arched a brow. "Like what?"

He trailed a hand down her neck, ending at the pendant still resting against her chest. "I should like to say, *wherever you go, I will goest*, but I think we both know the impracticalities of that. Perhaps, instead, we could just agree to let the other one know before we race off somewhere?"

"I can manage that." She hesitated, thinking of other things they needed to agree on. "I should tell you that I'm not a big fan of sharing," she admitted. "I know you frequently invited multiple people into your bed before—but that isn't for me." She had no idea what she'd say or do if he wanted to continue with his escapades.

Hawthorn smiled. "To be honest, I don't enjoy it that much either."

"You don't? Then why—"

"Safety in numbers, partly. If I pick multiple strangers, there's less chance one will be able to run me through. And because..."

"What?"

"I couldn't be with who I wanted to be with," he confessed. "I thought if I gorged on others, I'd feel less famished for you. For the record, it did not work."

"Is that why you'd crawl into my bed afterwards?"

"Yes," he admitted. "Begging for a crumb of you if I was denied a feast..."

"Gods, you're a fool," she said, shaking her head. "And I more so for not realising anything."

She claimed his mouth with hers, exchanging rules between kisses, vows of honesty and faithfulness and promises never to steal all the covers and give each other space and try to talk to one another in ways they hadn't been particularly good at in the past.

"No knives in the bed." Hawthorn suggested.

"No knives in the—"

"Juliana, my vicious love, you are quite dangerous on your own. I don't want to risk any bedroom accidents..." He ran a finger down her arm. "Unless, of course, we're both into that."

"Into what, exactly?"

"I... I quite enjoy it, sometimes, when you handle your knives," he confessed.

"You... enjoy it?"

"I have peculiar tastes, as it turns out. I don't actually want to be hurt, but I find the threat of it rather... stimulating."

"Stimulating?" Juliana's grin was wicked. Her hands clasped the dagger at her hip, and she flipped him over in a singular action, drawing the weapon out as she twisted. She raised the tip to Hawthorn's chin. His throat bobbed, eyes black and gleaming. He loosed a long, careful breath.

"Like this?" she asked.

"Yes," he said, voice rough, "just like that."

She moved the blade down his neck, as gently as if he were butter, slipping the knife under the metal clasps of his doublet and slowly, achingly, pinging each one free until the garment was splayed against the mattress.

"I won't rip your shirt," she promised, and went to place the dagger down.

Hawthorn grabbed her wrists. "No," he growled. "Fuck the shirt, and fuck me."

Juliana bit her lip, grinning, and brought the dagger back to the fabric. She started at the neck, gliding downwards in a swift, easy line, until the perfect, sculptured panes of stomach were exposed beneath.

She was unaccustomed to this ravenous kind of hunger. Sex had been fun before, a pleasure, a niggling craving rather than a frantic need. Now, she wanted him inside her, wanted to claim his flesh with hers, to devour him and be devoured. She went slick at the thought.

Hawthorn's hands sprung to her waist, no longer slow but desperate, claiming. Juliana flung the dagger to the floor, wrenching herself free of the bindings, all thumbs and fingers as they worked together to discard every scrap of clothing between them. Palms slid over torsos, arms, thighs. Fingers touched and teased and caressed. She couldn't decide where she wanted him more, what part of him to grab.

He seized her hair, winding it round his hand, and tugging back her head to get at her neck. His teeth nibbled at her ear, his tongue drifting down her throat, her collarbones.

Her fingers graced his chin, feather-soft. She couldn't get used to feeling him this way, couldn't quite let herself believe she was allowed to, that this moment wasn't fleeting but the first of many, hundred, *forever*. Her skin still trembled against his, tight, tiny goosebumps. When would it end? This strange, unquiet bliss, this fearful desperate want? The need to touch him, to be touched?

She wasn't sure she wanted it to end. Let her feel this way forever, even if it destroyed her.

Her hands drifted over his features, down his throat, over his shoulders, his back. Her tips traced the veins in his arms, every muscle, every sinew. She wanted to colour every inch of him with her fingerprints.

Mine, mine, mine.

Impossible. Ludicrous. *Real.*

The softest, briefest of smiles brushed Hawthorn's cheeks, devoid of all sin, all mischief. "You are thinking beautiful thoughts, wife, and I would hear them."

"I am thinking that I am an idiot for hating you for so long when I wanted you so badly... when I *still* want you. When I want you so much I think I'll die from it. When I want to touch you *everywhere*."

The sinfulness flickered back, although tempered with something else. "You have my full permission."

"I do so love to explore..." She raked her hands down his back so hard it was almost painful, and he dug his fingers into her flesh, murmuring incomprehensible words that somehow conveyed every thought he'd kept hidden all this time.

She bit the end of his ear, and whispered sweet words into him as her fingers explored the long, silken inches of him, making his breath hitch. Gasping, he flipped her over onto her back and put his elegant fingers to use, teasing and playing at her soft folds until she was a quivering, pulsing mess, begging to have him inside her.

They connected in a flurry of action, the kind that sent sensation stuttering, turning thought to putty. Desire raged inside her, his skin like fire. She brought his mouth to hers and kissed him until her lips went numb, legs locked around him, hips swaying beneath his.

This is so, so much better than fighting with him.

When it was over, she drew him to her damp breast, his fingers playing with the end of her hair. She never wanted to move from this spot, or move at all unless it was to yank him inside her again.

"I love you," she told him again.

Hawthorn grinned against her chest. "I believe you."

When she finally closed her eyes, it was to the sound of their shared heartbeat, and the knowledge that he'd still be here in the morning.

And always, always would be.

Excerpt from the Royal Records

Compiled by Chief Librarian Aoife Birchmoon, Year of Ardenthorn, I

KATHERINE MACDONALD

Prince Hawthorn married Ser Juliana Ardencourt on the 29th spring, in the year of Maytree 675, not long after his eighteenth birthday. The marriage marked the end of a curse that had plagued Hawthorn since his naming day. Scholars and soothsayers claimed that their union marked the beginning of a new golden age. Many courtiers were surprised at the union, the two having had a somewhat tempestuous relationship in the past, and believed at first that it was done for political gain. Despite the verbal animosity that continued between the two, it was plain to see that the two adored one another.

Decades of peace everywhere but at the dinner table followed the union. Ser Juliana herself led the charge to destroy what remained of King Ladrien's army, and then she and her husband travelled to the mortal realm to strengthen the relationships between the kingdoms, a journey that spanned the better part of a decade.

As had been predicted, Juliana became something between mortal and fae, aging far slower than her human companions and maintaining control over certain magic gifted only to the royal family.

Princess Aislinn Ardencourt was born to the couple in the year of Maytree 715, followed by Prince Beauregard Ardencourt in 717.

Shortly after, Queen Maytree abdicated in 720, in order to travel to the Summer Isles and enjoy her golden years.

The age of Ardenthorn has begun.

FOREST OF DREAMS AND WHISPERS

Epilogue

Ladrien sat in the ruins of the ancient winter court, little more than piles of blackened stone and rubble, and shivered down to his bones. He had never liked the cold. Even without the power to transform, the weaknesses of his dragonish half were ever-present. The cold scraped inside him.

He had lost everything. Everything he had worked to build for centuries, all because of a couple of *children* who hadn't even seen the change of a hundred years.

He had underestimated Juliana Ardencourt. Perhaps that was his mistake. Her father had raved about her—how she was smart and cunning, the finest swordsperson he had ever trained. Mortal parents often boasted about their children. They were usually wrong.

But Markham hadn't been. He'd been right to be proud.

Ladrien had pondered on the words of his banishment since it began, searching for a loophole. Love was out of the question. He neither wanted it nor knew how to get it.

But he would not sit here for a hundred years. Faerie needed him.

You will raise no armies, Prince Hawthorn had declared.

Ladrien thought of Markham and Juliana, and then, with a silent smile, an idea came to him at last.

If he could not raise an army, he'd raise something else instead.

Acknowledgements

Thanks as ever to the fabulous Lydia Russell and Chesney Infalt, the best writing buddies anyone could ask for. Thanks to Emily Dolan whose singular piece of description set this all off! Thanks also to Carly Aspinall for some of the suggestions of handicaps in the faerie tournament.

My beta readers, as always, deserved the highest praise for all their suggestions, so a massive thank you to Alice, Lucy, Mandy, Jess, Emma and Catherine. It wouldn't be the same without you, and I hope you love the finished product!

AFTERWORD

This story came to me in the oddest of ways. I was reading a really cool snowy scene with a banished prince in it, and thought, "hey, wouldn't a gender-swapped Snow Queen story be cool?"

I rushed out the rough idea, but quickly realised I quite fancied a whole series of gender-swapped fairy tales, darker and more 'fae' than my previous retellings, and that the brief concept I had for the Snow King would actually better suit the *end* of a series rather than the beginning. So what to pick now? I'd no plans to do another Sleeping Beauty retelling as I was quite happy with "Kingdom of Thorns" and couldn't think of a new spin to put on it (I've done four Beauty and the Beast retellings now, but they all have a different spin!) but I really liked the idea of a sleeping *prince*.

An idea started to form. Having him be rescued by a girl he has a somewhat love/hate relationship with was always part of the plan, but initially she was a princess from a neighbouring kingdom and the deal was she wouldn't *have* to marry him if she rescued him. However, I quickly decided I preferred the idea of him being rescued by a knight, someone he had spent a lot more time with in his youth.

The two were originally way more antagonistic towards one another, but I quickly realised that a relatively short journey through the woods was not going to be enough to erase years of hate (nor should we perhaps root for a couple that had been cruel to each other for so long) and instead their relationship morphed into one of more playful antagonism... where they've clearly liked each other for years but keep up the ruse of mutual dislike, with the journey finally giving them the space to act on those feelings. Juliana and Hawthorn ran away with the story, doing whatever they liked. Their first kiss wasn't supposed to happen until much later—but they had other ideas!

This is my longest book to date, but it truly wrote itself. I'm sad that their story is over, but will be looking forward to their multiple cameos in the rest of the series.

About the Author

Born and raised in Redditch, Worcestershire, to a couple of kick-ass parents, Katherine "Kate" Macdonald often bemoaned the fact that she would never be a successful author as "the key to good writing is an unhappy childhood".

Since her youth, Macdonald has always been a storyteller, inventing fantastically long and complicated tales to entertain her younger sister with on long drives. Some of these were written down, and others have been lost to the ethers of time somewhere along the A303.

With a degree in creative writing and eight years of teaching English under her belt, Macdonald thinks there's a slight possibility she might actually be able to write. She may be very wrong.

She currently lives in Devon with her manic toddler, in a charming Victorian terrace.

"Forest of Dreams and Whispers" is her 16th novel.

You can follow her at @KateMacAuthor, or subscribe to her website at www.katherinemacdonaldauthor.com to be notified of new releases and free review copies!

Also by Katherine Macdonald

The Phoenix Project Trilogy

Book I: Flight
Book II: Resurrection
Book III: Rebirth

In the "Fey Collection" series:

The Rose and the Thorn: A Beauty and the Beast Retelling
Kingdom of Thorns: A Sleeping Beauty Retelling
A Tale of Ice and Ash: A Snow White Retelling
A Song of Sea and Shore: A Little Mermaid Retelling
Heart of Thorns: A Beauty and the Beast Retelling
Of Snow and Scarlet: A Little Red Riding Hood Retelling

Standalones:

The Barnyard Princess: A Frog Prince Retelling

In the "Faeries of the Underworld" Duology:

Thief of Spring: A Hades and Persephone Retelling (Part One)
Queen of Night: A Hades and Persephone Retelling (Part Two)
Heart of Hades: A Hades and Persephone Retelling (Part One)
Heart of Tartarus: A Hades and Persephone Retelling (Part Two) Coming soon!

A Curse of Hope and Shadows

Part One
Part Two and Three (coming soon)

The Mechanical Kingdoms Quartet:

A Rose of Steel

Printed in Great Britain
by Amazon